WAS HE . . . AS AFRAID AS SHE?

Now, for the first time, she and Leo were truly alone. Silence stretched out, interrupted only by the popping sounds of the fire.

Just look at him, Anne. He's only a man.

More than that, he was her husband. Therein lay the crucial difference.

Go on. Look at him.

Slowly, Anne lifted her gaze. She started a little when she saw that Leo stood at the foot of the bed. She hadn't heard him move. Perhaps he had removed his shoes? She fought the absurd urge to peer over the side of the bed and see whether he was merely in his stockings or shod.

They stared at each other. More surprising than finding him standing so close was the glimmer of trepidation in his eyes. In the brief time she had known Leo, not once had he looked anything less than confident. It was a shock to see this extremely hale and potent man uncertain.

Was he . . . as afraid as she?

Books by Zoë Archer

The Blades of the Rose
Warrior
Scoundrel
Rebel
Stranger

The Hellraisers
Devil's Kiss
Demon's Bride

Published by Kensington Publishing Corporation

DEMON'S BRIDE

The Hellraisers

Zoë Archer

ZEBRA BOOKS
KENSINGTON PUBLISHING CORP.
http://www.kensingtonbooks.com

ZEBRA BOOKS are published by

Kensington Publishing Corp.
119 West 40th Street
New York, NY 10018

All Kensington titles, imprints and distributed lines are available at special quantity discounts for bulk purchases for sales promotion, premiums, fund-raising, educational or institutional use.

Special book excerpts or customized printings can also be created to fit specific needs. For details, write or phone the office of the Kensington Special Sales Manager: Attn. Special Sales Department. Kensington Publishing Corp., 119 West 40th Street, New York, NY 10018. Phone: 1-800-221-2647.

Zebra and the Z logo Reg. U.S. Pat. & TM Off.

ISBN-13: 978-1-4201-2228-2
ISBN-10: 1-4201-2228-2

First Printing: May 2012

10 9 8 7 6 5 4 3 2 1

Printed in the United States of America

To Zack, through the fire and the forge

Chapter 1

London, England, 1763

The Honorable Anne Hartfield had married a stranger. The thought drummed in her head all day, through the morning ceremony at Saint George's and the recitation of vows.

I, Anne Elizabeth, take thee, Leopold, to my wedded Husband, to have and to hold from this day forward, for better for worse, for richer for poorer, in sickness and in health, to love, cherish, and to obey, till death us do part, according to God's holy ordinance; and thereto I give thee my troth.

He had slipped a ring upon her finger, of rubies and diamonds that had been purchased the day before—it was no family heirloom, no treasure passed from one generation to the next, but pristine from the jeweler's workbench. It was beautiful, yet as Leopold Bailey had given her the ring, its red stones on the golden band reminded Anne of sunlight pierced by drops of blood.

With this Ring I thee wed, with my Body I thee worship, and with all my worldly Goods I thee endow: In the Name of the Father, and of the Son, and of the Holy Ghost. Amen.

They were married. She was no longer her father's responsibility, but everything of her keeping now relied upon her husband. The food she ate, the clothing covering her body. The bed in which she slept, which she would sometimes share with her husband when he so chose to exercise his rights and make use of her body.

The thought made her stomach pitch to her feet. This night would see her enter into the state of married women everywhere, leaving behind the solitude of virginity. She belonged to him now, his possession.

Those whom God hath joined together let no man put asunder.

She watched him now, this stranger who was now her husband for the rest of her living days. Leopold Bailey. He stood with a group of guests, and though the breakfast at his Bloomsbury home was well attended, finding him in the glittering crowd proved itself an easy task.

"Admiring your new prize?" Lady Byton followed Anne's gaze across the drawing room.

Heat spread through Anne's cheeks, and her father's cousin chuckled. "There's no shame in it, child, for he's worth admiration."

"Then we share an opinion," Anne said. She almost checked herself, then remembered that she was now a married woman, and had the liberty of speaking with greater boldness. Unwed girls hadn't freedom of opinion, for they were to be at all times agreeable. As Mrs. Bailey, she could opine as she wished. Though she did not know if her husband would encourage such behavior. Perhaps he would be one of those stern men who wanted only silence and obedience from his wife.

She rather hoped not.

"In my youth," said Lady Byton, "we would have called such a man a 'strapper,' and so he is. Mark me, child, you'll have the devil's own time in the bedchamber, but I warrant it will put more roses in your cheeks."

Lady Byton lived in the country.

Her cheeks already red, Anne studied her new husband. Her cousin's assessment, coarse as it was, proved correct. The drawing room of his Bloomsbury house was filled with the wealthiest and most influential of London Society, men of extraordinary power, and men of extraordinary affluence. Yet no one commanded attention as Leopold did.

He was not much taller than any of the other men, yet the eye sought him out with unerring frequency. Normally, he eschewed a wig and wore his sandy hair back in a simple queue—rather like a laborer—but today he marked the occasion by having his hair dressed and powdered.

Even in his wedding finery of gold velvet and cream satin, his lean, muscular build could not be disguised, nor the breadth of his shoulders or length of his legs. A few of the wedding breakfast guests were sportsmen, just as Anne's own brothers were, but Leopold carried his physicality in a way that suggested use and purpose rather than idle recreation.

Easy to imagine that Leopold was, in fact, the son of a saddler. Not a gentleman.

"Is his father here?" Lady Byton scanned the chamber. "With a son so handsome, surely the father is as well favored."

"The elder Mr. Bailey died two years ago."

Lady Byton clicked her tongue. "Such a disappointment."

"I imagine the greater disappointment belonged to Mr. Bailey."

"And the elder Mr. Bailey's wife?"

"She was likely disappointed by her husband's death, as well."

Lady Byton pursed her lips. "As a woman happily widowed, I beg you to reconsider that notion."

Anne had witnessed many marriages amongst the ranks of the gentry. A select few could be called truly happy; even fewer might be considered love matches. Love had no commerce when it came to marriage. Only in the pages of sentimental novels did girls and young men of standing find love. For herself, she hoped only to earn her husband's respect and to give it in return. That she was married at all was something of a miracle.

A cloud of gillyflower perfume announced the approaching presence of Anne's Aunt Louise before she even spoke a word. She enveloped Anne in a fragrant embrace, crying, "Oh, my child, I wish you happy on this wondrous day."

"My thanks, Aunt." Anne extracted herself from her aunt's arms. *Wondrous*. She supposed it was.

Aunt Louise and Lady Byton hailed from opposite sides of the family and, after curtsying, eyed each other warily like two strutting hens.

"Lud, Clarissa," Louise chirped to Lady Byton. "Is it really you? You are so altered from last we saw each other. Ah, well, I suppose all that country air has a rather *ripening* effect."

"You are much the same as when last we met," answered Lady Byton. She peered closer at Aunt Louise. "The paint is unchanged."

Anne supposed she had better avert a full-scale war whilst there was still time, or else the iced cakes would be used as mortars and the wedding breakfast table would serve as battlements. "I was just telling Lady Byton that my husband's mother resides in the country, and hasn't the constitution for travel."

"She sounds very delicate," said Aunt Louise, "for a woman from the lower orders."

Anne supposed that now she was Leopold's wife, she

would have to hear such comments frequently. "I have never met her, so I have no firsthand knowledge of her health. Only what Leopold relates to me."

Lady Byton's brows rose. "It is passing strange that you have not met your husband's mother. But," she added, "the whole courtship seemed to take place with extreme haste. No banns read. Everything done by special license, regardless of the expense." Her kinswoman glanced at Anne's silver-embroidered stomacher. "Perhaps you have acted quickly in anticipation of an event?"

The very idea nearly made Anne laugh. Her? Indulge in a dalliance? "You forget, cousin, how very little any man might have to gain by compromising me."

"A hard truth, child," agreed Aunt Louise. "A baron's daughter you might be, but the estate loses capital like a cup made of lace."

Lady Byton clearly felt the need to defend her side of the family. "But Anne has three brothers. Even the most profitable of titles would be hard-pressed in the keeping of all of them."

"Yes, however," smiled Aunt Louise with all the warmth of an adder, "I am obliged to note that the two younger boys must truly earn their bread through the military and the Church."

Leaving Anne with a paltry dowry and even smaller annual income. Soon after her coming-out, she began to realize the futility of a Season as, one by one, young men learned how little she could bring them, and they fell away, petals from a dying blossom.

"If you are not *enceinte*," said Lady Byton, pointedly turning from Aunt Louise, "then why the rapidity of the marriage?"

"Because Leopold wished it." Honestly, Anne did not know how or why the courtship had progressed as fast as it had. It seemed a blur to her now. Within a few meetings, she had found herself engaged and, only weeks after that, married. It was as though she had been playing blindman's buff: she'd been blindfolded and spun around, then she had grabbed the first person she could. Now she stood with sight and balance restored, the wife of a man she hardly knew.

As if sensing her watching him, Leopold turned, his gaze holding hers. Anne could not look away as he murmured something to the guests and then walked toward her, weaving through the guests. He moved beautifully, with a sleek animal fluidity that suggested barely restrained power. His gaze never left her, as if she were the prize he was determined to claim. The thought both thrilled and terrified.

She saw now how he had risen from his humble beginnings to who he was now: one of the wealthiest nontitled men in England. He permitted nothing to stand in his path.

Anne's pulse quickened as Leopold came to stand before her. Good Lord, how had she managed to wed this gorgeous stranger? He had none of the well-bred gentleman's softness, no insipid chin from generations of selective breeding. A bold jaw, high cheekbones, firm mouth that boasted a full lower lip. His morning shave had already lost its battle, and Anne could mark the faint trace where his beard gilded his cheeks and chin. As if the veneer of civility could not last long, and the marauder beneath came to the surface.

At eight and twenty, he was only five years older than she, yet he had the air of a man who had seen and knew the world. She had known . . . only this. London. The circles of the polite. What she understood of life outside her conscripted patterns came from books, yet she knew that the world as depicted on the printed page did not reflect true experience.

Her new husband was experienced. Even a sheltered young woman like her could see it.

"Ladies," he murmured, bowing.

Though Aunt Louise was surely on the other side of forty, and Lady Byton a good ten years older, both trilled and blushed as if barely out of the nursery. Anne could not fault their response. She was *married* to him, yet his nearness befuddled her senses to an alarming degree, and when he next spoke, her heartbeat raced.

"Might I speak with my lady wife in private?"

"Most certainly, Mr. Bailey," warbled Aunt Louise.

"Emphatically, Mr. Bailey," added Lady Byton. The two women nearly came to blows in their haste to curtsy prettily in their departure.

As her kinswomen drifted away, sudden panic gripped Anne. *Don't leave me alone with him!*

She pushed that thought away. This man was her husband now. They would be alone together a great deal. And in all their interactions, he was always courteous. She had nothing to fear.

"The wedding breakfast pleases you, my lady wife," he said. This was not a question, merely a statement of fact.

"It does, sir," she answered. "I commend your household for assembling such a feast in so short a time."

He turned to survey the long table that spanned the length of the chamber. Rather than look at the pyramids of iced cakes, the platters of roast pheasant, the bowls of negus, Anne gazed at her husband. He studied the table as if assessing its profitability, sharp and shrewd.

"It isn't enough," he said. "I'll have servants go to the shops and get more."

"No, please." Anne placed a hand on his sleeve. She felt solid muscle beneath his velvet coat, then snatched her hand back, shocked by the sudden intimacy of touch. During their brief courtship, she had taken his arm a time or two when walking, but that had been *before*. Before they were married, and the promise of his body existed only in theory rather than the soon-to-be-realized future.

She also did not know how he would respond to being contradicted.

"That is, sir," she murmured, "no one can fault you for your hospitality. There is plenty for all of the guests."

He looked unconvinced, so Anne continued. "There is such surplus, Lady Taplow is putting cake into her pockets. I wager her panniers are stuffed with bacon."

A smile curved at the corners of his mouth, softening the hardness of his expression. "I pity those who have to carry her home in a sedan chair. Perhaps we should send her in a dray."

"Drawn by draft horses."

His gaze now turned back to her, and she grew warm to be under his scrutiny. His deep-set eyes were clear gray, the sky moments after dawn, and they missed nothing. She rather felt like the table bearing the wedding feast, being assessed, her worth judged.

Apparently, whatever he saw when he looked at her pleased him, for his smile widened. "With the business of the day, I neglected to tell you how pretty you look."

"You are gracious, sir, and a flatterer." He might well compliment her on her appearance: everything she wore had been purchased by him, from her open sack gown of blue Spitalfields silk, to the silver lace frothing at the sleeves and pinned in her hair, to the pearls at her throat and the satin slippers on her feet. Even her fine West Indian cotton chemise was provided at his expense.

The whole of the wedding had been paid for by Leopold. All her father had provided was her.

"Not at all," Leopold said. "Plain speaking is my only form of address. I know no other way." His expression darkened slightly. "A fault of my birth."

"Honesty isn't a fault." She ducked her head. "Forgive

me, I talk too boldly, and would hate to have you regret our marriage before it is scarce two hours old."

"No." He touched his finger to her chin and gently raised her head. "Don't apologize for speaking your mind." His gaze warmed. "You're right. Honesty isn't a fault—in and out of business. And I encourage you to always say what you think."

Well—that was certainly different from the advice Anne had received from her mother. *Tell him what he wants to hear. Always agree, never contradict. That is how one maintains tranquility in marriage.*

Perhaps it was different amongst people without titles. She had so little experience with them, every moment was a discovery.

"If it pleases you, sir," she said.

"It does. It would also please me, Anne, if you called me 'Leo,' not 'sir.' 'Sir' feels . . . cold."

"Yes, sir . . . I mean, Leo." Her own parents called each other *my lord* and *my lady* or, when they were especially vexed with each other, *Lord Wansford* and *Lady Wansford*.

She and Leo fell into a silence that was not entirely comfortable. So much of him remained mysterious to her beyond only the barest outline of his history, and even that was cloaked in speculation and uncertainty. Together, they watched the room as people ate and drank and an occasional laugh floated through the room.

"I must admit that many of these guests are unknown to me," she finally said. Gentry she might be, but her family's circumstances had been reduced for so long that they seldom had the funds to make suitable appearances. New clothes cost money, as did tickets to the theater. "Are they all your friends?"

"Of the men in this room, I could claim less than half as acquaintances."

Her brows rose. "Then why—"

There was little warmth in his chuckle. "A business investment. That fellow, over by the sweetmeats." Leo nodded toward the man in question, a stout gentleman leaning on a cane as he selected one of the little confections. "He owns warehouses here and in Liverpool. By inviting him to my wedding festivities, he'll be more inclined to give a reduced rate to store cotton arriving in from the Colonies."

"Cotton shipments in which *you* have invested."

"Precisely." Leo turned his sharp gaze toward a lanky man in rust-colored satin. "That's Lord Medway. His estate is in the prime location for a canal that will help get tin from Cornish mines to London. He's been balking at the idea of cutting a canal, but after today and the amount of claret he's drinking, he might be favorable to the scheme."

"Not everyone must be here for the advancement of business, surely."

"Oh, no." He flicked a glance toward a cluster of people, men and women Anne vaguely recognized as being well above her in rank, including a duke and duchess, and two viscounts. "Seven years ago, none of those people would have admitted me or my father into their kitchens, let alone their ballrooms. Yet now they gather in *my* house, eating *my* food, drinking *my* wine."

The coldness of his tone startled her, as did the predatory animal lurking behind his wintry eyes. Good God, *whom* had she married?

"There must be some guests in attendance that are truly your friends," she protested.

At this, his expression thawed. "Over there, by the windows. *Those* men are my friends."

Anne followed his gaze, yet knew already who she would see. The only men other than her husband who drew attention. Certainly, even though the trio were merely conversing amongst themselves, all the guests kept glancing over at them warily as if they were dangerous beasts about to slip their tethers.

The Hellraisers.

Sheltered Anne might be, yet even she had heard of these men, her husband's closest associates. He was, in fact, one of their ranks. Whoever had access to a scandal sheet knew of the Hellraisers. Their exploits were well documented, and if only half of the stories were true, they lived very wild lives indeed. Carousing, gambling, racing, duels, and opera dancers.

They were never mentioned directly by name. *Lord W—y, habitué of the gaming tables. Lord R—l, a veteran of warfare against the French in the Colonies, lately seeing more action at certain establishments of pleasure in our fair metropolis. Mr. B—y, as feared at the Exchange as he is known for the noble company he keeps.*

These three Hellraisers were spotted without their companions Sir E F-S and the Hon. Mr. G—y in a den of fashionable iniquity, after which they retired to more private entertainments at the home of Lord R—l.

The one reason why men of such wicked reputation saw admittance to polite society was by virtue of their titles. Only Leo lacked a title, but his vast fortune admitted him where absence of breeding might deny.

Surely it must be wonderful to be a man, to have such freedom.

Yet she should not trust the scandal sheets. Everyone understood that they manufactured most of what they printed, and Anne would be foolish indeed if she attributed such wild behavior to her new husband. Not without learning who he *truly* was.

"Come, and I'll introduce you to them."

Before Anne could speak, Leo took her hand and led her across the room. He'd never held her hand before, and she felt the heat of his touch travel up her arm and through her body. His hand was large, the texture of his skin rough, and she felt fragile almost to the point of breaking in his grasp.

It wasn't an entirely pleasant sensation.

Distracted as she was by Leo's touch, she found herself nearing a trio of men she had read about many times, but never met.

Strange. As Anne approached them, she felt a odd humming sensation, as if passing through a spider's web made of dark, almost sinister energy. She fought the shudder that ran through her, and dismissed the thought as the product of nervous humors, or bridal trepidation.

Sinister energy, indeed. I'm merely hungry. Couldn't even finish my chocolate this morning.

She shook off her peculiar mood, and made herself smile politely as Leo performed the introductions.

"Anne, let me give you the questionable privilege of introducing my friends. This is the Honorable John Godfrey."

"My felicitations, Mrs. Bailey." Thin and gingery, Mr. Godfrey bowed over her hand, and it surprised Anne that a man with a scandalous reputation could look so scholarly. In snatches of overheard conversations, she had heard her brothers and father make mention of him, that he was a figure of considerable influence within the government. There had been undercurrents of something tight and edged in the voices of her family, something she might identify as fear, but it had been more tone than actual words spoken.

How could such a bookish man also be a profligate *and* a political threat? Surely she must have misheard, and the reports in the papers were scurrilous.

She curtsied her greeting, murmuring pleasantries.

"Here we have Sir Edmund Fawley-Smith," continued Leo.

"You illuminate the room, Mrs. Bailey." Sir Edmund offered her a very charming bow, and she could not help but smile at him. He was a very pleasant young gentleman, of shorter stature than the other Hellraisers, with kindly eyes and a rather rumpled appearance. Certainly *he* could not be a rake.

"And lastly, this is the extremely *dis*honorable Abraham Stirling, Lord Rothwell."

Anne turned to the final member of the group, fully anticipating that she would find him as undeserving of a rake's reputation as the other men. But that was not the case at all. She had actually seen caricatures of Baron Rothwell in a few news sheets, usually depicting him with his arms around whole seraglios of women, and Anne had believed the illustrator to be exercising a good deal of artistic license when it came to Lord Rothwell's appearance. Surely no actual man could be so darkly handsome, with a blade-sharp profile, black hair, and vivid blue eyes. Yet the illustrator had not exaggerated. With the exception of Leo, Anne had never beheld a man so physically arresting.

The only thing marring his masculine beauty was the large, ugly scar that traced from just beneath his right ear to disappear beneath the folds of his stock. It looked as though someone long ago had tried to cut Lord Rothwell's throat, and very nearly succeeded.

That Lord Rothwell stood before her now, bowing, proved that not only had the attacker *not* succeeded, but it was highly likely that Lord Rothwell had dispatched the assailant. Killed him. Looking into his glacial eyes, Anne could easily believe him capable of violence.

Violence, or seduction. Doubtless both.

"You have done England a great service, Mrs. Bailey," he said, straightening from his bow. Anne had to tilt her head back to look at him, for he was even taller than Leo.

"How so, Lord Rothwell?"

"By marrying this villain, you have removed a great danger from the London streets."

Leo scowled as Mr. Godfrey and Sir Edmund laughed. "I'm no more a danger than you, Bram."

Lord Rothwell spread his hands. "Thus you prove my thesis."

"*Quod erat demonstrandum*," said Mr. Godfrey, grinning.

Anne made herself smile, for though she did not understand precisely what the men discussed, she knew it would serve her well in married life to ingratiate herself as best she could with her husband's friends.

Still, something, or rather, some*one* seemed missing.

"Is Lord Whitney here?" she asked. The scandal sheets had been very specific in naming five men as Hellraisers: the four who stood before her now, and James Sherbourne, the Earl of Whitney, or *Lord W—y*. Wherever one of the Hellraisers went, the others were certain to follow.

She may as well have dropped a moldering carcass in the middle of the room. Whatever lightheartedness the men might have been feeling disappeared immediately. Everyone looked grim, and something very like grief flashed in Lord Rothwell's eyes.

"Oh, dear," Anne stammered. "He isn't . . . that is, I didn't know . . . has Lord Whitney passed on?" Mortified, she wanted to sink into the ground. "I'm so . . . sorry."

"Don't apologize." Leo patted her hand, but the gesture did not soothe her. "Whit . . . Lord Whitney is alive. Last I heard."

"Have you seen him lately?" Lord Rothwell put the question to her with surprising keenness, verging on an interrogation.

Four pairs of eyes fixed on her, all of them sharp and demanding. And her husband's gaze was hardest of all. Anne had to physically restrain herself from cringing.

"No," she answered at once. "I have seen Lord Whitney but a handful of times, the last of which was likely a year ago." She wished she could remember the specifics of the day, if only as an appeasement, but to be the object of such intense scrutiny rather unnerved her.

At her answer, the tension from the men lessened. Marginally.

Leo gave a tight nod. "It seems Lord Whitney is gone from here."

Gone from here could mean any number of things, yet Anne knew better than to press for an explanation. Whatever had happened, wherever Lord Whitney was, it left a cold shadow over the four men with her now. Including her husband. At his last mention of Lord Whitney's name, Leo absently rubbed at his shoulder, and frowned at the floor. What he saw was not the Axminster carpet, but dark, ominous scenes. Scenes from his past, shared with the other Hellraisers—but not her.

She had thought it before, but she truly believed it now: her husband was a stranger. A stranger with secrets.

"She's a bit undersized," said Bram. He and Leo stood off to the side of the drawing room, watching as dancers made their figures. As the day had worn on, and the sun had set, musicians had arrived. Footmen had moved the table, the carpets had been rolled up, the candles were lit, and dancing had begun.

A fine tension ran through Leo. He felt it in Bram, and the other Hellraisers, yet none of them wanted to speak of it on this day. Anne, unknowing, had spoken of the very issue—the very *person*—none wanted to discuss. The one who had been their closest ally and now threatened everything.

"Delicate," Leo corrected, forcing his mind toward less troubling subjects.

"I would have thought you might favor a more robust girl."

Over the rim of his glass, Leo watched his new wife

move through the patterns of a dance. It was the Friar and the Nun. Or maybe Gathering Peascods. He could never remember all the names of the dances, nor their figures. It mattered little—he never stayed at assemblies and balls long enough to dance, and other, more important thoughts filled his brain. The cost of transporting pepper from Sumatra. The profitability of shipping English ale to India.

Today, he'd done his duty and danced one figure with Anne, then quickly retired to the side of the chamber, leaving the celebrating to others, including his wife.

She *was* a delicate thing. When Leo had first seen Anne Hartfield at an assembly, she'd made little impression on him. Small of stature, her hair somewhere between blond and brunette, eyes more distinctive for their liveliness than their hazel color. There were other girls, girls of more vivid beauty and sparkling dispositions, who giggled and artfully fanned themselves whenever he made mildly flirtatious remarks. Anne had only smiled and looked away, as if uncertain how to respond.

Even now, partnered with one of her elder brothers, she moved tentatively through the steps of the dance, though it was part of every genteel girl's education to have a dancing master and learn to make pretty figures at assemblies. Her family's reduced circumstances were no secret, however, so perhaps she never had a dancing master.

"I'll own," he said lowly, "that when I decided it was time to wed, there had been other girls that first attracted my notice. But I came to see that Anne was perfect."

Bram looked skeptical. "Some of your Exchange logic?"

"I'm never without it. It was simply a matter of the best return for my investment."

"An aristocratic bride—I see the reasoning behind that decision."

As one of Leo's closest friends, Bram could read his heart well. Nor did Leo make much secret of his demands.

He burned for entry into a world long denied him. That could only be achieved by marrying a peer's daughter rather than a daughter of one of the wealthy ironmongers or heads of a trade corporation. Such a marriage might net him wealth, and valuable business connections. But he already had wealth. He had connections. What he wanted, demanded, could only be gained through blood ties.

He would not gain a title, but by the Devil's fire, he *would* have what his father had been denied: a place in Society.

And he refused to let Whit endanger that.

"Yet why not pick a bride with a fortune?" Bram asked. "Why the daughter of a baron treading the waters of genteel poverty?"

"For that very reason." When Bram continued to look unconvinced, Leo continued. "Had she come with a fortune of her own, one that matched or was greater than the one *I* possess, it would serve only to divide us. She would hold it over my head as proof of her superiority."

"I had no idea you were so mercenary, young Leopold."

Leo looked askance at Bram. "A lecture? From the man who has debauched most of the female populace of London?"

His friend chuckled, though the sound was more a shadowed representation of laughter rather than the thing itself. "No lecture. *All* of us Hellraisers live in glass houses."

"Damned drafty, those houses." Leo shrugged. "Yet they're better than dull, dense piles of stone."

Bram patted an ornate plaster embellishment on the wall behind him. Everything in Leo's home was new, this portion of Bloomsbury having been developed within the past few years. He had considered purchasing a townhome in Mayfair or Saint James's. He had the money. Yet he wanted his own place, something entirely his.

"Now you have your house *and* your aristocratic bride. What more could you want?"

Now it was Leo's turn to laugh. "There is always more. You, of all people, should know that."

Understanding darkened Bram's face. "Perhaps that is why Mr. Holliday picked *us* to be recipients of his gifts."

The mention of the Hellraisers' benefactor reminded Leo that the threat could no longer be ignored. "Find John. I'll collect Edmund, then we shall all meet in my study."

"Leave your wedding celebration?"

"For a few moments only. We must discuss Whit."

Bram's expression tightened. Of all of the Hellraisers, Bram had been closest to Whit. The betrayal had cut Bram deeply. Even months later, Leo saw the pain was still fresh.

Bram strode away in search of John, while Leo went to find Edmund. As he strolled through the chamber, guests continued to come up and wish him joy of his marriage. He accepted their felicitations, and felt a hard, sharp thrill to see his noble guests' silken finery strewn with crumbs and stained with wine from *his* table.

Eat and drink, you bastards. Stuff yourselves stupid, drink yourselves senseless. You'll be too fat and drunk to notice me tearing you to pieces.

He found Edmund watching the dancers and clapping along with the music.

"You aren't dancing," Leo noted. "You always dance."

"Now my dances are reserved for Rosalind."

"Dancing only with your wife? How provincial."

Edmund merely smiled. "With her, I am content to be the most unfashionable of men."

"You should have brought her."

At this, Edmund's usually cheerful expression dimmed. "Having her attend a social function such as this so soon . . ."

Leo nodded in understanding. Rosalind's first husband had died in a carriage accident not two months earlier. A month after that, she and Edmund had wed. There had been scandalized murmurs about how quickly the marriage had taken place. A few had even suspected that Edmund had somehow engineered the accident in order to finally gain the hand of the woman denied him years ago. The rumors never took seed—nobody could believe such an amiable man as Edmund could possibly do something so brutal and calculating.

But Leo knew the truth. As did Bram and John. And they would tell no one. For it was their truth, too. One far beyond the understanding of ordinary folk.

Whit also knew the truth. Yet he could do much worse than damage their reputations.

"Join me and Bram and John in the study," Leo said now. "We need to discuss the traitor."

Edmund nodded tightly, determination writ plain on his face. As Leo and Edmund skirted the edge of the chamber, the dance ended. Anne glided toward him with an anxious frown.

"Is everything well?" she asked.

"Private business, my dear. Between old friends," he added, with a glance toward Edmund.

"Of course." She was quick to make herself amenable, which oddly disturbed him. He supposed most men desired an acquiescent wife. Yet he found just then that a display of spine might suit Anne. He admired strength and determination in others—his wife would be no exception.

Hell, he hoped his choice in a bride hadn't been a mistake, guided by his own sense of retribution.

"Only," she added, "there is talk of putting us to bed soon, and it would be rather awkward if there was no groom to join me in the bedchamber." Pink flooded her cheeks, yet he was pleased to see that she did not look away, but held his gaze. Tremulously.

"You will find me at the head of the procession."

She smiled, relieved, and dipped into a curtsy. "I shall see you then."

"A very sweet girl," Edmund said after Anne moved away. He raised a brow. "How very unlike you."

Leo scowled. "I desire sweetness, too."

"Have a care with her." Edmund's normally genial expression grew serious. "Women are not trade routes to be aggressively negotiated."

"And my brutish peasant hands might crush her."

"Don't be an ass." Even affable Edmund could lose his temper. "Only, use that clever brain of yours to *see* your wife. What she thinks. What she feels. You will find it a better path to happiness."

Leo laughed. "I'm married now. Happiness has nothing to do with it."

Edmund shook his head, yet he followed as Leo led him from the chamber and down the corridor to his study. Sounds of music and merriment faded the deeper he went into his house. The sounds of an unknowing, innocent world, beholden to no one, subject only to reason and scientific principles. But Leo and the other Hellraisers knew differently.

A thought leapt into Leo's mind: What if Anne learned the truth about him? About the nature of the meeting he was about to have? What might she do?

He shrugged. If Anne ever discovered his secret, she could do nothing. *He* was the one with the power. Even if someone believed her allegations—which they never would—she had no leverage and could not harm him. No, the bigger threat came from Whit.

Within the book-lined room, he found Bram and John already there, illuminated by a single candle on his desk. Full night had fallen, and shadows were thick in the room, so that in the light of the candle, Leo and his friends appeared to be shades emerging from the Underworld.

Leo locked the door, and made sure all the windows were closed, the curtains drawn. With actions deliberate and ceremonial, he poured five glasses of brandy and handed them to his fellow Hellraisers.

"There's only four of us now," John said, eyeing the remaining glass.

As if Leo, or any of their company, could forget. That was what this private meeting was about. Whit's absence, and its tacit condemnation, howled like a cavern. Three months had passed since Whit had severed his ties with the Hellraisers, had urged Leo and John and Edmund to turn their backs on the source of their power. But Whit had been troubled, and misled. Especially by that Gypsy girl.

Leo had the scar on his shoulder as proof of his erstwhile friend's perfidy. Whit had made his choice, and no one had seen him these past months. Running scared, Leo supposed.

Only to himself did he admit that he missed Whit, his company, his counsel. Leo could not step into White's and see the hazard tables without thinking of Whit, for he had been a familiar figure there, wagering outrageous sums of money only for the thrill of risk. Gone now. All gone. Once inseparable, the five of them had been cleaved apart, never to be whole again.

Whit was a danger, one that had to be found and contained. And Leo knew the best way to find him, but he required assistance.

"For our guest," said Leo. He drew a breath, then spoke. "*Veni, geminus.*"

The candle guttered. Went out. The room became a black chasm, and the scent of burnt paper thickened in the air.

By touch, Leo struck a flint, lit a tinder, and brought it to the candle.

The doors to the study were locked, the windows shut. No one could get in or out of the room unnoticed.

Yet now a fifth man stood before Leo and the others. As always, the man wore elegant, expensive clothing, and he glittered as he bowed.

"Compliments, Hellraisers," the man said, smiling and making his leg. "And compliments from my master, the Devil."

Chapter 2

"The Devil?" Leo felt his mouth curl. "Your master's usually more discreet with his name. Last we were informed, he preferred to be known as 'Mr. Holliday.'"

The *geminus* smiled. Or rather, Leo had the sense that the thing smiled, for try as he might, he had never once truly beheld its face. It was always . . . blank, and Leo's gaze kept sliding away from it, as though trying to find purchase on a slick incline.

"He cannot resist a moment of theatricality, my master, and I am always obliging." The *geminus* eyed the three other Hellraisers. "Good sirs, this is a rare occasion to be summoned before the entire company."

"Not the entire company," said Bram tightly.

At this, the *geminus* made a clicking sound of displeasure. "Our prodigal. Lord Whitney."

"Thus my presence here, and not at my own wedding." The sounds of revelry could be heard only faintly through the door to the study, like vestiges of memory. "We need intelligence—the whereabouts of Whit. What can you or your master tell us?"

"Very little," said the *geminus*.

"Bloody nonsense." Cerebral as John usually was, he

also possessed a temper of quick and biting ferocity, and it snapped from him now like a whip. "We're to believe that the Devil himself—a being of unimaginable power— he and all his minions have not the means between them of locating one damned man?"

"His Gypsy girl, too," added Edmund.

"Without a lick of magic between them," Leo said.

"Lord Whitney did surrender his power to manipulate chance," the *geminus* conceded. "The Gypsy, however . . ." It shrugged. "She can still manipulate fire. *Her* ability did not come from my master. The one who bestowed that ability on her is also the one who shields Lord Whitney's location from my master."

"Damned mad Roman ghost," muttered Bram.

Its tone belying the studied indolence of its pose, the *geminus* pressed, "Has Valeria Livia Corva appeared to any of you of late?"

All of the Hellraisers, including Leo, answered, "Nay."

"Can't say as I miss her presence," said Leo. "Hovering at my bedside, babbling at me to turn my back on the Devil and renounce my magic." As though the words of an insane specter could possibly induce Leo to give up his gift of precognition. "I make my damned fortune investing in the future. And she thinks I'll willingly give up my ability to see that future? She *is* mad."

"Power," said John with a cutting smile. "No greater gift."

"Aye." Leo had dreamt about power, obsessed over it. And the Devil had given it to him. "And because of that, here I am, with the elite of Society celebrating my wedding to a peer's daughter."

Like hell would Leo willingly give up that power. To keep it, he would do *anything*.

"The ghost has been absent, however," noted Edmund. "Her strength's diminished."

"My master senses that she is but gathering her resources after she depleted them in Manchester."

"You were there," said Leo, turning to Bram.

"Witness to part of it, nothing more." Bram's voice was as dark as the shadows. "Whit and his Gypsy wench, they destroyed a gaming hell belonging to Mr. Holliday. Whit and the girl barely escaped with their lives. I saw a chance, a final chance, to bring him back to the Hellraisers. Talked to him. But the bastard remained adamant. Wanted all of us to give back our magic, and to join him in the fight against the Devil." The scorn in Bram's words left no question as to how he felt about Whit's entreaty.

"You should have used your gift of magic," John snapped. "Persuaded him to return to us."

"Don't you think I wanted to?" Bram fired back. "But I'd used it on him in Oxford, when he gave Leo that souvenir."

Leo's hand rubbed at his shoulder. The scar from the rapier blade had faded, but it would never disappear, nor the memory of the Hellraisers fighting Whit outside the Oxford tavern. The final break in their friendship, cauterized by the Gypsy girl's fire and Whit's steel. "You didn't have to force him to fight us. He didn't want to."

"Whit either stands with us, or he's our enemy. There's no middle ground. No *possibly*, no *perhaps*. Not when it comes to being a Hellraiser, and the power we have."

"Yet you didn't use that power on Whit in Manchester," John persisted. "It could have allied us once more."

Tightening his jaw, Bram glared first at John, then the *geminus*. "I can only use my ability once on someone. A limitation of which I had not been informed."

The *geminus* said, bland and mild, "The gifts my master has bestowed on each of you cannot be without boundary, else you may do yourselves a terrible injury."

"Considerate of your master," drawled Leo. His own

magic had its particular constraints, but he learned them quickly and made the necessary adjustments. In truth, Leo could not be overly critical of Mr. Holliday, for though there were restrictions to Leo's ability to see the future, the benefits far outweighed the limitations.

Leo knew one benefit: his wedding celebration happening at that very moment. He thought of Anne, his pretty, genteel bride, a woman he would never have had the temerity to talk to, let alone court and marry. Leo had grown up amidst the smell of leather and a single, smoky brazier filling a cramped little house. A saddler's son. But Adam Bailey had possessed ambition, and his son had even more.

The Demon of the Exchange. Even before he had received the gift of foreknowledge, Leo had earned this name. Fearless, ferocious, and uncompromising in his investments.

He made the wealthy peers shake in their silver-buckled shoes. Just as he desired.

His bride was afraid of him, too. He saw it in her eyes, the look of a woman confronting an animal she wasn't sure was tame.

He wasn't certain he wanted a wife who feared him. It seemed a petty, mean way of conducting a marriage, the sort of thing a bully desired—exerting one's might over a creature that constituted no threat.

Anne could not possibly hurt him. But there were others who could.

"How much danger does Whit pose?" he asked the *geminus*.

"If any of you gentlemen see Lord Whitney, do not engage with him. Summon me or any of my *gemini* brethren immediately, and we shall attend to the matter."

It won't tell us precisely how dangerous Whit is. Nor

that we should come into direct contact with him. Which means it's truly afraid.

"I'm keeping Rosalind," said Edmund, fierce. "Whatever's necessary, I'll do it."

"Whitehall is almost mine," John said. "Almost. But if I can't read others' thoughts, it could all be lost, like that." He snapped his fingers, the noise sharp in the quiet of the study. "I'll be no closer to a ranking Cabinet position than a damned pig farmer. I cannot have him, or any of you, compromise that."

Tension thickened in the room. Everyone glared at one another. Hell, they'd start scrapping with each other in a moment.

"When the time comes, all of us shall do what is needed to protect our magical gifts." Leo smoothed the scowl from his expression, and made himself smile. "For now, lads, be at ease. This isn't merely a counsel of war. It's an offer of thanks. For with assistance"—he nodded in turn at Bram, Edmund, John, and the *geminus*—"I was able to speed the process of my nuptials along, and bring sooner this happy day."

Bram's ability to persuade anyone to do anything had enabled Leo to get a special license rather than go through the lengthier process of having the banns read. Edmund had used his wife's distinguished connections to sufficiently pad the wedding feast with the wealthy and the powerful. John's contribution had been the reading of Anne's father's thoughts, which, combined with Leo's own intuitive ability to gauge people, enabled Leo to say precisely the right things to secure the hand of Lord Wansford's daughter. And, of course, it had been the gift of magic from the *geminus*'s master that increased Leo's fortune.

His wife knew none of this, naturally. She had no

understanding of his double life, nor the world in which she had now stepped.

Recognizing the joint efforts to hasten Leo's marriage, the hostility between the men slowly seeped away.

Though Edmund had not the ability to read minds, he seemed to know the train of Leo's thoughts. "How will you explain your markings to your bride?"

Leo's hand drifted to his back. "Markings?"

Bram snorted. "No need for coyness, Master Bailey. You know we all have them." He tapped his chest, just over his heart.

Edmund absently rubbed at his hip, and John pressed his knuckles to his ribs. Each of them, it seemed, carried the mark in different places upon their bodies.

The Devil's mark. Images of flame drawn upon his skin. They had appeared on Leo's back the day after he and the other Hellraisers had received Mr. Holliday's gifts. The mark had been much smaller then, confined to the area between his shoulder blades. Day by day, however, it had grown. Increased by an unseen hand. Fortunately, Leo's valet knew not to ask questions. Spinner was the only person who ever saw the markings. Leo was at all times careful not to bathe in the presence of others.

But soon his wife would see him unclothed.

"What say your courtesans and opera dancers when they see your markings?" Leo asked Bram.

His friend offered a careless shrug. "Nothing, of course. They are too well paid to offer opinions. And those that do venture to speak believe the markings to be some vestige of my time amongst the Natives in America, a primitive means of adorning the body. I do not bother to correct them."

"Your new wife may act as my Rosalind does," said Edmund. "She has seen the markings on me, naturally, but is far too decorous to speak of them."

Following Bram's example, Leo shrugged. "In a way, Anne's compliance has been purchased, like Bram's opera dancers. If I give her no explanation at all, she must be content."

"A sensible way to conduct a marriage," said John approvingly.

"As though you would have any experience on the subject," Edmund said with a shake of his head. He held his glass of brandy aloft. "As the only other married Hellraiser, I welcome Leo to the blessed state of matrimony."

"Better you than I." Yet John smiled, and also lifted his glass. "Felicitations."

Bram did not raise his glass, however. "Does this mean you shall become as dull as Edmund?"

"The dullard in question is every bit a Hellraiser," Edmund said, scowling. "Merely because I refrain from sticking my cock in every available quim doesn't signify I am any less of a Hellraiser."

"What's the point of *being* a Hellraiser, then?"

"Freedom," said Leo. "And from that freedom, power."

"The groom speaks good sense," John said. "And with that, I urge a truce between Bram and Edmund. We cannot afford any more dissention in our ranks."

Leo and the other men murmured in agreement.

"Then lift your glass, Bram," said John, "and wish Leo happy."

With a grudging smile, Bram did so.

Leo turned to the *geminus*. "The other glass is for you."

"You are all kindness." It bowed. "But the *gemini* do not partake of mortal food or drink."

"Just take the damned glass," growled Bram, "and join us in a toast. Don't have to drink a bloody drop."

"Of course, my lord." The creature was all solicitousness. "I am most eager to bestow my congratulations." It took the remaining glass.

"To Leo," said John.

"And Anne," added Edmund.

"May you each receive precisely what you deserve." This, from Bram.

"Good God," said Leo, "what an ominous toast."

Edmund hastily amended. "May you grow rich in wealth and happiness."

Leo grinned. "I *am* rich." In money, at any rate. Happiness would come . . . later.

"Rich*er*, then."

The *geminus* had its own offering. "My master's favor upon you and your new bride."

"To the bride and groom, Mr. and Mrs. Bailey." With John's words, everyone brought their glasses together. The sound chimed through the room like a brittle dream.

As the brandy was downed by everyone but the *geminus*, the creature asked, "My master would like to know when you anticipate returning to the Exchange."

"Bloody hell," sputtered Edmund. "The man is but hours newly married. Mr. Holliday cannot expect him to *work*. Not so soon."

Leo raised his hand. "Peace, Edmund."

"But you haven't even left for your bridal journey—"

"There isn't going to be a bridal journey."

"Why ever not?"

Leo shrugged. "Anne never asked for one, and I am disinclined to be away from business for so long."

Shocked, Edmund turned to Bram and John, looking for reinforcement.

"I am happily wedded to politics," said John. "The bachelor state is all I shall ever know."

Bram's mordant look made plain his feelings about the nature of matrimony.

Lacking support, all Edmund could do was splutter his

indignation. He shook his head and poured himself more brandy.

"Why should the Devil care whether or not Leo is at the Exchange?" John asked the *geminus*.

Again, Leo felt rather than saw the creature's cold smile. "The further building of Mr. Bailey's fortunes is always a concern of my master. And," it added, "my master does enjoy it greatly when Mr. Bailey compromises the fortunes of others."

"On that matter," said Leo, "your master and I are in agreement." For the pleasure in amassing wealth paled beside the lurid glow of bringing down those who held themselves superior to him. He could buy their estates and have surplus in his coffers, yet all the aristocracy saw when they looked at him was tannery dye staining his fingers. No matter that he'd scrubbed the discoloration away over a decade ago. No, he was nothing but a laborer, a saddler's son, and thus undeserving of the honor of their approval.

His body felt the familiar charge of energy when he contemplated whom he might destroy and by what means. Better to be the Demon of the Exchange than the Upstart Peasant.

He had money. He had an aristocratic wife. And he had magic bestowed upon him by the Devil.

And when the noblemen who sneered and spat came crawling to him on their bellies, pleading for loans, for mercy and compassion . . . he would laugh and kick them away, his boot in their faces, and tell stories to his father's headstone.

We've beaten them, Da. It was beautiful to see. Beautiful.

He would not waste precious time on something as inconsequential as a bridal journey. What was a tour of the Lake District compared to the destruction of a thousand years of privilege?

* * *

Anne anxiously scanned the drawing room. Still no sign of Leo. He had been sequestered in his study with his friends, and the guests began to notice. Of greater concern to her was his expression—dark and preoccupied. Something weighed on him. But what, and why on *this* day? She asked no one for answers and none came.

Falling back on years of schooling, Anne made herself circulate through the wedding feast, smiling and murmuring nonsensical pleasantries. A great deal of wine had been drunk, and the guests grew boisterous as the night deepened.

"Where's that blasted husband of yours?" Lord Runham stumbled into her path, red-faced and expansive. "'Sabout time to put you two to bed. Unless he don't fancy the job." He reached for her, this man old enough to be her father—who, in fact, was her father's friend. "Volunteer myself for the position."

Anne took a step back to evade Lord Runham's grasping hand. Then a lean, solid form stepped between her and the drunken baron. She had an impression of wide shoulders covered with golden velvet.

"No need. This is a duty I happily reserve for myself." Leo's words were affable but his tone was biting steel.

"To be sure." Lord Runham chortled, more in fear than merriment. Anne could not blame him for his alarm. The tension in Leo's posture and hardness in his voice left little doubt that he was but a hairbreadth away from violence. Almost as though he welcomed the opportunity.

"Pray, enjoy your wife's company," said Lord Runham. "I shall merely—" He didn't finish his sentence, but rather trundled away as quickly as his legs would allow.

Leo turned to face Anne, and she resisted the impulse to look down at her clasped hands. He was too imposing, too handsome, too . . . *everything*. How could she find him so attractive and so intimidating at the same time? Yet, sainted heavens, she did.

"Are you well?"

Her eyes widened at his heated tone. For a moment, she thought he might be angry with *her*, but then she saw that his anger was at her defense. It warmed her, though she could not be entirely comfortable in his presence.

"Other than a surfeit of iced cakes, I am perfectly well." She made herself smile. "I trust your . . . meeting was successful."

"Tolerably."

He seemed disinclined to say any more on the subject, and she was reluctant to press further. After all, their names were still drying on the parish register. She could not make demands of her husband so soon. According to her mother, at any rate. Throughout the day, Anne had received much advice from married women, most of it contradictory.

Be at all times silent and agreeable, else your husband will think you a termagant and shun your company.

Never allow your husband to dictate your actions or he will consider you weak and trifling, and shall not esteem you. Nothing ruins a marriage faster than lack of esteem between a man and his wife.

Which was it? Anne's head spun with words, so many words, sly winks, and knowing smirks. Up to this day, she had passed her life in relative anonymity. Now it seemed the whole of her existence became the fodder for dozens of opinions, scores of eyes. She felt rather like a newborn vole forced out into the light, naked, blind, wriggling. Ideal prey.

From across the overheated chamber, Anne's mother and several of her female relatives began walking toward her and Leo. The knowing smiles on their faces left little doubt as to their intention.

"I believe it is time for them to put us to . . . bed." Good Lord, she could barely get the word out, and she felt by turns hot and cold. The man standing beside her was about to join his body to hers in the most intimate way possible—and though she found him attractive, she barely knew him.

"This distresses you."

She did not want him to think her unwilling to perform her marital responsibilities. After all, she had been taught that therein lay a woman's primary function: the easing of a man's desires and the bearing of children.

"Not at all, sir . . . Leo. Only, there are certain aspects of a marriage that are . . . private. And this"—she waved her hand toward the advancing women—"makes it all so very . . . public."

"Then I'll tell them to go to the Devil," he answered at once.

A shocked laugh escaped her. "You can do no such thing."

He raised one brow. "This is *my* house. You are *my* wife. I'll do anything I bloody well please. And if it makes you uncomfortable to have the whole damned household shoving us into bed together, then it won't happen."

She stared at him. Many things he said astonished her. Not merely his rough language in the presence of a woman, but his willingness to flout convention. Gazing up into his cool gray eyes, Anne could see how such a man not only blazed a path for himself through the old, ancient forest of entitlement, but also how he had earned the name *Hellraiser*. A man who cared little for others' opinions, who did as he pleased—the world was his to use or discard as he wanted. Without a backward glance for the smoldering devastation he left behind.

What a heady power that must be. And he was willing to exercise it on her behalf.

"Truly, I do not mind."

"As you like." He shrugged, the pull of velvet across his shoulders a testament not only to the tailor's skill but the physicality of the man beneath the fabric. Pure feminine appreciation tugged low in her belly. What must he look like without layers of clothing?

She realized in a mix of panic and anticipation that she would find out very soon.

"Come, my child," Anne's mother sang out, nearing. "We must make you ready."

A chorus of cheers and some rather lewd suggestions resounded. Anne wondered if she might reduce to a pile of embarrassed ashes within the cage of her whalebone stays.

"Head up, my lady wife." Leo's whisper feathered warmly across her cheek, and edged excitement surged within her at the sensation. "Show 'em your spirit."

She tilted her chin up, determined to prove herself as brave as she wanted to be. For Leo's sake—and her own. This day marked her entry into true womanhood, and she was intent on crossing that threshold with a firm and un-wavering step.

As she put her shoulders back, Leo's gaze gleamed with admiration. He gave her a small nod, and she drew courage from it.

Anne allowed herself to be led away by her mother and her giggling kinswomen. The musicians sawed wildly on their instruments, filling the chamber with raucous sound, and the coarse laughter of men pushed Anne toward the door. Before she left, she sent one final glance over her shoulder, toward Leo. Men surrounded him, including the Hellraisers. A good thing Leo had a strong body, else he would have been on the floor from the force of the pounding on his back.

His darkened gaze met hers. Breath caught in her throat. Wickedly handsome. Her husband. Her body belonged to him now. *Who is he?*

And then she was pulled from the chamber. He disappeared from her sight. The next time she saw him, he would be there to take not just her maidenhead but the last vestiges of her innocence.

The voices in the corridor drew nearer. Men laughing and singing. Anne could not make out the words, though the few words she had been able to distinguish through the door had made her face heat. Soon, the men would be at the door, bringing with them her new husband.

"I hadn't expected this to be so . . . medieval."

Her mother ran an ebony-handled brush through her unbound hair, tugging hard enough to make Anne wince. "Traditional, Anne."

"And will everyone be back in the morning to examine the bedclothes?" Pain. There was going to be pain, and very soon. Her heart felt ready to detonate within her chest.

Her mother made that soft grunting noise she always made when annoyed. "There's no need for such vulgarity."

"Since the men outside seem to be taking care of that well enough."

Another grunt from her mother. "You might have spared yourself this. I have heard it is the modern fashion for newly wed couples to embark on a bridal journey immediately following the wedding breakfast."

"Leo did not suggest it." And as he was paying for everything else, from her garters to the wine, Anne had been loath to ask. Hearing the rowdy male guests approaching now, she began to question her diffidence.

"She looks beautiful, Eleanor." Aunt Louise sailed over

to where Anne stood in the middle of the bedchamber and idly toyed with the sleeve of Anne's silk nightgown. "How I envy you, child. There are few excitements in a woman's life like her first taste of her womanly duties."

"And how many times did you *first* taste them, Louise?" asked Lady Byton from her position on a footstool in the corner.

Before Aunt Louise could spit out a reply, Anne's mother said, "They are nearly here. To the bed, Anne, with haste."

Anne was herded to the bed, amidst much giggling from the women in the chamber. Her mother flipped back the heavy silk counterpane and pristine white sheets, and all but threw Anne between them. She arranged Anne's hair so that it covered her breasts. Anne supposed her mother's eagerness to see the marriage consummated stemmed from the desire to ensure no annulment. Once Anne became Leo's wife, she was no longer Lord and Lady Wansford's problem. The responsibility and cost of her upkeep fell to Leo.

Still, it was highly disturbing, contemplating her mother's eagerness to have Anne couple with a man. And she could not help but feel like a sacrificial animal, tied to a stake and bleating its distress before the inevitable doom. Was it going to hurt very much?

The door to the bedchamber slammed open. A crowd of men shoved Leo forward, though Anne could not see any of the Hellraisers amongst their numbers. Leo managed to keep his footing, despite the crowd's rough treatment of him. The song the men sang reached its conclusion, and between the presence of everyone in the bedchamber, the lyrics of the song, and the knowledge of what was about to happen, Anne had never blushed so furiously in her life.

Leo smiled and laughed, but Anne had the feeling he merely made the necessary adjustments to his face and

voice so that people would believe him in a good humor.
Yet even across the room, Anne saw impatience in his gaze.
As though he merely tolerated these antique practices, and
wanted to get on with the business at hand.

The business being the taking of Anne's virginity.

"Your bride awaits you," said Anne's mother.

In the doorway, Anne's father coughed.

At least *someone* was as discomfited as Anne. But it
did not give her much solace.

Leo's gaze moved to her, knowing and astute. She
dropped her own gaze to her hands folded on the counterpane. She wondered if he could see her heart pounding
against the silk of her nightdress, like a trapped moth. He
would touch her soon. She would know the weight of his
body on hers.

"My thanks, madam." His deep voice sent tremors of
fear and excitement through her. "And now, good night."
There was no denying it: her husband was dismissing
everyone in the chamber as though they were servants.

There were a few mumbles of disappointment. Clearly,
the guests wanted to draw out the rather public embarrassment a bit further, but Leo was having none of it. Anne
kept her gaze on her hands picking at the coverlet, but she
heard the sounds of many feet exiting the bedchamber,
some more ribaldry, and feminine giggling.

Then the sound of the door closing. And locking. Music
and laughter faded on the other side of the door as the
guests resumed their revelry without the bride and groom.

Now, for the first time, she and Leo were truly alone.
Silence stretched out, interrupted only by the popping
sounds of the fire.

Just look at him, Anne. He's only a man.

More than that, he was her husband. Therein lay the
crucial difference.

Go on. Look at him.

Slowly, Anne lifted her gaze. She started a little when she saw that Leo stood at the foot of the bed. She hadn't heard him move. Perhaps he had removed his shoes? She fought the absurd urge to peer over the side of the bed and see whether he was merely in his stockings or shod.

They stared at each other. More surprising than finding him standing so close was the glimmer of trepidation in his eyes. In the brief time she had known Leo, not once had he looked anything less than confident. It was a shock to see this extremely hale and potent man uncertain.

Was he . . . as afraid as she?

He started to drag his hand through his hair, then stopped and stared at it in disgust.

"I hate powder." He stalked away and through the door that led to a closet. Anne had seen the small chamber earlier, and noted it contained a copper bathing tub, a close stool, and a few other items for one's toilette.

She now heard the unmistakable sounds of clothing being removed. Velvet coat first, followed by the embroidered waistcoat. Was that the rustle of his shirt?

All of this disrobing was being done without the assistance of a valet. But this detail was unimportant compared to the very real truth that Leo Bailey was undressing in the very next room. With the door open.

Heat suffused her face, her limbs. Good Lord, he was taking off his breeches. She tried to picture him, his arms and legs being revealed as each garment came away—and found that she couldn't. Her mind simply shied away, protective. Anne had seen her brothers and their friends when they went for a bathe in the pond on their country estate. She had seen statuary and paintings, as well. She possessed a reasonable understanding of what the male body looked like without clothing. Like all girls, she was as fascinated as she was terrified by the idea.

How would such a body feel, so different from her

own? Would it be soft? Hard? Certainly hairier. And the male body underwent . . . changes . . . in order to have sexual congress. A married woman would doubtless be witness to those changes.

But that had all been *theory*. This was *real*, and not twenty feet away.

The sounds of splashing water trickled out from the closet. He was bathing. A pulse of arousal throbbed through her, unexpected and sudden.

As she waited, Anne tried to distract herself, and studied the bedchamber. Painted red paper covered the walls, the design depicting thickly knotted and thorny vines surmounted with carnivorous-looking flowers. The fabric comprising the bed hangings and window curtains must have been specially made, for its pattern matched the wall coverings. Two wing-backed chairs stood before the fire, and there was a large mahogany clothespress and an escritoire. Everything in the chamber revealed itself to be the finest quality. Expensive, and new.

But as for hints of the man who slept in this room, who he was, what he thought, if he had any interests or pastimes . . . Anne found none.

Perhaps she might discover books in one of the nightstands. She often had several books by her bedside—though she would never sleep in her bed at her parents' home again. She could not remember if she had packed those books in preparation for removing to Leo's house. The thought panicked her. She hoped the books were here, somewhere. As though finding an unanticipated friend in a far-distant land.

But surely Leo had a book or two at his bedside. The need to locate one such volume overwhelmed her. If she could find one, then perhaps it might give her the smallest intimation as to who this man was, this stranger she had married.

She leaned over and started to open the drawer on the nightstand.

"What are you looking for?"

She jerked up, gasping. Leo stood beside the bed, wrapped in a banyan of green-and-black silk, his damp hair loose about his shoulders. Anne had but a moment to take in a few details—his long, bare feet, the hollow of his throat, a sprinkle of dark golden hair across his chest— before the anger in his gaze blocked out all other impressions of him.

"Nothing, nothing." She didn't like the panic in her voice, or the way she pushed back into the pillows propped against the headboard. "Books, in truth."

He raised a brow. "Planning on reading?"

"I like to read before . . . bed." Her voice was thin, thready. Frightened.

Anger faded from his eyes. Replaced by something very like compassion. "This is all very strange for you."

"I imagine it is strange for *you*, as well. Unless . . . you have been married before?"

His laugh was unexpected, and genuine, and its warm contours helped soften the edges of her anxiety. "A new venture."

She imagined that marriage might be one of the few things he *hadn't* experienced.

The bed shifted as he sat down on the edge, his profile to her. He drew a breath, as if steadying himself. "Tell me, Anne. What do you know about what happens in the marriage bed?"

Don't stutter. Don't blush. He is a sophisticated man.

"I know the m . . . mechanics of it." *Curse it, what did I say about stuttering?*

He turned to her, a small smile curving his mouth. "*Mechanics* makes me think of grinding gears and pulleys. Though," he added, mostly to himself, "some might enjoy that."

She decided not to explore that last comment. "I know it can be very pleasurable for the man."

"For the woman, too." His smile warmed. "If done properly."

Oh, dear. "So . . . you've done it before."

"Few men get to my age without doing it at least once."

"When?"

"The first time, or the last time?"

She was uncertain she wanted to know the answer to either. Fragments from the scandal sheets jabbed into her thoughts, unsubtle suggestions about how the Hellraisers earned their reputations. Even Anne knew about *those women*. She had seen them at the theater, displaying themselves like gorgeous blooms in the hothouse of the private boxes, and the wealthy gentlemen that tended those blossoms, watering them with champagne and nourishing their soil with expensive trinkets. The women earned those trinkets, and Anne knew the means by which they did so.

Had Leo been one of those gentlemen? Did he know the company and bodies of courtesans? Would he continue to do so, even after their marriage?

Good God, attractive he might be, yet she really knew nothing about him.

She started at the touch of Leo's hand on hers, and she met his gaze. He drew a breath, as if steadying himself, and then leaned toward her.

Anne could do nothing but brace herself for what she knew was to happen next.

Chapter 3

He's going to kiss me. They had touched lips only once, impersonally, at the conclusion of the marriage ceremony. But this was to be a real kiss. A kiss between husband and wife. She felt as though she had been waiting for this moment forever, and wanted it, hungered for it, even as she was numb with anxiety.

She closed her eyes, and the sound of her blood in her ears was a rushing gale.

At the first brush of his mouth against hers, she jolted. Their noses bumped, hard. He pulled back.

Opening her eyes, she covered her mouth with her hands. "I'm so sorry."

He cradled his nose for a moment. "No damage done. Here." She braced herself for another attempt at a kiss. Instead, he ran his warm, long fingers across her cheek, then down her neck. He gazed at her with perplexed interest. His breath came faster, and a flush darkened his skin.

At his touch, shivers of sensation ran over her skin and echoed deep within her. It felt wondrous. It felt awful. She wanted this, wanted him, yet she had no idea who he truly was, and it was all so strange, so terribly strange.

His gaze intent, he moved closer to her. He angled his

body so that he faced her, and he filled her vision, every part of it, with the fire burning behind him.

This must be what rabbits feel when the hawk's shadow blocks the sun.

He braced one hand beside her thigh. His nearness overwhelmed her. With his other hand, he slid her hair over her shoulder, revealing the shape of her breast beneath the delicate nightgown. Her nipple made a pale point under the silk.

Leo stared at her breast, rapt as a scholar, and she could hardly catch her breath. No man had ever looked at her in this state of undress. Focus and desire sharpened Leo's face, and she felt pierced by it, by him, simply looking at her. At that moment nothing existed but the confines of the bed, and the truth that soon their bodies would be joined as intimately as possible.

Slowly, as if tracing a shadow, his hand moved from her shoulder. Down. The brush of his fingertips over her collarbone, the very top of her chest, and then lower. She bit back a gasp as his large, warm hand cupped her breast.

A rough sound came from deep within him, and an answering thrill shivered through her. His eyes were hot and sharp. When his thumb moved back and forth across her nipple, he watched the tightening bead with the intensity of a man searching for answers.

The rasp of silk and his thumb against her was exquisite, a gathering of terrifying sensation. She had learned, years ago, how to touch all the places on herself that gave pleasure, but it was so different having someone else touch her, a frightening drop into a dimly lit chasm.

"Anne," he rumbled. He lowered his head.

Another kiss. Could she do this properly? She closed her eyes.

His lips met hers, and she was grateful that she didn't jolt again. Instead, she kept herself still, willing herself to stop her mind, to simply *let* this happen. His lips were warm and firm, and they lightly moved back and forth over hers, coaxing response. The very tip of his tongue stroked against her mouth just as he grew bolder with his hand on her breast, his touch there deepening.

She was aware of everything: his mouth on hers, his harsh breath against her lips, the heat and size of his hand caressing her breast. Her own fear mingled with arousal in an alchemy she could not understand. It felt wondrous and odd and fearsome. She could not lift her hands from the counterpane. They seemed pinned like butterflies, her fingers spread, pushing down onto the bed. Part of her wanted to lift her hands and touch him, feel his sleek, hard body underneath the banyan. Part of her wanted to keep her hands flat, as if touching him were the final word spoken in an incantation that released an unknown magic.

The bed tilted as his long body stretched alongside hers. With one hand, he wove his fingers into her hair, cradling her head, and the hand that held her breast moved down with intent. The counterpane blocked its progress, and he shoved impatiently at the blanket until he found the curve of her waist. She gasped against his lips to feel the heat and strength of his hand on her. With her lips parted, he dipped his tongue into her mouth. Tastes flooded her—tobacco, wine, the flavor of a healthy male.

Oh, God, she felt *him* against her thigh. The hard thickness of his arousal. It was real, *he* was real, and a man, and she felt a rising need building within her, and she had never experienced such fear in her life, for Leo was different from her in every way. In her imaginings of this moment, she had seen herself as serenely acquiescent, almost detached. Instead, she shivered and wanted and was afraid.

His hand continued on its progress, stroking slowly from her waist to her hip. The lower his hand moved, the greater her shaking became, until she trembled so strongly that the vibrations from her body traveled into his hand and up his arm. Mortification burned her, for she knew he felt her fear. Her own breathing was a ragged sound, tattered as a scrap of lace in a gale, and tears gathered in her eyes.

Then . . . His touch disappeared. He angled away from her. For several moments, nothing happened. Anne waited and waited, until she felt ready to shatter. Finally, she opened her eyes.

He lay on his back, his breath coming in hard, quick exhalations. His hands lay on his thighs. As her gaze moved lower, she saw the banyan tented over his erection, and she quickly brought her gaze back up to his face.

A frown formed a deep line between his brows. The tightness in his jaw revealed an inner struggle.

Was he angry? With her? Why had he stopped? Too uncertain, Anne could say nothing. She felt awkward and gauche, lying beside him, her hands still splayed on the counterpane as she balanced precariously, midway between desire and terror.

At last, he broke the silence. "My parents married for love."

Of all the things for him to say, this was least expected. She struggled to align her thoughts, for they'd scattered in every direction like pins, and her body only now began to calm in its frantic trembling.

It took a moment for her to find her voice. "I didn't know."

Still staring at the canopy, he shook his head. "No reason why you would. She was a dairymaid, and she flirted with him when she passed the saddlery every day. He said she spilled so much milk from her pails—all her pretty curtsies—that every cat in the neighborhood sat on his roof. The cattery, he called his shop."

It seemed sweet and charming, far more so than the

ways in which brides were contracted for amongst the gentry, with calculated discussions of marriage portions and family connections.

"There's an advantage to being part of the lower orders." He turned his head and gave her a wry smile that did not fully warm his eyes. "Some apprentices marry their masters' daughters, but for the most part, we marry on the basis of what our hearts tell us. We have the privilege of time. Of nurturing the seedling of affection into something lush and verdant."

"That sounds . . . lovely." Her voice was barely more than a whisper, and a strange ache set up in her heart.

"It is. Or," he amended, "it would be. I am not a saddle maker and you are not a dairymaid."

"An impoverished baron's daughter and a self-made man." And they were already married.

Leo sighed, ran a hand over his jaw, then stood. The thick upright shape of his erection had begun to diminish. He walked to the clothespress and removed a long nightshirt. He eyed the garment with reluctance, then took it with him into the closet. A moment later, he emerged from the closet wearing the nightshirt, his banyan draped over his arm. The nightshirt was thinner than the banyan, and she watched the long, solid shapes of his limbs as they moved beneath the fabric. She saw the mass and shape of his manhood—that most fascinating and terrifying part of him—though his arousal had faded.

Slowly, he moved through the chamber, dousing the candles. She could not stop herself from staring at the taut forms of his buttocks as he crouched before the fire to bank the flames. When shadows shrouded the room, he padded over to the bed.

Anne quickly slid over when he got into bed. He filled it with his large, solid body, and she held herself rigid, trying not to roll toward him. She wanted to feel his body beside hers again, yet dreaded it, too. When he snuffed the bedside candle, the chamber went almost entirely dark, save for the lambent glow of the fire.

Perhaps they were going to take up where they'd left off a few moments ago. She wondered if she was supposed to do something. Disrobe, perhaps? Yet when she reached for the hem of her nightgown, his hand stopped her.

"Go to sleep, Anne." His voice was gruff in the darkness.

Did that mean they weren't going to . . . "I have displeased you."

"No. You please me fine." He let out a sound partway between a sigh and a growl. "But I've decided I can't behave as the gentry does, not when it comes to marriage. We barely know each other, and if I were to take your maidenhead on only truly a few hours' worth of acquaintance, then that makes me as cold and heartless as them."

She was gentry, but was far too stunned by his declaration to take umbrage. "Are we to have a chaste marriage?"

His laugh was rueful. "God, no. But I think it's for the best if we wait a little. Get to know each other more."

"Oh." Relief poured through her. Relief and . . . disappointment. Mainly, however, she felt a great burden lift.

He settled deeper under the covers, and it felt very odd, sharing a bed with a man—the size of him, his weight upon the mattress. Several inches separated their bodies, but she felt his ambient heat. Caught the traces of his skin's own scent.

If this weren't so strange, she might enjoy sleeping beside him. Unless . . . he didn't want to share a bed at all. She began to slide out from beneath the bedclothes, but his hand stopped her once more.

"Where are you going?" he demanded.

"To my bedchamber."

"This *is* your bedchamber."

Even in the darkness, she blinked at him. "I don't have my own bedroom?" Her parents slept apart. If her circle of friends was to be believed, all husbands and wives did.

"The idea that a husband and wife should sleep apart is ridiculous," he rumbled. "That's for aristos, not peasants like me." He tugged on her wrist, and she had no choice but to edge back beneath the covers. "Whatever our arrangement for now, know this, Anne. You are my wife. I am your husband. We will always share a bed."

Simple words, yet her heartbeat raced when she heard them. "As you like."

He released his grip on her, and exhaled. "Don't like it at all. Not now. But I will . . . at some point. Now sleep."

He continued to baffle her. Yet he was her husband, and according to the law and to the Church, that made him her master. "Good night, Leo."

"Good night, Anne."

He rolled over heavily. Within a few minutes, his breathing slowed and deepened. He slept.

Leaving her alone and awake, staring into the dark.

It didn't surprise Anne to wake up alone. She had slept alone her whole life, and to stretch in bed and find the space beside her empty was no different than any other morning. Except, as she stretched, her arms wide, her fingers did not meet the edge of the bed. And the sheets smelled of tobacco and spice, not lavender.

This was not her bed. She suddenly remembered: she was married now. Married, but a virgin. Leo had touched her, and it had been both wonderful and terrible, until fear had overtaken her with humiliating ferocity. He'd been kind, and stopped. They had then spent the whole of the night together, chaste as schoolfellows. Now he was gone.

Her eyes opened to images of menacing flowers and

vines tipped with thorns. The bed hangings. She pushed
the fabric back to reveal the room. Someone had come in
during the early hours to tend the fire, but now Anne was
by herself. The drawn curtains kept the chamber dark, and
it seemed that shadows congealed in the corners, trying to
take shape.

She shook her head at her foolishness. Merely an ad-
justment to life in a new house.

The gilt bronze clock on the mantel showed the time
to be well after nine. Not an unusual time for her to awaken,
but perhaps Leo liked to rise earlier. He probably waited
for her to join him for breakfast downstairs. Though their
marriage had begun in a rather . . . unconventional manner,
she did not want him thinking her indolent and spoiled. He
was a man of business, of industry. As his wife, she should
be just as industrious.

Anne slid out of bed. As she padded toward the closet
to make use of the close stool, the chill of the floor seeped
into her feet and up her legs. Baffling, that. The fire should
have taken the cold from the room.

After tending to her needs and washing up, she emerged
from the closet and found the curtains pulled back and an
apron-wearing girl waiting for her.

"Good morning, madam." The girl bobbed a curtsy. She
couldn't have been more than a year younger than Anne.
"I'm Meg, your maid."

Anne had always shared a maid with her mother, as the
family could not afford the expense of two, so to have one
all to herself seemed a tremendous luxury. It seemed odd,
though, that Meg had appeared without being summoned.
Perhaps things ran differently in a household that never
went into arrears and paid their servants on time.

"Has my clothing been unpacked?" Nearly all of her
garments had come straight from the mantua maker, but
some were hers from before.

"Yes, madam. Is there a particular gown you want?"

Anne realized she had no idea what constituted her new trousseau. Everything had been purchased so quickly, with hardly any consultation on her part. Still, she didn't fancy the idea of the servants knowing that she'd come to their master nearly penniless.

"I trust you, Meg," she said.

The girl brightened and hastened to the other clothes-press. Eventually, she emerged with an open gown of peach-and-green Indian cotton, as well as all necessary undergarments. Anne resisted the impulse to peer into the clothespress to see what other gowns had been purchased for her, just as she fought the urge to admire the quality and newness of the gown Meg now helped her into.

As Meg fastened the dress, Anne looked at herself in the cheval glass and felt as though she put on another woman's skin. The thought made her shudder, thinking that a woman's flayed body lay somewhere, its muscles and innards exposed as the corpse cooled. She had a sudden vision of an attic chamber, perhaps in this very house, where other brides' bodies hung.

You haven't married Bluebeard, for heaven's sake.

As if to counter her own fears, she said aloud, "Do hurry, Meg. I want to join my husband for breakfast."

The maid blinked up at her. "He's gone, madam."

Now it was Anne's turn to look blank. "Gone?"

"I only started working here last week, making ready for you, but the master always leaves the house by seven."

"Where does he go?"

"To Exchange Alley, I reckon." Meg glanced at her from beneath the frill of her mob cap, perplexed by Anne's ignorance of her own husband.

"Of course," Anne said, far more brightly than she felt. She pasted on a smile. "I'll just take chocolate and rolls in here, then."

"The master had Cook fix you a proper breakfast. Eggs, bacon, seed cakes. It's waiting for you downstairs."

She couldn't refuse, not without possibly insulting the cook. Since Anne would be responsible for consulting with the cook about meals, she must be politic and make herself eat a meal she did not truly want. "Sounds delightful."

After Meg finished her toilette, Anne quit the bedchamber. The hallway was very quiet, almost sepulchral in its stillness, barely interrupted by the sounds of servants attending to their daily tasks elsewhere in the house. If Anne had not left Meg in the bedchamber only a moment prior, she might believe herself completely alone. Maybe even the last person alive in the entire world.

Stop this ridiculous ghoulishness! She *never* indulged in thoughts of the macabre—she stayed clear of the hangings at Tyburn, and even went out of her way to avoid the occasional traitor's head piked on Temple Bar.

It was simply nervousness at her unfamiliar surroundings, and trepidation as a new wife. Last night had been very tumultuous, so there might be lingering emotions. But there was truly nothing to fear. These awkward first days would soon pass.

Yet as she made her way down the stairs, that prospect seemed dim. It felt even farther away as she entered the dining room. Without all the guests from the day before, the chamber was an empty cavern scoured by gray morning light. All signs of the wedding celebration were gone—not even a crumb or wine stain on the carpet. Almost as if it had never happened, save for the music and laughter ringing in Anne's remembrance like broken glass.

The large table was laid for one, and as Anne moved farther into the room, a footman hurried in from a side door to pull out her chair. She smiled her thanks and sat, and helped herself to far more food than she wanted. There was nothing she could do but force food down her throat as the footman stood in attendance. Everything tasted like pasteboard.

"Please tell Cook that the meal is delicious," she said to the footman, who bowed. "I trust we will have more exquisite dishes for supper."

"Suppose so," the footman said. "Seeing as how the master don't take no meals here, I wouldn't know."

"No meals at all?"

"Maybe a cold collation late at night, but he's often out."

"Are we to expect him today?"

The footman shrugged.

Leo's absence at the table and in the house was a silent humiliation. Had she so little to offer her husband beyond her bloodline that he willingly left their bed to attend to business? She had believed him compassionate when he'd forestalled the consummation of their marriage. Yet now, with her alone in his house, alone in every way, she wondered if it had been kindness or merely disinterest. If the scandal rags were to be believed, Leo was accustomed to wild living, indulging in every vice. Nothing checked his desires, his impulses.

Would he consider his wife another obstacle to ignore? He had said that he wanted them to wait, to learn each other before consummating their marriage. Perhaps without the inducement of his wife's body, there was little to interest him at home.

As she picked at the congealing remains of her breakfast, she felt a rush of blood to her cheeks. Disappointment—and anger—roiled within her. She had no expectations of marriage, yet even in her most hypothetical imaginings she had not anticipated being an afterthought to the man who claimed her hand. Clearly, however, that was how Leo saw her: a parenthesis.

Abruptly, she stood. The footman hurried to help her with her chair, yet she was halfway out the door.

As she climbed the stairs, resolution took shape. She would *make* herself essential to him. This house—its baleful silence, its icy shadows—she would find a way to transform it. He shunned his home. Yet under her care, home would become the warmth of the fire drawing him in from the cold night.

His hunting ground. Leo breathed in its aromas as a predator sniffed the air for the acidic scent of prey. The smell of coffee was the smell of money—brewing, percolating, waiting to be consumed. He barely needed the jolt of energy from the drink. All he required for strength was here, fed by the sights and sounds of Exchange Alley. And his own deeds gave him unstoppable momentum.

Leo strode down Lombard Street, its narrow confines bound on all sides by coffee houses that served as the financial heart of London, and thus, the world. New Jonathan's Coffee House. Garraway's. Lloyd's. Dozens, maybe scores more. Lombard Street and the cramped alleys of Cornhill and Birchin Lane demarcated the boundaries of the commercial kingdom. The air was thick with talk, hundreds of men's voices all crashing together in a din some might call discordant. To Leo, the sound rang as clear and sacred as an oratorio.

"Seven hundred shares of the coffee venture. No less."

"The demand for cotton only increases. You're a fool not to buy now."

"The Quakers have me by the stones, but there's no help for it. Our future is made of iron."

"There's Bailey, the Demon—if you're looking for deep pockets, he's your man. But mind, he asks scores of questions and is anything but a silent partner."

This made him smile. Rich gentlemen might mutely provide funds and collect returns, content with the fiction that, if they kept their interaction with actual business to a minimum, they would be less sullied. Leo didn't give a damn. He'd get as filthy as necessary to wring the greatest profits. He had no man of business. He did not deal with brokers or jobbers. Everything that needed doing, he did himself.

The sun had not yet topped the spires of Saint Paul's, yet the frenzy of the 'Change was at its height, and Leo in the thick of it. Precisely where he wanted—needed—to be. Within the few hours he had been here, he'd invested in a quarry whose slate tiles would be used to roof mill towns in the north, provided capital to ship English wheat to the Caribbean, and sold his shares in a Scottish timber venture. And the day wasn't half over. There was still so much to be done. Fortunes to be made—his.

"Oranges, Spanish oranges." A barefoot girl with a basket full of fruit picked her way through the crowd. Her cry could barely be heard above the clamor.

"I'll take one," Leo said.

"Two for a penny, sir. One for yourself, one for your wife?"

God, he *was* married now, wasn't he?

"Two, then," he said, handing the coin to the girl. She passed two oranges to him, like a dirty-footed goddess creating new suns. With the transaction finished, the girl moved on, her cry of "Oranges, Spanish oranges" soon swallowed by the din.

Leo pocketed the fruit. Though surrounded on all sides by men and chaos and noise, his mind drifted back to his house in Bloomsbury, and the woman who now lived there. Anne had been sleeping when he slipped from bed. In that expanse of white linen, she had looked very small, insubstantial. Yet one of her hands had been curled into a fist, as if ready to swing should she be attacked.

Had she been protecting herself from *him*? The thought

had troubled him, and he had summoned his valet and dressed quietly, careful to keep from waking her. She would arise later to find him gone.

Something edged and acute cut through him. It took several moments for him to recognize the feeling: regret. Or at least, he *believed* it to be regret, never having felt it before.

Perhaps he ought not to have left her. At the least, he might have woken her or left a note to let her know where he was. Damned strange. He'd been accountable to no one for a very long time. Even his fellow Hellraisers. To feel any sense of obligation, even to a wife, chafed. Yet he couldn't expect to marry and have nothing alter, could he?

Last night had been . . . puzzling. Disturbing. To feel her fear shuddering through her body and into his. He had expected some nerves on her part. Hell, there had been nerves on his part, as well. He'd never made love to a virgin before, and he'd wondered about the best possible means of doing so. Gentle, slow. That much he knew. Yet Anne had still been afraid.

His desire for her—that he felt even now, in this crowded, noisy alley—was unexpected, and a relief. Despite his ambition to marry a nobleman's daughter, he never would have given his name to a woman he could not want in his bed. Anne's quiet beauty stirred him; her intelligence and subtle humor intrigued him. As he had touched her and discovered her slim, soft body, he felt her respond. Not just with fear, but with hunger. There was promise, of what could be. He wanted to explore that, see where it led.

It was for these reasons that he had forced himself to wear a nightshirt, to hide his markings. Last night had shown him that what he had begun to learn of Anne, he discovered he actually liked. Which meant he would feel obligated to offer her an explanation for the markings—and that he was not certain he wanted to do.

What he *did* want was to see her again. He should go back.

"To hell with the *geminus*," he muttered to himself, "and the demands of Mr. Holliday."

The 'Change could do without him for a day, a week. And in that time, he and Anne could come to learn each other, become more than acquaintances. He had decided to wait on the consummation of their marriage until they knew each other better. He needed to learn more. That couldn't happen with him sequestered in the madness of Exchange Alley.

Though Leo's expertise at bedsport could not begin to match Bram's, he had a suspicion that, once her fear diminished and she was initiated into the realm of sexual pleasure, Anne would prove herself an eager student. She had a quickness of mind that revealed itself in her ready wit, in the keenness of her gaze. He'd touched and caressed her, discovering a hidden sensuality in his wife, a banked fire that needed a bit of encouragement to blaze to life.

But that fire would remain cool until he brought it forward. Which he could not do from miles away.

He'd return home now. Take Anne for a jaunt in the carriage. They'd stroll in Saint James's Park, perhaps have a mug of fresh milk from the cows that grazed there. Then they'd go back home for supper, and talk, maybe flirt a little over their meal. He knew a bit about flirting. Admittedly, not very much. Courtesans cared less for flirtation and more for generosity, which he had both in bed and out. Flirtation, though, was newer to him. Wordplay seemed to be involved, and compliments. Beyond that . . . he'd have to think of something.

Hopefully, the flirting stage would not last overlong. He was much more comfortable once the woman was already in bed. Last night had given him just a taste of Anne. Learning more about her body and what gave her pleasure . . . the prospect sounded damned pleasant. He already felt the quickening of his pulse, the heated edge of emergent desire.

Just as he turned to make his way back up Lombard and thence to Cheapside, he caught sight of Stephen Norwood emerging from a coffee house.

Destroy him.

The words, spoken silently by a voice not his own, wove through his mind like a trail of smoke. Thoughts of Anne were blotted out. All Leo saw was Norwood, the cheat. A year ago, they had been partners—Leo, Norwood, and two others—in an East Indian shipping venture. Norwood had gone behind Leo's back, urging the others to underreport the venture's profits, all the while wearing a wide betrayer's smile. Leo had caught wind of the scheme and extricated himself with as minimal damage as possible, never letting on that he knew of the deception.

Like a serpent, Leo had bided his time, waiting for the right moment to bring Norwood down with a flash of fang and mouth full of poison.

That time was now. Cold intent spread through Leo, originating between his shoulder blades and winding through his body, his limbs, and his mind.

Destroy him.

"Good to see you, old friend." He strode up and shook Norwood's hand.

The charlatan grinned. "Surprised to see you here today. Word is out that yesterday you took a wife."

Leo decided not to mention that he had *married* Anne, yet as to the *taking* of her . . . that would happen later. "A husband I may be, but the 'Change is my mistress, and I can never stray." He glanced toward the door of the coffee house Norwood had just exited. "You and I haven't spoken in far too long. Join me inside?"

Though he maintained his grin, Norwood's eyes were

chary. If he knew what Leo had planned, he had good cause for concern. But no one save another Hellraiser or the Devil himself could know what Leo intended.

"I have good intelligence on some new investment prospects." This was Leo's bait, for he was renowned, some might say notorious, for his faultless ability to select the best ventures. He'd been strong in business before gaining his gift of precognition. Now, he was unstoppable.

Wariness left Norwood's gaze, replaced by eager greed. "No greater pleasure than to renew our friendship."

They ducked into the coffee house and removed their tricorn hats. Inside, men of business hunched at battered wooden tables and crowded into settles. Brokers, jobbers, men seeking capital for their schemes, and those, like Leo, keen to invest in the next profitable ventures. The close air within the shop was thick with the smell of coffee and the sounds of speculation. London was an old city, a city built upon the detritus of centuries rotting into the earth. Yet here, in this coffee house, in the narrow, crowded alleys of the Exchange, men lived in the future. They dwelt in the possibility of what *could be*, what *might be*, and in that gauze-covered world of chance, they staked their fortunes.

Leo had an advantage no one else possessed. And that made him one of the most feared and respected men in the Exchange. Him. A saddler's son, who'd never drunk tea from fresh, unboiled leaves until he was fifteen years old.

He and Norwood managed to find a table, pushing aside the newspapers stacked there. As they sat, the proprietor flung two steaming mugs of coffee toward them and quickly trundled off.

"Have you change for a bob?" Leo asked Norwood. He held up a shilling.

"Only a tanner and thruppence."

"That shall suffice."

"Are you sure?" Norwood raised a brow, believing that the benefit would be all to him.

"Truly, it's satisfactory."

With a shrug, Norwood slid his coins across the table and accepted Leo's shilling. The moment Leo touched the coins, he smiled, for though he had lost three pennies in the exchange, he now gained something far more valuable.

To Norwood, and to all the men in the room, Leo sat at a table within the same coffee house. He did not rise up from his seat. He barely even moved, except to curl his fingers around the coins. Yet with just the brush of his fingers over the money's metallic surface, Leo's mind became a spyglass. Time folded in on itself, collapsing inward. Dizzying. The first few times Leo attempted this, he'd found the unexpected sensation unpleasant, like drinking too much whiskey too quickly. Now, he'd learned not only to anticipate the feeling, but to welcome it, for it meant that soon the future would be his.

Leo felt the rough wooden table beneath his fingertips, heard the voices of men around him, yet his eyes beheld not the coffee house but a distant port. Palm trees and golden-skinned people in colorful wraps. Tall-masted ships bobbing at anchor. Buildings both Oriental and European—no, not just European, but the tall, narrow facades of Dutch structures, and battlements. He knew this place, never having been there, but by reputation: Batavia, in the East Indies.

The lurid light spilling over the city's walls came not from the setting sun, but a ship burning in the harbor. Sailors tried to douse the flames. Their water buckets failed to stem the fire—it spread like a pestilence over the hull, up the masts, engulfing the sails. The sailors abandoned their task. They shoved themselves into jolly boats and dove overboard, and people on the shore could only watch as the ship became a black, shuddering skeleton, its expensive cargo turning to ash upon the water. The crew had escaped, but the pepper they shipped did not.

A disaster.

"Bailey?"

Norwood's voice broke the scene. Leo quickly pocketed the coins and the vision of distant calamity faded. He was back in a London coffee house, amidst news sheets and talk of business, with Norwood gazing curiously at him across the table. A phantom scent of burning wood and pepper pods remained in Leo's memory.

"Are you well, Bailey?"

"Forgive me. My mind . . . went somewhere else for a moment."

A knowing grin spread across Norwood's face. "Back to your new bride, I imagine."

Leo manufactured a smile. His ability to foresee financial disaster had been his particular gift from the Devil, a gift that remained a secret between Leo and the other Hellraisers. Anne would never learn of it—for many reasons.

"Are you at the 'Change today in search of new ventures?" he asked.

"There are several, all clamoring for my coin," answered Norwood, "and the matter remains only to discern which would be the wisest investment."

"I've more than a little intelligence in such matters. Tell me which have commandeered your attention."

Norwood raised a brow. "To what end? That you might seize an opportunity and leave me out in the cold?"

Leo placed a hand on his chest. "Injurious words. My offer was extended in friendship, that I might advise you." He glanced down at the heavy ruby he wore on his right ring finger. "And *I've* no need to cut you out of the profits, not when my own are so abundant. There is plenty to share."

If Norwood understood that Leo threw his own crime

back at him, he made no sign. Slowly, he nodded. "Everyone has said that lately your investments never fail."

Leo always possessed good sense, but with the Devil's gift, he had become infallible. The gold in his coffers and the country estate he had purchased for his mother's use testified to this.

"Unburden yourself," he urged Norwood. "Make use of my council."

After taking a sip of his coffee, the other man proceeded. "Three ventures have applied to me for investment funds. A housing development here in London, sugar from Barbados, or a pepper shipment from Batavia." He spread his hands. "They have all presented themselves in the best possible light, and I have done as much research into each business as feasible, yet I cannot decide which shall be the recipient of my capital. For I can invest in only one."

Leo kept his outward appearance calm. He crafted his expression into one of contemplation. Within, however, he felt the quick, exhilarating anticipation of a predator lying in wait. He had merely to let his prey wander farther into the kill zone, and the deed would be accomplished, his claws bright with blood.

"All three have their merits, their potential."

"But one must be better than the others, surely?"

How long could Leo toy with him? A pleasure to draw it out, knowing that the blow would come, or strike quickly, and then watch the carnage? Both appealed.

"Housing developments are certainly intriguing," he said. "Every day, more and more people come to London, looking for work beyond tenant farming. They all need places to live."

"So, that should be my investment?"

Leo feigned deliberation. Finally, he said, "Choose the pepper from Batavia. The appetite for spice goes unabated, and it always finds a buyer. With the desire for French cooking growing, especially amongst the swelling ranks of the bourgeoisie, such goods can only increase in value."

"Are you certain?" Norwood's brow pleated.

"A better investment cannot be found."

For a moment, Norwood simply stared at Leo, as if trying to make sense of a labyrinth. He released a breath. "You are . . . generous."

"This surprises you."

"No. Well . . . aye. You've something of a reputation."

"The Demon of the Exchange." Leo laughed at Norwood's pained expression. "I know every name I'm called." Including *upstart, peasant, lowborn bastard.* Leo had once overheard Norwood call him that. *The lowborn bastard won't know the difference in the balance sheets. A simple matter, and the profits are ours.*

Abruptly, Norwood pushed back from the table and stood. He held out his hand. "My thanks to you, Bailey. You've done me a kindness."

"Nothing kind about it." Leo resisted the impulse to crush Norwood's hand in his own, and merely shook it instead. "I have a very good feeling about your investment."

"I wish you great happiness in your marriage." With that, Norwood bowed before hurrying out of the coffee house.

Leo sat alone, with two cups of coffee growing cold, yet within, he was a volcano of hot, vicious joy. He took from his pocket Norwood's coins, the thruppence and tanner, and set them on the table.

Seeing the coins, the proprietor quickly walked over and hefted a steaming pot. "More coffee, sir?"

"Consider that a gratuity."

"All of it?"

"I've no use for the coin." Not anymore. It had given him precisely what he needed, for his gift of prescience required him to touch an article of money belonging to an individual, and from that, he would have a vision of their future financial disasters. Seldom did he not encounter a disaster, for they marked everyone's lives, and he'd gained most of his fortune since by counterinvesting. On the rare occasion when he saw no calamity, he knew the venture to be solid. Yet in the time that he'd gained this gift, he'd been witness to scores, perhaps hundreds, of catastrophes. Difficult now not to see disaster everywhere, lurking around corners and in the shadows of crumbling bridges.

The proprietor's mouth opened in surprise. "You are very generous, sir."

The second time in a handful of minutes Leo had been called such. But his generosity extended only to the coffee house owner. What he had offered Norwood served merely Leo's own appetite for vengeance.

Donning his hat, Leo stood. "Point of truth," he said to the proprietor, "I'm the most selfish bastard you'll ever meet."

"My wife's brother might have you beat, sir."

Leo's laugh was genuine. They came so seldom, the sound astonished him. He left the coffee house, energy and urgency in his step. He needed to counterinvest in shipments of pepper from Malabar—the price would surely go up after the destruction of the Batavian cargo—and then he needed to get to the pugilism academy. He trained there daily after leaving the 'Change. A necessary outlet, for nothing exhilarated him more than good, ruthless business, and the gentlemanly sports of fencing and riding held no appeal. Peasant blood flowed in his veins, demanding the most primitive, brutal means of release. To hit, and be hit in return, and then emerge the victor, his opponent's blood on his knuckles.

He wanted to crow about his victory, but the only people he could speak to of it were his fellow Hellraisers. Anne would never know. She *could not* know. The realization struck him, swift and unexpected. Only yesterday, he had believed that he would not care if she learned about his magic. Her opinion of him had not mattered, nor the need to offer explanations. Now, however . . . now he actually cared what she thought of him.

The thought disturbed him. He strode off to seek the un-complicated interaction of the boxing ring.

Chapter 4

Anne paced the corridor, watching night fall in thick black currents. Her skin felt tight and confining. She was a ghost haunting her own home. Aimless. Uneasy.

Keeping house for a man who seldom made use of it proved a more difficult task than she had anticipated. She had spoken to the cook about planning meals, only to learn that Leo sometimes took coffee in the mornings, but that constituted the whole of his requirements. The cook, in fact, had been painfully eager to talk with Anne, desperate for something to do. Just as Anne was. Yet she had no answers for the poor man. Could they expect guests? Possibly. Would the master be joining them for meals more often? Perhaps.

The clatter of carriage wheels on the street drew Anne to the window. But it was only the man who lived across the street. She watched as he alit from the carriage, and the door to his house opened. A woman stood there, her shadow thrown in jagged increments down the stairs. Her shade swallowed the man as he climbed up to her, then, with their arms looped, they went inside together, and the door closed. The carriage rolled on toward the mews.

Not a word from Leo all day. She'd had supper prepared and waiting for him at four. The hour had passed, and another, until there had been no choice but to eat alone, again, and have the remainder of the dishes shared amongst the servants.

The more hours passed, the more she thought of the previous night. Leo's warm hands and hotter gaze, the press of his body close to hers, and the even more intimate revelation about his parents' marriage. A tentative step toward knowing each other. Yet as the day crept forward and Leo's absence resounded in the empty halls of his home, she began to think of last night as a dream whose details faded after waking. Soon, she would begin to wonder if his touch and disclosure had happened at all.

Anne turned away from the window and resumed her restless pacing. Back and forth, crossing the landing that had a view of the entryway below. Everywhere her gaze fell, she found expensive objects. Axminster carpets, marble-topped tables with elaborately curved, gilded legs, Chinese porcelain. Brilliant things, glittering things. Soulless. Empty. Like elegant corpses.

She hugged herself and kept walking. These were idle fancies brought about by a day of inactivity. Seldom had she had so little to do, and so much time in which to do it.

Leo kept far more servants than her own family. Until yesterday, he was the house's sole occupant, and even then, he was rarely there. Between the abundance of servants and a master with few demands, Anne found herself superfluous. She'd been far busier at home—her old home. This is where she lived now. This richly furnished . . . mausoleum.

Sensation prickled along the back of her neck. The strangest feeling. As if she were being observed.

Anne spun around. "Meg?" She tried to recall the

names of other servants she had met today—Leo's valet, and the steward. "Spinner? Mr. Fowles?"

No answer. Nothing at all, until the middle candle in a three-branched candelabra abruptly went out. A curl of smoke drifted up to the ceiling.

She took one of the lit candles and used it to reignite the one in the middle. Yet the moment she replaced the taper, the middle candle went out again. It didn't gutter or flicker, as it might if there were a draft. It simply extinguished itself.

As if someone had blown it out.

A rolling clatter sounded on the street outside. Startled, her heart contracted, a painful grip in the center of her chest. Then came the footman's steps echoing across the checkerboard floor as he strode to the door and held it open. Anne drifted to the railing and looked down.

Cold air swirled in, and a man stood in the doorway. Light from the linkboy's torch outside made the man a figure of darkness, limned in fire. Tall, and broad-shouldered. He came into the entryway, sleek and sinister as night. She felt a clutch of instinctive fear, the urge to turn and run. Then light from the footman's candle touched the stranger's face and she saw it wasn't a stranger, no one to fear. Only her husband.

Though calling him *only* anything seemed paltry. For, as Leo strode into the house, removing his hat and caped coat and handing them to the footman, he looked up. Right at her. His storm gray eyes fixed on her with startling accuracy. The chandelier hanging in the domed entry bathed him in light, all the hard and handsome angles of his face, the long lines of his body. He wore the clothes of a gentleman, but the guise did not fool Anne. This was a dangerous man.

They stared at each other. It seemed to take a moment for Leo to place her, like running into an acquaintance after several years' absence. Then came recognition. He smiled, yet it did not much soften his face.

"Is that a bruise on your cheek?" Her voice sounded overloud, echoing in the foyer.

He reached up and absently touched his face. "I was in a fight."

Anne hurried down the stairs. "Footpads? Are you injured? We should summon the constabulary."

"And tell them I paid for the privilege."

She reached his side, tilting her head back to look at him in confusion. "Paid?"

"A pugilism academy." He held up his fist. Small cuts and bruises adorned his knuckles. "Every afternoon, after business at the 'Change is done. The man who did this to me looks much worse, but he was given a half crown for his troubles."

"Boxing." It made sense. The way he moved, how he held himself, as if expecting a fight at any moment, and not only ready to defend himself, but eager for the challenge. Of course, her supposition was all theory, but she had a rather good grasp of theoreticals. "I've never seen a boxing match."

He raised a brow. "Never?"

"Young ladies aren't encouraged to attend events where men in undress pummel one another. Though I've always been curious. It's a very ancient sport, isn't it?"

"I should take you."

Her mouth dropped open. "You can't."

He frowned. "It isn't illegal for a woman to attend a boxing match. In fact, I've heard that, once or twice, a woman was one of the pugilists. Next time a match is arranged, I'll take you."

"It will be quite scandalous." Her pulse came a little quicker to think about it. But not entirely from fear.

"Scandal doesn't bother me."

She looked at him, with the bruise on his face and the scabs on his knuckles, his sandy hair coming out from its queue, and suddenly understood that what made Leo so very dangerous wasn't his humble birth, nor his wealth, and not even his physicality. What truly made him dangerous was this: he honestly did not care what anyone else thought. And that gave him perfect freedom to do exactly what he pleased.

It was a thought both frightening and exciting.

Rather than address any of this, Anne said, "That bruise wants tending."

He merely shrugged. "I heal quickly."

"A meal for the victor, then?"

"Meal?" He looked blank.

"Food. One consumes it. Often at home. Though," she added, "I'm given to understand you seldom do."

"Little reason to."

"Until now." She wondered what he must think of her impertinence, yet she was unable to curb herself in his presence. His sense of liberation must be communicable.

He did not seem to mind, however. His smile actually warmed, becoming more genuine. "This must be the side of marriage that is so celebrated. A doting, fussing wife."

"I've little experience with the matter," she said, "having never had a wife before."

"Then we are equally innocent on the subject."

One word she would never choose to describe Leo: innocent. Even a rather sheltered young woman such as herself recognized that a whole life was lived behind the cool gray of Leo's eyes, a life utterly unknown to her.

She turned to the footman. "Ask Cook to prepare a collation for Mr. Bailey. Meat, cheese, bread. Wine. Some of the pie from this afternoon's supper."

The footman bowed and departed, leaving Anne and Leo standing alone in the chill of the vaulted foyer.

"Do you wish to bathe before eating, sir . . . Leo?" She caught the scent of fresh sweat from his skin, musky and clean, and fought to keep from drawing closer to his wool coat and inhaling deeply.

His smile turned rueful. "I did not know you had a supper prepared."

"It is a wife's duty to have meals ready."

"And a husband's folly if he forgets. Consider me chastised."

"I'll do nothing of the sort," she answered. "You aren't chastised in the slightest."

He chuckled. "Perhaps a little."

Anne gestured toward the stairs. "A bath? And then something to eat. I'm given to understand that is the common order of things."

"Behold your obedient husband." He turned to the stairs and brushed past her, his body large and warm. A shiver of awareness passed through her, like a fingertip drawn down her throat and between her breasts. She remembered the sensation of his hands on her, and the insistent press of his arousal. No, this was not to be a chaste marriage, but as to the when of its consummation . . . The promise filled her with dread. And eagerness.

At the foot of the stairs, he paused, his hand on the newel post. He gave a low laugh.

"A wife. A bath. A meal at home." He shook his head. "I'm becoming damned civilized."

As he continued up the stairs, Anne understood that no matter what Leo Bailey did, he would never be domesticated. He was, and always would be, wild.

"*This* is where we're supposed to eat?"

Anne noted the appalled expression on Leo's face as he surveyed the capacious dining chamber. He had bathed and changed into fresh clothes. In his pristine stock, snowy against his jaw, expertly cut green woolen coat, his hair dark, gleaming gold in the candlelight, he had transformed from a bruised brawler. But he didn't look a gentleman. No, in his restrained evening finery, he seemed a pirate prince contemplating future pillaging.

"You found no fault with the room yesterday."

"Because there were people everywhere. This." He waved his hand at the chamber, where a collation awaited him at the vast dining table, and two footmen stood in disinterested readiness. "All we need is a bear to bait."

"One of your footmen is a very big fellow. Perhaps he'd be willing to play the part of the bear."

With Anne on his arm, Leo brought them farther into the room. All the chandeliers had been lit—an expense she could scarcely fathom—yet this only illuminated how large and empty the dining chamber truly was. He frowned at the walls as if displeased by their distance, and the look was so commanding, she half expected the walls to simply get up and move closer just to please him.

"No wonder I never ate at home. Who could dine in here?"

"I did."

Her quiet words snared his attention. "Today."

"Yes, today. I broke my fast in this chamber, and dined, as well."

"Alone."

"There was a footman."

He shook his head, his frown deepening. "God, I'm an ass." He quirked an eyebrow at her. "This is the point in the exchange where you contradict me."

"I was given to understand that a good wife does not contradict her husband."

His scowl transformed into a smile that glittered in his eyes. "I think I've married an impertinent hoyden."

Her own lips curved. "No one has ever called me a hoyden before." And she rather liked it, for as a daughter of parents with little means, *subdued obedience* had been her byword. Being poor *and* an unmarried woman did not improve one's chances of being abided. "I suspect it's the low company I now keep."

The moment the words left her, she wanted to call them back. Leo's face shuttered at the perceived insult.

"I didn't—that's not what I mean." She gripped his sleeve. "It was a jest. Nothing more. I don't think of you as low."

"But I am," he said, words cool and impersonal. He withdrew his arm.

"Not truly. Low is defined by deeds, not blood."

His smile returned, only now it had a dark and cynical cast to it. "To repeat: I am."

She did not understand to what he referred, but the shadows in his eyes made her think perhaps she did not want to know. *Blast.* They had been heading toward something, a connection as tenuous as it was vital, and a few thoughtless words had torn it asunder.

Another realization dawned: he claimed not to care what others thought, and in many ways, he didn't, but there was still some part of him that bristled and brooded when his origins were derided. He lashed out when hurt, like a wounded beast. To keep her hand from being bitten off, she must proceed carefully.

"Grand though this chamber is," she said, searching for another topic, "it doesn't lend itself well to intimate suppers." She turned to one of the footmen. "Remove the collation to the parlor upstairs." The servant bowed, and he and the other footman began gathering up the plates and platters of food.

"There's a parlor upstairs?"

She exhaled. At the least, Leo's voice had lost its cold

timbre. "This house has a saloon, two parlors, a promenade, study, drawing room, and three bedchambers. I can draw you a map. I'm very good with them."

"No need. If I get lost, I'll whistle for you."

"Like a hound." She affected a sigh, though glad that his aloof, cutting mood had not lasted long. "Has any woman received a more romantic proposition?"

A mercurial man, her husband, for now he was grave. "I know little of romance. If it's pretty words and poesies you want, you'll have to find them in the pages of a novel."

"I don't read novels. Besides," she added, smiling, "I think we're doing well enough on our own. We do not need a histrionic novelist to tell us how to behave."

"Never did trust writers. A bunch of Grub Street scribblers paid to lie." Affable, he offered her his arm. "Shall we go up to dine, my lady wife?"

She placed her hand on his sleeve, and felt anew the jolt that came from touching his solid, sinewy form. "Let's. And I'll provide direction, should we get lost en route." At the least, she knew how to navigate the house. When it came to her husband, she found herself continually redrawing the map.

Leo never anticipated the pleasures of a meal at home. Until last night, his evenings had been spent in the company of his fellow Hellraisers. They had earned their name honestly—if such a thing could be done with honesty. Though he didn't possess the privilege of birth, he had that other opener of doors: money. With it, in the company of gently born scoundrels, he had experienced all that London had to offer. Wine, carousing, music. Women.

His taxonomy of women separated them into discrete categories. The *demimondaine* was the sort he knew best, and as a man of business, he appreciated the clear directives by which they led their lives. Some men liked to pretend that courtesans truly held affection for them. Leo was not one of those men. For all his manipulations at Exchange Alley, he liked dealings honest and with clear intent. So he paid courtesans for their time, their company, and never flattered himself that they found him handsome or charming. Only wealthy.

There were the wives and daughters of rich merchants and men of trade, but he seldom interacted with them. His ambitions lay elsewhere, even if he could increase his fortune tenfold by making a strategic marriage. Money he could make entirely on his own. He didn't need a wife to bring him that.

Also in his catalog were the women of the aristocracy. Staid matrons. Sly-eyed widows and bored, neglected wives—these were the sort who invited him into their beds, curious for a taste of the lower orders. He was happy to oblige. It gratified Leo to know that he vigorously pleasured women whose husbands sneered at him.

The delicate young ladies who played fortepiano and, by design, knew little of the world beyond the circumference of Mayfair—these he knew least of all. Wealth he possessed, but not reputation or bloodline, and genteel girls gave him wide berth. He did not mind overmuch, discovering in his limited conversations with them that they had been carefully instructed to have no opinions or use beyond silk-gowned broodmares. In his nights with the Hellraisers, the shortest portion of the evening was spent at aristocratic assemblies, for the company was dull and circumscribed, especially the young women.

Leo was young. And a man. When it came to female company, he wanted anything but dull and circumscribed.

To his surprise, this evening he learned that his young, aristocratic wife was neither of these things.

"Why not invest everything into a single trade?" she

asked, pouring him another glass of Bordeaux. "Concentrate all your interests in the development of a single product—perhaps even fund its advancement."

"Limiting one's investment into only one commodity means disaster comes when that trade fails."

"It might not fail, though, and the lion's portion of its profits go to you."

His smile was fashioned from witnessing many a disaster. Mr. Holliday's gift showed him nothing else. "At one time or another, most everything fails."

"How grim."

"Many things are." But not this conversation. For the past hour, as Anne had plied him with a cold supper, she had asked him many questions about his endeavors in Exchange Alley. She knew little of business, nor how one might buy and sell shares of things that only existed in theory, yet her mind had proved agile and eager for information.

Even the other Hellraisers had not shown as much interest or enthusiasm for his work.

Candlelight gilded her smooth face and the soft expanse of skin above the neckline of her peach silk gown, and her eyes were emerald one moment, topaz the next. He watched her hands as they floated over her wineglass, lively as birds.

Desire surged, low and tight in his belly. Pleasant in its demand and, surprisingly, pleasant in its deferral. He liked feeling it, the anticipation of what might be. For a long time, he had wanted certainties about the future, and thanks to the Devil, there were things about the future he knew with absolute authority. So he actually enjoyed not knowing entirely what the next few moments, or days, might bring. Including the pleasure of his wife's body as he came to know her heart and mind.

"Thus the necessity for diversification." He swirled the

wine in his glass, fashioning a small vortex. "If a cotton mill burns down, or the canal bringing iron becomes impassable, I have other sources of income."

"Yet any one of those ventures is also vulnerable to misfortune."

"Never the ones in which I invest." He could say this assuredly.

She tilted her head to one side, considering. "Never?"

"Not a one. So you've no fear of becoming destitute."

Her laugh was unexpectedly low and husky, sensuous for all its innocence. "I've already been destitute. I have no fear of that condition. But," she continued, "how is it that none of your investments suffer disappointment? If what you have said is true, that most everything meets with failure at some point, you must be either very sagacious or very lucky."

"A compound of both." The Devil's gift remained a secret known only to him and the other Hellraisers. As far as Anne and the rest of the world understood, the Devil was an abstract, an idea preached about on Sundays and on street corners, but never truly believed as real. If he told Anne of what had transpired beneath a Roman ruin three months earlier, she would have him committed to Bedlam. There was nothing to be gained by telling her.

No, she could not know. Her learning about his magic would jeopardize this tentative connection growing between them, and he found—to his surprise—he valued that connection too much to place it at risk.

"So it was luck *and* wisdom that saw you from a saddler's son to . . ." She waved her hand at the parlor, its walls covered in ivory damask, gilded carvings adorning the mirrors, moldings, and sconces. In truth, he found the style of the room to be oppressively ornate, but had permitted the designer to decorate the whole house as he pleased.

Naturally, the man had employed the most expensive designs and artisans.

Leo had been home too infrequently to be bothered. So long as his house had displayed his wealth, he did not care.

Now, however, seeing Anne like a bryony amongst rotten hothouse roses, he found that he did.

Abruptly, he got to his feet. Anne blinked up at him in confusion, until he came around to pull out her chair. "This room feels choked. There's a garden out back. At least," he amended, "I believe there is one."

"It has paths and a fountain, though it is a little barren so early in the year." She rose, and he caught her scent of green meadow and young woman.

He had an urge to place his mouth at the juncture of her neck and her shoulder. But it was too soon. Instead, he strode to the door and said to the footman waiting outside, "Have Mrs. Bailey's maid fetch a cloak for her mistress. And don't light torches in the garden." After the glare of indoors, he wanted the darkness.

He turned back to Anne. "You don't mind." Leo realized he spoke this more as a directive than a question, but he wanted out of this room, out of the house. And he wanted her with him.

"I often walked in the garden at night. After the chaos of the day, it gave me some peace."

He would scarce recognize peace if it shot him in the face.

In a moment, Anne's maid appeared with a sapphire woolen cloak. Leo took the cloak from the maid, dismissing her with a nod. He stepped close to Anne and, with a flourish, draped the garment around her slim shoulders. A flush of awareness pinked her cheeks as he worked the fastening at her throat. *Good.* He wanted her affected by him, for he found himself growing more and more responsive to her.

Claiming his glass of wine, he offered her his arm. Her

fingers rested lightly on his sleeve. Had his other hand not been occupied with his glass, he would have clasped her fingers closer. A testing, to see whether she would retreat, or push forward. Yet without the slightest provocation on his part, her hold became more secure, fingers curving with purpose around his forearm.

Desire knifed through him. He mentally shook himself. *I'm a sodding boy again.* A time in his life when just the fan of a girl's eyelash could rouse his cock. Now, years later, only the firmer press of Anne's fingers on his arm caused him to respond.

"Comfortable?" He wasn't.

At her nod, they walked downstairs and then out together. Brittle air scented with smoke and fog bit at exposed skin, but after the close heat of indoors, Leo welcomed the bite. He led her down pathways paved with crushed shells. Accustomed more to purposeful striding than a placid stroll, Leo forced himself into an even, steady pace, feeling the cold air abrade his lungs.

Bare-branched privet hedges squatted beside the path, and Leo could just make out in the darkness the skeletal arms of espaliered fruit trees reaching toward the sky. He tried to remember what might grow in the neat rectangular beds and found that he could not.

"In the spring, this will be a very pretty spot." Anne spoke softly, a deference to night and its muted expectation. "Broom, and Sweet William, and candytuft. The pear trees will have lovely white flowers."

It was the first he knew of it, or even what fruit the trees might bear.

"We had no garden," he said. "The saddlery shared a common yard with a potter and a chandler, and we lived behind the shop. The yard was just that, a square of dirt. It smelled of wax, clay, and leather."

"That's where you played?"

He snorted. "No play. From the time I could hold a pair of shears, I helped my da. Schooling first, then work. Da wanted to be sure I knew my letters. He didn't, not until he reached four and forty."

Leo had never spoken of this to anyone, not even Edmund or Whit. They knew many aspects of his low birth, but never such intimate details, and it surprised Leo that he talked so openly to Anne now. The false affinity created by darkness.

As if sensing this, a cloud over the moon abruptly shifted and icy light spilled into the garden, washing away the intimate dark. In the light, he felt exposed, the distance between him and his wife all too evident. Moonlight drove them apart, for now he had nowhere to hide.

He cursed himself for being so unguarded. Surely she'd mock him for being the son of an illiterate. He readied for her cutting words, telling himself that he didn't care what she thought of his humble blood.

"Your father must have taught himself," she said instead.

Leo's steps slowed a little, surprised by her response. "He did. Sat at the kitchen table with a hornbook, struggling to sound out the Lord's Prayer."

"With such a determined son, I expect no less from the father." Esteem warmed her voice.

Leo felt as though he'd taken a punch to the chest. To steady himself, he took a drink of wine. He had expected bafflement from her, or outright disdain. But not this . . . admiration. Especially not in the clarity of a barren, moonlight-blasted garden. Yet she saw him fully, and liked what she saw.

"No one more determined than Adam Bailey," he said after a moment. "*Was* as determined." Leo's father had died as he lived: working. Always wanting more. A trait shared by his only living son.

Leo had advantages his father did not. More wealth, a

greater understanding of the exigencies of business. And magic, given to him by the Devil.

Leo would use his every power to seize whatever he wanted.

As if frustrated by the growing bond between him and Anne, clouds slid across the face of the moon, blotting out its light. The garden sank back into darkness.

"Fifteen shillings a week. That's what he made." The same amount Leo carried in his pocket wherever he went. "Hardly more than subsistence."

"Something altered your circumstances."

"A rich man's fancy." The irony hardly escaped him. "He gave my father a commission. A bloody *big* commission that meant pulling me from school so I could help complete it in time. The man wanted a dozen racing saddles. And he wanted them within a month. So we made the damned things, my father, my mother, and me. I was ten at the time. We had to hire the coffin-builder's wagon to make the delivery." Sometimes he woke from dreams to find his fingers holding a phantom awl.

"The man must have been quite fond of horseflesh," Anne murmured.

"He owned two horses only, to pull his carriage. Said that he'd been thinking about taking up racing, and wanted to be prepared, should he ever indulge the whim."

Anne's laugh was wry. "No wonder you think all noblemen are fools."

He stopped and faced her. "I never said that."

"Those words specifically? No." Some light escaped the house, tracing the line of her cheek and curve of her ear as she stared up at him. Her gaze was alert, unblinking. "Yet it's there, just the same. Your opinion of the upper classes is . . . low."

"They haven't given me much cause to believe otherwise." Memories of university lacerated him. He still heard

the taunts of the noblemen and gentlemen commoners,
how they'd called him *scum* and *upstart vulgarian* and
emptied their chamber pots onto his bed when he was out
attending the classes they disdained. The burning shame
of those days still charred him around the edges.

He had returned home after one term, swearing never
to go back. After that, he had worked beside his father
once more, only by then work meant not the saddlery but
Exchange Alley.

She dropped her gaze, yet only slightly, before looking
up again. "So, those of noble birth are all the same person
wearing different masks?"

Her voice held a bite, faint, but there, and he respected
her for it.

"There are . . . exceptions."

"And I am indeed *grateful* you made an exception for
me." She moved away from him. "I find myself chilled. I'll
return inside."

He caught her wrist as she turned, and drew her back.
"Neither of us is who others suppose us to be."

She gave this consideration, which was more than he
had given her. "These past few days have been educational."

"For both of us." He still believed most aristos to be
spoiled buffoons, but he was sage enough to admit when
there was something to learn. Mostly, he was learning the
intricacies of his wife. "Stay out here with me. Please," he
remembered to add.

Her wrist slid from his grasp, and for a moment, he
thought she would storm back into the house. Instead, she
looked pointedly at his arm, which he offered. She accepted, and they resumed their stroll, with the sounds of
crunching shells beneath their feet and the distant tolling
of Saint George's bell marking the hour.

Ten o'clock. Bram would be at the Snake and Sextant,

the usual meeting place for the Hellraisers before they ventured out for the night's exploits. Edmund went out seldom, now that he had the wife he had coveted. John often had dealings at Whitehall that kept him late. Which meant that Bram was alone. Unless Leo joined him.

He waited for the feeling of restlessness that always presaged his evening entertainment. The need to do and see more and more. An unceasing appetite for the pleasures afforded by wealth.

Part of him felt he should go, merely on principle. Prove to himself that marriage had not changed him, nor the essence of himself.

Yet jagged and uncertain their conversations might be, he found himself enjoying Anne's company. He liked talking with her. If he required a rationale, he could tell himself that he merely wanted to speed up the process of rogering his wife. And he did want that. But she was more than a receptacle or ornament. A person. Entire and genuine. Soft, but not fragile. Innocent, yet not immature.

There could be much more to Anne than he had first accounted—a thought both alarming and intriguing.

Since the subject seemed to interest her, he said, "The money my father earned from the commission was substantial. More than he could make in a year. But he didn't put it back into the saddlery. He invested it instead. In a shipment of Indian cotton."

"I didn't realize saddle makers knew so much of overseas trade."

"They don't. My father would go to the pub and have someone read him the newspaper. Got his imagination sparked by tales of wealthy nabobs and all the faraway places making such wondrous things. He wanted to be a part of that."

"It was a bold thing to do," Anne said quietly. "Invest when he had so little experience with it."

"The neighbors called him a fool for pissing away a year's earnings, and all for a bit of Oriental cloth. Their smirks died when he earned thrice what he had invested."

"What a fine day that must have been for you." She smiled.

He remembered it vividly. The letter that came from London. Leo reading the letter aloud as his father stared at the banknotes stacked on their single, rough table. His mother's tears. And his father's vow that he would invest again, and again, until they could have butter on their bread and fresh tea in their cups. His father had contracted a sickness that day, a sickness for the future. Leo caught it, too. A fever in his blood, one he hoped would never be cured.

"By the time I was fifteen," he said, "we were more than comfortable. We were rich. And every day, I grow richer."

"Gaining you everything you want."

He chuckled at that. "There is always more."

"Never enough?" She glanced up at him through her lashes.

"When I become the wealthiest man in England, perhaps then." But he doubted it. He stiffened when he caught the soft music of her chuckle. "You think my ambition ridiculous."

She shook her head. "You mistake me. My laughter is for the peculiarities of circumstance. Yesterday, I found myself married to a man I barely know. And today, I learn that this man and I share something unexpected."

"We share a name now." And a bed, though they had only slept in this bed.

"Something else. For I realized just now"—she moved to stand before him—"that the saddler's son and the poor baron's daughter are more than husband and wife." A rueful smile curved her lips. "We have both stood outside the assembly hall, watching the dancers." She glanced toward the house. "Now it's time to go inside."

Chapter 5

After the revelations of the evening, Anne had anticipated Leo might press the moment and claim his husbandly rights. A shivering sense of excitement and apprehension had accompanied her over the course of the night, that uneasy comingling of want and fear. Yet when they had lain side by side in bed, he had done nothing more than kiss her cheek before turning over and falling quickly, deeply asleep.

Leaving her again to stare off into the darkness, her mind churning.

This morning, she heard him stir, and the quiet exchange between him and his valet. She sat up when Spinner left the chamber.

"Did I wake you?" Leo frowned in concern as he tugged on the cuffs of his dark blue coat. Its slim cut emphasized the leanness of his form, the breadth of his shoulders, and with the early morning light seeping in beneath the curtains, he was a crisp, handsome herald of day.

I cannot believe I am married to this man.

"Last night gave me much to think about," she said.

He drifted closer to the bed. She felt acutely conscious of her rumpled nightgown, her state of near undress, when he had armored himself in impeccable tailoring. She sat in bed, whilst he stood. Their inequality unsettled her.

"I would like to help," she said.

"Help." He spoke the word as if uncertain of its meaning.

She made herself meet his gaze. "You and I, we're not precisely desirables amongst the ranks of Society. I have breeding and connection, but no wealth. You have fortune, but no pedigree. Each of us with something the other lacks. Before we wed, I was apprised by my father of the monthly allowance you settled on me." The amount still stunned her. She could not possibly spend it within the course of twelve months, let alone one. "So you have given me what I lacked before our marriage, and I want to do the same for you."

He raised a brow. "I want nothing given from obligation."

"Not obligation—a desire to *help*." She fought frustration. What a stubborn man, determined to see everything as a battle. "There are men of the gentry with whom you could form connections. Men of power and influence."

"I know many of those men, and they're little willing to accept me as one of theirs."

"It's in the approach. If you go at them head-on, they become cornered dogs, snarling and bristling. But a slower side advance might yield better response. Perhaps not a tail wagging, but at least a tentative sniff. That is far better than a bite."

A smile tilted the corner of his mouth. "I believe you are calling these noblemen sons of bitches."

She bit back a shocked laugh. "Some men of science theorize that humans are merely animals. I've been to assemblies—my conclusion is that animals are more civilized."

"How do you propose we tame these savage dogs?"

"Through the bitches—I mean, the wives."

"Bitches," Leo confirmed.

Again, Anne found herself appalled . . . and also thrilled by his candor. "A few morning calls on the right wives could secure us any number of advantages. Including invitations to private gatherings and dinner."

Outsider Leo might be, but he recognized the benefit of dining with select company. Alliances fashioned over the roast, and confederacy shaped between after-dinner glasses of brandy. Anne actually disliked paying calls, and had found them exceedingly tedious when her mother dragged her along on them. Either the conversations were full of meaningless prattle, or else scandals were dragged forth with all the glee of a resurrectionist procuring a corpse.

"Seldom have I received dinner invitations," he noted.

"Single men might not. There *are* advantages to marriage."

His gaze, suddenly hot, raked over her, and she struggled to keep from folding her arms protectively across her chest. Yet deep within her, a quick flare of response ignited.

"I'm aware of some of the advantages," he murmured.

Anne dropped her gaze. Last night, as he had slept, she stared at the shapes his body made beneath the bedclothes, their solidity and strength. He heated the bed far more than any warming pan, and as the night's chill had seeped into the room, she had wanted to press herself against him. Only partly for warmth.

"Doors may open for you now. Married men are seen as more respectable than bachelors." She traced the knotted pattern on the counterpane. "Less threatening, too."

Leo made a soft noise, something akin to a laugh, though absent of any humor. "Perception and the truth seldom overlap."

She glanced up. "*Are* you a threat?"

"To you, never."

Some comfort in that, yet she did not miss what was couched in his response. But his gaze warmed as he looked down at her.

"You would do that—pay calls, wrangle invitations—for me?" He sounded bewildered, a man little used to kindness.

"We are married now. If we do not take care of each other, who shall?" It was more than matrimonial duty, however. She had heard the hurt throbbing beneath his words last night, the wounds that pained him still, despite, or because of, his pride. And pride Leo had in abundance. Not unlike the lion with which he shared a name.

Here was something she could provide for Leo. Something he could neither be born into nor buy. She discovered she wanted to give him something. For all the abundance of things in his home, his clothespress full of expensive garments, even those Hellraisers he called friends, he had very little truly his own, bestowed on him simply for the gratification of giving.

"I . . ." He searched for words, perplexed. And then, "Thank you."

Her cheeks heated, her pleasure intensified by the simplicity and honesty of his language.

With slow ceremony, he took her hand in his. Turned it so that her knuckles faced up. His gaze held hers, and she felt herself planted firmly where she sat, unable to move or even breathe. Then, unhurriedly, he bent and pressed his lips to the backs of her fingers.

It was not an unmannerly kiss. Not lascivious or coarse. Yet for all that, the touch of his firm, warm lips to her fingers sent dragon coils of hunger twisting through her. A contraction of want tightened between her thighs.

"I would say that you're too good for me," he said, his breath its own caress on her skin, "but I want good things." With equal leisure, he released her hand and straightened.

At the very least, the tightness in his jaw revealed that the courtly gesture had affected him, too.

For a moment, they simply stared at each other, spinning the fine threads between them into something stronger.

"I do have a request of you," he said finally.

She nodded, eager.

His gaze shifted away and followed the thorny convolutions painted upon the wallpaper. "Ever since my father made his fortune and sent me away to school, I developed . . . well . . . one might call it an odd habit. A compulsion, you might say. I've become a collector. A collector of coins."

"That does not sound very odd. Many men collect coins—ancient coins, or from other countries." Her own father had been too lacking in resources to have anything remotely resembling a gentleman's cabinet of curiosities. Rather than accrue small treasures, antiquities or animal bones, her father collected letters demanding payment. Occasionally, those debts would be paid.

"The coins I collect aren't rare," said Leo. "They're quite ordinary. Except for the fact that they belong to other people."

"I do not follow."

Leo dipped his hand into his pocket and produced a handful of change. He set the coins upon the counterpane, arranging them beside her leg in a neat line. Commonplace currency: farthings, pennies, shillings.

"This." He pointed to a sixpence. "Belonged to Lord Huyton. This." He nudged a ha'penny. "Lord Feering's." Leo saw the question in her eyes, and answered, laughing, "I didn't *steal* them. Merely asked for change and it was given."

"But . . . why?"

He shrugged. "It's hard to explain. I suppose having something that was once so difficult to obtain is part of it.

Now I have coin in profusion, but I like owning something that belonged to one of the gentry. Something so mundane, but important." Leo gave a wry smile. "Now I sound like I should be in Bedlam."

"No, it makes sense." And it did, in a peculiar way. "Both you and these gentlemen having use of coins. Despite everything that they say, all their prejudice, the need for coins makes you equals. It confirms what they might never acknowledge."

His eyes narrowed as he looked at her. "Something in an aristocratic girl's education must make them astute. Yet," he added thoughtfully, "I suspect it isn't the education, but the girl that makes the difference."

"Living one's life dependent on others' goodwill, one learns to make a close study of one's environment." She had seen hardly anything of the larger world, but that which she knew, she understood very well.

"I congratulate myself for making such a wise decision in my choice of a bride."

"By all means," she replied, "take credit for my perspicacity."

He chuckled, but his gaze drifted from her face back down to the coins. And then she understood.

"You would like me to collect some coins for you," she deduced.

"There are certain men whose coins I want."

At first, Anne thought to refuse. She could not fault Leo for his idiosyncrasies. Almost everyone had them, including herself. Yet his was a mania altogether private, something between himself and his desires.

Still, it was such a small thing. And if it helped forge a stronger bond between her and Leo, she knew her directive.

"If you write their names down for me," she said after a pause, "and if they're married, I'll gather coins for you."

She was not particularly adept at making idle, pleasant conversation, and had not the slightest understanding how she might obtain these coins, but she had faith in her wits. A solution might present itself.

"The coins must come from the men themselves. Not their wives or children or servants."

Here was an added complication, and frankly, one even more eccentric than she had anticipated. "If that's what you wish."

He seemed surprised that she agreed. "Truly? You'll do this?"

"It might be an enjoyable challenge."

He moved so quickly, Anne had no chance to react. One moment he stood beside the bed, and the next, he leaned over her, his large hands cupping her head, tilting it back. He kissed her. Not the tentative exploration of the wedding night, but a full, sumptuous kiss, demanding and carnal. His lips were ravenous on hers.

For a moment, she could do nothing but let it happen, stunned into immobility. Then instinct and need guided her. She slid her hands up his arms, to hold tight to his hard shoulders. Her lips parted, inviting him in, and he took the kiss deeper.

This was . . . extraordinary. Beyond any kiss she had ever received, the few times she had gotten them. Not just two mouths meeting, but a complete submersion into sensation. Only his hands and his lips touched her, yet she felt him, felt him everywhere. In the rush of her blood and softness of her flesh. Most especially between her legs and the tips of her breasts, now achingly sensitive. Leo kissed as he lived: without compromise, without quarter.

His tongue swept into her mouth. She touched it with her own, and Leo groaned.

She could not stop her response, the primal surge of desire. But fear sharpened the edge of that desire. It was too much. She was overwhelmed. He'd devour her, and she would not only be powerless to prevent it, she would present herself on a silver charger, the willing animal eager to be feasted upon until only bones remained. She already sat in bed. It would be easy, very easy, for him to pull her down and put his weight atop hers. Claim her fully.

A sound escaped her, a moan partway between arousal and terror.

At once, he pulled his mouth away.

His gaze, bright and hot, held hers. He looked as stunned as she felt. As though neither of them could comprehend what had just happened.

For a moment, he seemed on the verge of taking her mouth again. His fingers tightened in her hair. Abruptly, he let go, yet she felt the strength in him it took to do so. He stepped back, until a respectable distance of several feet separated them.

"I'll write that list up for you." His voice had hoarsened, and she caught the trace of a rough accent. The saddler's son emerging from beneath a carefully cultivated luster.

He turned and strode to the door and opened it. There, one hand braced on the frame, he paused. He did not turn around. "Expect me home for dinner."

Then he was gone, closing the door behind him. Anne's only company was the coins, their blank metallic faces staring up at her, offering not a single answer.

The carriage waited for him outside, and he leapt into it. At his nod, the footman closed the door and called up to the coachman, "Drive on."

They clattered their way east toward Exchange Alley, but Leo did not see the familiar streets of High Holborn, Chancery Lane, nor any of the others. His mind was with

Anne in Bloomsbury, and his body wanted to be there, as well.

Hell, what had come over him? His intentions to take things slowly with her had burned away. He hadn't even planned on kissing her mouth at all, for it had been enough to kiss her hand. Yet impulse and need had taken over. Once unleashed, it became a battle to rein it in again.

She had thrown him. He prepared himself always for eventualities, outcomes, options. The Devil's gift showed him the future, and there he often dwelt. Even without this gift, Leo could chart what was, what would be. Yet Anne continued to defy his expectations.

At first, he'd regretted telling his wife about his past, his father, fearing it made him vulnerable. But it had drawn them closer together, revealing unexpected similarities, as if the tide ebbed to uncover a hidden house beneath the waves.

Yet he knew that if he revealed his magic to her, everything they had been building together would crumble. There would be no warm acceptance, no understanding. Only fear. Perhaps even disgust.

No—he must keep his secrets.

He planned to use their strengthening connection by slowly building toward physical intimacy. It seemed the best, soundest plan.

Had she been anyone other than herself, that plan would have unfolded just as he desired. Yet what she had said this morning, what she offered . . . no one had ever given him as much. He knew she did not want to pay calls and try to ingratiate herself with the wives of the highest elite. It was more than her overcoming natural shyness. It meant forcibly pulling herself from the shadows into the glare of artificial suns, suns that burned more often than warmed.

Logically, he saw how she might benefit herself by Leo gaining alliances with rich, powerful men. As his status increased, so would hers. But he knew her motivations were different. Her help was for *him*, and no one else.

And she would get coins for him. Coins that would show him future disasters. She had no idea what the coins revealed to him, how he used them to advance his own fortunes whilst ruining another's. Yet she would get the coins for him because she thought it would make him . . . happy. He tried to remember the last time anyone had done anything for him without an ulterior purpose, or simply because it would bring him joy. Even his father's gifts—a pearl-handled folding knife, a book of quotations—had been to advance Leo within the eyes of the world. And the Hellraisers were a bunch of selfish bastards, just like him, offering companionship but gobbling down experiences as fast as they could be devoured.

He'd thought himself too cynical, too jaded to feel much beyond his own mercenary desires. He was unaccustomed to feeling gratitude. Yet Anne's offer had pierced him like a golden blade.

And she had looked so damned enticing, still rumpled from sleep, her pretty face touched by morning light. That same morning light had revealed the silken shape of her body beneath her nightgown, and he had been struck with the visceral memory of her breast in his hand, its soft, perfect weight. Desire and something else, something that might have been tenderness, flooded him, and he had acted. Kissed her.

The carriage jounced as it turned onto Fleet Street. Traffic thickened as he moved farther into the heart of the city, the core of London. Yet as the carriage was forced to slow, Leo's pulse sped.

That kiss . . . Before her fear had emerged, Anne had been so responsive, so eager. Her kiss was untried, yet what art it lacked was more than compensated by enthusi-asm. He'd suspected that she contained far more passion than she even realized, and he was right. It had taken every ounce of control he possessed not to climb onto the bed, gathering her soft, willing body against him. Show her how to wind her legs around his waist as he undid the buttons on his breeches. Make her fully his. He had never hungered for innocence until that moment.

Only her sound of fright had stopped him. Barely.

He had made a vow to himself. One he would not break. He might not have married for love, like his parents, but by hell, he would not conduct his marriage as the aristos did. When he took Anne's maidenhead, no fear would exist between them.

She deserved better than an impersonal, calculated fuck. He discovered he liked her too much to treat her like chattel. So he now rode toward Exchange Alley with a faintly aching cock and the taste of her in his mouth.

His smile mocked only himself. At last, Leo Bailey had developed ethics. And his cock hated him for it.

Traffic stalled, and Leo poked his head out the carriage window to see what caused the delay. An overturned cart blocked the street. Two men argued fiercely, their faces red, as bystanders watched. One of the men swung at the other. Within a moment, the street filled with brawling.

The carriage rocked as the horse grew agitated. From his seat, the driver called down to Leo, "Sorry, sir, but we're jammed. Oi! Get off!" The coachman knocked down a man trying to climb up onto his perch.

Leo bit back an oath of impatience. He hadn't time for this. Occasional scuffles in the streets were as common as rats, but this altercation went beyond the usual fracas. It seemed as though it hadn't taken much to make the little fight explode into a much bigger brawl. Yet he needed to get to the Exchange. Business hours had already begun. Missing important deals infuriated him.

"I'll walk the rest of the way, Dawkins."

"Are you sure, sir? It's—down from there, you son of a whore—a bit rough."

Leo smiled grimly, and opened the carriage door.

Amazing what a bit of brawling could do for one's humor. As Leo wended his way up Queen Street and then turned on to Poultry, he shook out his fist. Fortunately, he knew how to throw a punch, and the ache in his hand had already begun to subside. No one in that melee had expected a gent in a fine private coach to come out swinging. But he had, and laid out three big men for their trouble. He had cleared a path for himself.

Now he had to stop himself from whistling. He hadn't been able to obtain physical release with his wife, but fighting in the street offered more brutal means.

He reached the entrance to Exchange Alley off Cornhill. Three men waited for him. Hellraisers. Bram made a tall, dark shape against the sunlit street, and both Edmund and John glanced around with tense, strained expressions.

"What in the name of God has you out of bed so early?" The hour had barely reached eight o'clock. "Unless you haven't been to bed yet."

"Bram and John roused me from mine," Edmund muttered.

The shadows under John and Bram's eyes confirmed that neither had gone home last night. Leo realized that, for the first time in . . . as long as he could remember, he hadn't joined in for the evening's debauchery. He had been at home. With Anne.

And he hadn't missed going out, not a bit.

"It's business hours, lads," he said. "If there's carousing to be done, it must wait 'til later."

Bram shook his head, and Leo saw that the drawn cast

that honed his friend's already sharp features came not from a night's dissipated revels, but something else. Something troubling.

Nerves tightened along the back of Leo's neck and his pleasant mood burst like a blister.

He glanced around. Men of business who knew him well were casting him and the other Hellraisers speculative glances. Leo's presence at the 'Change was common, but his dissolute friends' attendance was noteworthy.

"There's a tavern in an alley off Threadneedle. The Cormorant. I'll meet you there in a quarter of an hour."

His friends dispersed, trailing shadows. Leo spent a few minutes chatting with acquaintants, maintaining the illusion that all was well, even as he knew otherwise. Eventually, he drifted away and toward Threadneedle Street. He hated missing any potential deals, but he had no choice. The Hellraisers would not seek him out at this hour unless the situation were dire.

Less crowded than a coffee house, the Cormorant tavern still held a few patrons. One man slept with his head on the table, beside his tankard. Another puffed on a pipe by the fire, watching smoke rings drift up to the stained ceiling. The Hellraisers occupied the settles in the corner, and they stared at their mugs with hard, wary expressions, as if anticipating an attack.

Leo sat next to John. He grunted his thanks when the tapster brought a grimy mug of ale, though he had no thirst for it.

"Whit's been spotted," Bram said without preamble. "Here, in London."

Leo clenched his hands into fists. "When?"

"Don't know. John and I only heard about it last night."

"We ran into Chilton at the Theatre Royal," said John. "He asked why Whit wasn't with us, as he had seen him just that morning on Westminster Bridge, with a pretty Gypsy girl on his arm. Whit asked Chilton about us, wanted to know what we had been doing."

"And Chilton told him," added Bram.

Leo swore. He considered taking a drink of his ale just to steady himself, but something floated on the drink's surface, and he pushed it away.

Damn it. *Damn.*

"What do you think he wants?" Edmund gnawed on his thumbnail, as he always did when anxious.

"Same as he's always wanted—to take our gifts." John's fingers beat a staccato rhythm on the tabletop.

"He hasn't the power to do so." Yet Bram did not sound as confident as his words attested.

"Not that we know of." Leo crossed his arms over his chest. "It's been months since Bram saw him in Manchester. Not even Mr. Holliday has been able to keep track of him. Anything might have happened in the interval."

"We can't let him take our gifts. We *cannot.*" A note of panic threaded into Edmund's voice. Unlike the broader-reaching gifts that John, Bram, and Leo had received, Edmund had received one, and one alone: Rosalind.

Bram scowled. "Just last night I used my gift to persuade my way into Lady Hadlow's bed. She was always too devoted to her husband, even if he's in India."

"As a married man," said Edmund, "I find your actions deplorable."

"Because, before Rosalind, you only fucked widows and courtesans?" Bram snorted. "You forget, I once saw you sneaking off with the very married Augustine Colford." When Edmund continued to sulk, Bram added, "For all her fidelity, Lady Hadlow did not complain when I brought her to climax four times."

"There's more at stake than your damned cock." John growled. "Yesterday afternoon, I read the mind of the Earl of Northington, the damned Lord Chancellor, and learned his plans for the treaty with France. Without Mr. Holliday's gift, I wouldn't know a bloody thing. I'd be merely another *normal* man," he sneered.

Dissention was never difficult to come by with the Hellraisers, but Leo needed to stop it before they degenerated into an outright scrum. "No one is taking anything. There are four of us, and one of him."

"And the Gypsy," added John. "The ghost, too. If she has reappeared."

"Doesn't matter," said Bram. "Between us four Hellraisers and his less-than-reliable confederates, the odds favor us."

"Whit always did like steep odds." Leo smiled darkly. "But this is one gamble he cannot win."

"You have a scheme in mind," said Bram.

"Continuously." Leaning forward, Leo braced his elbows on the table. "Whit might not be able to mount a full-scale frontal assault. He knows that he cannot beat us all. If I were him, I would seek out allies, wherever I could find them. All that remains to us is to ensure that he makes no allegiances."

John's fingers slowed their beat as he began to understand Leo's intent. "Ostracize him."

"If Whit is not received anywhere in London, if he becomes a pariah, then he is left to his own frail resources."

Still, Bram looked skeptical. "*Frail* was not the word I would have used to describe Whit in Manchester. He had no magic, 'tis true, but he seemed stronger than ever. Especially with that damned girl at his side. As if he could level mountains with thought alone."

John snorted. "False confidence engendered by a bit of quim. Doubtless he has begun to realize that, outside of the bedchamber, a Gypsy girl makes for an inferior companion. He could be weakening even now."

"We cut Whit off from any source of support," said Leo, "leave him with nary a friend, so he has no reinforcements."

Clearly heartened by this idea, Edmund brightened. "That should not prove overly difficult. His habits at the gaming tables seldom won him friends—beyond us, of course."

"A few well-placed tales of cheating and theft," Leo continued, "and the deed is done. There've already been rumors about him ruining lordlings and reckless gentlemen. Some more kindling on that fire, and we will smoke him out."

Yet Bram was not entirely satisfied. "And then?"

"And then . . . when Whit has nowhere to turn, he will either flee, or attempt to make a stand. At which point"—he smiled grimly at the other Hellraisers—"we will render him no longer a threat. By any means at our disposal."

A sheet of paper awaited Anne at breakfast. On it, in Leo's bold, masculine scrawl, was a list of names. She took her tea and rolls in the upstairs parlor rather than the cavernous dining chamber, and as she sipped from her cup, she considered the list.

All of the names she knew, some better than others. Impoverished her family might be, but their breeding was matchless, their connections impeccable. A few barbs might be lobbed in Anne's direction, given that she had married so far beneath her rank, yet a baron's daughter she remained. Barring any real scandal, she ought to be admitted to anyone's home. Welcomed, even.

She picked apart a roll and reviewed the list. Leo had selected the highest-ranking members of Society, men of ancient lineage. Anne mulled over their names, sensing that something connected them, something she could not quite identify, yet lingered at the back of her mind like a distant storm. Dark clouds massing on the horizon.

But what was it? What linked the names on the list?

Anne shook her head. Again, she let fancy run rampant. Leo had revealed much this morning, giving her glimpses of a self she suspected he showed few, if any. How much of his past did his friends know? Men seldom unburdened themselves to one another, as if, like the basest pack of animals, they feared a show of vulnerability meant a challenger would disembowel them and claim dominance.

What Leo had said to her today had been spoken in trust. She could not repay that trust with suspicion. Already she knew her acceptance pleased him. Her mouth and body still resonated with the heat of his kiss.

God, if that kiss was any gauge of what she ought to expect when they finally consummated their marriage ... no wonder she battled fear. For the effects of Leo's desire could leave her a smoldering ruin. And she might gratefully welcome the conflagration.

Cheeks burning, heat pooling low in her belly, Anne tried to compose herself with a sip of tea. Yet the liquid was too hot, and she burned her tongue. Everything, it seemed, burned her.

She spent the remainder of the morning in correspondence. As she sat at an escritoire in the opulently furnished drawing room, no noise in the chamber but for the scratching of her pen across the foolscap and the pop of the fire, Anne thought she heard a rustling, and the sound of a footstep just behind her. Startled, she dropped her pen, spattering ink across the paper.

She turned in her seat, expecting to see either Meg or one of the servants. No one. The chamber had one occupant: her.

Instinctively, she looked toward the mounted sconces, but the candles were unlit. There was nothing to extinguish.

Chiding herself, Anne sprinkled sand onto the paper in the hopes of salvaging it. The contents of her letter were not irreplaceable, but she was too used to frugal living to readily lose a sheet of foolscap. Paper was dear.

Now she could afford as much foolscap as she desired, and in her letters she would not have to cross her lines anymore as a means of using less paper.

Anne sighed. The letter was beyond repair, and her thoughts too scattered to attempt anything resembling coherent correspondence. Checking the hour, she saw that she was well within polite boundaries for paying calls. She may as well begin crossing names off Leo's list. No sense in delaying.

Lord Newstead seemed the best candidate with which to begin. Lady Newstead was close in age to Anne, and married only a year. She and Anne might find elements of parallel over which they might form, if not friendship, then a better sense of acquaintanceship. Keeping this strategy in mind, Anne donned her hat and, with Meg in tow, stepped outside.

The sky was mottled, gray clouds streaking the cold blue sky, and an air of hushed waiting hung over the street.

"Mr. Bailey has taken the carriage." The footman waiting in attendance by the door seemed apologetic, as if having only one carriage seemed a breach of decorum. Anne's family had to share their carriage with two other families, which kept impromptu journeys to a minimum. "I can summon a hack for you, madam."

It seemed a dreadful expense, when a sedan chair would suit the same purpose, but she had to remind herself that expense little mattered anymore. She glanced down the street. "I do not see any hackneys." In truth, almost no one was out, apart from a sweep with his brushes.

"Two streets over, there's loads of traffic. I'll just run over. Back in a moment, madam."

"You may have an admirer, Meg," Anne said once the footman had run off. "He seemed most eager to show himself at an advantage."

The maid sniffed. "As if a lady's maid would ever hold truck with a *footman*. It takes more than a fine pair of calves to turn my head." Yet Meg cast lingering glances in the direction which the footman had disappeared.

An icy wind spun down the street. Anne shivered.

"This weather is changeable." Meg gazed critically toward the sky. "Shall I fetch a shawl for you, madam?"

At Anne's nod, the maid hurried up the stairs and then into the house. Anne stood by herself, rubbing her hands on her arms. The sweep had turned the corner. No one else occupied the street. She was alone.

"Mrs. Bailey."

Anne spun around.

Not five feet from her stood a tall, brown-haired man, his clothing fine but verging on threadbare. His brilliant blue eyes shone with intelligence, and though he never took his gaze from her, he seemed acutely aware of his surroundings, as if sensing enemies all around. At his side was a young woman of exotic origin, her skin dusky, her eyes as black as her hair. Like the man, the exotic girl had an air of wariness about her. They had the guarded manner of fugitives.

Though Anne did not recognize the girl, she knew the man by reputation alone.

Her voice came out little more than a croak. "Lord Whitney."

Chapter 6

The street had been empty, yet Lord Whitney and his companion had just noiselessly appeared. "My . . . my husband is not at home."

"It's *you* we want to speak with," said the young woman. Large golden hoops hung from her ears, necklaces draped around her neck, and rings adorned her fingers. Anne had never been this close to a Gypsy in her life, though she had seen them at Bartholomew Fair doing trick riding and telling fortunes.

"Time is in short supply." Lord Whitney stepped closer, and Anne took an instinctive step back.

"Time for what?"

"To warn you."

Unease crawled up Anne's neck. "Truly, perhaps you should return when Leo is home."

"Leo is the one you should be afraid of."

Anne did not like the alert tension in Lord Whitney's stance, nor the way the Gypsy woman kept glancing around the street. Perhaps the Gypsy was ill, for her body gave off a tremendous amount of heat. Perhaps both the woman *and* Lord Whitney were both ill, for they had a kind of fever in their eyes.

"He has been nothing but kind to me," Anne said.

Lord Whitney and the Gypsy exchanged speaking glances. "She doesn't know," said the Gypsy.

"Know what?" Anne's anxiety gave edge to her temper. "These riddles you speak are tiresome."

"Leo has—" Lord Whitney broke off when the front door opened.

Anne turned to see Meg standing at the top of the stairs, an Indian shawl in hand. "Madam?"

Glancing back at Lord Whitney and his companion, Anne jolted in surprise when she found no sign of them.

"Did you see them?" Anne asked when Meg came down the steps.

"I heard you speaking with someone, but when I came out, you were alone." The maid's forehead wrinkled in concern as she draped the shawl around Anne's shoulders. "Are you well, madam?"

Anne pressed a hand to her forehead. Had she just imagined that entire bizarre conversation? Manufacturing Lord Whitney—a man she barely knew—and a Gypsy woman—whom she knew not at all? If she had invented that scenario, she could not understand where the details came from, nor why she would construct the person of a Gypsy out of her own imagination.

Perhaps I'm *the one with fever.*

"I do not know." She pulled the shawl close around her shoulders.

Carriage wheels rattling broke the street's silence. The footman ran beside a hackney coach, and he smiled with ruddy-faced pride at his work when both he and the vehicle stopped in front of the house.

"The missus isn't going to need that." Meg deflated the footman's satisfaction. "She's ill, and must have rest." Realizing her presumption, the maid turned to Anne. "That's right, isn't it, madam?"

Anne did not feel sick in the slightest, yet she must be, to believe she had conversed with people who were not truly there. And she had had that peculiar incident earlier in the drawing room, that sense of being watched. This morning had been a collection of eldritch moments. "Yes. I think I will lie down."

The footman looked crestfallen as Meg led Anne up the stairs. At the top of the stairs, before going inside, Anne glanced back out to the street. Movement near the mews caught her eye, yet when she peered closer, all she saw were shadows caused by shifting clouds. Shaking her head at the strange convolutions of her mind, she went inside.

Meg lit candles against the onset of darkness. Yet as soon as the maid left Anne's chamber, the same thing happened. One by one, the candles went out. Not wanting to summon Meg for something she could easily accomplish on her own, Anne tried to relight the candles, but they continued to extinguish themselves. She checked the windows. They remained secure. The door to her chamber stayed closed. There were no drafts, no gusts. Again, she had the oddest sensation that something, some*one* blew the candles out. Yet she was completely alone.

On the third try, the candles stayed lit, as though whoever had blown them out either left or grew weary of their labors. She gazed around the room, uneasy.

Full dark fell by the time Anne heard Leo's footsteps on the stairs. She set her book aside as he entered the bedchamber, looking slightly windblown yet striking nonetheless.

Seeing her reclining in bed, he took long strides until he stood beside her.

"What ails you?" He sat down and, frowning with concern, took her hand between his.

"Nothing. A momentary complaint." Indeed, after spending the remainder of the day in bed, with the walls of the chamber—of the house itself—close about her, restlessness danced through her. She barely remembered the incident outside the house, and now began to wonder if all of it had been some strange, momentary folly brought about by too little sleep and too much idleness.

Yet Leo was solicitous. "I'll fetch a physician."

"It isn't necessary. Truly, Leo, if there was a crisis, it has passed." He looked skeptical, but she could be as obstinate as he, when required. She tried for a diversionary tactic. "I hope your day of trade and commerce proved fruitful."

If she had not been studying the angles and contours of his face, she might have missed the slight movement of his gaze—the barest flick to the side. But her husband was at all times a subject of fascination, and so she did see this tiny movement, and could only wonder what it meant.

"A hectic day." He smiled, and pressed her hands closer within his.

It was not precisely an answer, but she decided not to push for specifics, since she did not want an accounting of her own actions today. They would maintain a mutual blindness.

As they gazed at each other, realization crept over them both. The last time they had been in each other's company, he had kissed her. The kiss resonated now like unheard music, the beat of a drum steady and compelling beneath the silence. Her gaze drifted to his mouth, just as his did to hers. Both of them wondering, each asking themselves, *Did that truly happen? Could it happen again?*

Beneath his hands, the pulse in her wrists quickened.

He released his clasp of her hands. As if to distract himself from the potential of his wife in bed, he glanced over to the small table beside the bed. Extending his long body so that he stretched over her, he took hold of some of the squares of thick paper piled there. His body spread warmth through hers as his torso brushed hers.

He straightened, his cheek darkening beneath golden stubble. Riffling through the cards, he read aloud. "*Mr. and Mrs. Samuel Bingham. Sir Frederic and Lady Wells. The Lord and Lady Overbury humbly request the honor of your presence.*" He looked up at her, baffled. "What are these?"

"Calling cards. Invitations. Sending them is rather a mania for Society. The cards arrive every morning, especially after a wedding. Have you never received them?"

"Some requests to dine from business associates but not this. Never anything so . . . reputable." He seemed unused to speaking such a word.

She laughed. "My nefarious respectability. I am afraid you may have caught it from me, like fever."

"Have you responded to any of these invitations?"

"Not as of yet. I wanted to consult with you first. I did not know if you would want to attend such . . . reputable entertainments."

He stared at the cards as though he held messages from beyond the grave. Cautious, curious. "This world," he murmured. "It's strange to me."

It touched her that this man, so proud and forthright, could feel even the slightest whisper of trepidation, and that he trusted her enough to reveal it.

"What you need," she said, "is a guide."

A separate world existed in the respectable hours of evening, one with which Leo rarely rubbed shoulders. Lit by hundreds of candles, it was brighter than the world Leo knew, and yet more obscure.

He and Anne stood at the side of a large chamber, watching the complex convolutions of human relations—

the subtle gestures, the layered discourse with more gradations than shale. The room itself showed signs of recent remodeling, for Leo noticed plaster dust collecting against the ornamental baseboards, but the interactions within its walls bore the weight of history.

A small assembly at the home of Lord Overbury. There were refreshments and mannerly games of ombre and a girl in the corner picking out a pretty tune on a fortepiano. The guests were rich, genteel, powerful, and far, far from the company Leo normally kept. He had attended a few events like this with the Hellraisers, but he had paid such gatherings little heed, his thoughts on wilder sport later in the evening. Now, he finally observed that the movements of the aristocrats were even more cunning and artful than anything he had witnessed or engaged in at the Exchange.

By angling his body just so, one guest indicated that he refused to acknowledge another's presence. A woman whispered into another woman's ear as they both watched a laughing female guest. Three men stood in a group, their conversation as portentous as their waistcoats. The very air buzzed with influence.

"I feel like a naturalist accompanying a Royal Society expedition."

Anne smiled over the rim of her glass. "There's more treachery here than in the jungles of Suriname or Guiana."

"Spoken as one having experience with both places."

"Not personal experience." She glanced away. "Barons' daughters are seldom taken on Royal Society expeditions."

He suddenly found her much more fascinating than the tangled encounters of the assembly. His gaze traced the slim line of her neck as she kept her face averted. "But you want to go. To Suriname or Guiana."

She shrugged. "Having never been on a ship in my life, especially traveling somewhere over four thousand miles away, I couldn't say if I would find the experience enjoyable."

Interesting that she would know the distance between England and the distant northern coast of South America, when few men let alone women could locate Portugal on a map.

"There is no way to know until you try," he said.

"I am not a fanciful person." She turned back and her eyes were very clear. "I don't entertain ideas that cannot come to pass."

"Yet . . ."

"Yet." His wife glanced around the chamber, as if concerned any of the guests might be within earshot. Seeing that no one paid too much attention, she continued. "I don't long to travel. Not so far. However, on the rare occasions I was given pin money, I spent it at print shops on the Strand. On maps."

He could only regard his wife with genuine surprise. "Maps. Of South America."

"Or the Colonies, or Africa, or the East Indies. Maps of anywhere. Even England. It isn't the places so much as the drawing of the maps."

"I had not pegged you for a lover of cartography."

She studied him, looking, he believed, for signs of mockery or dismissal. Yet what she saw in his face must have encouraged her, for she admitted, "It is . . . an interest of mine."

"An unusual interest for a young woman."

"I had not cultivated it on purpose. It just seemed to happen." She smiled softly, an inward smile at some remembrance. "I recollect the day, I couldn't have been more than eight, and I was with my father at a print shop. The printer was trying to get my father to buy a map of the Colonies. A special reduced price because the map was no longer accurate. New discoveries had been made, territory west of a great river, and there were new settlements, too. It fascinated me that something as stable and immense as land, as a whole country, could suddenly change. Not because of an earthquake or a flood, but because of human knowledge."

She caught herself. Her voice had grown stronger, less hesitant, as she had spoken. Her eyes gleamed, and the flush in her cheeks came not from the wine nor the overheated room, but from the fire of her passion.

Leo was enthralled. The quiet beauty of his wife became altogether vibrant. And it wasn't unnoticed. He glowered at several men who sent her admiring glances, and they averted their gazes quickly.

"Did your father buy the map?"

She shook her head. "Such things were unnecessary, and the expense profligate. In truth," she confessed, "I never had enough money to buy maps, but I did annoy the shopkeeper by endlessly browsing."

"Thus your knowledge of far-flung places."

"The same places from which you buy your coffee, cotton, and spices." She waited, then glanced at him, a faint crease between her brows. "Well?"

"Well, what?"

"This is when you chide me for my decidedly unfeminine interests. My parents certainly did."

Leo's sudden, unadulterated laugh drew more curious glances from the assembly's guests. "Hell, I'm the very last person to lecture anyone on acceptable behavior."

"Your opinion might change when I tell you something very wicked."

He said nothing, merely waited.

She lowered her voice. "When I was thirteen, I . . ." After a deep breath, she pushed on, so that her words came out in a rush. "I stole a map."

"How?"

"I was in the print shop, looking at a map of the Moluccas. It was beautiful, but so costly. A customer came in and distracted the proprietor. That's when I did it. Ran out the door with the map. The proprietor didn't even notice, he did not cry thief or summon the watch. Even so, I never went back."

"And you threw away the map. Your ill-gotten gains."

Her eyes widened. "Lord, no. I kept it under my bed and pored over it every chance I had. Until my younger brother grew spiteful and tore it up." She stared at Leo. "Are you not . . . shocked? Appalled?"

"It would take far more than a single act of theft to appall me. Besides," he added, smiling, "I like having a secret about you. It's something private, only for us." A darker heat stole into his voice, deepening it.

The blush in her cheeks grew brilliant. In her saffron-colored gown, canary diamonds at her throat and hanging from her ears, she held the pure luster of sunshine.

"The way that I know about your coins," she murmured.

He blinked. A few words from her transported him from the radiance of her allure to the shadows of foreseen disasters. Her luminosity to the darkness of his Devil-given power. And Whit threatened everything—his power, his strengthening relationship with Anne. Yet Leo had no intention of allowing Whit to destroy all that Leo had created for himself.

"Like that, yes." Talk of his gift sharpened his resolve. He eyed the guests. Many of them had potential for exploitation, either by benefit of their deep coffers or because they had been vocal in their denouncement of social climbers like Leo. Others he didn't know, but wanted to—for he seldom let an opportunity to make use of someone pass.

Spotting Lord Overbury, Leo turned to Anne. "Excuse me for a moment. I want to speak with someone." At her murmured agreement, Leo took his leave and made his way to his host for the evening.

The viscount gave a polite but aloof nod at Leo's approach. Anne's birth might have gained him entrance to Overbury's home, yet Leo and the viscount would never be considered friends.

After giving his own restrained bow, Leo said, "My lord, I require your assistance."

"However may I be of assistance, Mr. Bailey?" Overbury's eyes scanned the room, his offer of help hardly more than a token.

"I actually possess magical power."

His interest piqued, the viscount raised his brows. "You do?"

"My wife is of similar disbelief." Leo addressed Overbury. "The only means I have to demonstrate my power requires a coin." He patted his pockets, making a pantomime of looking shamefaced. "All my coins are at home. Play the champion and give me one of yours."

Overbury produced a thruppence from the pocket of his satin waistcoat and handed it to Leo. "Show me this magic of yours."

"I have the coin here." He held it up for the viscount's inspection, then closed his fingers around the coin. "And now, it has disappeared." His hand opened, revealing that it was, in fact, empty.

The viscount made a sound of astonishment.

"Ah, wait, here it is again." Leo plucked the coin from beneath the lace of Overbury's jabot, and his host chortled.

"Clever, Bailey. You must show me how to perform that trick."

"'Tis no trick, my lord. Magic. Which I now must show my wife."

With the sounds of Overbury's chuckle behind him, Leo wended his way back to Anne.

"An ingenious way to get another coin." She smiled, and when Leo performed the same trick for her as he had for Overbury, her smile turned to a charming laugh. "I did not know you were a conjurer."

"Sleight of hand, nothing more." His words were glib, yet a tempest filled his mind. He saw cane fields washed away by a Caribbean storm, and a plantation house half buried beneath a wall of mud as the people within the house fled and palm trees bent double from the hurricane's wind. The odor of sodden sugar clogged his nostrils—noxiously sweet and damp. Yet he breathed it in deeply, for it was the smell of privilege's destruction.

"Perhaps you might teach me." Anne's voice perforated his vision, and he blinked to clear it from his thoughts.

He was not in Bermuda, watching the future destruction of Overbury's sugar crop, but at an assembly in the viscount's Mayfair mansion. He slipped the thruppence into his pocket. "I can. Later. Who's that nob over there?" He nodded toward a gent in embroidered satin, his coat cut unfashionably full.

Anne smothered a shocked laugh at his language. "The Earl of Toombe. He's the eldest son of the Marquess of Gough."

"Rich?"

"Uncommonly so. There's rumors he has thirty thousand pounds a year. His estate is in Buckinghamshire. I don't know how he votes in Parliament," she added, smiling.

"Children?"

"Two married daughters, three sons. His oldest son is the Viscount Berrow."

A name Leo knew from the Exchange. Leo had encouraged the viscount to invest in new cotton-milling equipment, which had more than tripled the mill's output. Suitably armed with information, he now eyed Berrow's father.

Leo tucked Anne's hand into the crook of his arm.

"We'll talk with him." He took a stride forward, then stopped when he noticed Anne staying rooted to the spot.

"We cannot simply walk up to him and start a conversation," she protested. "Not even to perform some legerdemain."

"Why the devil not?"

"I only know Lord Toombe by reputation, but I've never had a formal introduction. And our hosts tonight have not introduced us yet!"

"Our hosts are busy." Lord and Lady Overbury were now drinking and flirting, respectively. He tugged on Anne's hand. "Following ceremonial codes of conduct is idiotic. This is the modern era, not the Age of Chivalry."

Still, she looked uncertain. He might have simply towed his wife behind him, or gone on without her. But he wanted her to make the choice.

After a moment's hesitation, she matched her step with his. "It *is* rather absurd, to pretend someone doesn't exist unless you adhere to a set of outdated rules."

As they crossed the chamber together, her step grew more confident, her chin tilted higher. When Leo first saw Anne, months ago, she had been standing at the side of a chamber, much like this one, at an assembly very similar. It had been one of the few times Leo had attended such a gathering and paid any attention. He preferred wilder masquerades and revelries where the company was decidedly less virginal.

Yet something about the shy girl watching the festivities had intrigued him, even as she hung back from the entertainment and spoke only when spoken to. Then, she had been the suggestion of potential. Now, as they walked together toward the phenomenally wealthy earl, throwing off convention like dried carapaces, he could actually see her change, grow bold. She felt the eyes of the guests upon her, and she did not shrink. She soaked in their attention as if it were her due.

That night, he had seen aristocratic breeding in the fine structure of her face. This evening, her bearing came not just from bloodlines, but from action and confidence.

What was that sensation in him? That strange, rising warmth? A new kind of magic? No.

Respect. Not self-admiration, in what he could achieve or earn or buy, but appreciation of *her*, and that he could help fashion her metamorphosis.

He stopped in front of the earl. The older man stared at him, baffled. Leo stuck out his free hand. "Lord Toombe. Leo Bailey. My wife, Anne."

The earl, still mystified, shook Leo's hand, and bowed to Anne. "Do I know you, sir?"

"Your son and I are friends." Which was not precisely true, but Leo considered netting Berrow a handsome profit a decent foundation for friendship. "A singularly intelligent fellow."

Everyone is gratified to hear their children praised, and Toombe proved no different. He smiled, self-congratulatory. "He reminds me of my father, with his brains."

"You are too modest, my lord," Anne said. "The resemblance between Lord Berrow and yourself is remarkable. Both in appearance and acumen."

As Toombe blustered his approval, Leo's admiration of his wife grew to encompass the whole of the chamber. She possessed a natural instinct for finessing a potential target, no prompting required. Catching the approbation in Leo's gaze, she glowed with pride in herself.

When Leo and Anne strolled away ten minutes later, they had been invited to Toombe's for dinner the following Sunday. Three other men and their wives would be attending the dinner as well, three men with expansive pockets and an untapped interest in commercial enterprise.

Anne's eyes gleamed. "That was . . . exhilarating."

"Nothing gets the blood moving like stalking one's prey." He felt his own surging, not just from hooking an invitation to a wealthy peer's home, but because his wife had worked with him in perfect harmony.

Her brows rose. "Prey? Is that how you see these men?"

"Those Suriname jungles follow the same principles. To survive, one must see everything and everyone as either a threat or sustenance."

"Quite mercenary."

He slanted her a grin. "Exactly. We see to our own interests. Come," he cajoled, guiding her to stand by the windows at one end of the chamber. "You knew precisely what our purpose was, and you fought the battle flawlessly."

"My part was very minor," she demurred.

"I'll have no false modesty, not from my wife." He watched the guests, but was acutely conscious of Anne's hand on his arm, her slender form beneath silk, panniers, and stays. "Negotiating business deals—that is my expertise. You, however, understand the nuances of polite society. You guided the conversation without appearing to. Toombe honestly thinks that inviting us to dinner had been *his* idea."

At first, it seemed as though she would protest again, but then she pursed her lips and allowed herself the faintest trace of conceit. "It *was* rather well done of me."

He laughed. God, he found her more and more delightful, as unexpected as a butterfly amongst moths. "If you have given me the ailment of respectability, it's only fair that I corrupt you."

They gazed at each other. With her eyes bright, her cheeks flushed, she looked like a woman eager for ravishment. He quickly assessed the chamber. There was a folding screen in one corner. He could draw her behind the screen, kiss her again, and see if this morning's heat was atypical, or something he could coax forth once more.

He liked knowing things. Futures, investments, strategies. But nothing seemed more worth knowing than whether or not he could kiss his wife breathless with desire.

Something in his eyes must have given him away, for her smile faded and a look of anxious expectancy crossed her face.

Yes, he'd lead her away now—

A familiar voice said his name. "Leo, what the devil are you doing *here*?"

He smothered a curse and turned to find John staring at him in utter astonishment.

"Conducting the world's most discreet robbery," Leo answered.

"Mrs. Bailey." John offered Anne a bow, and she curtsied in return. He glanced at the guests within the chamber. "This circle is a good deal more sober than your normal company."

"Spoken as a constituent of my normal company."

"*Are* you so scandalous, then?" asked Anne.

Before John could answer, Leo said to him, "You never mentioned associating with this crowd."

John narrowed his eyes. "I have interests beyond your understanding of me. Lord Overbury hosts some of the most influential figures in the government."

Thus, John's presence. It made sense, yet Leo knew his friend better from late-night horse races and houses of pleasure than electoral races and Houses of Parliament.

"Please pardon me, gentlemen." Anne disengaged her hand from his arm, and he felt a strange compulsion to snatch it back again.

"Are you well?" he asked. Though she had insisted that

she had recovered from whatever mysterious ailment had troubled her earlier, he didn't want to risk a relapse.

"Yes, yes certainly. I just need to . . ." She glanced toward the corridor, which led to the ladies' retiring room.

Within the chamber they now stood, servants were removing furniture and rolling up rugs in preparation for dancing. Anne saw this, and said, "Perhaps when I return, we might dance."

"I don't know the steps," Leo said.

"I could teach you."

"Many things I'm willing to try, but I'd sooner kiss John than learn to dance in public."

"Flattering," drawled John.

Yet Anne looked disappointed. Clearly, the girl who had hesitantly danced at their wedding celebration had transformed into a woman more comfortable in herself. Leo felt his own stab of remorse. He wanted to please her.

"John, you had a dancing master."

Seeing the direction Leo was heading, John spread his hands. "Monsieur Desceliers never had a less apt pupil than I. It is rumored that, in despair, he fled back to the Continent and became a rat catcher. Or a drunkard. Or both."

"I do not want to cause mass drunkenness," said Anne. "Nor would I appreciate the spectacle of my husband kissing anyone but me." She blushed, but did not lower her gaze. "We shall save the dancing for another occasion. Pardon me, gentlemen."

Both Leo and John bowed as she took her leave. Leo watched her as she circled the room, noticing how she kept her chin tilted up, her tread confident. When they had come in, less than an hour earlier, she had kept her chin tucked low, and her step had hesitated. She grew before his very eyes, as if he could somehow watch a rose unfurl its petals within the span of a moment.

"Oh, for the love of sin," muttered John.

Leo tore his gaze away as Anne left the chamber. "The hell are you going on about?"

"You'll be as bad as Edmund soon." John batted his eyes.

Leo scowled. "Edmund is besotted."

To which John only gave him a very droll look.

To which Leo gave John a very rude hand gesture.

John smirked, but his humor did not last. In the glare of candlelight, his long, thin face and deeply set eyes looked almost macabre. "How fared you the rest of the day? Did you accomplish what you needed to do?"

Sobering, Leo answered, "Whit won't be received at any of the gaming clubs. Not White's, nor Boodle's, nor the others. It took just a handful of suggestions that he played dishonestly, a few fraudulent written testimonials, and a promise to make several valuable investments on behalf of the club managers."

John nodded, pleased. "I went to several of the taverns and coffee houses he frequented. Did much the same." His smile widened. "Reading minds gives one tremendous insight. It makes it so much easier to say to exactly what one needs in order to render a particular result."

"What am I thinking now?" *John's a scary bastard.*

His friend glowered. "You know I cannot read the thoughts of the Hellraisers. One of my gift's limitations. Further," he added, "you were probably thinking something boorish about me. The gift's other limitation is that I cannot read thoughts if they are about me."

"Seems our mutual friend Mr. Holliday gave us all slightly flawed gifts," Leo murmured.

"Of course he did. Only an idiot would bestow unlimited power on someone."

"And Mr. Holliday is certainly not an idiot."

"He chose us as the recipients of his gifts, did he not?" John grinned. "Clearly, he possesses superior intelligence."

The dancers gathered in the middle of the chamber,

forming rows for a set. They looked like troops assembling for war, troops clad in silk, armed with cutting glances instead of sabers.

Leo's attention wavered as he saw Anne reenter the chamber. Her gown was not the brightest in the room, nor did she wear the most jewels, and there were other women who might be called more beautiful, but when she paused at the entrance of the room, he could not look anywhere but at her. Just as her gaze automatically found him. Warmth spread through him when she smiled in response.

And he was not alone in his attention. She drew the gazes of many at the assembly, especially the younger men. One of the bucks approached her, hand out. Asking for a dance. Anne immediately looked to Leo—seeking permission.

Leo's first instinct was to cross the room and plant his fist in the bloke's face. He already felt his hand curl in preparation.

But this was not the street. Nor even the pugilism academy. A punch laying the gent out might satisfy Leo, but damn it, he had to at least *pretend* to be civilized.

More to the point, Anne wanted to dance. The buck with the padded calves offered to dance with her, when Leo could not.

His neck felt stiff as whalebone as he nodded, the barest inclination of his head, granting her leave to accept the offer.

She looked momentarily surprised, then took the gent's hand. Leo ground his teeth together as she and her partner took the floor. They faced each other. The air began, and Anne curtsied as her partner bowed. Leo did not miss the way the gent's eyes strayed to the soft shapes of Anne's silken breasts above the neckline of her gown. He calculated interest rates to keep himself from tackling the bloke.

"Christ," muttered John. "You haven't heard a sodding word I've spoken."

"Something about Whitehall, something concerning Bram and Edmund." Yet Leo continued to watch Anne as the dance began, and the dancers moved in their intricate patterns.

John exhaled in annoyance. "Only a few days ago, you talked of her like a promising piece of land, and now you stare at her as if she were the North Star."

"I don't need her to find my direction." In truth, he saw that his sense of direction had already begun to alter since their wedding night. He felt himself gently veering off course.

"She's only a woman."

"She's also my wife—and far more complex than I had thought."

John snorted. "I've yet to meet any women of complexity."

A corner of Leo's mouth turned up. "Perhaps you need to reconsider the female company you keep."

"Hell, the very last thing I crave is an added complication. I have my work in Whitehall, and if I want for female company, 'tis an easy matter to purchase precisely the kind I desire."

Not so long ago, Leo held the same outlook. The edges were beginning to fray. He wondered—should he rush to stop the tear, or allow the fabric of his existence to be rent apart?

He knew two things: Whit would not be allowed to take his magical gift from him. For it brought Leo far more power than he had ever anticipated, and with that power, he could give Anne more and more. He found he wanted as much as he could grab, not for himself alone, but for her. A new development.

The other thing Leo knew: he couldn't watch his wife dance with another man any longer.

Without saying another word to John, he strode away,

directly into the movement of the dance. The dancers stared at him, their patterns stuttering to a stop in half-finished arcs and turns. He shouldered past Anne's partner. A vicious satisfaction in seeing the nob stagger. Then Leo stood before Anne.

She, too, stared at him, her eyes wide, her hand suspended as she waited for the next form in the dance.

Leo took her hand in his, and stalked from the dance floor, towing her behind him. Like roaches, guests skittered out of his path. He moved on, out of the chamber, into the hallway.

"Get Mrs. Bailey's cloak," he snapped to a waiting footman. "And summon my carriage."

As the servant darted off, Anne said, "That was rude."

"I'll give him a generous vail." One always tipped servants when visiting another's house, and Leo tipped liberally.

"Not the footman."

He turned to face Anne as they stood in the entryway of Lord Overbury's home. Leo searched her face for anger, even as he knew he didn't care whether or not she was angry. He had acted, primal instinct pushing his body into motion, heedless of consequence.

Her eyes were bright. But not with anger. Something far more visceral. Excitement.

"Tomorrow." He advanced on her, stalking her, yet she did not back up in fear. She met him straight on, until their bodies were less than an inch apart. "You teach me how to dance."

"You have taken a sudden interest in it."

He shook his head. "If anyone partners my wife, it will be *me*, and no other."

Color stained her cheeks. "Dancing exclusively with one's spouse is considered unfashionable at best. Gauche at worst."

"Don't. Bloody. Care." He brought his mouth down on hers. Her lips were soft, silky. And eager.

Her fingers threaded into his hair, holding him close, as she met his kiss. In the span of a day, already transformation had begun. For she knew him now—not perfectly, not entirely, just as he still did not fully know her—but *this*, the touch of lips to lips and the consuming of each other, *this* was known and explored further.

His blood was fire, his body instantly awakened and aware. He gathered her close and hated the elaborate cage of her gown, for he could not feel her completely, locked as she was in stays, panniers, and petticoats. The rustling of her silken dress sounded louder than a tempest. It maddened him, suggesting the movement of her body beneath her clothing.

He walked her backward, until the wall met her back. Pressed himself against her. This primitive need—it overwhelmed him. Never had the hunger for a woman been greater, the demand to take, and to give, in return. His cock was thick and impatient as he positioned himself between her legs, and as he rocked up, she gave a low, soft moan.

Hellfire, he wanted her. Like this. Now.

"My gracious!"

Leo swung around, snarling. Lord and Lady Overbury stood nearby, frozen in shock as they took in the sight of their guests on the verge of coupling right in the foyer. Several other guests gathered behind them. And the footman, holding Anne's cloak.

Releasing Anne, Leo held out his hand toward the servant. The footman hurried forward with the cloak. Leo took it from him, then draped it around a stunned Anne's shoulders.

"My carriage ready?"

The footman nodded and held open the front door. Leo flung a shilling at him before tucking Anne's hand into the crook of his arm. They strode from the entryway, out into the night. He did not wait for the footman to open the waiting carriage door, but tore it open and helped Anne inside. With her seated, Leo threw himself into the carriage, sitting opposite his wife.

As the footman shut the carriage door behind them, Leo caught a glimpse of the assembly guests all standing in the doorway of Overbury's house. They stared at the carriage as if it were the vehicle of the Devil himself. Leo smirked. They had no idea.

He rapped on the roof of the carriage, and it drove away, heading northeast toward Bloomsbury.

In the shifting shadows within the carriage, Leo's arousal did not diminish. It grew only stronger. He thought about reaching across the space of the vehicle and gripping Anne about the waist, hauling her over so that she straddled him. Sex in a carriage could be damned enjoyable.

But a slight movement captured his attention. Anne was shivering within her cloak. And not from the cold.

Damn it. He had scared her. Again.

"You've nothing to fear from me." His voice was rough, and he heard the hard consonants of his old accent.

When she spoke, her words were soft, barely audible above the rattle of the carriage wheels on the cobbles. "It's what *I* want that frightens me."

Chapter 7

Anne felt a change during the ride back to Bloomsbury. A crisis point, after which nothing would be the same. She didn't know if it was him, or her. Perhaps they were both transformed. The carriage ride felt both interminable and brief. Across from her sat Leo, and passing torchlight flickered on and off his face. One moment, he became a vision of golden masculinity, the next steeped him in darkness, save for the gleam of his eyes. Both aspects frightened and intrigued her.

For the whole of the ride, he did not attempt to touch her. Neither spoke. Despite the chill outside, the atmosphere within the carriage felt hotter and heavier than any tropics. She breathed in, and felt every one of her nerves absorb the heat.

From the time she left her home this evening to now, she had transformed in a way even she did not fully understand. She felt the profundity of her body, its taut anticipation, and also the barely leashed hunger in his.

"Sit beside me," she said into the darkness.

"Can't." His voice was an almost subterranean rumble. "I touch you, I won't stop. And I'll not take your virginity in a carriage."

Anne did not know one *could* engage in lovemaking in a carriage. Now that he had introduced the idea, though, her mind filled with possibilities. It wasn't capacious, but surely there was room enough, and the curtains could be drawn . . .

"Stop." He scrubbed a hand over his face. "I know what you're thinking, and if you keep thinking it, I'll make it happen."

"Perhaps I want you to." God! She could hardly believe she had said that! Yet this night was abounding with possibility, just as she was.

Leo growled a curse. "Not in a damned carriage. Not the first time."

A sultry need spread through her when she considered that at some point in the future, he might very well take her in a carriage. Or she might take him. Anything could happen.

She felt giddy with power. Hers, and his. For she had discovered her own potential at Lord Overbury's. She had revealed her deepest secrets to Leo: that her love of cartography had led to thievery. Yet he had not chastised her, nor expressed disgust at her actions. He *admired* her for all of that, and she learned to value herself.

Never before this night had men looked at her the way Leo had. And he wasn't the only one with frank interest in his gaze. When she stopped concerning herself with how others saw her, suddenly there were men everywhere, even asking her to dance.

She drew a visceral, primitive thrill from watching Leo stalk across the chamber to claim her, taking her away from her dancing partner. Nothing refined or cultured in his behavior. He simply took what he wanted. And what he wanted was her.

He still did. And Lord save her, she wanted him.

At last the carriage rolled to a stop outside their home.

Before the footman could come and open the door, Leo already had thrown it wide and had leapt down. He reached in for her. His hands spanned her waist, swinging her down onto the sidewalk. She had no awareness of the street, of the servants, of anything but him staring down at her.

"You aren't afraid."

She shook her head. "Not anymore."

Animal need flared in his storm gray eyes, and his hands tightened around her waist. "To hell with waiting."

He released his clasp of her middle, only to thread his fingers with hers, then took the steps with long-legged strides. Fortunately, Anne felt the same urgency, and kept pace. In a moment, they were inside and hurrying up the stairs leading to their bedchamber.

Leo pushed the door open. Only the fire was lit, and the room held a dark, flickering glamour, like stories of ancient fairy kingdoms beneath the hills. In those stories, young girls wandered into the kingdoms, lured by sinister, beautiful Fae princes to become ageless consorts. Their families in the mortal world mourned their disappearance, little knowing the truth behind the loss.

As Leo drew her deeper into the bedchamber, its red walls bathed in firelight, she felt herself one of those folktale girls beneath the hills, and could not mind that she would never again see the sun.

Meg appeared in the doorway.

"I don't need you tonight." Anne's gaze never left Leo.

"But your gown—"

"I'll see to it," said Leo. He, too, did not look away, but stared at Anne with fire in his eyes as they stood by the foot of the bed. "Close the door."

If Meg answered or did as she was bade, Anne never knew. She saw only Leo, heard only the harsh rasp of his breathing and the thick beat of her heart.

Leo stepped toward her. She met him halfway.

Anne wrapped her arms around his wide, hard shoulders, sank her fingers into his hair after tugging it free of its queue. His hands splayed across her back, pulling her tight against him. They were large, and rough, yet she felt both fragile and resilient beneath them. They each drew in a breath, taking air from each other, and their mouths met.

What had begun in the Overburys' foyer served merely as prelude. The heat and need that had been building gradually over days, weeks, lifetimes finally ignited. Their lips shaped each other's, testing, tasting. Exploratory and claiming. She felt his hunger, his demand, and it didn't frighten her. Her own desire did not send her, shivering and protective, into herself. She drew on their mutual need, took sustenance from it.

His tongue slicked inside her mouth, and she stroked it with her own. His response came in his growl, and his hand moving down her back to pull her hips snug against his own. As snug as he could, given the mass of her skirts, panniers, and petticoats.

He broke the kiss with a snarl. "I need to *feel* you, damn it. *See* you."

They both battled with her clothing, undoing the hooks beneath her stomacher, loosening ties, undoing tapes. Together, they peeled away rustling layers of silk, the gown pooling on the floor. She stepped out of her shed clothing, kicking off her heeled slippers, and stood before him in her underclothes.

Craving his touch once more, she moved toward him, but he gently held her back.

"Let me see you, Anne. Let me see my prize."

Her face flamed with a combination of embarrassment and desire, yet she kept herself still and let him look his fill. He was all bestial hunger as he stared at her, his gaze roving over her with hot possession. She knew she could

show herself like this to him—these past days had shaped
a trust between them, and she gave herself to that trust.

The cotton of her chemise was thin as a sigh, her peach-
hued nipples and dark golden curls between her legs
plainly visible. Light as it was, the gauzy fabric still felt
heavy against her skin. She saw in Leo's ravenous gaze
that she was beautiful, and it fed her power.

She stepped closer, and his hands came up, roaming
over her body, stroking along her shoulders, down her
arms, tracing patterns between her breasts and the curve
of her belly. His touch filled her with sharpening crests
of need. When he cupped her breasts and teased her nipples into harder points, awareness coalesced into an exquisite ache.

Wanting more, she rose up on her toes and kissed him,
open-mouthed. They groaned at the sensation. He took
and he gave, and as her hands gripped his shoulders, the
trembling she felt was not merely her own, but *his*. This,
too, strengthened her, and she pressed closer, rubbing her
thighs and the tips of her breasts against him.

Hotter air touched her as he gathered up and discarded
her chemise.

She was utterly exposed. Instinctive modesty made her
turn away, crossing her arms over her chest.

"No, no." He gently turned her to face him. "This is me.
This is what we've made between us."

His gaze burned hot, yet beneath shone tenderness and
acceptance.

Drawing a breath, she let her arms lower to her sides.
Allowing him to see her.

He recognized what this meant, and as he looked his
fill, she saw both his sensual hunger and his pleasure in
her trust. Yet he did not simply look. He stepped toward
her, and then his broad hands were everywhere, caressing her naked skin. Her back. The curve of her buttocks.

Her breasts. Her skin became unbearably sensitive, yet the flood of sensation was too good, too wondrous, and she couldn't find words to make him stop. She didn't want him to stop.

She moved to untie her garters and roll down her stockings.

"Leave them." His fingers trailed over the ribbons and silk, then higher, to the bare flesh of her thighs. "Soft here. So damned soft. And here"—his fingers glided higher, and she tensed in anticipation—"softer still."

Her arms wrapped around him. She held herself in readiness, dizzy with the feel of his still-clothed body against her own naked skin, the tremors of need that wracked them both.

Then his fingers found her. Her most intimate place. She cried out in pleasure, the sudden and yet inevitable beauty of it. He stroked her, spreading wetness, learning her secrets.

"Ah, Leo." She writhed against him.

"Have you done this, Anne?" His voice was hoarse, demanding. "Have you touched yourself? Made yourself come?"

With anyone else, the questions would have embarrassed her, yet she knew this man, her husband, and to hear him speak thus and answer in kind felt precisely right.

"Yes." She gasped into his mouth. "Yet it was never like this."

He groaned. "Spread your legs. Give me more."

This was to be a night of discovery. She had often wondered how it must feel to stand on the deck of a ship and see an unknown coastline approach, never before encountered. The fear and excitement of new territory. Part of her wanted to stay within the confines of safety, her narrow world. But here was a chance to be the explorer she had longed to be. Summoning her courage, she whispered, "Let me touch you, too."

His gaze flared, recognizing her bravado. Yet he shook his head. "Your pleasure first." He walked them back to the bed, and guided her to drape beside him. As she lay on her back, he propped himself up on his side. He cupped the back of her head with one hand, and with the other, he dipped between her legs.

She arced as he caressed her, her legs flung wide, her hands buried in his hair. If she did not hold tight, she was certain she would float up and never stop. His touch was relentless, tender. He circled and rubbed at her pearl. Two of his fingers stroked her cleft, lightly sinking inside, testing only the opening. Everything inside her tightened in preparation.

"Leo, I—"

"*Yes.*"

It grew within her, a rising sensation that originated between her legs yet permeated every part of her. She craved it; she feared it.

"Give me your trust." He continued to stroke her, drawing her forth. "As I give you mine."

She saw the truth of this in his face, tight with need, yet open and unafraid. Him, only him.

The climax demolished her. And built her stronger. It filled her body with a pleasure that seemed too much to bear, yet she took it, took what it gave her, what Leo drew from her body. She could not even scream. Her mouth opened. No noise came out. Only a silent cry of release that was too intense for sound.

"Never," she murmured when she could speak. "Never like that."

A look of harsh triumph crossed his face. "Mine to give you. Everything else—gowns, money—those are only *things*. Anyone can have things. But *this*. *This* is more.

This is ours." He slowly sank a finger deep into her tight passage, and she gasped at the new sensation. It took her several breaths before her body eased, permitting him access.

When he added a second finger, stretching her, she winced and sucked in a breath.

He stopped immediately, his fingers still within her, but motionless.

She wanted to retreat, but would not permit herself to hide. "Keep going." She lifted her hips. "I want everything."

For a moment, he remained immobile. And then he grew sharper, darker as his gaze burned. His fingers left her, and he rose up to stand beside the bed, tearing at his garments as if they were on fire.

He stared at her as, layer by layer, he undressed. All his exquisite tailoring meant nothing, just an impediment. His coat, his waistcoat. He peeled off his stockings, revealing thickly muscled calves. It took him two attempts to undo the buttons fastening his breeches. When, at last, the buttons slipped free, he shoved his breeches down along with his smallclothes.

Anne could not look away from his erect penis. She had never before seen an aroused man, and the sight was far more compelling than any statue or painting. He was thick and slightly curved, with a gleaming, broad head.

His low chuckle brought her attention back up to his face. "I knew it."

"Knew what?"

"You were a zephyr waiting to become a tempest."

She was wry. "Another investment pays off."

Yet he shook his head. "This isn't business. We waited for a reason. So it could be more than cold commerce."

"I am assuredly not cold."

Leo grasped the hem of his shirt, the only article of clothing he still wore. Then hesitated, frowning.

Desire made her audacious. She knew what his body felt like beneath his clothing, and understood that it would rival even the sunrise for beauty. "Don't be shy. Let me see you, too."

"I have . . . marks."

"It does not matter."

To her disappointment, he lowered his hands. "Not yet." Then he knelt on the bed and lowered himself beside her. She would have voiced her complaint—that it did not matter to her if he had scars or any disfigurement, because to her, he would never be anything other than magnificent—but his kiss stole her words.

They wrapped around each other, and she discovered she loved the contrast of his muscular, hairy legs with her soft, smooth limbs. The burning heat of his body soaked into hers, even with his shirt between them, and as their mouths met and devoured, his erection pushed insistently toward her. He left slick trails on her belly. Leo rolled them over, positioning himself above her, then slid his penis between her folds, teasing without entering her.

It felt so strange, to have someone other than herself give her pleasure, conferring such personal demands to another. Yet it made sense, for if anyone could touch her so intimately, it must be Leo.

He touched her like this; pleasure built again, pushing away lingering traces of apprehension.

"Kiss me," he said, a hoarse demand.

She arched up, her open mouth to his. At the same time, he thrust into her.

Pain and pleasure collided. She had no sense of which was which. They were the same. And, oh, he was thick within her, filling her. He was everywhere inside her. A moment's panic. It was too much. She would be lost. He was too hard, too male, too *everything*.

Yet after that initial thrust, he was still, and Anne willed her eyes open to see him above her. His face contorted, torn between pleasure and anguish. He held himself back savagely as her body learned the feel of his. The only sounds in the chamber were the muted pops of the fire, and his harsh breathing.

She relaxed into the sensation, allowing herself to experience this newness, for it was exotic, his body within hers. Yet true and right. Fear ebbed. Pleasure took its place.

Tentative, Anne brought her legs up, and wrapped them around his. His eyes flew open, silver and bright. He groaned her name. In response, she curled her fingers into his shoulders, feeling the bunch and strain of muscle beneath the cambric.

"I want . . ."

"Tell me," he urged gravely.

An experiment: She tilted her hips. He moved within her. Pleasure followed, streaking through her hotly. "More."

"You can bear it."

"Anything."

He took her mouth, kissing her deeply. And his body began to move. Sliding forward, gliding back. She had imagined this moment many times—what it would be like to have a man inside her—and the truth far outpaced what she had envisioned. For the shadowy man of her imagination had no true will of his own, no real need. But Leo did. He had strength and hunger, entirely his own, and these she felt with every movement of his narrow hips.

She was not still, could not be passive. Her body had its own will. She met his thrusts, and pulled him tighter. Pain limned the edges of sensation; it swirled through her in a spiral of dark and light.

The world spun further, and she realized that Leo had actually turned over onto his back with her clasped against him, his body still deep inside hers. He sat up and edged backward, until he leaned against the carved headboard and Anne straddled him. The posture was altogether wicked, for it allowed her to see everything—him, his face harsh with need, the shirt clinging to his slick torso and arms. She saw herself, too, nude save for her garters and stockings.

He gripped her hips. "Look down."

She did. What she saw made her gasp.

"That's my cock." His voice was no more than a snarl. "*Mine*. Inside you. Can you see that?"

"I . . . can."

"Watch." He pulled back a little, and she saw inches of his . . . cock . . . sliding out of her. Then he surged forward, and she moaned to see him sink into her, disappearing all the way to the root. Had she not witnessed it with her own eyes, she would never have believed she could contain his length, yet she saw and felt and knew.

She was truly his wife, in every way. Just as he was her husband, in all meanings.

"Now." He released his bruising hold on her hips, and grasped the headboard, his arms outstretched. His eyes glittered. "*You* take us there, Anne. Show me. Show us both."

"I don't—"

"You do." His jaw tightened. "The whole time. It's been there. In you."

For a moment, she hesitated, uncertain. It came to her: an image of herself this very night, crossing the floor of the assembly, her chin tipped up. She had been seen by everyone, and drew strength from it. It gathered in her now, her capability. Leo had shown her the path, and she walked it using the strength of her own legs.

Had he wanted to, he could have lain her down and taken her, controlling every movement and sensation. But he wanted more than that, more from her. A challenge. She would meet that challenge.

Settling her hands on his shoulders, Anne pulled her hips up, just a little. Again, that wondrous sliding within her. Then she sank down. As she did, her pearl rubbed against him.

"Oh." She dragged in a breath. "That's . . ."

"Yes." The cords of his neck stood out.

Anne moved again, and once again. She discovered angles, speeds. Her hands clutched him tightly, so tightly she feared she might tear his shirt and mark his skin. Part of her *wanted* to mark him, but she did not want to cause him pain. She grabbed the headboard, as well, and saw his knuckles whiten.

Rational thought slipped away. Anne rode him. He stretched beneath her, arching up. Her gasps joined with his groans, and the room resonated with the sounds of flesh meeting flesh.

This time, when her climax arrived, she could not be silent. At her scream, his hands released the headboard. He seized her hips, his head fell back, and his whole body went rigid.

He had never looked more beautiful, carved as a statue.

Finally, release faded, loosening its grip on both of them. They could only pant and stare at each other, sated and amazed.

Concepts, thoughts, words—all vanished. She knew only the resonance of her body and the feel of him against, and within, her. Gradual as a feather drifting in circles to earth, she regained use of her mind.

She wondered: What was one supposed to say in a situation like this? *Thank you?* It seemed a paltry phrase to enclose a world far bigger than any atlas.

So she let actions and silence serve her better. Her fingers cramped as she released the headboard, but they relaxed as she cupped his face. His stubble prickled against her palms.

He stared at her, grave, marveling, yet when she lowered her mouth to his, his eyes drifted shut, and he took her kiss readily.

We are outcasts no longer.

He didn't want to, but Leo needed to get up from the bed. Reluctantly, he disentangled his limbs from Anne's, and left her murmuring and drowsy as he padded into the closet. By the light of a single taper, he stripped off his shirt. He took a cloth and dipped it in the water-filled basin. With movements made hasty from eagerness to return to her, he cleaned himself off.

Blood streaked over his cock. Not much, but enough to prove that, for all her responsiveness and innate sensuality, he was Anne's first lover.

First and only. For himself, he was glad of his experience, if only to have made it good for her. Thinking of her sighs and moans, the way she moved, the pleasure she took from him, his cock stirred. He wanted more.

A folded nightshirt awaited him on a small table. God, he hated having to wear it.

He walked to the glass on the table, adjusted it to get the right angle. Turning, he looked over his shoulder to see the reflection of his back.

Images of flames covered his skin there. They appeared to be drawn directly on his flesh with black ink, yet he knew that nothing could wash them away. The flames began just below his nape, spread across his shoulders, and twisted down along the length of his spine.

He did not regret his gifts from Mr. Holliday, but something about the image of flames writhing across his skin made him feel sick dread.

His resolve strengthened never to let Anne see the markings, nor understand their meaning.

Which meant he would be forced either to make love to her in utter darkness, or to wear a damned shirt when he did. And though he had always slept nude, he had to endure wearing this sodding nightshirt like some doddering old man.

He turned away from the mirror. Sleeping in a nightshirt was a small sacrifice if it meant having Anne beside him. He quickly tugged the thing on, then took a fresh cloth and dampened it. After blowing out the candle, he returned to the bedchamber.

Anne stretched out atop the bedclothes, sleek and soft and delicious as she lay on her stomach. She had taken the last of the pins from her hair, and the mass of it spread around her in silken profusion. At his approach, she smiled. Something seized within him, something tight in his chest.

Wife. He felt he understood the meaning of the word now, its significance. By giving her his name, he had pledged to her his care, his protection. And he vowed it to himself now, more binding than any words spoken by a reverend.

Seeing the cloth in his hand, she reached for it, but he held it away.

"Let me," he said.

As she turned over and leaned back on her elbows, the embers of desire roused. She was beautiful to look upon—her lush breasts tipped with coral, the curve of her belly, her pretty little quim, the suppleness of her arms and legs. Her body held more strength than one would have guessed, for she had gripped him hard. He was glad of it. Rather than pliancy, he wanted strength to match his own.

"I like how you look at me now," she murmured.

His gaze flew up to hers. The stain of passion still tinted her cheeks, and she wore a timeless little smile. It pleased him, knowing he put that smile upon her lips, that she could be so free with him.

"I like looking at you." He curled one leg under him as he sat beside her. Carefully, in slow, tender circles, he ran the cloth over her. He frowned at the smears of blood at the tops of her thighs. "It hurt."

"Some. Less than I thought it might."

"But it felt good, too." The need to please her burned hotly through him—as strong as his need to build his fortune on the Exchange. Stronger.

"No new bride has less cause for complaint." She placed her hand atop his. "Truly, Leo. It was . . . a marvel. Sensations I could never have conceived."

"You *may* conceive." Finished with his task, he set the cloth aside and stretched out alongside her. He placed his hand over her belly.

Her lips curved. "That *is* the purpose of marriage."

"Trying to make children has its own enticements."

She wound her arms around his neck and smiled up at him. "In truth, I hope a child comes later. Much later. For I am selfish enough to want you all to myself."

"Nothing wrong with self-interest." He pulled her close, his hands cupping the sweet roundness of her arse. The fragrance of her skin enthralled him, sweet and musky with the lingering traces of sex. With *their* sex. He pressed his face into the juncture of her neck and shoulder, nuzzling. She murmured encouragement. Her limbs made a delectable rustling in the bedclothes.

He wanted her again. The time he had waited to consummate their marriage fell away in gathering desire. Each day he had come to know her better and better, so that, for the first time, when he seated his body within a woman's, he felt not just the pull of animal need, but a deeper communion. It had been more than simple release. It had been a bestowing of pleasure, a joining.

His cock thickened. He thought perhaps it might be too soon, that she would be sore, but she cupped him close, her leg thrown over his hip.

"Leo." Her voice was velvet.

"Mm." He trailed his lips across her neck, and bit lightly on her earlobe. She shivered and burrowed closer. Her hands were bolder now, roaming over his arms, his back, even down to his buttocks. Against her skin, he smiled. She was indeed a tempest, too long confined to a teacup, but now released.

"A request."

He did not hesitate to answer. "Anything."

"When you take a mistress, don't let me find out."

His head lifted, and he stared down at her. "What?"

She did not look away, and her expression was grave. "Your mistress."

"I don't have a mistress."

Her tension eased minutely. "But you *will* take one. All men of means have them."

"Who the hell told you that?"

"My mother. And . . . others. One hears things." Her lashes lowered. "Every married man known to my family keeps women. Lord Haverbrook spends more time with his mistress, Mrs. Delphi, than he does with Lady Haverbrook. The Earl of Macclestone had his bastard son educated at Cambridge."

Leo only stared at her.

"It's how things are. The only recourse for wives is acceptance." She raised her gaze once more, and a storm stirred within. Only a few days earlier, she would have been too guarded to reveal this much of herself, yet now things had changed, *they* had changed, and she spoke with strength. "When you *do* take a mistress, keep silent. I don't wish for ignorance, but of this, it's preferable to knowledge. Thinking of you, doing *this*"—she glanced down at their entwined bodies—"with anyone other than me is . . . insupportable."

Leo, who seldom found himself at a loss for words when finessing deals on Exchange Alley, discovered he could not speak. Not for a full minute. At last, however, he gained his voice.

"Mark me, Anne. I have no mistress. Never did, and never will."

Her eyes rounded. "All men—"

"Not all. Not me." When she began to protest, he would not allow her to continue. "My body is yours. Only yours. If that makes me a baseborn peasant, that's what I am."

"That is not how I think of you."

He knew this, and it weighted his words. "*You* are my wife. *I* am your husband. We shall know the pleasures of no one else's flesh but each other's." The very thought of touching a different woman made him feel sick. And the idea that she might have another man kiss her, let alone make love to her . . . he'd never experienced such rage.

"Only you." She held his gaze. "That is all I want."

"Good," he said, lowering his mouth to hers. He wanted their bare torsos pressed together, but knew it could never be. He had to keep his secrets. If ever she discovered the truth, he would lose her, and that he could not allow. "For I find that when it comes to sharing my wife, I'm damned miserly."

Anne walked in a temple. It was a strange temple, its walls solid stone, and stone loomed overhead. Torchlight flickered, and she saw that the temple was actually *underground*. Or perhaps set within a hill or mountain. She did not know the where of the place, nor how she came to be there. One moment, she had been lying in Leo's arms, warm, replete, her body tired and her heart full to bursting. Then she was here, in this place.

The stone floor chilled her bare feet, and she clutched herself close to stay warm. Columns had been carved into the walls. At one end of the temple stood an altar, surrounded by bronze lamps. Cautiously, she approached, then recoiled. A lamb had been sacrificed. Recently. Its body splayed across the altar, steaming, and blood dripped onto the ground.

"You see yourself there."

Anne spun around. A woman stood a few feet away. She wore a tunic in the Roman style, with golden brooches pinned at her shoulders, and her dark hair was piled atop her head in elaborate curls. She stepped closer, the torchlight revealing her to be a woman of lustrous, aristocratic beauty, her gaze proud and cunning—and urgent.

"To what am I being sacrificed?" asked Anne.

"Him."

"Leo?"

The Roman woman shook her head. "He is but the instrument of your oblation. The blade plunged into your heart."

Instinctively, Anne's hand crept between her breasts, shielding herself. "I do not understand the purpose of this sacrifice."

"He serves another. The Dark One." The temple turned to mist and became an elegant chamber with gilt friezes upon the walls. In the middle of the room stood a stylishly dressed man with white hair and irises as pale as diamonds. The guise of the elegant man melted away like liquefying flesh, revealing a humanlike creature of immense height, its skin the color of ash, curving horns atop its head scraping the mural on the ceiling and its cloven hooves tearing the Kidderminster carpet. The eyes remained the same, pale, cold. Ablaze with power and malevolence.

"He has never seen the Dark One's true face," continued the Roman. A priestess, she must be. A witch. "And on the day he does, it will be too late. His doom shall be sealed, and with him, the doom of countless others." The elegant chamber shattered into pieces like broken glass. Anne shielded herself from the shards. When she lifted her arms, she saw the world ablaze. Cities leveled. A never-ending war. Famine and misery. And over all of it, the horned beast watched and applauded.

This scene crumbled away, and Anne and the priestess stood once more within the temple.

"My allies are too few," said the Roman. "This half-world imprisons me, and only two willing fighters exist in your realm. Not enough. We need others to wage war." The priestess turned her gaze to Anne. "Powerful warriors."

Anne held up her hands, palms up. "I have nothing. No power of my own, and am certainly no warrior."

The Roman's eyes glittered as she advanced. "Strength lies within you. As for the rest, I shall bring it forth."

Anne backed up, until she felt slickness under her feet. Blood from the sacrifice. "No."

"Think you there is a choice?" The priestess looked scornful. "Death is your only other option."

"I want out of this place. I want to go home." Anne sounded small and terrified, precisely how she felt.

"We have not the time for this," snapped the woman. "My hold here weakens." As she spoke, the edges of the temple blurred and grew hazy. "There is no safety at home. You sense this, and my warning presence. That place is a haven for wickedness."

"Not Leo."

The Roman's mouth twisted into a cruel smile. "He is

most wicked of all. The Devil's operative who makes the world ready for his master."

Not the same man who held her, who gave her so much, who believed in her strength even when Anne had been uncertain it existed at all. "I don't believe you."

The priestess made a sound of irritation as more of the temple turned to smoke. "Time draws apace."

She raised her hands and chanted. Anne did not understand the words, though some sounded vaguely familiar. *Tempestas, ventus, maleficus.* The air grew colder. A wind began to gust. It swirled, its movement marked by eddies of dust. Torches flickered. Faster and fiercer blew the wind, cold and lacerating, until it howled like the gates of Hell being opened.

Anne staggered, fighting to keep standing, yet the wind had the force of a storm, pushing her back.

The wind screamed, and the priestess's voice raised to a shriek, her words barely audible above the tumult. She curled her hands into fists, and the wind spun around her, gathering, collecting. Building momentum. Her hair came loose from its elaborate arrangement, her tunic billowed, and her eyes blazed as she chanted.

Then she opened her hands and *shoved* the wind toward Anne.

Certain she would be torn apart by the vicious storm, Anne darted to the side. But too late. The wind slammed into her. She stumbled against the altar and fell to her knees. The pain of impact was nothing compared to the sensation of bitter, cutting wind reaching into her, filling her veins, pushing through her.

She screamed. The torches guttered and went out, sinking the room in darkness.

"Anne?"

She jolted, then felt Leo's large, warm hand on her thigh. There was a hiss of a tinder being struck, then the flare of lit candle. It took a moment for her eyes to adjust to the light, but when they did, she discovered herself sitting upright in bed. Leo stared up at her, concern furrowing his brow.

"A nightmare?"

Yes, that's what it had been. Only that. She looked around. No underground temple. No bloody altar. And no Roman priestess speaking of things Anne could not understand. There was no howling wind, nor even a breeze. The bedchamber was warm and still.

"I think so." She resisted the impulse to check her feet to see if they were sticky with blood.

"You're bone cold." He drew her down beside him, surrounding her with his heat. He felt so solid, so real and alive, and Anne relaxed into him. "Better?"

She drew from his warmth, his substance. Her body slowly thawed.

A peculiar ache resounded through her, but she dismissed it as the aftereffects of very thorough, very enthusiastic lovemaking. In time, she might grow used to such physical activity, but she hoped and rather believed she would not. How could she grow accustomed to so much sensation, to a man like Leo?

"Better." Still, when he began to nibble along her jaw, she added with regret, "I think . . . I may be a little sore."

He chuckled. "Madam, your husband is a brute."

"Which is one of his more charming qualities."

Leo gazed over her face. "Tell me what you need, sweetheart. How to keep the nightmares at bay."

It was strange, she was seldom plagued by bad dreams, and this one had been particularly vivid. Yet Leo's presence shoved away the last vestiges of the nightmare.

She snuggled closer. "Having you here is enough."

He pulled away just enough to blow out the candle, then wrapped his arms around her.

"Sleep well, sweetheart."

"And you," she said, then added shyly, "my dear."

His arms tightened, holding her closer. They lay together. Anne felt the gentle, rhythmic rise and fall of his chest as he drifted into sleep, and it lulled her. The darkness felt more comfortable now, everything secure, everything as it should be. Because of him.

Yet as sleep began to claim her, the priestess's words echoed in her head.

He is most wicked of all. The Devil's operative who makes the world ready for his master.

Chapter 8

The world spread beneath Leo's hands. Seas, continents, nations. The span of his hand covered the whole of an ocean. If he so desired, he could crush all of it into a ball and consign it to the fire. He grinned.

"Have an interest in maps, do you, sir?"

Leo glanced up from his perusal of the map spread out on a table. The shop's proprietor watched him with an eager smile. "I begin to."

"My shop has all that you could desire. The very latest. The Americas, the East Indies. Even the newest geographical surveys of England. Here." The proprietor hurried behind a curtain and emerged with a globe upon a turned oak stand, surmounted by a brass meridian. "Just come from France, sir. A beautiful example."

He set the globe down on another table and waved Leo over to it. "Can't do any finer than this. The latest in the cartographer's art, and a stunning addition to the home of a distinguished, worldly gentleman."

Leo peered down at the globe. The cartouche was in French, so he could not read it. He rested his finger atop the dot marked *Moscou*. How many souls beneath his finger? Giving the globe a push, he watched the world spin on its axis, the passage of days in a matter of seconds. A godlike power.

"My purchases today will not be for myself," he murmured.

"A friend, then."

Smiling, Leo moved away from the spinning globe. He perused charts hanging on the walls, with the shopkeeper trailing after him. "I believe so. My wife."

The proprietor frowned. "Would they be for your wife, or a friend?"

"She is both." It surprised him, but there was the truth of it. Anne was more to him than could be conveyed in the simple term *wife*. She accepted him as he was, and did not look for weaknesses to exploit. What she admired in him was . . . *him*.

"Beg pardon, sir, but you mean to say, you would give maps to your *wife*?"

Leo looked at the shopkeeper, and the man shrank beneath the coldness of his expression. "That is exactly what I intend to do. I'll take my coin elsewhere."

"Oh, no, sir. No, no." Seeing the fineness of Leo's clothing, the rings upon his fingers, the proprietor was all solicitousness. "I think 'tis a wonderful thing for a man to dote on his wife, indulge her every fancy."

It was more than a fancy for Anne, her love of maps. She considered not just the things themselves, something pretty or curious to be idly looked up, but what they signified, what they *meant*. It troubled him how little he had credited her when first he began to pay court. She had been merely an instrument to aid in his objectives. And he had been a fool to think her so easily rendered into a discrete, uncomplicated category.

All this, before he had known the sweet pleasures of her body. Now he had, and the world was new.

The proprietor gestured to a small chamber, separated by a curtain. "The best merchandise lays within, sir."

Leo nodded and entered the chamber. He would give Anne the best. Anything she wanted, she would have.

The scent of paper enriched the air. Stacks of charts and maps lay atop tables and collected in V-shaped stands. Neat scrolls of parchment rested in cubbies built into the walls. Every sheet of paper represented a part of the globe, whole civilizations, and lives lost to the cause of exploration. But the world needed to be known, and in so knowing, owned. Leo understood this impulse, this covetousness. Always, it had been centered on his demands and what he could attain for himself. Now, he wanted everything for Anne.

"Here, sir." The shop owner pulled a map of South America from one of the stands. "Taken from the most recent voyage. Mark the profusion of rivers. Most prodigious."

Leo did not know much of cartography, but he trusted his own judgment. "I will find what I need. On my own."

With a bow, the proprietor backed from the chamber. As he did, he drew the curtain, affording Leo privacy.

Leo made a thorough, careful survey of the contents of the room. He knew many of the places on the maps, for England served as the heart to the beast of commerce, pumping blood in the form of money and merchandise through the veins of global enterprise. Bending to study a map of the West Indies, he examined the multitude of islands dotting the Caribbean Sea. Barbados, Saint-Domingue, Hispañola. Growing the cane that sweetened the world's tea, and distilling the rum that spun the world's head.

"A marvelous place, the West Indies."

Leo glanced up. The *geminus* leaned against a table. It had its arms folded across its chest, its legs crossed in a posture of perfect, gentlemanly leisure. Having gained

Leo's attention, it pushed away from the table and joined him in the perusal of the Caribbean map.

"I've never been," Leo answered.

"Some call it a paradise." The *geminus* chuckled. "My master particularly enjoys it."

"The sultry climate."

"The atmosphere is in all ways pleasing to him. Particularly that of the plantations."

Leo replaced the map and selected another, this one of the Barbary Coast. Tiny ships sailed atop a painted sea, their sails billowing. Pirates, maybe, preying upon the hordes of merchant ships and their holds laden with wealth.

"I am surprised to see you at this place," said the *geminus*. "Trading is ongoing at the Exchange, and yet you are here."

Without looking up from the map, Leo replied, "My time is my own. How I spend it is my choice."

The *geminus* gave another indulgent chuckle. "Of course. One cannot engage in business every waking moment. Yet . . ."

"Yet?"

"Now that you possess knowledge of Lord Overbury's imminent disaster, would you not be better served putting that knowledge to use?"

"Counterinvest." Leo straightened and pulled the map of the Caribbean out of the stand once more. He had seen Overbury's plantation destroyed by storm, a future calamity that could easily be taken advantage of. His ever-present hunger stirred at the thought.

"At the very least," agreed the *geminus*. "My master knows how exceedingly clever you are at exploiting weakness." When Leo did not immediately respond, the *geminus* continued. "It was clear that Overbury had no love for you, nor others of your class. Had it not been for your advantageous marriage to an aristocrat, you would never have been invited into his home. Indeed, I overheard him say to Lord Devere that he wasn't surprised by your use of sleight of hand, since it is the perfect skill for someone born *of the streets*. And that you deserved a wife who came to you very nearly a *beggar.*"

Familiar hot rage poured through Leo, its origin somewhere between his shoulder blades and spreading throughout his body, tight and burning. He looked down to see that he had crushed the map he held. "I did not see you there last night."

"I am often close."

The calm that had enveloped Leo all morning singed away. Overbury's insult could not stand. The slur against Leo was no surprise, but that Overbury dared to slander Anne . . . "The beef-fed bastard won't live out the rest of the day." He stalked toward the curtain, ready to race to the man's doorstep and punch him bloody.

"Hold, sir." The *geminus* stepped into his path. "There are more effective ways of hurting Lord Overbury. Ways that will keep you out of Tyburn, and ensure the nobleman's suffering."

Leo fought for calm. Damn it, the *geminus* was right. Though Leo craved blood, money might serve the same purpose. He could manipulate the marketplace against Overbury, ensuring that his loss would be even greater. If Leo acted prudently, he could make certain that the nobleman's losses gutted his estate. Overbury might not be forced to become a mudlark, scavenging in the slime-draped banks of the Thames, but he'd feel his fall, and painfully.

Today's plan had been to finish at the map shop, then return home to present Anne with an abundance of gifts. He thought to gladly accept her thanks by taking her to bed, and so pass the day in communion with her body.

That plan could not stand. Overbury must be crushed, and Anne avenged.

He stepped around the *geminus*. "I set out for the Exchange now."

"Sir? Were you speaking to me?" The proprietor held the curtain back and peered into the chamber with a cautious expression.

"I was talking to my—" Leo turned, and frowned. The *geminus* was gone.

"To . . ." The shopkeeper's gaze slid to the crumpled map, his eyes widening. "Afraid you are going to have to pay for that, sir."

Leo always carried cash. He unfolded several banknotes and shoved them into the proprietor's hands, and the man sputtered his surprise.

"This is too much!"

"For the ruined map, and more. I want your finest wares delivered to my home. The globe and any other map you feel would please a devoted scholar of cartography. Anything you believe is the best, I want. And if that cash isn't enough, bill me for the rest."

As the shopkeeper babbled in thanks, Leo scribbled his direction on a piece of paper. Then he strode from the shop. He was known as the Demon of the Exchange. Today, he would be the Demon of Vengeance.

Anne accepted the dish of tea from Lady Kirton with a murmured thanks. She and the countess sat in a little parlor, a small table bearing an even smaller plate of biscuits between them. Anne nibbled on one of the biscuits. It was stale.

The parlor itself was a fine enough room, with a portrait of Lady Kirton's favorite spaniel taking pride of place on the wall, but it was clear this room was not often used

for entertaining callers. A larger, more elegant chamber
served more frequently for guests. Anne had seen it as she
had been led up by the footman. She did not merit the
better parlor.

"Married life must agree with you, my dear." Lady Kirton
eyed Anne over the rim of her dish. "I have seldom seen you
looking so well. Though you do appear a little tired."

Anne fought not to blush. She did feel different today,
weary but full of wild energy. It was all she could do to
keep seated. Images from the previous night—and early
this morning—kept stealing into her thoughts. Leo's hands.
His mouth. His . . . cock. All bringing her pleasure. And she
had given him pleasure, too.

He had kept her thoroughly, deliciously occupied, and
if that had not exhausted her, then her troubling dream
would have. Normally, when she did recall her dreams,
they faded over the course of the day. Not so this one.
Anne could still feel sticky blood on her feet, could describe in detail every pleat in the Roman priestess's gown,
and remembered all that had been said.

*He has never seen the Dark One's true face. And on the
day he does, it will be too late.*

"Mrs. Bailey?"

Anne's attention snapped back to the present. "Apologies, my lady. Indeed, I am a little weary, but I find your
company altogether delightful."

"The first weeks of marriage can be quite taxing." The
older woman spoke from wellsprings of experience. "In
time, the novelty wears off, and we wives are left in
blessed peace."

Anne hoped not. The more she knew of Leo, the more
of him she wanted. And it seemed the feeling was mutual.

How very different her marriage was from others of her
class! How full of wonderful potential! It exceeded her
every expectation.

Yet her memories were darkened by the dream that had followed. That temple. The images of an evil being bringing death and destruction. And the awful storm being slammed into her body.

Anne gulped at her tea, striving for warmth. "I have heard that a husband's interest wavers."

"If one is fortunate." Lady Kirton smiled thinly. Having met the ill-tempered Lord Kirton, Anne could understand why it was preferable to keep him at a distance.

"For the present," Anne said, "I do enjoy having my husband's favor."

The countess sniffed. "Though he lacks any sort of breeding, when it comes to fortune and appearance, your husband *is* generously endowed."

It took Anne's supreme force of will to keep from saying something extremely unpleasant. She had a purpose here, and could not allow herself distractions.

"Though I know in time he will behave as all men do, in the interim I strive to keep things amusing between us." She affected a conspiratorial giggle. "Shall I tell you how?"

Lady Kirton's veneer of polite boredom fell away, and she leaned in close. "Yes, do."

"I like to play little practical jokes on him."

Though clearly this was not quite the response the countess had been hoping for, she still looked interested. "Practical jokes?"

"Mr. Bailey is *so* very observant. It amuses me to see what he does and does not notice. For example, I replace his brandy with sherry and his Bordeaux with burgundy."

"I'm surprised a man of his pedigree knows the difference."

Anne dug her nails into her hand to stop herself from slapping Lady Kirton. "He notices. And there is another trifling game I like to play." She edged closer and lowered her voice. "Money is indeed a pressing concern of his."

"Naturally," drawled the countess.

Anne forced her bared teeth into a semblance of a smile. "He often keeps coins in the table beside the bed. It's extremely droll to replace the coins with the exact same amount, but in different denominations, and then wait to see if he recognizes the discrepancy. Observe." From her purse, she pulled a handful of coins. "I have here a thruppence and two shillings. I shall use them to replace the six ha'pennies and two tanners that I know my husband keeps in his desk. Or," she said, "perhaps you might like to try the same little jape on Lord Kirton."

The countess sat back, stunned. "*I?* On *Lord Kirton?*"

"With such an amusing trick, it might rekindle some of the newlywed's spirit in your husband."

Lady Kirton looked dubious. "Truly?"

"La, yes." Anne giggled. "I assure you, whenever Mr. Bailey catches on to my jest, it puts him into a very agreeable humor."

The countess considered this, tapping one finger against her chin. Some faded memory of past passion must have revived, for her pale cheeks turned pink. At last, she said, "Perhaps I shall."

"Oh, marvelous!" Anne clutched her purse tightly. "Can you think of a place where Lord Kirton keeps his coin?"

"His desk in the library." Lady Kirton stood eagerly. "I can fetch them in an instant. A moment, Mrs. Bailey." She hurried out the door to the parlor, leaving Anne alone.

Smiling to herself, Anne set down her dish of tea. She rose up from the settee and drifted around the parlor, idly examining the room. The portrait of the dog drew her attention; paintings were costly, and she wondered what sort of person immortalized an animal.

She realized that in the whole of Leo's house, there were a few paintings of landscapes, some hunting scenes, but not a single portrait. No grim ancestors staring out from the walls. Not even a picture of Leo's father or mother. Her husband had no history. He created himself, whole and entire, as if he were both Zeus *and* Athena, springing forth fully formed from his own mind.

A demilune table was positioned directly beneath the portrait of the dog. Lit candles were arrayed atop the table, struggling against the overcast day. As Anne neared the picture, the candles guttered. When she halted her advance, the candles stopped flickering. The room was still and silent, the windows shut tight, and not a breeze or draft whistled.

Anne took another step forward. The candles flickered. She took one more step. The candles went out. Twists of smoke rose to the ceiling.

It was as though *she* were the breeze that extinguished the flames. Frowning, Anne crossed to the fire burning in a small hearth. As she drew closer, the blaze sputtered and popped, despite the screen arrayed in front of it. She walked quickly to the fire. It shuddered as if harried by a wind. Then it choked out, leaving only smoldering ashes.

Anne stared down at the ashes. Her dream assailed her—the windstorm conjured by the priestess, and the wind crashing into her own body, absorbing it.

It had been a dream. Nothing more. Yet Anne gazed at her hands as if she could not quite place them, as if they belonged to someone else, and were grafted on to her body.

"This *will* be amusing." Lady Kirton sailed back into the parlor, her hands cupped around an assortment of coins. She held them out to Anne.

Anne blinked.

"The substitution," prompted the countess. "Some of Lord Kirton's coins for the same amount in different denominations."

Anne shook herself. There was a purpose in her coming here. "Yes. Let's make the exchange."

Lady Kirton frowned at the now smoldering hearth. "Those useless servants. Cannot make a decent fire."

Saying nothing, Anne took her seat. Lady Kirton did the same, and counted out twenty-seven pence' worth of coins, which Anne traded for her two shillings and thruppence. Anne felt a visceral thrill when the countess placed her coins in her hand. The woman had no idea what she had willingly agreed to do, believing herself the instigator of an entertaining prank. But Anne had manipulated Lady Kirton to do precisely what she wanted.

If this was anything like the sort of excitement Leo felt when finessing a deal at Exchange Alley, no wonder he devoted himself to work. She could get quite addicted to the stimulation.

"I cannot wait to see Lord Kirton's face when he discovers my cleverness." Lady Kirton gave a sly smile. "He was in a fever to marry me, those many years ago. Not merely for my fortune. I had been known as quite a beauty." She patted her powdered curls. "Perhaps this may reignite that *tendre*."

Anne rose, tucking her purse into her pocket. "Do keep me informed, my lady." Though she rather hoped that she did not receive any excessively detailed descriptions. "Now, I thank you for your affability in welcoming me into your home, but I have several more calls to pay."

"The obligations of a new wife." Lady Kirton sighed. "Enjoy these early days, child. You will soon discover that the man you thought you married is someone else entirely."

With a small shiver, Anne asked, "Why would you say that?"

The countess shrugged. "We all of us pretend to be different people in order to make ourselves agreeable to our spouses. But the illusion soon drops away. 'Tis the nature of marriage. Then it becomes a matter of adjusting expectations."

"I will take that under advisement. My lady." Anne dipped a curtsy and was led by a footman back downstairs.

Leo had taken a hackney that morning, leaving her use of their own carriage, and it now waited for her outside. As the footman held the carriage door open, something within caught her attention.

A letter, placed upon the seat.

"Who put that there?"

The footman shrugged. "I didn't see anyone, madam." He turned to the driver. "You see somebody put a letter in the carriage?"

The coachman only shook his head.

"Never mind." Anne gave the footman a vail, though she was careful to keep some of Lord Kirton's coins for Leo, then climbed into the carriage. As the door closed and the carriage drove away, she picked up the letter. The name *Mrs. Bailey* had been written across the front, but with no direction.

Someone had placed the letter in the carriage without being seen—someone of dark skill. She pressed back into the seat and drew the blinds, yet she could not rid herself of the sensation that she was being watched.

Madam,

I am given to understand that you have been contacted by Valeria Livia Corva. I wager she has confused you more than elucidated. Have patience with her, as existing over a millennia trapped between the realm of the living and the dead tends to confound one's wits.

As I have not been trapped between these realms, my mind is a degree sharper than Livia's,

*and I must illuminate that which she has left dark.
Thus shall I to my purpose.*

*Mrs. Bailey, your husband is not the man you
believe him to be. He and the other Hellraisers
all share a wicked partnership. Once I counted
myself one of their compatriots, but wisdom, and
an audacious Gypsy woman, prevailed. All of us
Hellraisers were blinded by arrogance and greed.
We made a bargain, gaining gifts but never
understanding the price.*

The price was our souls.

*In short, Mrs. Bailey, we forged a pact with the
Devil.*

*Likely, you think me mad, and with good reason.
Yet my pen conveys the truth, difficult as it may be
to accept. My gift had been the ability to manipulate
fortune, for I could control probability to suit my
needs. As a gamester, no greater ability exists. I
have since surrendered this ability, and with great
joy. The other Hellraisers, however, retain their
bequests so bestowed upon them by the Devil.*

*John gained the facility to comprehend
thoughts.*

*Bram received the power to persuade anyone to
do his bidding.*

Edmund was bestowed Rosalind.

*And Leo has the ability to see what has not yet
transpired.*

*Well may you think me deranged for proposing
such outrageous allegations, yet my claims are
factual. Indeed, not so long ago, I battled the Devil
and the Hellraisers, both. Upon Leo's shoulder is
a scar which I made with the point of a rapier
blade. If I may presume, you may observe it in the
intimacies of nuptial life.*

Your husband is in monstrous danger. If he is not already consumed by the Devil's evil, soon shall he be. All of the Hellraisers are being consumed. As they fall, as their dark power grows, they become threats not merely to themselves, but to the world.

This cannot stand.

You shall find me and Zora at the Black Lion Inn, in Richmond. Do not dally in seeking us out, for the danger to you and Leo increases with every passing moment.

Three things I urge you: do not speak of this missive to anyone; destroy this letter upon reading it; find Zora and I quickly. We face now a war for Leo's soul, as well as the fate of millions. In this, we are your sole allies.

> *I remain,*
> *Your servant, & c.*
> *James Sherbourne, Earl of Whitney*

She lost count of the number of times she read the letter. A dozen, at least. She moved from shock, to fear, to indignation, to anger. To pity.

Anne sat on the settee in her bedchamber, the letter in her lap. She glanced from it to the rain-streaked windows.

Lord Whitney was mad. That much was plain. Who else but one destined for Bedlam might pen such a letter, with allegations too preposterous to be considered? The *Devil*? Truly?

Like most women of her acquaintance, Anne went to church on Sundays. She sat through sermons, the reverend admonishing the congregation about sin, temptation, wickedness. Evil. These things existed in the hearts of man. One couldn't walk down the streets of London without seeing proof. But she never truly believed there was an *actual* Devil. He was a metaphor, nothing more.

That Lord Whitney believed the Devil was real . . . that might be excused as a religious mania. Perhaps he had fallen out with the Hellraisers because of newfound spiritual beliefs. He could be one of those fire-and-brimstone Calvinists. Many former sinners found redemption and comfort in the arms of an angry God.

Yet there was more, far more, than simple religious conviction in Lord Whitney's letter. He was not speaking metaphorically. Nor even as one trying to convert former friends. No, this was insanity. The depths of his madness were unfathomable.

She watched rain streak down the glass, the gray city beyond. Shivering a little, she stood to prod the fire. As she neared, the flames snapped and guttered.

She frowned, and pulled her shawl of Indian cotton closer about her shoulders. She had thought that perhaps this strangeness was confined to Lady Kirton's home. But it seemed to have followed her back to Bloomsbury.

Lord Whitney had to be mad. That could be the only explanation for his letter. She felt a small comfort in knowing that he *had*, in fact, approached her the other day and was no construct of her own unbalanced mind. Yet this comfort was small compared to the dozens and dozens of questions now tumbling through her mind.

Quickly, before the fire could go out, Anne strode to it and threw the letter onto the flames. She backed up, watching the paper writhe as it burned. Like a soul in Hell. Leo's soul?

Stop it. Do not give Lord Whitney's lunacy any *credence.*

Men did not sell their souls to the Devil. Not literally. They did not gain magic power as a result of this bargain. Magic did not exist. She lived in a world of coal and clockworks. It had been decades since witches were burned. Every day were made new discoveries in the realm of natural science. Lectures were given nightly by distinguished men of learning on those very subjects.

And there were maps, wondrous maps, of new lands. For every new inch of land charted, fear and superstition retreated, replaced by rational thought. Maps embraced the progressive, the enlightened, one of the reasons why they fascinated her. Magic and superstition—relics of older ages—had been supplanted by the modern era.

Life was about the present. The present meant her life with her husband, Leo. As of last night, they had begun to form a true connection, not just of legalities, but of their hearts.

Lord Whitney was a stranger. His mad words could not touch her. They *would not*.

Yet the red walls of the bedchamber felt too close, the vines snaking up the wall coverings forming a cage. She strode from the room. Some of her books had arrived from her parents' house, and waited in the library to be unpacked. That would serve to occupy her.

Walking down the corridor toward the stairs, she passed lit sconces and candelabras. They all flickered as she passed, just as they had at Lady Kirton's.

Magic?

Anne scowled. Magic was not real. She was real. Leo was real. This house and everything within it—all real. Everything that Lord Whitney alleged was false. Perhaps there had been a bad falling-out between him and the other Hellraisers, and he simply sought a means of hurting them. What better way than driving a wedge between Leo and his wife?

She descended the stairs and headed toward the library, resolve in her step. If Lord Whitney thought her some empty-headed girl easily swayed by suggestion, he must reconsider. Leo had shown Anne that her own strength had value. She refused to surrender it to Lord Whitney's manipulations.

Inside the library, she found a small crate of her books. She called a footman to open the crate, and after he did, she sorted through the few tomes. All of the books had been secondhand, their pages already thumbed, the bindings coming undone.

A man's purposeful stride sounded in the corridor. Her pulse sped, for she knew the tread, yet she made herself sit in the wing-backed chair and wait, rather than rush out to meet him.

Leo's long, muscular form filled the doorway. The light from the candles within the library did not fully reach him, and with the glow of the sconces in the hallway behind him, he made a dark, imposing shape.

Anne half rose, unable to keep seated. What was it that made her heart pound: Excitement? Pleasure? Fear?

No, not fear. She pushed that aside as Leo came into the room. He wore a hard, cold expression, as if he had leveled dozens of enemies and burned to bring down more. Then he saw her, and smiled.

Doubt melted away at that smile and the warmth in his gaze.

She started to speak, but before a word left her, he came forward and wrapped her in his arms. His clothing held the chill of outside, yet beneath was the heat of his body. He brought his mouth down onto hers.

Anne leaned up, pressing herself into him.

This was real. *This* was true—his arms around her, his hand coming up to cradle her head.

"Missed you," he murmured into her mouth.

"And I, you."

He touched his forehead to hers. "I brought you something." He stepped away, then moved to the doorway and spoke into the corridor. "Now."

Several footmen entered. Two of them carried crates, and the other one held a large, flat wooden box. At Leo's direction, all of the items were placed upon the desk by the windows. The footmen filed out.

Leo took a large ebony-handled knife from the top drawer of the desk. He pried the tops of the crates open and pulled out handfuls of straw.

Curious, Anne drifted closer. Her mouth opened soundlessly when Leo reached into the crate and drew out the most beautiful thing she had ever seen.

A globe.

He set it on the desk, yet before she could form words or truly comprehend what lay before her, he performed the same task on the other crate. Another globe emerged from the packing—but this one depicted constellations rather than the Earth.

"Yours." He nodded toward the two globes. When she did not move, his brow furrowed in a rare display of uncertainty. "You don't like them."

"No, I—" She shook her head. "I don't know where to begin, which one to look at first."

"Start with the Earth, then work your way to the heavens."

She did. Her finger traced over the coastline of Eastern Africa, from Cape Horn, past Madagascar, to the Gulf of the Arabian Sea. There were names she did not recognize, rivers she did not know. How the world had changed, and she did not even realize it!

In a daze, she moved to the celestial map. Here, myths arrayed themselves in an eternal dance—vain Cassiopeia, brutal Hercules, the fallen hunter Orion—tales of hubris and loss told in the language of stars.

Still unable to truly speak, Anne could only gaze at Leo.

The cost of the globes had to be phenomenal, for they were large and modern. And beautiful.

"There's more." He flipped open the brass catches on the flat wooden box, and opened the lid.

This time, Anne *did* gasp.

Maps filled the box. She could not stop herself from moving in front of Leo and pulling out map after map. The Americas, the Baltic Sea, China and the Japans.

"There are dozens of maps in here." She lay them out upon the desk, but they were so numerous, their edges overlapped, a world folding in on itself. She wanted to spend hours studying each and every one. She could barely comprehend any of it.

"Are there enough? I can get more."

She stared at him. "This is . . . this is . . ." Her voice trailed off. "You have given me the world." Beyond that, with the maps, he had brought her the rational word, banishing fear.

"They please you." Pure male pride illuminated him, and he seemed to grow even taller.

"*Please* is too mild a word. Leo, you overwhelm me." It was more than the expense, though she knew the price to be astronomical. He had heard her, listened to her. "There is no gift equal to this."

"Good." His gaze was warm as he trailed a finger along the line of her jaw.

"I have something for you, too."

His brows rose, and he looked almost comically surprised. "For me?"

"It isn't half so extraordinary as what you have provided, nor as numerous. But . . ." She reached into her pockets. "Guess which hand."

After a moment's deliberation, he picked her left hand. She held it out.

"Three shillings seven," he said, counting the coins.

"From Lord Daleford. Now pick the right hand."

He did. "Two shillings thruppence."

"From Lord Kirton."

Leo stared at her hands, then up at her face, his expression one of wonderment. "You did it."

She nodded. "I must own, it was rather . . . exciting, finding a means of extracting the coins. Rather cunning of me." Her cheeks heated, and she studied him. "They please you," she echoed.

"More than please me." He laid his palms over hers, covering them and the coins. For a moment, his gaze went far-off, as if briefly distracted by a thought or memory, but they quickly cleared, and all he seemed to see was her. "I'm more than overwhelmed, Anne. I'm . . . humbled."

It shocked her, the truth of his words. She thought nothing and no one could ever breach his pride, this fierce man who admitted no weakness, no impediment. Yet a handful of coins had done just that. *She* had done it.

"I don't want you humble." She threaded her fingers with his, so their hands clasped. "I want you precisely as you are."

His eyes closed; his jaw tightened. Something passed through him, a wave of ferocious energy, and an answering power responded in her. In silence, they called out to each other. In silence, they responded.

He opened his eyes. What she saw there—her breath caught. Leo, the man. Without ramparts, fortifications, constructed identities. The saddler's son.

This was the finest gift of all. Not expensive maps and globes, but him. She understood that she alone had ever seen him this way. And it appeared to frighten him a little.

"Observe." She pulled out a map. "The last a map I saw of North America was Mitchell's, over eight years ago. There are far more places with names between now and then."

Apprehension dimmed in his gaze. "The spread of civilization."

"In your case," she said, smiling, "new opportunities for investment."

"I ought to invest in cartography." He studied the boundaries delineated on the map. "For all this will change with the end of the war with France. Will you take a commission?"

Anne laughed. "I have merely an appreciation for mapmaking, not an aptitude."

His gaze flicked up to her. "I'll hire men to teach you, if you desire."

She laughed again, thinking he jested, but saw his sincerity. "Studying them contents me. If you wish to have a map drawn, it would be far wiser to engage an experienced cartographer."

"As you wish. But if you change your mind, you've but to say the word." He bent to examine the map once more. She stared at his lowered head, his hair pulled back into a simple queue, yet burnished as gold.

He would give her everything, just as she would hold nothing back from him. She believed herself utterly open to him, yet she knew this was not entirely true.

She had not informed him of Lord Whitney's letter, and its secret lay in her heart like a waiting poison.

Chapter 9

He was in a fever of impatience. He left Exchange Alley as soon as business had concluded for the day. Normally, he stayed until the last bleary trader or investment seeker staggered from the coffee houses. He had been the first to arrive, last to leave.

Now, he strode down Lombard, the sun still high. It had been a good day's work. Between his own instincts and his visions of the future, he would net himself a very fine profit. But he had not been working entirely on his own. Anne provided him with a steady stream of coins from England's most ancient and esteemed families. Lord Kirton, who had publicly called Leo a "baseborn scoundrel," would find his investment in South American coffee to be a poor one after hurricanes destroyed his crops. Leo had counterinvested in another coffee harvest. His fortunes would rise, and Kirton would suffer.

Leo walked quickly toward home, barely hearing the tolling of Saint Mary-le-Bow's bells. Over the past week, since he and Anne had consummated their marriage, he had become a man on a rack, torn between two needs.

Building his fortune, destroying his enemies—these were the demands of the day. He awoke every morning in a fever of impatience, needing to devastate those in his path, to have *more*. It fueled his daylight hours, like tinder thrown upon flame, yet the fire's demands never ceased. He wanted his coffers overflowing, and the power to crush those who opposed him, consigning them to a life of humiliation and poverty. The greater his fortune, the more power he wielded. And he would use it like a vengeful god.

The demands of the night, those were the sweet to his days' metallic taste. Even now, hastening through the streets of London, past Gray's Inn, need to see Anne pulsed through him.

This week with Anne . . . He'd never experienced its like. Their bedsport was delicious, especially as they both grew more confident with each other. Every night, after exhausting himself and her, he sank into a profound slumber, his arms wrapped around her, soft and slumberous and murmuring contentment.

Oh, but it was more, so much more, than the pleasure their bodies gave each other. With her, he found himself . . . comfortable. For the first time in perhaps the whole of his life. All of his other identities—upstart, knave—fell away. She did not judge him for his choices, had no expectations for him to be anything other than himself. Even with the Hellraisers, he kept part of himself guarded as he acted the part of rake and libertine.

He played no roles with Anne. For the first time in his life, he simply *was*. The way she wanted him.

A man could grow used to that. A man might want that plainness of self every day, every moment.

As he turned onto Southampton Row, his step quick, he felt the force of his two hungers drumming through him. His hunger for power never ceased, could not be sated. It was the cold bite of steel always present.

Anne was his other hunger, yet this was a pleasurable desire. Pursuing and feeding it became its own reward.

Someone called his name. Leo intended to ignore the man, but hurried footsteps sounded behind him. "I say, Bailey!"

It was Robbins, a coal magnate with whom Leo had done business with many times before. And to great profit. With an inward sigh, Leo stopped, allowing Robbins to catch up with him.

"Afternoon," Leo said, trying to remain civil, though he merely felt impatience to be home.

Robbins puffed, his face reddened, then grinned. "No wonder you put all the other men of commerce to shame. It seems you are always going to or from the Exchange."

"There is no spontaneous generation for money," answered Leo. "Someone must be there to make it."

"Yes, however, one needs to enjoy the fruits of one's labors."

"So I do." Leo thought of Anne's joy when he gave her the maps and globes, and had never enjoyed his wealth more.

"But when? You're coming from the Exchange now, and just last night, I saw you at Crowe's Coffee House, in discussion with Vere and Delfort, the cotton importers."

Leo frowned. "I was at home with my wife last night. You must be mistaken."

Yet Robbins seemed adamant. "Think I can't recognize the Demon of the Exchange?"

Leo grew truly irritated. He just wanted to get home to see Anne, not argue with Robbins as to where he was or was not last night. Leo knew exactly where he had been—studying maps, having supper, and then making love with his wife.

"Get yourself to Bond Street and be fitted for a pair of spectacles." He strode away, ignoring Robbins's stuttered shock at being dismissed so rudely.

Anticipation coursed through him as he reached home. The moment a footman opened the door, Leo asked,

"Where is my wife?" Already striding up the stairs, he threw the servant his hat and overcoat.

"She's in the downstairs parlor, sir. With a visitor."

Leo stopped, his hand on the railing. "Who's the visitor?"

"Lord Wansford, sir."

His father-in-law. The first call the man had paid since Leo had wed his daughter. Frowning, Leo turned and headed back down the stairs. This was not how Leo had planned on spending the afternoon.

Yet he felt a buoyancy within him when he saw Anne in the parlor, perched there on the sofa, a dish of tea in her hand, with cool city light in her hair and along her shoulders. She set down her tea and rose to meet him, smiling.

"Here you are," she murmured.

What was this strange sensation? This sharp tug in the center of his chest? God, was it . . . did he feel . . . *happiness*?

He reached for her, but remembered just in time that they weren't alone. A brief kiss had to content him, and then he turned to face Lord Wansford.

The man was everything Leo's father had not been. Round, where his father had been lean. Complacent, where his father had been determined. And at the end of his life, his father's clothing had all been impeccable. Plain, but expertly made, and new. The embroidery on Wansford's waistcoat blurred as its stitches came up, and the lace at his wrists bore stains of wine and tobacco. A shabby man, his father-in-law.

"An unexpected honor," Leo said, bowing.

Wansford returned the bow. "No, you are kindness itself to receive me."

"You can see your daughter is well cared for."

Anne blushed, tugging on the kerchief she had tucked into the neck of her gown. Leo's teeth had left faint red marks upon the juncture of her neck and shoulder, and her moans still resounded in his ears.

"Oh, Anne." The baron seemed surprised to recall that his daughter was in the room. "Yes, yes, I'm glad to see you hale. Your mother sends her regards. And I see you're looking very . . . prosperous, my child." He eyed the gold-and-emerald pendant hanging from her choker.

"I have what I need, Father." Her eyes never left Leo's.

The baron shifted from foot to foot. Leo waited. When someone wanted something, all one had to do was wait.

"Bailey, I wondered, that is, I was thinking, if you had a spare moment. We might have a chat." Wansford's gaze slid to his daughter. "Privately."

"Anything you say to me can be said in front of Anne."

Her father reddened. "I rather think the subject indelicate for ladies."

Before Leo could insist on Wansford's candor, Anne spoke. "I'm certain I can find something that needs mending or perhaps a fatuous romantic novel to read." She glided to the door, then curtsied as she took her leave.

Leo's humor darkened. He had nearly run through the streets of London to get home to her, but the pleasure of her company had to be delayed because of her damned father.

The baron turned to him and opened his mouth to speak.

"In my study," Leo clipped. At least he kept good brandy there.

Wansford followed him down the corridor to the study. There, Leo poured them both drinks and settled behind his desk. He sipped at his brandy. The baron bolted down his own liquor and took a seat.

Leo felt a shifting within, his other self coming to the fore. It roused, its appetite fathomless, even here in his own home. Without Anne to tame that creature, he became ravenous, merciless.

After fidgeting with his knuckles, Wansford finally spoke. "You do very well for yourself, don't you, Bailey?"

"We had this discussion already. When I was negotiating for the hand of your daughter." Though *negotiate* was not quite the word for it, since she brought no wealth to the marriage. No *material* wealth. Little had he known that the true value of Anne came not from her breeding and connections, but from the woman herself.

The more Leo came to know her, the less he respected her father. What kind of man simply sold his daughter to whatever deep pocket would have her? No woman deserved that fate, especially not Anne.

Wansford looked abashed. "We never spoke of specifics."

"I've no intention of giving you specifics. My coffers are *my* concern. No one else's."

"They say that you have a rare gift."

Leo frowned. Surely Wansford wasn't talking of Leo's gift of prophecy. No one but the other Hellraisers knew of it.

"A gift with . . . investing." The baron spoke the word as if it held a faintly rancid taste, and for men like him, it did. Wealth came from the land. Only commoners earned their fortunes through trade.

Leo shrugged. "I know my way around Exchange Alley."

"The Demon of the Exchange."

"The demon who is married to your daughter." Leo leaned forward, bracing his elbows on his desk. "There are only a finite number of hours in the day, and I make good use of them. So speak, Wansford. Tell me what you want."

The baron eyed his glass, as though wishing it held more. Leo made no move to refill it.

"I would like to make an . . . investment."

"In trade?" Leo raised a brow.

Wansford nodded, uncomfortable. "The estate is failing. My sons stand to inherit nothing but arrears upon my death. For all that I'm not a very clever fellow, I know I ought to do better by them."

Not a word about Anne. But then, she was now Leo's problem.

"Now you seek to supplement your finances with a bit of plebian commerce."

Another nod from Wansford.

"You came to me, because . . ." Leo knew the answer, but he enjoyed hearing it from the baron's mouth.

"No one knows the Exchange like you do," answered Wansford. "No one has profited as you have."

"I'm to be your intermediary." Leo contemplated this. He never acted on anyone's behalf. All his investments had been for himself alone. He was no one's broker.

By using a go-between, Wansford wouldn't have to sully his hands through the Exchange.

"I already have the scheme picked out. An iron mine in Gloucestershire. Someone told me that it cannot fail."

"Everything fails," said Leo.

"Nothing in which you invest ever does."

True enough. But Leo had an advantage no one else possessed. "Tell me why I should help you."

Wansford had not been expecting this. He sat with a look of dumbstruck bafflement, having fully anticipated Leo's eagerness to be of assistance. The man probably thought Leo felt indebted to him. In a way, Leo was, for he had been given Anne. Yet having gained his prize, he looked with disgust upon the man who had surrendered her so easily.

"It is the Christian—"

Leo held up a hand. "No homilies. They fall on deaf ears."

The baron stared down at his feet. Leo had seen the paste buckles adorning his shoes, and knew Wansford looked at them now, chipped and dull.

"You have no reason to," he said at last. "Only consider." He looked up, and Leo saw age and weariness creasing the corners of his eyes, a life of genteel poverty slowly, slowly grinding him down. "Though I did little to help Anne, I *am* her father. She came from *me*. I cannot claim any of her virtues as my creation, yet there is a part of me that exists in her, however small. That must have some value."

For a long time, Leo studied the baron. Wansford shifted and looked away, uncomfortable.

"For Anne's sake," Leo finally said. "She would take it very hard if her father went to the Marshalsea."

Wansford became all effusion. "Thank you, Bailey. My eternal thanks."

Leo waved off this rhapsody. "I need one thing from you."

"Anything."

"A coin."

The baron furrowed his brow. "Coin?"

"A ha'penny, a farthing. Anything." Usually, Leo obtained coins with more finesse, but he hadn't the humor for that today. He simply needed to see Wansford's financial future and be on with his business.

"I . . . I have nothing." The baron patted his pockets. "Buy everything on credit."

Of course he did. Aristos lived on credit. If they could get credit for the air they breathed, they would, but fortunately, air happened to be free.

"The next time you see me," said Leo, "bring me a coin."

"What denomination?"

"It doesn't bloody matter."

Wansford appeared as if he was about to ask *why* Leo wanted a coin, but thought better of it. "Of course."

"In the interim, I'll do some investigating of this iron mine. See how it's shaping up." Leo *did* have abilities beyond his magic.

"Whatever guidance you can provide will be most appreciated." The baron started to rise.

"One thing, Wansford. What do you intend to invest?"

The baron sank back down to his chair. "Pardon?"

"You cannot simply amble toward a venture and say, 'I want to invest in you,' and provide no funding. There has to be actual money involved, or some other form of capital. And offering your word as a gentleman won't suffice."

"Ah."

"Yes. Ah."

Silence descended.

"Supposing," began Wansford, "supposing you lent me the funds."

"On what security?"

"You know I shall pay you back. If all your investments succeed, then the money is as good as yours."

Leo shook his head. "Unsound, to hold faith to something that doesn't yet exist."

The baron compressed his lips into a line. "You leave me little choice. I *do* have something to use as collateral." He stared at Leo. "My estate."

Crossing his arms over his chest, Leo gazed at his father-in-law. The Wansford baronial estate did not amount to much—a leaky-roofed manor with poor yield on its crops—yet the significance of the place could not be discounted. Land was everything. Ancestral land held even more symbolic value. An aristocrat could not exist without his estate. He became as empty and fragile as a soap bubble.

For Wansford to offer up his estate to Leo . . . The man

had to be desperate. And Leo was just bastard enough to exploit his desperation.

He held out his hand. The baron stared at it as though it were a viper poised to strike.

"This is how *gentlemen* seal bargains," Leo said.

Wansford shook his hand, but released it quickly. "You will not mention this to Anne?"

"Of course I'll tell her about it." Leo stood. "I don't keep secrets from her." As he said this, the irony of his words congealed in his chest.

The baron looked dubious, yet he saw that Leo wasn't to be dissuaded. He rose from his chair. "I thank you." He edged toward the door.

"Anne can join us again. You'll stay for dinner."

"Ah, no. I have . . . engagements."

What sort of engagements an impoverished nobleman might have, Leo could not hazard a guess. He did not care. A footman answered his summons, and escorted Wansford to the door.

Leaving Leo to contemplate the complicated knotwork of his life. Until now, he had kept Anne separate from the commerce that ruled his life. Yet now, they were tied together. Loops and twists irrevocably bound, with no beginning, and no end.

Anxiety coursed through her. This was a test, and she must pass it.

Anne gazed down the length of the dining table. Her first foray into the realm of hosting guests for dinner, and she wanted everything to succeed. For her sake, and that of her husband.

She might have spared herself some apprehension, as the guests were Leo's closest friends and perhaps less likely to judge harshly. Or that made her every action doubly scrutinized. If she said that she did not care about these men's opinions, she would speak false.

Flickering candlelight gleamed on platters of roast venison, pheasant with chestnuts, fricassee of mushrooms. Dark wine filled the glasses.

Masculine voices and laughter ringed the table. Anne had brothers, yet she never felt so fully immersed in male company as she was this night.

The Hellraisers sat at her table. They all insisted she call them by their Christian names, yet it did not make them any less intimidating or foreign, visitors from a nighttime realm, bearing shadows and an air of wildness. Even the substantial dining room could barely contain the dark, vivid energy that radiated from all of them—including her husband.

Lord Whitney's words burned at the back of her mind, acrid and scorching. The men at her table were the Devil's legion. Or so one madman would have her believe. She did not want to view the Hellraisers through the mist of Lord Whitney's insanity—yet it clung to her like plague-bearing vapor.

"Missed you at the boxing match the other night." John chided Leo.

Her husband lounged like an indolent pasha in his chair, his fingers draped over the rim of his glass. "I was busy."

John's gaze flicked to Anne, then back to Leo. "I've a strong suspicion of what occupied you."

Her cheeks warmed, and she sipped her wine. She was not so sophisticated as to discuss such private matters so publicly, even with her husband's close friends. Friends who almost certainly led lives of utter dissipation. Would it shock these men to learn that much of the time Leo spent with her was in conversation? Oh, they made good use of their nuptial bed. *Very* good use. Yet they shared an intimacy that went beyond their bodies—something she doubted his friends appreciated, let alone understood.

"Shame, though," continued John. "The match was spectacular. It went forty-one rounds, and ended only when McGill could no longer see, from all the blood in his eyes."

"This hardly seems an appropriate topic," said Edmund. "With ladies present."

The woman sitting beside him merely smiled. Several times over the course of the evening, Anne simply forgot that Rosalind was in attendance. The pretty, fair-haired woman spoke but a handful of words, and these only when addressed directly. Perhaps she was shy. Yet Edmund's wife kept a bright, wide smile on her face the whole of the night, her gaze cheerful but vacant.

Anne had met Rosalind before, during her previous marriage. She had been witty, given to wordplay, and a respected hostess of levees. But now . . . Rosalind seemed empty, as if whatever had animated her before had drained away.

Lord Whitney's letter was still inscribed in Anne's memory. *Edmund was given Rosalind.* Like a child given a doll on Christmas. A pretty doll with no life of its own, merely propped up at the table and fed imaginary pudding.

Ridiculous. One cannot use magic to effect such a transformation. There is no *magic.*

"The subject of pugilism doesn't trouble me," Anne said. "Leo has been telling me all about it, and it sounds fascinating."

"Violent," said Edmund, "and bloody."

Anne noted the wine in their glasses. "Most ancient traditions are."

"Like marriage." This, from Bram, sprawled at the farther end of the table. He took what light there was in the room, seeming to draw it into himself so that surrounding him was the absence of light, a palpable darkness.

"Spoken as one with no experience in the matter," said Leo wryly.

Bram's chuckle held little warmth. "To the contrary, I know much of married life."

"Married *women*," said John.

"Which provides me with an ample survey. Faithlessness is not reserved for men. Few women hold true to their vows."

"Where *you* are concerned." John smirked. "You are, indeed, very persuasive."

When Bram's arctic, calculating gaze fell on Anne, she made herself return the look, though she felt a cold shrinking inside her. "Perhaps, Mrs. Bailey, you might like to—"

"*No*." Leo's voice was no more than a growl. He sat forward, his fists braced against the table. His eyes blazed.

Anne expected him to launch himself across the table and beat his friend into a pile of bones and viscera.

Though Bram continued to sprawl in his chair, his whole body tensed, gathering strength. Anne had felt the hard, hewn muscles of her husband's body; he would fight with brutal, efficient power. Few men could best him. She understood this with intrinsic knowledge. Yet she also understood that, if anyone could match Leo's strength, it would be Bram.

They were wolves, circling each other. Ready to pounce and rip out each other's throats.

Good God. Her very first dinner party was about to erupt into a brawl. The influence of dark magic?

"With such an abundance of opportunity," said Edmund, "Bram may cast his net *further afield*."

The thick tension in the room untangled. Both Leo and Bram eased their postures. Minutely. But enough.

Bram shrugged. "There are some who find the condition of marriage tolerable. Like Edmund, or young Leo. Far be it for me to disrupt such a happy state of affairs."

"Which reminds me," said John, "Ancroft announced his engagement."

"Again?" Leo shook his head. "This will be his third."

"His future brides have a habit of eloping with other men."

"Perhaps he owns an inn in Gretna Green," suggested Bram, "and can profit from the jilting."

Good-humored banter resumed amongst the men. As they talked, Anne could only wonder. What had Bram been about to suggest to her? And why had Leo been so adamant that Bram not make that suggestion?

Bram received the power to persuade anyone to do his bidding.

Surely not. One could not force another to obey their will. That would exist in the unreal realm of the Otherworldly.

If Lord Whitney had spoken the truth, that meant that John could read others' minds. And Leo . . . could see the future.

She stared at her husband. In the candlelight, he was beautiful and gleaming, and whenever his gaze caught hers, she felt the tug of connection. A shared understanding, for not only did their bodies know each other now and the pleasure they gave each other, but their attachment went beyond the physical. They spent drowsing hours talking of many things, both fanciful and weighty.

He had told her of her father's request, and his agreement to serve as broker. He even disclosed that her father had offered the estate as collateral. A shocking turn of events, and yet, not so shocking, for every day creditors came dunning. She was, in truth, more surprised that Leo had agreed to help. Instinct told her that it was not concern for her father that motivated Leo. *She* had been the motivation.

For a man who positioned himself in continual combat with the world, with her, his generosity knew no limit.

Yet still, some part of himself he kept locked away. She could not fathom what—if she had any questions about himself, he answered. No evasions or half-truths. Not that she could sense. Beneath it all, though, he still seemed as much a stranger as he had been on their wedding day. And the more intimacy they shared, the greater this discrepancy felt.

She might be able to discover more about him through knowing his friends. As the conversation fell into an amiable lull, Anne directed her words at John. "Leo tells me you are active in politics."

"Rather a passion of mine," he answered. "The era wherein the king held all the power is long over. This country is controlled by ministers and secretaries."

"God help us all," muttered Leo.

John's mouth curled. "God is not part of the process."

"Not with your hands in everyone's dealings."

Anne asked, "What lies on the horizon? Peace, I hope." The war with France had been costly, both in terms of money and human lives. As she spoke, she saw Bram absently rub at the scar along his throat, and she recalled that he had been a soldier in the Colonies, fighting in that very war. He had paid a price, as well.

"There's to be a treaty, and an exchange of territories in the coming months. Some secretly oppose the treaty, but they shan't provide an obstacle, for all their cabals to prevent it."

"Secretly? You must be kept in confidence, to know this."

"In a manner," he drawled.

Bram gave an amused snort but, at her questioning look, merely drank his wine.

She felt as though two conversations occurred simultaneously, yet she could understand only one of them, the other spoken in a language too subtle to be grasped.

More courses followed, more talk. The cook had been

eager to display his talents, and Anne felt some comfort that her guests would not leave her table hungry. There were French ragoos, and beef collops, cakes, and fruits out of season, and Anne could only pick at her food. A fine tension tangled in her belly. Something hung over the table, something billowing and shadowed, that drew its strength from the four men who ate and laughed with hard animal gleams in their eyes. Was it only fancy? Or was it more?

Surely Lord Whitney had written his letter with a branding iron rather than a quill, for his words seared her, even now. Bargains with the Devil. Sinister magic. Phenomena reserved for sermons and lurid tales.

When, at last, it came time for the women to adjourn to the parlor, Anne did so with an inward sigh of relief. The men got to their feet as she stood. Rosalind watched with that same overbright smile, yet she did not rise.

"Beloved," murmured Edmund. "Go with Mrs. Bailey."

"Of course, my dearest." Rosalind stood and glided after Anne.

As Anne crossed to the door, Leo never took his gaze from her. She felt it like a trail of fire between her shoulders as she left the room. A new sensation, and an uncanny one.

Tea and ratafia awaited them in the parlor. The room felt hot and small, confining where the dining room had been a chill cavern. Rosalind sat placidly on a settee and stared off at nothing.

"May I offer you something to drink?" Anne desperately wanted some of Leo's potent brandy, but it must wait until later. When Rosalind did not answer, only continued to gaze into the air, Anne asked louder, "Tea? Spirits?"

"Oh . . . tea, I suppose. Do you think that's what Edmund would want me to have?"

"I'm sure he wants you to have whatever it is *you* want." Yet Rosalind stared at her, blank as snow. So Anne poured her a dish of tea. For herself, she took the ratafia.

Moments went by as she and Rosalind sat together silently. The other woman took sips at regular intervals, like a wound-up automaton that mirrored human movement, yet without thought.

"How are your writing endeavors?"

Rosalind blinked. "Writing?"

"Some time ago, you hosted a levee. You were gracious enough to invite me. I remember you read an original composition, some verses about the war between the sexes. It was much admired amongst the company for its acuity and imagination."

"I do not remember."

"This was . . . before. During your . . . other marriage."

Yet Rosalind merely shook her head. "I do not remember anything, really, before Edmund." She smiled.

Anne attempted to return the smile, but her efforts did not succeed. Fortunately, Rosalind did not notice. She merely returned to drinking her congou, placid.

This, from a woman renowned for her wit? Again, Lord Whitney's letter reverberated through her, its many assertions that she had been so quick to dismiss as the work of a faulty or devious mind. How could Anne possibly believe him? How could she trust him?

Nearby candles guttered, the flames turning to smoke.

Valeria Livia Corva. The name wove into her thoughts. A Roman woman's name.

Anne had burned Lord Whitney's letter, but rather than destroying it, the contents of the missive became stronger, more potent. Like an offering to a dark god.

How could Lord Whitney possibly know about Anne's dream of the Roman woman?

The parlor tilted as her head spun, the air thick and close. She needed fresh, cool wind. Outside, in the garden. Yes—to go outside, that would clear her head and help make sense of the morass in which she'd sunk.

"Will you excuse me for a moment?"

Rosalind merely smiled, and so Anne quickly left the chamber on unsteady legs. She tottered down the stairs, then moved through the darkened corridor that led to the garden. As she walked, she passed the closed door of the dining room, hearing the rumble of male voices. The Hellraisers in private discussion.

She hesitated. No footmen stood in attendance in the hallway. Rosalind remained upstairs. Anne was alone.

She pressed her ear to the door. Thick wood muted sound, and she had more a general sense of different men speaking than their actual words. The low rumble of Bram. Edmund's measured pace. And Leo—his voice she knew now almost as well as her own. In the depths of night, she had heard him speak words both tender and demanding, had heard him hoarse with passion, and drowsy with satiation. In a room crowded with a hundred men's voices, she would find his, unerring.

He spoke now, and Anne pressed even closer, trying to divine his words.

". . . asked around . . . no one . . . as if Whit . . . vanished."

Oh, God. They spoke of Lord Whitney. She wrapped her arms around herself, but did not move away from the door.

". . . certain?" That was John, cutting and precise.

". . . only Mr. Holliday . . . yet he has been mute . . ."

It seemed as though Edmund spoke next. ". . . safe, then?"

"Never safe," said Bram.

". . . remain alert . . . notify the others if . . ."

"Madam?"

Anne whirled to face one of the footmen, a decanter in each of his hands. Bringing more wine for the gentlemen.

Of a certain, news would spread amongst the servants that the lady of the house was caught listening at doors like a housemaid. The question remained whether Leo would hear this news, passed from the servants' table to the valet, and from the valet to the master. Little help for it. Either Leo would know, or he would not. And then . . . she did not know what then.

Secrets. They kept building, widening a chasm between her and Leo.

Anne stepped back from the door, and moved deeper into the shadows of the corridor. "Go on. Bring the gentlemen their wine."

She turned and walked out into the garden, out into the cold. She had no shawl, and shivered in her silk gown, yet she did not want to return inside. Not yet.

Shells crunched beneath her delicate slippers, digging through the flimsy sole to stab into her feet. She could go nowhere on such fragile shoes. Within minutes, they would be torn to pieces on London's rough streets. Yet she wanted to run, and run far. To a place where the sun shone and revealed everything. Where she could laugh at shadows, dismiss them, destroy them.

Anne wrapped her arms around herself. She felt the burden of secrets along her shoulders, the heavy press of concealment and uncertainty. She longed for the comfort of maps and their defined borders—but even this solace was illusory. Maps could be drawn only when men took to the seas, facing uncertainty. How often did those sailors stand upon the deck of a ship and see the stain of an approaching storm? And how often did they have no choice but to sail into the teeth of that storm?

Anne suddenly felt a kinship with those nameless sailors, for now she stood at the railing and saw the portentous black clouds of a storm nearing. She could not outpace its fury or circumnavigate around it. It must strike. She hoped she would not drown.

Chapter 10

"I received a letter from Lord Whitney."

Leo paused in the act of pulling off his coat. He stood in the middle of the bedchamber, the candles extinguished, only the fire in the grate illuminating the room. Anne hovered near the foot of the bed, still in her gown of heavy green silk, her hair up, her eyes wide.

"What?" He could not have heard correctly.

Anne wrapped her hands around a bedpost, like a woman clinging to a treetop as floodwaters rose around her. "Lord Whitney. He put a letter for me in the carriage."

"When?"

"Several days ago."

Leo went very still. "Why have you said nothing until now?"

Her hands tightened around the bedpost. "I wanted to forget."

"Show it to me."

"I burned it."

He strode to her, and though she did not shrink away, he saw the smallest wince in her face. "Tell me what it said."

At this, her wide gaze slid away. "I cannot remember."

Leo knew a lie when it was spoken. He witnessed many

of them on the Exchange. Never did he expect to see the same prevarication from his own wife. Something in his chest hurt, and he spoke around its cutting edges. "Anne."

She was no hardened man of commerce, no gamester. Of everyone he knew, including himself, she was the most truthful. And falsehood could not last long within her. Firelight gleamed in her eyes as she returned her gaze to him.

"Mad allegations," she finally admitted. "Too outlandish to be believed."

"Tell me."

"He said . . . that you and the other Hellraisers had made a bargain with the Devil. That you each gained powers in exchange for your souls, and . . . you've unleashed a terrible evil upon the world. A growing danger. But that is all ludicrous. A Bedlamite's ravings." She forced out a laugh, hollow as a husk.

Fire coursed through Leo. His heart slammed inside his chest, and every inch of him tensed, ready for battle. A momentary paralysis. It did not last, for he had to act.

He strode to the bedchamber door and threw it open. "Munslow," he bellowed, calling for the head footman. The hour was late, the remains of the dinner already cleared away, the house put to rights. Leo shouted again for the footman.

The servant appeared a moment later, buttoning his waistcoat and smoothing his wig. "Sir?"

"Have you seen Lord Whitney?"

"No, sir. Not recently, sir."

"Or a Gypsy woman?"

"Not her neither."

Leo could not feel any sense of relief. Simply because Whit had not been seen did not mean his threat was any less present. He'd put a damned letter in Leo's carriage. For Leo's *wife* to find. Fury tore through him, his body shaking with it. Leo's fears were coming to pass. No. *No*. Whit would take *nothing* from him, especially Anne.

"He isn't welcome in my home," Leo said. "If any servant sees Lord Whitney, even a glimpse, they must tell me immediately. I want at least three footmen to accompany Mrs. Bailey whenever she goes out. The biggest and strongest we have. Hire more, if necessary. I can apply to my boxing salon. I want bruisers, brutes. If I am not present, they must be with her at all times when she leaves the house."

From behind him, Anne spoke. "Leo, I—"

"And if Lord Whitney should attempt to approach her, he must be stopped. You understand. There is to be no communication between him and Mrs. Bailey. None. Do whatever is necessary to keep him from talking with her."

The head footman nodded. Like most footmen, Munslow was young, tall, and strong, and the ready shine in his gaze showed that he welcomed the chance to brawl.

"Tell the rest of the servants to keep a watchful eye. Housemaids, coachmen. All of them. And if anyone sees anything, I am to be notified at once."

"Yes, sir."

Leo sent Munslow off with a jerk of his head. It did not matter to Leo what the head footman told the rest of the servants. If they thought him mad, or wondered at his reasoning. All that mattered was keeping Whit away. From Anne, above all.

Turning back to her, Leo shut the door behind him. Locked it. The protection offered by the lock was minimal, but he would seize any means of warding off the man Leo once considered one of his closest friends.

Leo advanced on Anne. She continued to hold fast to the bedpost, her features drawn tight.

"Should Whit attempt to contact you again," he said, "tell

me. If I am not here, send a running footman to Exchange Alley. Swear that you will do it."

Her eyes were round, her cheeks pale, even in the hot gleam of the firelight. "He speaks nonsense, doesn't he? There is no Devil. Not truly."

"Swear it." He stepped closer.

She released her death's grip on the bedpost, and though he could see the furious beat of her pulse in her neck, and heard her agitated breathing, she did not shrink away. "This is not what we have built together." She tipped her chin up. "All this time. We've made more, you and I, than a husband who threatens and a wife who meekly obeys."

"Whit is *dangerous*, Anne. Understand? He is a threat to everyone. You and I, especially."

"Why?" she cried. "What is it that he threatens?"

Leo's jaw tightened. "Everything."

He would not allow it. He refused. Leo had built his entire life with his own hands. From the foundations laid by his father, he had constructed an existence, borne the weight upon his own shoulders, his hands scraped raw and bloody. Whatever he possessed belonged to him on the strength of his will. A foolish, lazy man would have squandered the Devil's gifts on ephemeral pleasures, but not Leo. He took the granted power and became even stronger, more ruthless, more determined.

Like hell would he sit idly by as Whit tried to steal from him.

Anne. His own *wife*. The woman he had come to know almost as well as his own heartbeat. By revealing the truth, Whit wanted to take her away.

Leo's rage knew no limitation. *Never*.

"Nothing," he amended, his voice barely more than a growl, "and no one will take you from me."

"I am not leaving."

To keep her, he would commit any crime, destroy anyone who sought to tear them apart. For now that she was in his life, he could not imagine it without her. He would bind her to him, as he was bound to her.

"I cannot . . ." He struggled to speak. "No one means more to me than you do."

The wariness in her gaze sifted away. "Leo—"

Words were not enough. He was a man who spoke plainly, and had no interest or skill in constructing artful webs of words. There was nothing he could say that could equal what he felt within the innermost reaches of himself. So he had to use his body to do what his words could not.

He closed the remaining distance between them. Their bodies pressed close, and against his abdomen he felt the swift contraction of her own stomach as she drew in a sharp breath. He threaded his fingers into her hair, cradling the back of her head, and tipped her chin up. Her lips parted. For a moment, they only stared at each other, gazes locked. Her eyes were the shifting hues of forest shadows, holding depths few ever realized.

But he knew. He saw and he understood.

On a groan, he brought his mouth down onto hers. Fear of losing her sharpened everything, and he wanted all he could take. He was ravenous, his hunger sudden and unchecked. She tasted of almonds and sweet woman. And she met his kiss with her own need. Their tongues stroked as their mouths opened. Each velvet touch spread desire through him.

She had lost her tentativeness. They both had. Over the course of the week, they had gained knowledge and confidence. How to touch each other. How to make demands and how to satisfy those demands.

She gripped his shoulders, rising up on her toes to press tight against the aching length of his body. They swallowed each other's breath as the kiss went even deeper. A desperation in both of them, straining toward something, as if by the heat of their desire, they could burn away doubt.

Needing more, wanting all of her, he walked her backward until her legs met the edge of the bed. One hand he slid from her hair, down her neck, feeling the softness of her flesh and the thrum of blood beneath. He urged her down to sit on the edge of the mattress, though his mouth never left hers as he bent over her and she leaned up into him.

Pins and ties lined the front of her gown. His hands became huge and clumsy as he fumbled with these tiny, feminine fastenings. They seemed deliberately designed to bewilder and confound a man. Yet he had an ally. Anne also worked at her gown, her fingers making quicker labor of the fastenings. Until, with a sigh, the green silk came open, the stomacher peeled back like a fruit ready to be savored.

Beneath were her stays and chemise. He growled at these impediments, wanting the touch of her bare skin. He took his lips from hers and trailed hungry kisses down her throat, over the bows of her collarbone, and along the floral, lush flesh of her breasts, rising in silken curves above the stiff stays. She gasped into his hair as he touched her with his mouth and hands, dipping below the top edge of the stays to find, like treasure, the tight points of her nipples.

He'd never known greed like this. Not for a person. It filled him with dizzy madness, his body hard and aching in its hunger. And he needed her pleasure, too, with a voracity that outpaced his own demands for sensation.

Whit would not steal her from him. Leo would ensure it, branding her with his body.

They pulled at each other's clothes. Her hands were quick and clever as she shoved his coat to the floor, as she plucked at the silk-covered buttons that ran down the length of his waistcoat. Each brush of her fingers against the tight muscles of his torso sent knives of pleasure through him.

He found the ties of her stays. Loosened them just enough to tug the stays down, so her breasts were free and luxuriant beneath the tissue-thin cotton of her chemise. He broke the narrow ribbon threading through the chemise's neck, and pulled this down, as well. Baring her breasts.

She still wore her gown, her stays, yet with a small, vital core of nudity, her breasts exposed to him, her nipples succulent. As though he, and only he, could ever know her like this, the prize of her body beneath her clothing. She gazed up at him, eyes heavy-lidded. Her hands had been tugging on his shirt, pulling it from the waistband of his breeches, but they stopped now. She reached for his hands. Then placed them onto her breasts, his hands covering her. She arched up into his touch.

Leo sank to his knees. He seized her mouth again with his as he stroked her breasts. He circled her nipples, teasing them into even harder points. Then took them between his fingers, rolling, lightly pinching. Her gasp drew his own breath.

"Leo, yes."

Nothing in the world felt like her. Nothing matched her as she writhed and moaned, a silken tempest. And when he licked her nipples, one and then the other, drawing them into his mouth, she clutched at his head.

Her skirts rustled as her legs eased open. He felt the press of her knees against his sides, her feet attempting to hook around his calves, yet hindered by the swaths of silk. Against the front of his breeches, his cock strained.

Hell. He couldn't have enough. He needed more.

"I want you," he rasped against her skin. "Let me have you."

He urged her back, until she rested on her elbows, her legs draped over the edge of the bed. He continued to kneel between her legs. With shaking hands, he gathered up her skirts. They filled his hands with silk the color of spring, whispering a woman's secrets, layer upon layer, her body restless beneath. Until he uncovered her legs.

He plucked her slippers from her feet and dropped them to the carpet. Stroking up her legs, he untied her garters and drew down her stockings. These, too, he let slip to the carpet, and they lay like discarded reveries, bearing the echoed shape of her legs. Such delicious legs, smooth and pale. He had to touch them. He did, gliding over her flesh, feeling her tremble and tense.

"I love your hands on me," she whispered. "Their size. Their feel. Just a little rough." She shivered.

"I love to touch you." And he did. He stroked her legs with hot possession. Then peeled away her drawers.

He hissed in a breath. All around her were rivers of silk, yet here, here she was bared to him. He allowed himself a moment to admire her, the soft golden curls, the rosy flesh, ripe and ready. But it took far more control than he possessed to simply look. His thumb rubbed along her folds, and she gasped as he discovered sleek wetness.

"Give me everything, Anne."

In response, she spread her legs wider.

With an animal sound, he bent down and put his mouth on her. Her taste flooded him, rich and sweetly musky, and the feel of her against his lips and tongue engulfed him in sensation.

This. This private joy, this secret pleasure. It belonged to them alone. No one and nothing would take that from him.

He teased, he delved. Hands spread over her thighs, he kissed her intimately, sucking and licking. She dug her heels into the small of his back. Her elbows gave out as she splayed across the bed, fingers woven into his hair.

And when he drew her clit between his lips, she pulled him tight against her. He sank his fingers deep.

She bowed up and cried out her release, a long, liquid sound that filled him with wild pleasure. Yet he was not satisfied, not until he brought her to the edge and over again, and again.

At last, she fell back, gasping, arms outflung, legs spread.

"More," she panted. "I want more of you."

"Yes." He began pulling off his remaining clothing—stockings, gaping waistcoat—but when he reached his shirt, he paused.

His marks. He could not show her, especially now, with Whit's poison in the air. But he had to feel her bare flesh against his. Craved it.

He strode to the fire and banked it, extinguishing every last glowing ember, until it was nothing more than charcoal. Not a gleam of light shone. Still, the chamber was not dark enough. He paced to the windows and tugged the curtains closed, cutting off the wan moonlight and faint glow from London's streets.

Turning back, he was satisfied. The chamber lay in utter darkness, black as the depths of the ocean.

He found her through sound, the soft rustling as she removed the last of her garments. Inflamed through sound alone, Leo tore off his clothes, shedding them like regret. He pushed through the darkness until he found himself at the bed. He touched the counterpane, the rumpled sheets, and then her, kneeling in the center of the bed.

On his knees, he moved over the mattress, feeling it dip beneath his heavier weight. He edged toward her, and when their bodies pressed against each other, length to length, finally, utterly stripped, they both moaned. God, the feel of her breasts against his bare chest, her curved belly to his flat abdomen, the whole of her—he was dizzy and demanding, aflame with need.

He gripped her buttocks, urging her even closer. His cock was thick and nestled tight against her. Unashamed, she cupped her hips to his, and her mouth opened to his when he claimed a kiss.

The edges of fear crept into sensation. He could lose this. Lose her.

No—he was a born ruffian. He fought for what he wanted. Anne was *his*.

With rough tenderness, he tipped them both, until she lay back on the bed and he stretched over her. Sight was gone, and all he knew was touch, sound, scent. As he stroked her everywhere, with her own hands bold in their caresses, he submerged himself in sensation. Her skin, her fragrance.

He positioned himself between her legs, hooking one over his arm. Her breathing came in fast, shallow gulps, her hips angling up.

Leo rubbed the length of his cock along her opening, coating himself with slickness. Then surged into her.

He lost himself in pleasure. Everywhere was her, tight and hot and wet, gripping him. He pulled back, then slid forward, sheathing himself. She moaned his name.

His will and his body wanted the same thing: her. He thrust, his hips moving, and sweat filmed him as he gave his entire self to this, to her. Anne made luscious, lascivious sounds, as lost to pleasure as he. He wanted to keep her here, where nothing existed but them and the communion they shared. Minds, bodies. All.

Fierce demand wanted everything. Abruptly, he withdrew, and she mewled a protest. Yet when he turned her over so she was on her stomach, her protest dissolved. He urged her hips up, gripping her, but kept one hand on the middle of her back.

They had experimented over the past week with different postures, even this one, but not until this moment had the position been imbued with such animal need, such raw hunger. He had usually gone into her gently, tenderly. Yet now, his control slipped. He was desire and want.

He surged inside her. And again. His thrusts were rough, and she met him stroke for stroke, pushing her hips back into his, gripping him tightly from within. Desperation marked their movements, as if they could demolish fear and uncertainty through the pleasure they created, as if the heat of their bodies could raze the twisting spirals of doubt, of mistrust. A foolish hope, but one they both chased as they gave themselves to each other.

But even this could not last. He felt his climax near, could not stave it off. So his hand left her back and glided down, over her stomach, until he found her bud and stroked it. Tight little circles that drew gasps and moans from her, straining eagerly. And then she cried out once more in release—a sound that drove him directly into the teeth of his own climax.

It tore from him, hot and unforgiving, excruciating pleasure. He poured into her, her name on his lips, on his heart.

Only when the very last of his release faded, only when she was lax and supple, only then did he withdraw. He pulled back the blankets and covered them both, his arms around her waist. They lay together, bodies slick, hearts pounding. He brushed his mouth back and forth across her damp nape, delicate hairs soft against his lips.

Neither spoke. Silence lay as thick as the darkness. He'd never made love to a woman the way he had just loved Anne. He'd never felt such a storm of emotion, frantic and furious. He'd never needed anyone as he needed her. If the Devil's magic was ripped from him, he could suffer any financial loss, knowing he could regain what was taken. He could never regain her. And that filled him with a panicked savagery, the likes of which were unknown to him.

Yet he could speak none of this. Instead, he held

her close, as close as two people could be, damp flesh clinging, limbs intertwined, and still he felt the chasm between them widen.

"This way." One hand on the small of her back, Leo guided Anne up the stairs of the Theatre Royal, Drury Lane. They passed women in wide, sparkling gowns, men in jewel-hued satin coats. Powder, sweat, and perfume scented the air. Everywhere was talk, talk. So many voices. All of them bright and sharp as shattered crystal.

"One more flight," Leo said.

She moved up the stairs, threading through the crowds. They passed the lobby for the pit, and then the first gallery. There were clothes of every variety, all mingling together as everyone searched out their seats. From stained frieze, worn every day, to gleaming moiré silk, perhaps donned for the very first time this night.

As she and Leo climbed the stairs, they passed men who knew him. No one stopped to speak with him, only nodded with chary respect and moved on. She wondered: was it respect or fear she saw in the other men's eyes? Fear of him. Her husband.

They reached a landing, and Leo directed her down a corridor lined with doors. He pushed one open and waved her in.

"We have arrived."

Anne stepped into the box. Curtains hung on the walls, and a bench was pushed up to the railing. She swayed forward to stand at the rail. Chandeliers glittered from the high, ornate roof, and gilded sconces threw more smoky light into the echoing theater. People filled every available space: boxes, pit, galleries, orchestra. A seething mass that laughed and shouted and jostled with a hard recklessness.

Leo stood beside her. She did not need to gaze at him

to know how cuttingly handsome he looked this night. In his dark gray velvet coat and breeches, his red lustring waistcoat embroidered with twisting vines, his tawny hair pulled back with a tie of black silk—no man compared with him. From her high vantage, Anne could see the many admiring glances he received from women in other boxes, even from the women in the upper gallery.

"That is where I usually sat." She pointed to the rows of benches in the first gallery. Up there were the tradesmen, the professionals.

"Not there?" He nodded at the amphitheater, situated beneath the first gallery, where the fine ladies of quality fanned themselves and gossiped.

"Only if we came after the third act." Later entry meant paying half price. When she wanted to see the earlier acts, she had to elbow her way into the first gallery instead, beside the ranks of the mercers and Grub Street scribblers.

The whole of the theater echoed the tight regulations of class, for no one ventured where they were not welcome. Young noblemen and officers kept to the benches of the pit, where they could strut, paw prostitutes and orange sellers, and enjoy all the privileges of sex and birth. Less rowdy nobility gathered in the amphitheater. Then came the galleries—the first for tradesmen, the second for servants and ordinary people. The varying price of the seats enforced hierarchy, but tacit understanding did far more to keep everyone apart.

"We didn't go to the theater," Leo said, watching the crowds assemble. "Even after my father had made his fortune. He thought it frivolous, a waste of time and money."

"Then this is your first time in a box, too." Only the very wealthy took boxes, visible to the entire theater, as much part of the spectacle as what transpired on stage.

He shook his head. "Bram always found us one." He nodded toward a box across the theater, empty at the moment. "We all came together, after supper. They're probably all at the Snake and Sextant now. John and Bram anyway."

At the mention of the other Hellraisers, Anne felt the strings of her nerves tighten further. She attempted a smile, yet it was brittle and could not be long sustained.

Leo pushed back the bench in their box, and seated Anne before settling beside her. She noted the neat movement of his wrists as he flicked the long tails of his coat out of the way. In all things, he was efficient, tolerating no excess or unnecessary showmanship.

"We are the subject of scrutiny." Anne tipped her folded, ebony-handled fan toward the many faces turned in their direction. "You are notorious."

"Perhaps, but *you* are the one who draws attention, not me."

She glanced down at her ruby brocade gown, gold lace frothing at the sleeves and low neckline. Still, she had not acclimated herself to wearing such fine clothing. "Is something amiss with my dress?"

He smiled. "Only that you look stunning in it. *That* is what has everyone intrigued. They are all wondering about the identity of the beautiful woman, and how a knave like me could be so fortunate."

"Your skill with compliments grows daily." She flicked open her fan and waved it, stirring hot air against her face.

"Only because I've reason to give them."

Who were these people? These shimmering, shallow people she and Leo had become tonight? Words came from their mouths, but the words were empty, facile. Their emptiness echoed in direct opposition to what was not being said. For it lay between them, the river of doubt, that would drown them if they ventured even a toe into its waters. Fast and deadly, its currents, and so she and her husband stared at each other across the rapids, mouthing pleasantries over its roar.

After the performance at the Theatre Royal, they would proceed on to Ranelagh and its famed rotunda. She had never been, nor to Vauxhall with its Chinese temple and clockwork wonders, and felt no desire to go now, but Leo was determined to fill their hours with as many pleasures as possible—as if to distract her from the black abyss at the heart of their marriage.

The discordant orchestra silenced as a man strode onto the stage, shouting about the evening's program.

"The performance is about to begin," Leo murmured.

His breath upon her neck traveled warmly through her body, drawing forth memories of the night before, its furious passion. Only in absolute darkness had he finally stripped bare, so she knew him by touch alone. And in that heightened sensitivity, she discovered something upon the hard, solid muscles of his shoulder.

A scar. Thin, as if made by a rapier's point.

Just as Lord Whitney had described.

Having a scar upon one's shoulder did not constitute evidence that one was in league with the Devil. It meant only that, at some past moment, Leo had been wounded by a sword. And Lord Whitney knew about the wound.

And yet . . . And yet . . .

Anne gazed at Leo as he sat back to watch a flock of dancers in gauzy skirts take the stage. A chorus of hoots rose up from the pit. Long and sleek on the bench, Leo observed the dancers with a cool remove, as if indeed witnessing the behavior of a species of pretty, giddy birds. He watched the theatergoers with the same detachment. But when he looked at her, his wintry gaze warmed, and her heart responded with a painful, sweet throb.

I have fallen in love with my husband. But, God help me, I do not trust him.

* * *

People came and went across the stage. The dancers flung themselves around with more flamboyance than grace. A man came out and belted comic songs, earning him roars of approval. Then painted backdrops of Italian gardens were propped against the back wall of the stage, and a clot of actors pranced out, mouthing words of intrigue.

Many times in the past, Anne had sat in the gallery and wondered about the experience of sitting in a box. The unobstructed view of the stage. The even better view of the theatergoers. How marvelous, she had thought. What a rarified place, untouched by deprivation, rich with delight.

Now she sat in one of those boxes. She could see everything, everyone. And she felt herself utterly removed, as if she were encased in glass. She could not smile or laugh. There were only the thorned vines knotted around her heart, piercing her with every breath.

Yet she was not alone in her disquiet. Throughout the theater, the crowds stirred, restless, ill at ease. The theater was never a calm place, but this night, it felt volatile. Voices from the crowd came too loud, people shoved one another. Tears from women, angry words from men, as if everyone tapped into a font of bitterness beneath the floorboards.

"There's Bram and John," Leo murmured.

She glanced across the theater and saw the two men come into a box. Heads turned at their entrance, and no wonder. They were striking men, both tall, commanding attention by their presence alone. John escorted a lady in a low-cut yellow gown, and Bram ushered in two women. Courtesans, clearly, by their gaudy laughter.

As Anne watched, the Hellraisers took their seats, the courtesans fluttering around them. Bram whispered something to one of the women and she giggled, nestling closer, while the other toyed with the buttons of his waistcoat. John seemed less engaged in the actions of his companion, spending his time surveying the crowds with an icy, critical eye. When his gaze fell on her and Leo, Anne suppressed a shiver.

Can he hear my thoughts? Does he know what I think, even across the expanse of the theater?

Leo raised a hand in greeting, but kept his seat.

She was glad he did not want to join his friends in their box. For at the Hellraisers' entrance, the crowd grew yet more restless. The actors could barely be heard, bawling their lines above the growing din.

"An ill feeling tonight." Leo frowned and leaned forward, scanning the theater. He looked down into the pit. Perhaps he recognized some faces there, for his expression tightened. He stood and placed his hand on her elbow. "Time to leave."

Anne rose, grateful. She needed out of this place. Yet as she got to her feet, a girl down in the pit shouted.

Two orange sellers struggled. One of the girls had her hands wrapped around the throat of the other, whilst her opponent gripped her hair. Men close by tried to separate the orange sellers, but the girls could not be pulled away. They struggled with each other, knocking into the people around them. Like a pebble dropped in a lake, their violence rippled outward, as men in the pit began to fight one another. Elbows and fists were thrown. Someone drew a sword.

Several men threw a bench onto the stage. The actors scurried back, and shielded themselves as more benches came flying up. The actors fled into the wings as men clambered onto the stage.

Women in the amphitheater screamed. The galleries erupted. People strained to reach the exits, their progress impeded by brawls. What had been, moments earlier, simply a theater now became a scene of chaos. Even the boxes exploded into violence.

"Goddamn it." Leo wrapped an arm around Anne's shoulders and urged her back.

A man's hands appeared at the railing of the box. He began to haul himself up, his eyes glassy and wild.

Leo released Anne, stepped forward, and slammed his fist into the intruder's face. The man toppled backward, falling into the surging crowd below.

In an instant, Leo was with her again. Grim-faced, he guided her to the back of the box. He paused next to the door.

"Do not leave my side." He drew a pistol from inside his coat.

Anne stared at the weapon. Her husband looked very comfortable holding it. Her gaze never leaving the gun, she managed a nod.

Leo checked to make sure the gun was primed, then returned it to his coat. Lips compressed into a tight line, he eased the door open. The narrow corridor was full of people, some running, some fighting. An impassable morass.

"We cannot make it," she said.

"I *am* getting you out of here." Resolution hardened his voice.

Intuitively, Anne knew the safest place was beside him. She pressed close and, at his signal, moved with him as he pushed his way through the corridor.

He cleared a path, shoving aside those who got in his way. Around her churned insanity, the thin veneer of civilization shattered like the wood and broken glass beneath her feet. She could scarce believe that these people, many in damask and lace, brawled like beasts. But there was Lady Corsley raking her nails down Mrs. Seaham's face. And there was Sir Fredrick Tilford, trading punches with a top government minister. These were only the people Anne knew. Merchants, physicians, costermongers. Rank and profession made no difference—everyone had succumbed to madness.

And there were other faces, too. In the hectic blur, she thought she saw twisted, inhuman visages, the flash of talons, the gleam of fangs. Yet she could never gain a better look, for the crowd would surge, and she saw only more rioters.

God, would she and Leo survive the night?

He cut steady progress down the stairs. When a man stepped into his path, fists swinging, Leo rammed his own fist into the man's chest, then knocked him back with a blow to the jaw. As Leo shepherded her from one level to the next, he continuously beat away attacks. He moved with lethal grace, swift and clean. No extraneous movement, no attempts at showmanship. His was a violence of intent, of purpose, and it was brutally beautiful to see him fight.

Anne felt a sharp tug on the train of her gown. She staggered backward, and found herself suddenly facing a wall and pinned against it, a man's hulking form pressed into her back.

"Pretty bird," he said, his breath rank and hot in her ear. Coarse hands fumbled with her clothing.

She did not have thought to scream. Instead, ferocious instinct gripped her. She took her folded fan and rammed it hard into what she hoped was her attacker's eye. She must have succeeded, for he howled in agony and released her. Anne pushed back from the wall in time to see her assailant fall to the floor. He disappeared from her sight as panicked audience members scrambled around and on him.

A hand closed around her wrist. She spun, swinging out with her fan. But it was Leo, his face an icy mask. He neatly ducked, avoiding her blow. Before she could apologize, he was pulling her behind him.

"When we get out of here," he threw over his shoulder, "I'm teaching you how to throw a punch. A fan does no bloody good."

She might have mentioned that her fan had caused a grown man a good deal of pain. Might have, but she could find no words to speak, no thoughts to think other than they must get out of this place before it was torn to the ground, before the candles were knocked over and the building went up in a curtain of smoke and flame.

At last, they made it down to the ground-floor lobby. Chaos was thick here. Anne had never seen so many people brawling before. She caught glimpses of blood on the floor. Men's shouts and women's screams thickened the air. There, on the other side of the lobby, were Bram and John. While John ducked and wove through the crowd, Bram had his rapier out, and he slashed at a group of advancing men. As skilled as Leo was with his fists, so Bram was with his sword, and she understood now how he had survived the long-ago attack in the Colonies. Even to her untrained eyes, she saw few could best him with steel.

There again—strange faces swirled within the crowd. Unearthly faces that came straight from the depths of a nightmare. Yet they vanished before she could verify whether they were real or products of wild imagination.

Leo tugged her forward, carving a route for them both to the doors. Closer and closer they crept, their progress impeded by the hundreds of others all fighting to also get free. There were too many people trying to get through too small a space. Someone cried out as he was trampled in the doorway.

Leo encircled Anne with his arms. His heart beat hard against hers. "Hold tight to me," he said.

She wrapped her own arms around his waist. Felt the

solidness and heat of him through his damp clothing. And she clung to him as he barreled through the door. His arms served as a protective cage, keeping her from being crushed.

Then, at last, they were out. Yet here was little better than inside, for the riot had spread into the streets, drawing in those who had not been in the theater. Those within spilled onto the street in every direction, and those on the outside met them in a fierce clash.

Another surge of people shoved against her and Leo. Her grasp around his waist broke. Suddenly she was alone in the mob. She was caught on a tide of humanity, noise and pandemonium on every side. Perhaps those strange creatures she had thought she saw were truly part of the throng, were moving closer to her. Though she fought against it, shouting for Leo, the flood was too strong. She was borne away, deeper into the storm.

Chapter 11

He had to find her. Everywhere was noise, anarchy. Windows shattered and voices shouted. Leo had seen mobs, knew what they were capable of, the sudden violence that razed buildings and caused men to turn to animals. It never took much in London to incite a riot.

Add demons to the mix, and what followed was inevitable.

Demons. Damn him. *Demons.* Real, and inciting the crowds to violence. He had seen the creatures in the pit. Things with horns and fangs. Yet they were disguised somehow, wearing the clothing of ordinary humans. No one else had noticed, but Leo recognized the beasts for what they were. Part of his bonds with the Devil, he could only assume. It did not matter how he knew the things for what they were. What mattered was getting Anne out of the theater—yet he had been too late.

Now some of the city's most esteemed residents were brawling in the streets like Saint Giles rowdies, and on the cobbles lay a few insensate people, trampled by the feet of hundreds. Having broken the chain about its neck, humanity went wild.

Leo shoved through the crowd, searching for Anne.

He roared her name. The noise was too great to hear if she responded.

Fear unlike anything he'd experienced throbbed through him. *Demons* were out there. Creatures of darkest magic. They might have her. She could be hurt, or worse . . .

No. *No.* He would find her.

But where the hell was she? He scanned the mob massed on Russell Street outside the theater. There. He caught a flash of light brown hair and ruby silk, before it disappeared into the crowd spilling into other streets.

He plowed through anyone in his path, his gaze fixed on where he'd last seen her. As he did, he cursed his useless gift of foresight, which showed him only financial disasters but could not help him in this, his greatest moment of need.

Nearing where he had spotted her, the rioters still thick around him, he finally heard her, calling his name. He shouted back to her, but could not catch her response or if she even knew he was nearby. But it gave him a sense of where she might be. Off Russell Street, and into the twisting, dark lanes surrounding the theater.

He moved into a narrow, shadowed street, where the crowd thinned. At the farther end of the street, he saw her at last. Three men had her, pulling on her arms as she struggled to break free. They tugged her into an alley.

Rage blackened thought. He bolted down the street, shouldering aside anyone in his way, seeing nothing but where Anne had been a moment ago. He did not pause at the entrance to the alley. It was almost pitch black, and stank of rotting mutton, but he plunged in.

Four darker shapes revealed where Anne battled against her captors. Judging by the sounds of struggle, she was putting up an admirable fight.

"Filthy rogues," she snarled. "Swine."

He could not see, but so long as she kept talking, he

knew where she was. And his presence had not been noticed by the bastards who had her. That gave him one advantage. His other advantage lay in his coat pocket, but he had only one shot, and in dark, close quarters, he could not run the risk of missing and accidentally hitting her.

He merged with the shadows, slipping forward unseen. Then, at the precise moment, he launched himself into the fray.

Tackling one of the men, Leo grappled with the assailant, getting a sense of the man's size, his position. Leo rammed his fist into the man's face, and his opponent went down with a groan.

Anne cried out a warning as two others rushed him. Darkness helped and hindered as he repulsed their attack. He grunted as one man's fist connected with his shoulder, but Leo knew the ways of street fighting. Long before he began training at the boxing salon, he had been a hot-tempered young man in countless brawls.

He wrestled now with the attackers in rough, ugly combat. No art here, only the desire to hurt, and survive. In the darkness, they fought, threw punches, kicked. But the assailants did not have Leo's motivation, for he fought not just for himself, but Anne. He punched one of the men in the side of the head. The attacker formed a dark lump as he crumpled to the ground.

Leaving Leo with two remaining opponents. He heard Anne's angry curses as she continued to fight against one of the men.

He could not wait for the next attack. His hand brushed against a broken board lying on the pavement, and he grabbed it. Noting the sounds of his adversary's shoes on the cobbles, he shot forward, swinging the board. It must have connected with the man's stomach, for he made retching sounds. Using the noise as guidance, Leo struck the gagging man under the chin, knocking him backward.

The board broke in Leo's hands as the man groaned. He did not rise again.

Only one bastard left. The son of a bitch who had Anne. But Leo could not attack—he might hurt her in the process.

"Don't know who you are, bloke," the man sneered. "But I'm taking this here piece."

"I'm the piece's *husband.*" Leo's old, coarse accent had returned but he did not give a damn.

The man chuckled. "Tonight she gets a new man."

"No she bloody won't," Anne spat.

"Anne, with your free hand, grab his little finger," commanded Leo.

By the sounds of the man's grunting, Leo understood she had done what he asked.

"Now pull back. Hard."

Her attacker yelped. "No—"

Anne did not hesitate. A sharp cracking sound filled the alley, followed immediately by the man's scream.

"Get to the wall," Leo directed.

"I'm there," she said a moment later.

As soon as the words left her mouth, Leo attacked. He threw himself toward where he suspected the man would be. And he was not wrong. Finding him in the darkness, Leo rained punches down on him, mercilessly hammering at Anne's would-be attacker. The injury to the man's hand made him reckless and angry, and while his punches weren't accurate, they packed a great deal of power. Leo lost his breath as he took a fist to the chest. He recovered, gasping, his own fury blazing.

He riddled the bastard with hits, until Leo felt his own hands wet with the other man's blood. It wasn't enough. Leo wanted more. He kept up his barrage. Finally, Leo heard the man fall to the ground. Leo continued his assault, the demand for more and more blood urging him on.

Nothing would satisfy him but destruction. He picked the man's head up, ready to smash it to the pavement.

Anne's touch on his shoulder stopped him. "He's not hitting back."

"Don't care." Leo's voice was rough in his throat, someone else's voice.

She tugged on his coat. "The way is clear."

Reluctant, he loosened his grip on the man's head. Though he did not smash it on the cobbles, he did let it drop, and it hit the ground with a thick, meaty sound.

He straightened, his body screaming with demands for more violence. Only Anne's arms around him kept the beast within at bay. She urged him toward the entry to the alley, stepping over the prone bodies of the other men.

At the entrance to the alley, Leo stopped. He heard one of the men stagger to his feet behind them. A metallic hissing echoed in the narrow space—the sound of a knife being drawn. And then footsteps rushed toward them. Leo whirled around.

A brief flash lit the alley, followed by the bark of a pistol. Powder scented the air. There was a groan, and then the sound of a body tumbling to the ground.

Leo lowered his pistol.

"Is he dead?" asked Anne.

"Don't know. Don't care."

A brief pause, then: "I don't, either."

Leo tucked his gun back into his coat. He threaded his fingers with Anne's. Together, they ran off into the night.

．

Dawn lightened the sky to the color of ash. Leo watched the coming of day from a wing-backed chair in his study. He still wore his clothing from the night before, though there were tears at the shoulders and elbows. A gentleman's finery was not cut for brawling. But despite the plush carpets at his feet or the morocco-bound books lining the shelves of his study, he was not and never would be a gentleman.

He was glad.

Curled into a ball in the other wing-backed chair, with a blanket tucked around her, dozed Anne. She had not changed out of her gown, either. In the half-light of morning, her face was pale, and her lashes formed dark fringes against her cheeks. At her feet tipped a half-empty glass of brandy, the same he had pressed on her as soon as they had returned home last night.

The flames in the fireplace burned bright and hot, casting warmth. Though she had fought bravely, she shivered the whole way back to Bloomsbury. Yet she refused to go to bed. So he tried to make her as comfortable as possible here, in the study, which meant a strong fire and brandy. He had moved her chair close to the fireplace so she might warm quickly. At least her shivering had stopped.

Leo studied the raw patches on his knuckles. His hand ached a little. He welcomed the ache, for it meant that he had done exactly what he needed to in order to secure Anne's safety. He had not fought like a gentleman. He'd broken men's faces and splattered their blood upon the ground. He had shot someone. Perhaps killed him. And left the scene without a blemish of concern on his heart. Not the actions of a man of genteel birth.

He did not care. All that mattered was that Anne was safe.

Leo pushed up from his chair. He stoked the fire, then strode to the window. He braced his hands on the inside casing and stared out at the approach of morning. There had been a time when he knew this hour of the day because it meant he was just coming home from his night's revels. It had left him enough time to bolt down some coffee before heading back out again to the Exchange. Little reason to keep him home, for his house in Bloomsbury was costly but empty.

Never did he think he would be awake at this hour because he had battled through a riot.

He glanced over his shoulder. Anne still slept. Fitfully, but deep enough.

With no eyes on him, Leo at last gave in. His head hung down between his outstretched arms, and a shudder passed through him.

God. *God.* He had come so bloody close to losing her.

His mind reared back from the possibility. Thinking it felt like a cold knife cutting him into large, bleeding pieces.

And with Whit out there, somewhere, last night's dangers were but a foretaste of possible disaster. He might have even been in the mob, waiting for his moment to strike, to steal her away.

Leo swung away from the window, lest he smash his fist through the glass.

A soft tap sounded on the door. Leo strode over and opened it, careful to keep his steps quiet.

The head footman, Munslow, stood in the hallway, and Leo moved out to meet him. "Brought a morning paper, as you asked, sir."

Leo took the newspaper and scanned the front page. Wet ink smeared on his fingers, but he could still read it. *Most shocking Violence and Disorder at Drury-Lane Theatre transpired yesterday evening, the Cause of which is yet Undetermined. Three Deaths are reported with greater numbers of Injury, including a Sergeant of His Majesty's 15th Regiment of Light Dragoons. It is noted by the Author of this article that lately such grievous Events are occurring with greater and greater Frequency in this noble City . . .*

Reading on, Leo found an extensive list of localized

disorders, from fights all around town to an increase in arson, theft, and even murder.

"What do you know of this?" He held the paper in front of Munslow, who peered at the type.

"Can't say if that's all true, sir." The footman scratched beneath his wig. "But it has been rough out there. On his half-day, Davy Jenks, who waits for the gent across the street, he got beat by a gang with truncheons. And the fire brigade were summoned only two nights ago when someone tried to burn down Mrs. Lee's pie shop on Smithy Street. Lately, seems like all of London's become Bedlam. Don't need to pay to see lunatics—not when everyone's mad."

Leo frowned. "I haven't heard any of this."

The footman offered a half smile. "Well, sir, seeing as how you been busy with the missus, it might've missed your attention."

Leo thrust the newspaper back into Munslow's hands. "Bring coffee. And something to eat for when Mrs. Bailey wakes."

The footman bowed and hurried off. Quietly, Leo went back into the study, picking over what Munslow had said. The footman had no cause to lie. And Leo remembered how, not very long ago, he'd been caught in a melee on his way to the Exchange. He had been wrapped too deeply in his own concerns to notice, but thinking on it now, images flickered through his mind. Of thrown fists and broken windows and weeping women and slack-faced men, spread all throughout the city like rot. *London's going mad.*

Why now? What was the cause? It was never a peaceful place, but something was stirring up poison.

Across his back, his flesh grew heated. Unease tightened his belly.

Despite the heat on his back, the room itself felt chilled. And no wonder. The fire had gone out. It had been blazing not a few minutes prior. Now it was cold, its embers faintly smoking.

He crossed and pulled the tinderbox down from the mantel. Using a flint, he lit some tinder, and so brought the fire back to life again. He crouched, watching the flames for a moment, their shift and dance.

Turning his head, he saw Anne gazing at him. They stared at each other, mute.

At that moment, he wanted nothing more than to tell her everything: the gift he had received from the Devil, the true threat that Whit represented. No more secrets between them. Only the truth of themselves.

Yet even if she *did* believe him, he could not predict what her response might be. Disgust, horror. Terror. All possibilities ended with her fleeing. None with her cleaving to him, swearing eternal devotion.

She must never know. Her innocence had to be preserved.

He stroked his hand down the side of her face. She leaned into his touch, but her gaze stayed fixed on his.

"That trick you showed me last night," she said. "With the man's finger—breaking it so he would let me go. I want you to show me more."

He knew dozens, if not hundreds, of ways to hurt a man. Part of his less-than-genteel education. Ladies did not know how to jam their thumbs into a man's throat or ram an elbow in a man's groin. He did not care if Anne was a lady. Keeping her safe—that was all that mattered.

"We'll start later today," he said. "After you get some rest."

She clasped his wrist. "Show me now."

Before he could speak, another tap sounded on the door. It must be the breakfast he'd sent for. He straightened up from his crouch. "Enter."

Munslow opened the door, but he did not have a tray with him. "Beg pardon, sir. Lord Wansford is come calling."

"My father?" Anne glanced at the clock on the mantel, which showed the hour to be barely past seven. "He is never up this early."

"I would've told him you weren't taking callers, sir, but he seemed insistent, and you and the missus *are* awake."

Leo frowned. Of all the times to deal with his father-in-law, the morning after escaping a deadly rampage ranked at the bottom of a very long list. Still, if he was here this early, it must be important.

"Give Mrs. Bailey a moment to retire, and then show him in."

Anne rose. "I want to stay."

"Show him in now. And bring that coffee."

The footman bowed. "Yes, sir."

When they were alone, Anne looked at her reflection in the pier glass over the mantel. During the night, the pins had escaped her hair, and now it spilled over her shoulders and down her back in tangled caramel waves. She briefly fussed with her hair, but the struggle did not last long. "I look like I was in a riot."

He came to stand behind her and gathered up the mass of her hair so he might press a kiss to the back of her neck. "You were. And you look beautiful."

"Like a ruffian."

They stared at each other in the glass, their mirror selves. His own hair was undone from its queue, stubble roughened his cheeks, his clothes were torn, and his hands curved over her shoulders showed red, raw knuckles.

"A well-suited couple," he said, and as he'd hoped, she smiled.

The footman's reflection appeared in the mirror. "Lord Wansford."

A moment later, the baron stepped into the study. He visibly started when he saw not only Leo, but Anne, both of them looking ragged.

"Good God," Wansford exclaimed. "Were you accosted by bandits?"

"There was a riot at Drury Lane last night." Leo did not bother bowing. "It's in the papers."

"We do not receive the newspaper," murmured Anne.

"*He* doesn't get the paper," Leo said. "*We* do." He drew a breath. "Tell me your business, Wansford. It's late, or early, and my wife and I are tired."

The baron tugged on his threadbare waistcoat, pulling it across the expanse of his belly. From his pocket, he pulled a coin. "I came to bring you this."

Leo stared at the penny for a moment. His mind was both acutely sharp and also misty, but he recalled his purpose. From the corner of his eye, he saw Anne frown. She clearly did not expect Leo's coin-collecting "pastime" to extend to her own family.

He was too weary and tense to provide an explanation. Instead, he strode across the study and plucked the coin from his father-in-law's hand.

A falling sensation as the vision pulled him in. It was dark, and oppressively close. On every side was solid rock. Veins of glinting ore threaded through the rock, and by the light of flickering lanterns he recognized the ore: iron. A mining tunnel. Grimy-faced men wielded picks, the sound a relentless *chip-chip-chip* as they hacked the ore from its prison. No sense of day or night in the tunnel, or any time at all passing, for there was always iron, and more iron to be pried free from the earth.

Someone shouted as a tremor passed through the thick stone walls. The tremor grew. It turned into a hard buckling, rock sifting down in larger and larger chunks. Men yelled, shoving each other in their haste to flee. But most could not escape. The walls collapsed. The ability to breathe vanished. The lanterns went out, and everything became darkness and sound and choking airlessness and the grind of rock upon the fragile bodies of men.

"Leo?"

A touch upon his arm, and he snapped back into the room. No crushing rock. No darkness and the screams of those trapped. Only his study in Bloomsbury, with its paneled walls and indifferent furniture.

Anne gazed up at him with concern, her hand upon his forearm. Her father also stared at him, anxious.

Leo dragged air into his lungs and pushed back the suffocating remnants of the vision. It lingered, though, in black tendrils wrapped through his mind and body.

He offered a smile to Anne. "Only tired."

"You have your coin," said Wansford, "for whatever reason. Now will you invest in that iron mine on my behalf?"

Leo opened his mouth to tell the baron that he would *not* sink money into a venture that would suffer a catastrophic collapse. "The weather continues to be damp," he said instead.

Wansford gave him a puzzled frown. "Usually it is, this time of year. But what of the mine?"

Again, Leo tried to speak, to warn the baron against the mining venture. "Will you stay for breakfast?"

"I've taken mine already." Wansford scowled. "See here, Bailey, you must say at once whether you will serve as my intermediary. You agreed to it already, and I shall look unkindly on it should you renege now."

"Perhaps we ought to get some rest," suggested Anne, "and we can resume this conversation at another time."

"It must be today," her father said. "For it is the last day the venture will accept investors."

Leo heard their voices as if from a great distance. Words formed in his mind, words he intended to say, and yet as much as he fought, he could not get them into his mouth and spoken aloud. It felt like a vise, crushing him, and his vision swam.

He must tell Wansford to avoid the investment, but for some reason, he could not speak. The room tilted as he staggered to his desk. Anne's concerned voice floated around him, yet he grabbed a sheet of foolscap and a quill. A dip of the nib in ink, and he readied his hand to write his warning.

The sharpened nib touched the paper. He moved his hand, willing the words to move from his thoughts to his pen.

ABCDEFG. There are ships at anchor in Portsmouth. O, what a jolly lad is he.

Spattering ink like black blood, the quill fell from his fingers. He stared at his hand as though it belonged to someone else. Powerless in his own body.

Anne appeared at his side, a pleat of worry between her brows. She looked at the sheet of foolscap, the nonsense he had scribbled there, and her face paled. "I should summon the physician." She ran her hands over his torso. "Perhaps you suffered an injury last night. You need to be attended."

"I'm fine." But he wasn't. The Devil had given him a gift, a gift that he had always exploited to his own benefit. It had never failed him, not once. And indeed, it worked perfectly this morning. Save for one critical element: he couldn't warn Wansford about the mining disaster.

He had never needed to caution anyone before. Never knew this one fatal flaw in his gift. Now he did.

As he stared at his wide-eyed wife and her father, coldness seeped through him. If this vital failing existed in what he once thought infallible, what other damned defects existed in his agreement with the Devil? Of a certain, they must be there. Any investor knew that one flaw led to another, and another. Until what had once appeared to be a perfect opportunity became merely the presage to disaster.

* * *

She did not want him to go out. Something clearly was not right with her husband. Not illness, precisely, but a profound sense of *wrong*, as if he found himself inhabiting another man's life. Surely it was on account of their exhaustion. Yet he would not remain at home.

"I have to get to the Exchange." Standing by the glass in their bedchamber, he shrugged into a coat of dark blue wool. His hair was still wet from his bath, yet he had not shaved, and he looked as dangerous as a primed pistol, ready to fire.

"Then I will come with you." She plucked at the ribbons fastening her wrapper. A few minutes was all she required to change from her dishabille into something suitable for the outdoors.

His hand stayed hers. "I need you to stay here."

"Because it is scandalous if a lady goes to Exchange Alley?"

He scowled. "Don't give a damn about scandal. I only want you safe."

"The safest place for me is with you."

Yet he shook his head. "Not after last night. Not with London verging on chaos." He stepped back, and she felt the strained brittleness of the connection between them. "You're safer at home, behind these walls. Munslow is here, and a dozen footmen. No one will be able to hurt you."

His concern touched her, though a little, venomous voice whispered, *Is it the rioters he fears, or Lord Whitney?*

She had no answer. She could not explain what had transpired in the study with her father, the strange humor that had gripped Leo. He had spoken of inanities, written nonsense—alarming in and of themselves. But most frightening was the look on his face, the confusion and angry powerlessness. So utterly unlike him.

Something *was* happening, something strange and terrible, and yet nowhere could she find meaning.

Leo brushed a kiss across her mouth, and she saw it again, fleeting, in the gunmetal of his eyes: doubt. A doubt that unnerved him deeply.

"I'll return soon. And when I get back, we'll begin your fighting education." Then he was gone, his footsteps sounding in the hallway, down the stairs, and finally out the door.

The fire in the bedchamber sputtered, and died.

God, why could she not keep a fire lit? She grabbed a china figurine of a drowsing shepherd, and threw it into the fireplace with a frustrated cry.

A moment later, a footman appeared at the door, drawn by the sound of shattering porcelain. "Madam?"

"An accident. But don't send a maid to clean it. Not yet."

The footman bowed and retreated. Anne sank down to the carpet, exhausted, despairing. She felt herself in a cavern. All around her was darkness, and she had neither candle nor lantern to light her way. Her only option was to stumble forward, hoping she did not fall and suffer a fatal injury.

They had just finished dinner. The servants had cleared away the dishes, and the candles burned low as a distant clock struck the hour. It had been a meal marked by silence, the sounds limited to the clink of knives against china, wine poured in goblets. She had tried to speak, to draw Leo out, yet every thrown lure was met with distracted responses. A word or two was all he had managed, his gaze withdrawn and preoccupied.

Anne rose from the table. Leo did the same. They went up together. In the hallway, he guided her toward the parlor.

"I'm for bed." Weariness oppressed her.

"You should have rested when I went out."

"Rest was impossible."

"The bedchamber door was closed, else I would've come in."

She could only manage a shrug, unwilling to tell him that she needed distance to make sense of the uncertainty twisting within her. Gazing up at his hard, handsome face now, gentled slightly with concern for her, she wondered how the plays she used to watch from the theater gallery could have been so very misguided. They ended when the two lovers pledged their devotion to each other, and with that, all obstacles fell away. As though love were the answer, demolishing every impediment.

What lies those sentimental dramas were. For her heart cracked and bled.

Leo frowned—he was an astute man. He had to feel it, too.

"Sir," said an approaching footman. "Lord Wansford has returned. He would speak with you."

"Bring him up to the parlor." He turned to Anne. "I'll see you in our chamber."

"I'll join you in the parlor." She had not forgotten the strange scene from that morning.

His gaze turned opaque. Yet he offered her his arm, and together they went to await her father.

He came into the chamber, bearing the cold air of evening and an angry expression. "The deuce, Bailey?" Her father's gaze shot to her, as if too late remembering he was not to use such language in the presence of a lady.

"Wansford." Leo did not get up from where he was draped against a settee. Nor did he offer her father a glass of brandy.

"You said you would invest in that iron mine. And yet you did not."

"No."

Anne stared at her husband. He kept his gaze on the brandy in his glass, contemplating it. His face was a mask.

"Why the Devil not?" demanded her father.

She could not stop her small flinch at those words, and saw Leo's mouth tighten, as well. Still staring at his drink, he seemed about to speak, but whatever he meant to say appeared to lodge in his throat. He took a drink, swallowing hard, then set the glass down on a low table.

"I made a better investment."

"We agreed—"

"I said I would investigate the Gloucestershire mine. I did not consent to invest in it."

Her father reddened. "The opportunity is lost."

"If Leo did not make the investment," Anne said, "he must have a good reason for doing so." That was one reliable truth about her husband: in matters of business, he always acted in the best self-interest.

"You will still earn a profit, Wansford," said Leo. "I made a counterinvestment in another iron mine."

"Why not the Gloucestershire mine?"

"I don't need to explain my decision." Leo's voice was sharp, his gaze likewise cutting. Her father recoiled at the tone. "But mark me, you *will* make a profit. That is a certainty."

A look of confusion crossed her father's face. He seemed uncertain how to respond. Leo continued to stare at him, his gaze unblinking and cold.

Ultimately, her father said, "I will respect your judgment."

Leo's mouth twisted. "How gratifying."

"These past hours have been very taxing." Anne rose up from her seat and urged her father toward the door. "It's time for you to go."

His head jerked like a puppet. "Yes. Yes, I should . . . I ought to . . ." But he did not know what he should or ought to do. He peered around her, and produced a smile for Leo. "My thanks."

The response was merely a flick of Leo's wrist. Though he continued to lounge on the settee, tension coiled through him, as though he were a hairbreadth away from tearing the chamber apart.

"Good night, Father." Anne gave him a dutiful kiss on the cheek, catching a thread of his scent of reboiled tea and adulterated tobacco.

He muttered a farewell, then followed a footman down the corridor. As his footsteps retreated, Anne shut the door to the parlor, then pressed her back against it, facing her husband. He stared into empty air.

"That was kind of you to make a better investment."

Once more, that bitter twist of his mouth. "Nothing kind about it. It was *my* capital."

"Against *his* estate. If the venture had not succeeded, you nonetheless would have emerged the richer."

"As I said, a more advantageous opportunity presented itself."

She studied the long lines of his body, her gaze moving up to trace the clean delineation of his profile, the curve of his lower lip. A sweet agony to look upon him.

"I wish you would let me into your confidence."

His gaze snapped up to hers. "You know everything."

"Who can we be honest with," she said quietly, "if not each other?"

He stared at his hands, the rows of healing wounds on his knuckles. "I've told you everything I can."

Which was not an answer, and they both knew it.

Chapter 12

Leo waited until shadows swathed the house. He left Anne upstairs, deeply asleep. They had not spoken much after her father had quit the house. What words had been said aloud were terse, strained. Yet the whole of the evening, he wanted to clutch her close, to bury his face in her hair and draw her scent deep into his lungs. To whisper the things that weighed heavy within him.

Instead, they had sat far apart, mute, and even in the bedchamber, they had moved around the room like strangers encased in glass. They had lain beside each other with intimate formality. Smothering darkness pressed down, leaving words and touches stillborn.

Now Anne slept. He hated having to leave her, limbs soft, skin warm and fragrant. But his business could not wait.

Slipping on his banyan, Leo padded through the dark corridors of his house, and down the stairs. A lone footman drowsed by the front door. The servant did not stir as Leo passed through the foyer. The place was still as a tomb.

In cold and darkness, he entered his study. He did not bother lighting a fire, but he lit a candle and set it on the end of his desk.

"*Veni, geminus,*" he said.

The scent of burnt paper stained the air. And then there stood the *geminus*, dressed for an evening out, like any man of means. Leo tried to stare hard at the thing's face, yet his gaze continually slid away.

"Such a pleasure," the *geminus* said, bowing, a smile in its voice.

Leo folded his arms across his chest. "Time for answers."

"I am in all things obliging. Whatever you desire shall be yours."

"The truth," said Leo tightly. "Neither you nor your Mr. Holliday ever told me about the flaw in my gift."

"Flaw?" The *geminus* chuckled. "Not a flaw, but merely a limitation."

"The name you give it doesn't matter. What *does* matter is that I couldn't tell Wansford about the mining disaster. I couldn't even warn the damned mine owners when I went down to the Exchange." Leo had approached the men at the coffee house, determined to tell them that there would be loss of life if they did not take precautions. And he had stood there like a dullard, spouting nonsense about the best kind of fish to eat, whilst the mine owners stared at him, baffled.

He had tried to write, just as he'd done with Wansford. Again, only nonsense came from his pen. There had been nothing he could do. No way to prevent the disaster.

"Such events cannot be averted," answered the *geminus*. "Even my master cannot stop it."

Leo stalked toward the creature. "None of this was told to me."

"Why should it?" The *geminus* spread its hands. "Until now, it has served you exactly as you desired. Have you not profited, and profited well, from this gift?"

Leo dragged in a breath. Only one answer: he had.

"It matters naught," continued the *geminus*, its tone appeasing, "this tiny aspect of what is a most generous gift.

So you cannot prevent what is foreseen. What of it? You can still reap profits the likes of which are unknown to all mortal men. Your wealth and power continue to grow. Those men you consider your enemies continue to fall. There is nothing you cannot have. Nothing," it added, "you cannot give to your wife."

Damn it, but the *geminus* was a sly bastard. Leo knew the thing manipulated him, said precisely what he needed to hear. He was aware of the creature's machinations, yet they played upon him, just the same.

He fought against the subtle trap the *geminus* wove. "That doesn't change the fact that, even if I didn't want to stop the mine from collapsing, I couldn't warn Wansford not to invest in it."

The *geminus* shrugged. "Again, 'tis trifling. The man is no friend of yours. Further, with your knowledge of the imminent misfortune, you made a counterinvestment that shall yield very agreeably, to both you *and* to him. I see no difficulty."

Surely the Devil and his underlings must practice their art at the Exchange, for this creature spoke honeyed words intended to beguile. Had Leo not trained himself well in the art of deception, he might have ceded to the *geminus*'s blandishments.

"The underhandedness of this whole business makes me wonder: what else are you not telling me? What hidden traps does the Devil have in store?"

The *geminus* made a shocked sound. "Sir, you wound me and my master. He has been most generous, and here you cast aspersions."

"He's been called worse, and by far more than me."

The *geminus* strolled away toward the fireplace. With a wave of its hand, the kindling blazed. Firelight limned the outline of the *geminus*, the rest of it naught but shadow. It studied the flames for a moment.

"It is time," the *geminus* said, "for a reward."

Leo frowned. Of all the responses he'd anticipated, this was not one he'd considered. "Why?" he demanded.

"Because you have served my master well."

His frown deepening to a scowl, Leo said, "I serve no one. I act in my own best interest."

"Of course," the *geminus* answered quickly. "You are your own man. A quality my master admires greatly. What I meant to say is that you have made my master exceedingly proud. The ruthlessness you display at the Exchange, the men whose lives you destroy . . . all of this pleases my master. Thus, he desires to give you a reward, in recognition of your good works."

"Tell me about this reward."

"Greater power. Should you so desire it. You will be able to see farther into the future, decades, and to trigger this ability, you will no longer require coins, but simply *any* object belonging to your intended prey." Laughing, the creature said, "Is this not a wondrous gift? And most generous of my master to offer it?"

Leo turned the idea over and over in his mind. Tempting, indeed. Obtaining items owned by his quarry would be an easy matter. The cuff of a coat during a handshake. Inspecting a gentleman's ornate walking stick. The rewards would be even greater than before, his power immense. Anything he desired—his. Anything Anne could ever possibly wish for—hers.

The old order, based on ancestry and blood, would crumble. He could fashion a new world, where a man's value was based on his deeds, not birth. Any who opposed him and this new world would see themselves utterly crushed, smashed to powder beneath the relentless grindstone of progress, with his shoulder pushing the stone forward.

"Yes, you see my master offers you a most marvelous

power." The *geminus* moved from the fire, its footsteps muffled by the carpet. "Speak but a word, and it is yours."

"Tell me the price."

"It has no cost, sir."

"There is always a cost."

The *geminus* tutted. "Time on the Exchange has made you chary. What I ask is merely a trifle."

Leo narrowed his eyes. "I gave you one, months ago. At the temple." In order for him and all the other Hellraisers to receive their gifts, they had been required to present tokens. Leo had given the *geminus* a snuffbox, which had been a minor loss indeed, as he never took snuff, only kept the thing as part of a gentleman's effects.

"One more. Anything shall suffice."

Glancing around the room, Leo espied a tortoiseshell-and-silver quill stand on his desk. He removed the sharpened, waiting quill, and held the stand.

"Yes," said the *geminus*.

Leo had no remembrance of buying the thing. A memory did come to him, though: the battered pewter quill stand and matching ink pot his father used. The pride in his father's face when he would take up his pen and write, and how happy it made Adam Bailey to see his son make use of it as though the act of writing was itself a commonplace skill, not something painfully acquired later in life.

It had cost his father a week's earnings to buy that pewter quill stand, and it had already been well used by the time he'd purchased it from the chandler.

The ornate object Leo now held likely cost ten times the quill stand his father had bought. And yet, he didn't care about this thing at all. It meant nothing. As for the dented pewter writing accessories once belonging to his father, those were kept securely in a strongbox in a locked drawer of Leo's desk. Only Anne knew of their whereabouts, their significance, for he had shown them to her, and she had handled them with the respect one saved for sacred relics.

This was why she meant so much to Leo, why he had to keep her with him at all costs. Only she understood what he valued. Only she accepted every part of him.

Staring at the expensive trinket in his hand, Leo wondered: what would his father do in this situation? He might refuse the Devil's offer of power. Or he might seize any advantage given to him, for his father had been at all times ambitious. This was the greatest bequest he left for his son—the need to rise ever higher.

His back heated as greed surged through him. He wanted to take, to claim. Everything he could. For himself, for Anne. For the memory of Adam Bailey.

He glanced up. The *geminus* stood before him, though Leo had not heard it move. It held out its hand.

"That thing has no value," the *geminus* said. "But what my master offers is inestimable."

Leo's fingers tightened around the quill stand. Then released. He placed the object in the *geminus*'s hand. The creature immediately put the quill stand in its coat pocket.

"A wise choice."

"When will this gift take effect?"

"Immediately."

To test this, Leo considered taking something from the footman dozing in the entryway, but he had little care for the fortunes of a servant. It must wait until the morrow, when the Exchange opened and Leo could prey upon any number of men.

"If our business for the evening is concluded, I shall away." The *geminus* practically sang with good spirits. It strolled toward the door and opened it.

"You have no need of doors," said Leo.

"Ah, but sometimes I find them amusing, sir, and my humor is too pleasant to waste on tedious appearing and disappearing. I believe I shall take a stroll in your garden. Such a place at night will suit my fancy."

Leo shrugged. His thoughts were too occupied with whom he should meet tomorrow at the Exchange, what fortunes he would make for himself, and whose he would demolish. "As you wish."

"Good night, sir. And may I say again how very gratified my master is made by your continued efforts on his behalf."

"I act on my own behalf."

The *geminus* smiled, or so Leo sensed. "That you do, sir." With that, it quit the study, closing the door behind it. A moment later, Leo heard its footsteps outside on the garden path.

Leo stood alone in the chamber, searching within himself for a sense of his new power. He could not perceive it, not yet, but he felt its potential. Damn, but he wished the sun would rise so the day's work could begin. If only *that* were one of his abilities. He felt sorely tempted to run up to the bedchamber and wake Anne, tell her of his greater power. Yet he could not. At the least, he wanted to see her, hold her. His greed for more encompassed them both.

After dousing the fire and candle, he returned upstairs. He threw off his banyan and walked toward the bed.

"Leo?" Anne's whisper floated through the darkness.

He settled between the covers and pulled her close, fighting the urge to reveal what new gift had been given to him. They would both reap the benefits. "You sound surprised."

"I thought you were in the garden."

He stilled. "I was in my study. Some work needed attending."

"But . . . I just saw you out there." She edged back, away from him. "I heard footsteps outside, and you weren't in bed, so I looked out and there you were, walking up and down the garden."

The *geminus*. He hoped she did not mistake the creature for a would-be burglar, and want to summon the constabulary. "The gardener, perhaps."

"No. The moon came out, and I saw your face. It was *you*. I know my own husband. But you weren't wearing your nightclothes, you were fully dressed."

Leo was out of bed in an instant. He threw back the curtains and peered into the garden. No one was there. Not the *geminus*, and not the gardener Leo had invented. He glanced back at Anne, moonlight turning her to silver and shadow, caution in her gaze.

She had seen the *geminus*, and thought it was him. It could not be possible.

Memory like a knife pierced him. Months earlier, Whit had deserted the Hellraisers. They had fought on Saint George's Fields, guided there to intercept Whit by his *geminus*. Whit had pointed at that *geminus*, told his friends to look at the thing as if expecting a revelation. When none came, when they had seen naught but a faceless creature, Whit had despaired, and turned his back on them. The Gypsy girl with him *had* seen something, though.

The same as Anne had seen. Whit's *geminus* looked like Whit. And the *geminus* who answered Leo's summons was *his* double.

And there had been Robbins, who had insisted on seeing Leo at a coffee house when Leo had been, in fact, home.

Hot pain shot through his left calf. As though he were being branded. He staggered into the small closet and fumbled for a candle. It flared to life with a hiss. Hand faintly shaking, he held the light up to see his calf.

Just above the ankle: an image of a flame.

"Leo." Anne's voice was very close, right outside the door to the closet. "Tell me what is going on. If something is wrong, I need to know."

Using his fingers, Leo snuffed the candle's flame. He

did not bother wetting his fingertips, simply crushed out the fire with his bare skin. But if there was pain, he did not feel it. He felt only the thick, choking smoke of approaching doom.

"Nothing." He left the small chamber and found Anne waiting for him, ghostly in her night rail, and beautiful. His arms wrapped around her, pulling her close, and he rasped, "Nothing is wrong."

Anne threaded her way through the cramped alleys, dodging men in sober woolen coats and tricorns, their faces serious as though the fate of nations weighed on the next few hours. Which it did, in a fashion. For her many discussions with Leo had revealed to her that commerce comprised the blood of statehood. Money flowed through England's veins. Should it cease to flow, death would follow, and decay.

Yet the men she passed were not too deeply involved with business that they did not see her. She attracted many curious stares, and one gentleman in a full-bottomed wig stopped outright in his tracks to gawk at her.

Pulling her cloak closer, Anne gave the gentleman a polite, cool nod, but kept walking. A footman trailed close behind her.

"At which of these coffee houses will I find my husband?"

The footman shrugged. "He always leaves the carriage and walks in. I never even been here before."

Meaning Anne had no guide for this new, masculine world of Exchange Alley. A cartographic challenge, then. The native populace always knew where they were, but it was left to the cartographer to learn the landscape.

The scent of coffee and the sounds of men's voices thickened the air. Everyone walked with great purpose, else they huddled close in grave conversation. Signs adorned each storefront. LLOYD'S. NEW UNION. NEW JONATHAN'S. JERUSALEM. Inside, a continual supply of coffee and newspapers was provided. A far distant country from the gossip and idleness of genteel women. A palpable energy buzzed, making her heart beat faster.

Or perhaps it was not the energy of the place, but Anne's errand.

She ducked her head into one coffee house, and scanned the crowd within. Startled eyes turned to her. So many men, but none were Leo. Moving down the street, she peered into another, yet the results were the same. The process repeated itself, again and again.

"Are you sure he is here?" she asked the footman.

"Coachman told me he dropped Mr. Bailey here this morning."

There was no help for it but to ask. She stopped a man hurrying by. "Excuse me, sir."

The man took in the details of her clothing, her fine cloak, her soft hands. He blinked in surprise. "Madam?"

"I seek Leopold Bailey."

He frowned. "The Demon? You'd best keep away from him, madam, for he's been on a tear these past days. Either makes a man laugh with joy or weep with despair, as the humor takes him. A demon, indeed."

"That *demon* is my husband."

"Beg pardon, madam." The man gave her a shamefaced bow. "At this time of day, you'll find him at the Albatross. Which is just around the corner. Third shop on the left."

Anne murmured her thanks and walked on. Each step made her pulse drum harder.

A sign painted with a large seabird told her she had found the place she sought. She gazed through the dust-streaked windows. Her heart leapt up to lodge in her throat. There he was, sitting at a table with three other men. The men listened intently to whatever it was Leo said, nodding and scribbling in small notebooks.

Gathering her courage, Anne moved to the door. "Wait out here," she told the footman. Then she walked inside.

Smoke from countless pipes striped the walls, and the floorboards tilted unevenly. Tables were jammed close together, men huddled around them, and she heard words such as *interest*, *profit margin*, and *dividends*. She knew what those words meant now. Yet this still was a strange and alien place.

Anne kept her gaze fixed on her husband's tawny head, and his wide shoulders. His back was to the door, so he did not see her approach. The men seated with him did, and one by one, they fell silent and stared as she neared.

Leo turned, frowning. His expression shifted to one of pleasure. Followed by fierce concern. He rose in a single, sinuous motion and stepped close.

"Something has happened," he said. "Are you ill? Hurt?"

She shook her head, though she did feel both ill and injured. "We must speak."

"Not here." He took her hand and led her from the coffee house, without saying a word of farewell to the men with whom he had been conversing. "There's a tea shop not far." His stride long, he strode down the alley, Anne hurrying to keep up.

They left the close alleys and coffee houses, and walked on until he guided her into a shop with a clean bow window. Here, the air smelled of congou and butter, and framed prints of pastoral bridges adorned the walls. Though the hour was still early for ladies of fashion, there were yet a few women gathered at the tables, their calico gowns of good but not exceptional quality, their hair and hats artfully arranged by an unseen maid. The wives of the merchants who worked a few streets away.

She and Leo took the table in the corner. Dishes of tea

appeared before them, served by a rosy-cheeked girl. Anne watched the leaves swirl within her cup, caught in miniature vortices.

"I'm half sick with worry," Leo said. "And you're pale as frost. Tell me what has upset you."

To give herself a moment to compose herself, she took a sip of tea. "The mine," she said at last.

Leo's expression tightened. He leaned back. "Your father's investment is safe."

"I don't give a damn about the investment."

Several feminine gasps sounded in the quiet of the tea shop.

Lowering her voice, Anne said, "There was a collapse at the iron mine in Gloucestershire."

"Word circulated this morning." His gaze was shuttered. "Three men died. How did you learn of it?"

She would not look away from his storm gray eyes. "I had one of the footmen making inquiries, keeping me abreast of any developments."

"Then you and I know the same things."

"You know far more than I do." She leaned over the table. "Such as: the cave-in at the mine."

Cold sickness spread through her when he did not deny this. He looked away, his jaw tight.

"How? How could you know? Unless . . ." She swallowed. "It was planned. Deliberate sabotage."

His gaze snapped back to hers, angry. "Not deliberate. Simply . . . an act of God." A bitter laugh escaped him.

"Men were *killed*. Somehow you knew. And did not try to stop it."

"I tried. But couldn't." Self-recrimination roughened his voice.

"How, Leo? How did you know?"

"Doesn't matter."

She stared at him. "I cannot believe you would say that. To me, out of everyone."

The agony in his eyes carved her apart. "It has to be this way."

"You've shown me that we can shape the world as we see fit, make it bend to *our* will. Whatever secrets you keep, you do so for your own benefit." Eyes hot, she pushed back from the table and headed for the door, ignoring the stares of the tea shop patrons.

Leo's hand formed an iron band around her upper arm as he stood next to her. "Stay here," he bit out to the footman.

Anne had no idea where they walked, until they emerged on the embankment. A dank, thick scent rose up from the dark Thames, and close by came the din of London Bridge. Vessels plied the water, tall-masted ships at anchor, and small rowboats ferrying people through the dangerous currents beneath the bridge.

She felt a choking sensation in her throat, as she and Leo faced each other. The treacherous river was to his back.

What Lord Whitney had said, it could not be true. It *could not*, for if he did speak the truth, it meant that the Devil was real, that there was actual magic in the world, and wickedness embodied. It meant that not only was there genuine evil, but her husband had willingly bargained with it.

Her heart and mind reared back.

"I swear to you, Anne," he said now. "Nothing between us is any different."

"You've no idea how much I want to believe that."

He reached out and ran the back of his fingers over her cheek. His gaze was bleak. "We can make it so."

His fingers drifted up from her cheek to wind through her hair. Oh, she loved his hands, broad and rough. She loved the strength of him, and how, when he touched her, his eyes flashed silver. Seeing her, seeing *into* her. A simple touch, yet with it, she felt the chaos of the city retreat, the perilous river recede.

A curl tumbled down as he tugged a ribbon free. He

stroked the coil of hair, longing in his eyes, but then his gaze turned distracted as he wound the ribbon around his finger.

He seemed to visibly withdraw. His body remained precisely as it was, but his mind went elsewhere.

She recognized the look. He had appeared much the same when her father had brought him a coin. Right before Leo told her father he would not invest in the mine.

"What do you see?" she asked.

His focus returned, a sudden sharpening of awareness. He became wary, guarded—of her. As though she concealed a dagger in the folds of her skirt.

"I see my wife." Yet he dropped his hand and the ribbon slid from his fingers. It gleamed in a satiny curve as it fell to the ground, where it lay in the mud.

"That is exactly what I am, Leo. Your wife." She stared up at him. "The one person you should trust above all others." *Tell me*, she willed him with her gaze. *Whatever it is, I must know.* Yet she feared his honesty.

He took several paces away from her. Then turned, and cautiously approached, as if uncertain whether or not she would bolt away. She stood her ground. They faced each other, scarce inches between them, testing each other, testing themselves. His hand came up to cup the back of her head. She tilted her face up. In slow, slow degrees, he brought his mouth to hers. With the sound of the surging river enveloping them, she felt herself slide beneath a tide of yearning, wishing life could be as simple as a kiss.

They held tight to each other, until someone shouted lewd encouragements.

"Go to Hell," Leo snarled to the waterman on his skiff.

"Ain't you heard, guv'nor?" The waterman chortled. "We're *all* goin' to Hell." He poled his flat-bottomed boat on, chuckling all the while.

Leo said nothing, but it was clear that if the waterman had been within reach, Leo would have made him suffer.

Her husband stared at the Thames—the boats and ships upon it, bringing his cargo and wealth, the swarms of people skimming across the surface of the water like insects, and the buildings and warehouses crouched on the banks. He gazed at it all as if he could burn everything down with only a look. Anne half expected to see flames burst to life along the masts bobbing at anchor.

He faced her. "Everything will be all right."

Yet it was clear that even he did not believe his hollow words.

He ensconced himself in a dockside tavern, having lost his taste for commerce on this day. She had gone home— or so he imagined, for they had talked little as they returned her to the waiting carriage. Her hand had been light on his arm as they had walked, her gaze abstracted. Vast troves of unspoken words lay between them. As he had handed her into the carriage, she had slipped from his grasp like smoke. He'd watched her drive away, though he wanted to shout after her, *Stay*.

Now he stared at the empty tankard before him. Two men diced by the fire. Another whittled what appeared to be a piece of bone, peering at his handiwork through one eye.

"Another drink, sir?"

He waved the tapster off, but tossed him a coin for good measure. Drink would not straighten his head. Answers came scarce at the bottom of a tankard.

The *geminus* had spoken true. Any object now gave him access to what would be—including a ribbon belonging to his wife. Until then, he had only looked into the futures of those he sought to undermine or exploit. No longer being beholden to coins gave him an even greater advantage. And a yet larger hunger for more. He could not find satiety. A profit of a thousand pounds meant nothing. His demand refused appeasement, as though a monstrous serpent lived within him, consuming everything, including himself.

Her ribbon lay in the mud. It had shown him a future he did not want to see. Anne, speaking with the Roman ghost. The ally of Whit, and enemy of the Hellraisers. There was nothing Leo could do to stop this future from happening. He could not warn his wife. His only option was to wait, and he despised waiting.

A shadow darkened his table. Without looking up, Leo knew exactly who cast it. His body tensed.

"You aren't impervious to bullets," he said, "for all your Gypsy's magic."

He did glance up then to see the man he'd once called friend. It had been months since last he had seen him. Whit looked a little thinner, but not haggard. Far from it. When Leo had known Whit, he'd been indolent, indulged by birth and circumstance, finding his one real spark at the gaming tables. Now, he was sharp as vengeance, his gaze alert to everything around him.

"Nor can your gift of prophecy deflect a blade." Whit's hand rest lightly on the pommel of his saber, his nobleman's privilege. "Prior history has proven so."

Leo resisted the urge to rub the scar on his shoulder. When Whit had turned his back on the Hellraisers, there had been a fight in Oxford. The rapier that had wounded Leo had, in fact, belonged to Bram, but Whit had manipulated luck to cause the injury.

"Both of us could mortally wound the other," said Leo softly. "But who will be first? Shall we wager on it?"

"I came to warn you," Whit replied, resisting the lure, "not kill you."

Leo's chuckle was low and rueful. "Assuming that you're faster with your sword than I am with my pistol."

"The danger to you and your wife grows hourly, and yet you waste time with braggadocio."

Leo shot to his feet and grabbed Whit's neck cloth. The tavern fell silent. "Threaten her, and I *will* kill you."

"Goddamn it, Leo, *you* are the one who threatens her, not me." Whit shoved against him, but Leo would not release his hold.

Whit spoke, low and quick. "What the hell do you think the price of your gift was? What do you think we all bargained in exchange for that magic? Our *souls*."

Leo narrowed his eyes and released Whit. "I still have a soul." He could feel it within himself, and its bright aching resonance whenever he was near Anne.

"Every day, you lose more and more of it." When he saw that Leo meant to contradict him, Whit continued. "The markings that appeared after we made our bargain—they are growing. From one night to the next, they spread across your skin. The more they grow, the more of you they cover, the more your soul is taken. Until there is nothing left. Until you belong to the Devil completely, and you are damned."

The marking of flame on his calf was growing daily, and now it reached almost up to the back of his knee.

His legs urged him to move. Leo shouldered past Whit and went out into the street. Whit followed. Leo did not know where he headed, only that he must keep moving.

Whit kept pace as Leo walked, his stride equally long. "You feel it. The Devil's hunger, constantly craving the destruction of others. As the markings grow, so does his hold on you. You will become his puppet, his minion. I know this, because it happened to me, as well. As it is happening to all of the Hellraisers."

"Don't know why I should trust you," Leo said on a growl. "You've proven yourself a traitor already."

They dodged heavy drays rattling down to the wharf, and dogs nosing in the heaps of rubbish.

"If not for the sake of your soul," Whit said, "then for the sake of your wife."

"Leave her out of this," snarled Leo. Simply hearing Whit speak of Anne set Leo into a killing humor.

"It is *you* who have involved her." Whit grabbed Leo's shoulder and swung him around so they faced each other. "For I tell you truly, Leo, you aren't merely losing your soul, you are losing *her.*"

Leo shook himself out of Whit's grasp, but he felt as if he'd been stabbed through. He glanced down, just to be certain that he hadn't. It wasn't Whit's blade that wounded him, but his words.

"This association with the Devil will cost you everything," continued Whit. "Your life, your fortune, your soul. Your love." He peered closer. "You *do* love your wife, don't you?"

Leo stood utterly still. His heart beat thickly in his chest.

"I do." The realization scoured him.

"Then if you won't fight for yourself, fight for her." Shouting by the docks drew Whit's attention. He glanced around, wary. "London is not safe. And the Hellraisers are to blame."

"Mankind has always been treacherous. That isn't the fault of the Hellraisers."

"The Hellraisers have worsened a chronic illness," said Whit. "Hastening society toward early collapse. And one of the first casualties will be your marriage."

Leo inhaled sharply. "If that is true . . ." His jaw tightened. "I have to find a cure."

Whit backed toward an alley. "I cannot stay longer. But when you are ready, you will find me."

"Whit, damn it—"

"Hurry," was all Whit said, and then ducked into the alley.

Leo ran after him, but there was no one in the passageway. He stood alone.

Chapter 13

She did not go straight home. Thinking about returning there, with its hollow chambers and shadowed corners, reminded Anne too much of the emptiness of her marriage. What could have been a warm, welcoming place became instead an unfulfilled promise. So she asked the coachman to drive around London, circling aimlessly.

At one point, the carriage drove past her parents' town-home on Portland Street. A faded little building tucked between grander structures, an impoverished relative at an elegant dinner. She immediately discarded the idea of going to see her mother and father, taking shelter with them from the chaos of her life. They could offer no solace, no haven. Even if she did go in and confess everything—her fears, her frantic, dying hope—they would never believe her. She, herself, could not believe the thoughts she now entertained.

Leo cannot be in league with the Devil. The Devil is not real. Magic is not real.

Yet her faith in the world as she knew it crumbled away, with each day, with each hour.

The carriage drove on.

Everything spun out of control. She watched the

streets roll past—Saint Martin's Lane, Oxford Street, the Knightsbridge Turnpike as they headed west and out toward the new development of Kensington—seeing only a world off its axis, and her unable to right it, to stop the mad whirl.

"Sun's going down, madam," the coachman called from his seat. "Don't think the master would want you out after dark."

There was nowhere to go but home. It wasn't home, in truth, but a house she occupied. "Very well."

By the time she reached Bloomsbury, dusk lay in hazy folds, and the few lamps that had been lit threw flickering shadows across the streets.

Inside, the house held light, but little warmth.

She handed her cloak to a nearby footman. "Is my husband home?"

"Not yet, madam. Dinner is nearly ready, so Cook tells me."

She had no appetite. "Excellent. Tell him to serve as soon as my husband returns."

The footman bowed. "Very good, madam."

Inwardly, she cringed. Making dinner plans, as though she and Leo could sit together at table and converse over Whitstable oysters and seed cakes like any married couple. The thought of the plates, the cutlery, the meaningless exchanges she and Leo would make when the weight of greater questions bore down with a relentless, killing force—it made something inside her curl up and shudder.

She could not sit in a parlor and occupy herself with a book or pore over her trove of maps and globes. She could not spend a moment within these ornate walls. Yet she could not go out. Only one place offered a degree of relief.

Her footsteps took her out into the garden. The time of year was still too early for any growth, everything remained barren and bare, but at the least she had no walls around her, no roof threatening to crush her. She paced quickly up and down the paths, feeling like an animal in a menagerie.

She pressed back farther into the recesses of the garden, where the shadows deepened in the twilight gloom. A small arbor formed a dark cove, hidden from view, and she sat down upon a stone bench tucked within it, determined to gather her thoughts.

She stared at the thorned branches of what would be roses. Nothing could coalesce in her mind, for every time she sought to understand what was truly happening, staunch reason tried to assert itself. All that remained were fleeting impressions, half-glimpsed truths, and thwarted hopes. With a violent intensity, she wished she and Leo could go back to those days leading up to and just after the consummation of their marriage. For she saw what they *could be* together—were it not for the darkness that gathered around him like a mantle.

A shimmering radiance drew her attention. It appeared as no more than a flicker of light beside the empty flower bed. And then grew larger, like a spark becoming a flame.

Anne dug the heels of her hands into her eyes. She must be tired, having slept hardly at all these past nights, and her vision played her false.

Yet as she took her hands from her eyes, the light remained. Grew even larger. Until it was the height of a person. It coalesced from a nebulous radiance into . . . a woman's hazy form.

Anne shot to her feet. Her heart thudded in her chest. Yet she could not run. She simply gaped as the woman sharpened, grew focused, her limbs and facial features emerging from the light.

"Oh, God," Anne rasped. For the woman wore ancient Roman clothing. She had proud, aristocratic features and cunning dark eyes. And she stared directly at Anne.

The same woman from her dream.

Anne dug her nails into her palms, and fissures of pain threaded up her arms. She was truly awake. The ghostly woman who shimmered in the garden was *real*.

Which meant that everything else—Lord Whitney's accusations, the existence of the Devil, Leo's use of magic—all of it was real, too.

"You believe now." The specter's words sounded as though they came from a great distance. The ghost was *talking*. "At last you believe."

"Who . . . are you?" Anne hoped that the ghost would not answer, for that meant it was not sentient, and did not truly converse with her.

"Valeria Livia Corva," said the specter, killing Anne's hope. "Livia, as I am known. We have met before, as well you know. Now my strength has grown. Thus, I appear before you—though time is fleeting." She took a step—or rather, floated—closer. "Come, there is much to do."

Anne edged backward. "Leave. Go away. I don't want you here."

The ghost frowned. "What is this delay? The battle is nigh, I have given you the weapons you need. We must act. *Now.*"

"None of this makes sense." Moving farther back, Anne felt the edge of the stone bench against her legs. It was all so similar to her dream, but she was assuredly not asleep, much as she wished that to be so. "Whatever it is you want of me, I won't do it."

Livia scowled. "Are you *his*, then?"

"I'm no one's."

"There is no neutrality. A side must be chosen." Her hands made patterns in the air, and Anne bit back a yelp of surprise when a glowing image appeared, hovering in the space between her and the ghost.

She stared at the image, eyes wide. There stood Leo, and all of the Hellraisers, in the same temple of which Anne had dreamt. And there was the elegant, diamond-eyed man, receiving small objects from each of the men, including her husband.

"Reckless men." Livia's mouth twisted. "They transformed themselves from merely debauched to truly wicked, the enemies of virtue and honor. Gained magic, yet lost their souls."

The same magic of which Lord Whitney spoke.

"The pact is written upon your husband's flesh," said the ghost.

"Leo keeps his skin covered." She had foolishly thought the cause was discomfiture over birthmarks or disfigurement.

Livia's smile was pitiless. "Hiding evidence of his crime."

Anne assembled the pieces: Leo's infallibility with investments, everything that had transpired with her father. His refusal to let her see his bare skin. She felt ill. More than an illness of her body, but a sickness down to the depths of her soul. The only man she ever loved was a fiend.

"Leo is . . . damned?"

The ghost spoke brutally, coldly. "The world is damned with him. Gaining souls, the Dark One's power strengthens. His influence spreads like plague."

"The riot," Anne murmured to herself. She *had* seen creatures in the theater, demonic beasts. Leo must have seen them, too, for he had tried to get them out of the theater before the creatures could strike. He knew. He *knew.* He was part of that madness, perhaps even the engineer.

"A foretaste of what is to come," answered Livia. The image of the Hellraisers shifted, becoming a hellish landscape of flame and destruction. It was London. Fire engulfed the city, consuming Saint Paul's Cathedral, Buckingham House, Westminster Bridge. People ran to flee the inferno, whilst others looted and committed horrible acts. And demonic creatures swarmed the streets and skies, turning London into a true hell on earth.

Leo would make that happen.

The specter waved a hand, and the images of a destroyed London mercifully vanished. "Our magic is the fortification, but we must take up arms at once. I have given you the power once belonging to the Druid sorceress. Her magic I stole for my own selfish use, but it is yours now."

Anne did not know anything of Druid sorceresses. Shaking her head, she said, "I've no magic."

Livia's mouth curved. "You make this assertion? Daily, you have seen evidence."

"The candles," Anne whispered. "The fire." It had begun the morning after her dream. When alone, she could not keep a fire lit. Candles guttered and went out. Because . . . she possessed magic. She stared down at her hands.

Power within *her*? Magic. She reached into herself, searching. Surely she could feel it, if magic imbued her body.

She gasped, for there, faint but true, came the flutter of power in her veins, tucked into the secret corners of herself. A cool, blue energy swirled like currents of wind.

"Such a spell comes with a cost. Not until this moment could I appear before you and summon you to battle. Yet I am here now, and you are ready." The ghost hovered nearer, her expression determined, merciless.

Anne's pulse beat thickly in her throat, and she could barely speak. "I do not . . . how can I . . ."

"I have *armed* you, and yet you still require me to devise the battle's plan? Can you not formulate your own attack?"

Anne felt the blood leach from her face. "I won't harm Leo."

"The greater good demands—"

"No." The ground beneath Anne shifted as her head

spun. Her life had become a nightmare. The Devil. Magic. Doom. "I chose none of this."

"It has chosen *you*, fragile mortal." Livia scoffed. "This female has none of the strength of the other, the girl of flame. Oh, for a better ally."

"I am *not* your ally. I am nothing."

"That is of a certain, should you continue on with your mewling protests. As the world collapses, you shall be burnt alive. And the man you call husband will watch and laugh. The crisis point is here. Either you are my ally, or my enemy. Make your decision *now*."

Anne choked, bile rising in her throat. She staggered forward, then ran toward the house, seeking safety yet knowing that none was to be found.

He raced into the entryway of the house, the cold of early evening spreading an ache through his bones. As Leo handed his greatcoat and hat to the footman, Anne ran into the foyer. She skidded to a stop when she saw him, her face ashen, eyes wide and dark.

Leo understood at once. Wordlessly, he stepped forward and took hold of her wrist, then strode up the stairs, pulling her behind him.

She did not speak, either, not until they reached the bedchamber. He closed and locked the door behind them.

The candles sputtered. Went out. Likewise the fire. Darkness enveloped the room, the only light coming from the last remnants of a dying sun.

In her pearl-gray gown, Anne made a pale shape, a ghost of herself. She kept nearly the whole of the chamber between them, as if holding herself out of striking distance.

"The Roman priestess," he said, toneless, "she spoke with you."

A choked sob broke from her. "Then it's true." She

turned away, pressing her hands and forehead against the wall behind her. "I kept hoping, wishing. God, this cannot be happening."

He stared at the slim, straight lines of her back, his gaze tracing down the heavy pleat of fabric that ran from her shoulders to the floor. "It began long before we ever met."

She made another strangled, wounded sound, and it pierced him straight through. "The whole time you courted me," she said, "knowing I was to be your wife. Knowing you would bring me into *this*. Leo, what have you done?"

"You don't understand." Now that this moment was at hand, he felt hollow, bereft. A man facing the ruination and loss of everything. It slipped from his grasp, no matter how tight he clutched at it. He wanted to crush her to him, bind her close.

She whirled to face him. "*Make* me understand."

A tap sounded on the door.

"Get the hell out of here," Leo roared.

"Sir," said the footman on the other side of the door, "I'm sorry, he said it was urgent and must speak with you immediately."

Leo stalked to the door and threw it open. "Send the bastard away, whoever he is. And if you disrupt me and my wife again, I will throw you out of my damned house."

"Yes, sir." The servant gulped. "Only . . . he said I was to give you this." He held out his hand. A ribbon encrusted with dried mud lay curled in his palm.

Anne's ribbon. From the riverbank earlier that day.

Leo stared at it for a moment. "Where is he?" he asked tightly, pocketing the ribbon.

"He told me he'd wait in your study, sir."

Leo drew a breath. He could not leave Anne now, but this had to be attended to. "Tell him I'll be down presently."

The footman nodded, looking relieved that his job was not at risk, and hurried away.

Turning back to face the darkness of the bedchamber, Leo looked for Anne. She was pressed into the corner of the room, preserving the distance between them.

"I'll return," he said. "A few minutes only."

"You cannot leave." Her voice was thin, strained. "Not *now*."

"This is important."

She made a disbelieving laugh. "So is this."

He was racked between necessity and longing, wanting to stay, yet knowing that he could not. "I have to go."

"Leo—"

Before she could convince him otherwise, he turned and strode from the bedchamber. He hastened down the stairs, then along the corridor, until he reached his study. Leo opened the door.

Waiting for him was not Whit, as he had expected. The man who stood before the fire, glowering at him, was *him*. Save for the clothing he wore, the man was identical to Leo in every way, from his size, face, hair and eye color, to the way he stood, balanced lightly on the balls of his feet as if readying for an attack. Leo's double.

"My master is extremely displeased," the man snapped.

He wasn't a man at all. It was his *geminus*.

Everything made a terrible sense now. Everything became clear. He understood what he must do.

Leo stepped inside and shut the door behind him.

"The situation is intolerable." The *geminus* strode toward him, its face contorted with anger.

But its face was Leo's face, and he knew in that moment how it must feel to be on the receiving end of his rage. Torn between fascination and horror, he stood his ground as the creature who was his exact likeness paced nearer. No wonder so few ever opposed him—in the full of his anger, he appeared utterly merciless.

And so he had been. In almost all aspects of his life. Anne remained the lone exception.

Thoughts of her spurred him on now.

"The situation isn't intolerable," he said, his voice cutting. "It's ending."

The *geminus* halted its advance. Its mouth twisted. "You made a bargain, and you will honor that bargain."

"Honor? Poor choice of words, coming from you."

The *geminus* glowered. "And a word of which *you* are unfamiliar. Have you not profited, and well, from the advantage my master bestowed upon you? Is not all of this"—it waved its hands at the study, the shelves of books, the expensive carpets, the heavy desk of imported wood—"the culmination of your power?"

"I don't need the Devil's magic to succeed." Nearly everything in the house, and the house itself, had been purchased before Leo had received his gift.

"Mark me well, *mortal*," the *geminus* spat, "it is a small matter to my master to take all of this away from you. *Everything* can be taken away."

Leo tensed. "What the hell are you threatening?"

"Precisely. Hell." Seeing that it had Leo's complete attention, the creature smirked. "My master does not tolerate sedition within his ranks. Sever ties with Lord Whitney. Should you see him again, kill him. And bring your wife to heel. You are her lord and master. Bend her to your will."

Leo hated having anyone tell him what to do. Yet fury warred with fear. "If I don't?"

The *geminus* moved to the fire, then reached into the flames. Leo hissed as searing pain blazed up his left hand and arm, and as he stared at his hand, the skin reddened and blistered. Turning back to face him, the *geminus* held a tongue of flame in its palm.

Leo stared as the flame grew larger, hovering above the *geminus*'s hand. The flames shifted, forming shapes out of fire. Figures emerged. His house appeared, only to tumble down into a smoking ruin. Yet he did not truly feel terror until Anne's likeness appeared in the flames. A host of demonic creatures attacked, and he could do nothing but watch as the beasts dragged her away toward a ravenous abyss.

"Goddamn you." He snarled, striding nearer.

The flame and images vanished from the *geminus*'s grasp. Pain receded by bare degrees from Leo's hand, but rage and horror sank talons into him.

"Damn *you*," the *geminus* corrected. "That is a given. Yet you shall damn *her*, as well, if my master's will is disobeyed."

Fury poured through Leo, white-hot. Most of it directed at himself.

He'd been stubbornly heedless, convinced of his own supremacy. A bloody thick-headed fool. To think that *his* gain outweighed any consequence, that nothing mattered but *his* advancement and the destruction of those he saw as his enemies.

And to drag Anne down with him . . .

It was insupportable. He clenched his hands into fists. "Do not threaten her."

The *geminus* gave an ugly laugh. "What leverage have you? My master's power is vast, and yours a trifle by comparison."

"But your power is not so great." Leo stalked to the *geminus* and wrapped his hand around its throat. He squeezed tightly.

And felt himself choking.

His fingers uncurled from the creature's throat. The moment he released it, his own breath returned.

Both he and the *geminus* panted and coughed, and the creature wheezed, "No business investment . . . is undertaken without . . . insurance." Regaining more breath, it chuckled. "I am made from you. The other side of your coin. Hurt me in any way, and you hurt yourself."

Black swam in Leo's vision. He despised being backed into a corner, but the one who had put him in this position was himself. The architect of his own plight.

The *geminus* became all solicitousness. "Come, it needn't be antagonistic between us. If you but heed my master's command, your rewards will increase tenfold. You may enjoy a life superior to a king or emperor. And your wife shall be your empress. No harm shall come to her. Nay, she will thrive, and bear you fine, healthy sons—each of them destined for greatness unparalleled. Is that not a fair bargain? To gain so much, and for such a small cost."

"Bring Anne under my control," Leo recited, "and cut ties with Whit."

"Your rewards would be handsome, if you were to eliminate Lord Whitney. Say, lure him into your confidence, and so dispatch him."

"Let's speak plainly. You want me to kill him."

The *geminus* smiled at Leo, and the uncanniness of being smiled at by himself made his gut clench. "Ah, my master always did enjoy your directness. So, have we reached an accord?"

"I—"

The door to the study banged open, and the fire sputtered. Anne stood at the threshold.

"Leo, send your visitor away. We must talk—" Her words died as she looked past him to the *geminus*. Color leached from her face. "Oh, my God."

"Hello, my dear," murmured the *geminus*. "At last I have the pleasure of meeting you."

What she saw before her was impossible. Leo in the study. Not Leo, singular, but two identical men, both of them not merely *resembling* her husband, but *were* her husband. Save for their difference in dress, the men in the study were mirror images of each other.

He had no twin brother. This she knew.

Then who, or *what*, was this other man?

Her gaze darted back and forth between the men. One was dressed in the same clothing she had seen Leo wearing throughout the day—dark brown coat, waistcoat of green wool, buff breeches tucked into tall, glossy boots—and the other was clad in a gentleman's bronze velvet ditto suit, the buckles on his shoes clearly not paste. Aside from these surface differences, she could not tell the men apart.

No—that wasn't true. One looked at her with agony in his storm gray gaze, the other smiled at her, but his eyes revealed a profound, bitter coldness, as if she were no more than a grub found wriggling through the flour.

"What is this?" she rasped.

"A fortuitous encounter," said the Leo in velvet. God, even his voice was the same, with the barest hint of a rough accent in the hard consonants. He took a step toward her. "If I may—"

The other Leo moved to block his path, his face darkening in fury. "Don't bloody touch her."

The cold one smirked. "We have already proven that your threats hold no weight. I was merely going to suggest—"

"Suggest *nothing*." The rage in this Leo's face outpaced the vengeful wrath she had seen from him in the riot at the theater. And it terrified her as her mind struggled to understand what she saw before her.

He turned back to her. "Anne," he said gently, the way one might speak to a frightened horse, "it's me. Your husband. Leo."

"Then who is *he*?"

His mouth tightened. "My *geminus*."

"I don't know what that is."

"You're a clever girl," drawled the other Leo, the *geminus*. "Surely you can hazard a guess. Only consider: I came into being one very eventful night three months ago."

According to Livia, that was when Leo and the other Hellraisers made their pact with the Devil, exchanging tokens for their sinister magic. This *thing* sprang into existence from that exchange. Looking at it now, she saw in its wintry gaze the most malevolent parts of Leo—rage, contempt, hatred. Drawn forth from him, and given flesh.

"It's you." She stared at her husband, who stared back with anguish. She could only imagine she looked equally ravaged. "Your dark counterpart."

"Ah, you *are* clever." Yet the *geminus* looked far from pleased by this notion.

Anne's hand rose to her throat. "God, Leo, what have you done?"

"What I thought I must," he rasped.

The *geminus* clicked its tongue. "Let us not stray from the subject at hand. Now that you are here, we may as well discuss vital matters." It attempted to move closer to her, and again, Leo lunged into its path, blocking its advance.

"I said, *Don't. Bloody. Touch. Her.*"

The heat and violence of his words made Anne edge back. She had never seen Leo this angry, and his rage was a terrible thing, savage as a blood-maddened wolf. Everything became a peril, especially the man she knew as husband. What did he want from her? What would he do? Anything was possible, and all of it awful.

She needed safety. She had to run away, to protect herself. As her emotions churned, energy gathered within her, a swirling maelstrom collecting throughout her body, potent and blue.

Leo turned to her, his expression torn between fury and desperation. "Anne, please—" He took a step toward her, one hand outstretched.

"No!"

Anne flung her own hands out, warding off an attack. As she did so, she felt the energy within her release, pouring out of her in a furious gale. Both Leo and the *geminus* flew backward, pushed away on a current of violent air *that came from her hands.*

The *geminus* slammed into the desk. Leo careened into the bookcase lining the far wall. Both groaned at the hard impact, then fell to the floor, sprawling on the carpet.

Anne stared down at her hands in horror, then at the two figures lying upon the floor. She had done that. Pushed them both away using a power that came from within her. *Madness.*

Leo groaned again. He pushed himself up onto his hands and knees. Raised his head to look at her. The pain etched into his sternly handsome face made her want to go to him, comfort him, and she was appalled at herself.

"Anne," he rasped.

She turned and fled.

She did not know where she ran. She knew only that she must run far. Put the whole nightmare behind her, as if, by the motion and momentum of her body, she could outpace the truth. The truth that scoured her with its ghastliness.

My husband is in league with the Devil.

Anne ran through the streets of Bloomsbury, past elegant homes and leafy parks. Night covered the city, and lamps threw out fitful light. As she passed, the lamps extinguished. Linkboys' torches sputtered. Even candles she espied through windows guttered and died as she ran by. She sped into darkness.

London became a city of deepest shadow, the city in which she had spent almost her entire life made strange and frightening. Every face she passed seemed to be Leo's, or some demonic creature. She remembered the things she thought she had seen in the riot, the fiendish beasts in the crowd. Those had been real, and even now, they could be out here, searching for her.

Running, she passed a group of men.

"Where are you going, madam? Are you in distress? Shall I fetch a constable?"

She shied away from outstretched hands, seeing clutching grasps, and raced on. Those men could be disguised demons. They could be men also in confederation with the Devil, their words of supposed kindness a trap.

She had no means of protecting herself. Not from the demons. Not from Leo. And not from herself. Something lived within her, a power she did not understand.

Winded, her stays a hard cage that crushed the breath from her, Anne stopped in an empty square and struggled for air.

Her head spun. Where could she go? With whom could she seek refuge? Not her parents. Numerous acquaintances were scattered throughout, in Marylebone, in Soho and Saint James's. The idea that she could sit in someone's parlor and explain to them that her husband had made a compact with the Devil, thus creating a sinister double of himself, and she had to flee for her very life—if she wound up in chains at Bedlam, she ought to consider herself fortunate.

Where, then? When she had not a single ally.

Ally.

Lord Whitney. He had known all along. Had tried to warn her. She must go to him; he would help.

You shall find me and Zora at the Black Lion Inn, in Richmond.

She fought to get her bearings in the darkness. She might be in Mayfair, if the impassive, towering buildings around her were any indicator. Her heart sank. Richmond stood miles away to the west, past Hyde Park, past Kensington, past even Chiswick—on the other side of the river.

Coin to pay for her journey she had none. A bitter irony, considering the number of coins she had procured for Leo.

Coins. Leo had asked her to obtain them for him. Could it be that he needed them to utilize his magic to prophesize? She remembered that he'd demanded a coin from her father before making the mining investment. If that was true . . . She had *helped* him. Abetted his use of evil power. And like a spaniel eager to please, she had done it.

Nausea roiled through her. He had used her. Deceived her. She had done it to make him happy, never knowing to what wickedness she contributed.

It wasn't all for Leo's benefit, whispered a voice deep within her. *You* liked *playing tricks on those disdainful, pompous women. You* enjoyed *it.*

She shoved that traitorous thought from her mind. It did her no favors, not now. Easier, simpler, to think of Leo as the villain and herself the wronged innocent.

What she needed was to reach Richmond, and Lord Whitney. Leo might be in pursuit of her. She could not dally.

Holding her aching side, Anne turned toward what she hoped was west and ran. Yet she was a lady, little used to running, and her slippers were meant for soft carpets or gleaming parquet floors, not rough pavement and cobblestones. She might as well have foolscap strapped to her feet for all the protection her slippers gave her. So her progress crept along, as she kept slowing to catch her breath and to ease off her throbbing feet.

London seemed infinite, the night equally huge. Every dark shape made her jump. Each rustle of wind through the elm leaves caused her heart to pound. She was sick, and weary, and terrified, and she despaired of ever arriving at Richmond.

Prayers were sent up to whatever deity might be listening, that she could reach Lord Whitney, and soon.

Anne stumbled down the road, until she found herself at the edge of a large grassy plain, a pitiless, colorless moon overhead illuminating paths, trees. A trio of buildings formed fanciful shapes against the sky, including a tower that soared high above the grass, a series of curiously roofed structures stacked one atop the other. Moonlight gleamed off its green-and-white-tiled roof. She realized at once where she was: the Royal Botanic Gardens at Kew. The tower was the Pagoda, built recently, and distantly she espied the domed roof and minarets of the Mosque. The Alhambra and its extravagant latticed railing and cupola made up the third structure.

It was all so deliberately, obstinately whimsical—buildings designed to be novelties, things meant for the enjoyment of London's pleasure seekers, whose lives never touched the kind of horror that Anne now faced.

She hated those buildings, their playful indifference. A bitter desire clutched her; she wanted to burn them down, laugh at their ashes.

Instead, she staggered toward them. Though her heart urged her to keep running, her body demanded rest, and she needed out of the cold. She tottered inside the Alhambra, shadows dulled its brightly painted arches and columns. Only when she sank down onto the ground, her legs unable to bear her weight any further, did she at last give in to tears.

Chapter 14

He heard her footsteps racing down the hallway and the front door open. She ran from him. Leo tried to stand, to force his legs to follow, but dizziness overwhelmed him. He felt the twin pain of being thrown not just against the bookcase, but the hurt of the *geminus* as it was flung against the desk. The creature lay on the floor, unmoving.

He could not believe the power that had come from her, sudden and unknown. *She threw me and the* geminus *across the room.* His surprise knew no limits.

Blackness swam in his vision. He tried to push it aside, as he pushed all obstacles out of his path. In this, though, his body overruled his will, and he slumped to the floor.

"Sir? Sir?" Munslow gently shook him. Leo opened his eyes to see a pair of polished but well-worn buckled shoes. "Shall I fetch a physician, sir?"

Leo sat up, groaning. Munslow stood close by, gazing down at him with a worried frown, whilst more servants gathered in the doorway of the study, peering in like curious birds.

Turning his throbbing head to look at his desk, Leo saw that the *geminus* was gone. He tried to focus on the clock on the mantel, but his head spun.

"My wife," he rasped.

The head footman shot an anxious glance over his shoulder, toward the other servants. A girl Leo recognized as Anne's maid shook her head.

"Gone, sir."

"How long?" Leo forced himself to standing, his whole body aflame, his head aching.

Munslow could only offer a shrug.

Leo pushed past him and the gathered servants as he staggered from the study. He barely heard Munslow's calls to him, the nervous offers of bringing in a physician. As he lurched up the stairs, he shouted, "Have my horse saddled and ready to ride."

"Sir?"

"Do it." Leo gained the top of the stairs. His head still pounded, but the floor became steadier, and he ran into the bedchamber.

He would not allow himself to look at the bed, to think about the life shared between him and Anne that now lay in ruins. He had an aim, a purpose; he would not falter.

Her clothespress. He strode to it and threw open the doors. Gowns of every color and fabric lay in neat arrangement. They carried the sweet fragrance of her body, the echo of her shape. Plunging his hand between the gowns, his fingers brushed against smooth cotton, the pleats of ribbons.

The room around him vanished. He found himself in a darkened pavilion, though the night could not fully disguise the brightly painted arches and columns. And there, on the ground, curled into a ball—Anne.

The vision dissolved. Once more, he stood in his own bedchamber, and Anne was gone.

If ever he had been glad of his Devil-begotten power, nothing compared to his appreciation for it now. For without it, he would never know where to find his wife, and this was his lone aim. Without her . . .

No. He refused to think of it. Instead, he ran back downstairs to the study. There, he loaded his brace of pistols, then slipped them into shoulder-belt holsters and slung the whole of it across his chest. His primed hunting musket hung across his back. Into the top of his boot, he sheathed a knife. Damn that he could not carry a sword. Any means of attack or defense, he would use—he would never use them against Anne, but London after dark was not safe, now worse than ever. The riot at the theater remained lodged in his brain like a thorn.

He started to stride from the room, but froze in his tracks when he saw the *geminus*. Not the *geminus*, he realized, but his own reflection in a glass. The man who stared back at him bore no resemblance to the wealthy businessman he had fashioned for himself. His hair undone, his expression wild and fierce, heavily armed, he looked every inch the brute the aristocrats claimed him to be. Good. Now was not the time for aping the manners of the gentry. Now was for survival, for reclaiming what he had foolishly lost.

He left the study. His saddled bay gelding waited for him outside his house. Leo snatched the reins from the groom and, without a word, kicked the horse into a gallop.

Tearing through the streets of Bloomsbury, bent low over the horse's neck, he saw nothing but the roads ahead. Each beat of his mount's hooves was the pound of his heart. Fear and anger and need clawed at him. Nothing in his mind made sense, only the single directive: *Find her, find her.*

It took too long, but eventually the vast shadowed expanse of Kew Gardens rose up before him. He'd come here before on a rare daylight expedition with the other Hellraisers, yet they had not tarried, for artificial ruins and ornamental follies held no interest for men such as they. Far better were the pleasure gardens of Vauxhall and Ranelagh. Now Leo sent up a fervent prayer of thanks that he had come to Kew, for he knew precisely where to find his fleeing wife.

He galloped up to the Alhambra and flung himself down from the saddle. With long strides, he sped into the building, terror thick in his throat, shortening his breath. He found Anne still curled on the ground, eyes closed. Another spike of fear stabbed him. Was she hurt? Worse?

But he saw her shudder, and her own breathing came in a low, frantic rhythm. Trembling movement flickered behind her eyelids. She slept. Only then did he gain the ability to draw air into himself again. Relief poured through him, sending his head spinning once more. He thought he might black out again, but he forced himself to remain standing.

His boots echoed sharply beneath the vaulted ceiling as he took a step toward Anne.

She came instantly awake. And when she saw him, saw his face and the weapons he carried, she sat up and scrambled backward on her hands.

He thought he understood pain of every variety. Physical, he had felt many times in his life, in brawls and fights. Whit's rapier in his shoulder. The body-jarring agony of being slammed into a bookcase. And burying his father had reduced him to spending weeks at the bottom of a decanter, as he fought to think of life without the massive presence of Adam Bailey.

Yet none of those moments of pain could ever match what he felt as Anne now looked at him with fear and despair. The misery of betrayal shone in her eyes like poison in a fresh mountain lake. And the poison burned him from the inside out.

"Anne—" He took a step toward her.

"Don't come near me." She flung up her hands, and a gust of cold air buffeted him.

They both stared at her hands as she lowered them. She, with wide-eyed shock, and him warily.

"That is . . . new," he said, cautious.

She continued to gaze at her upturned hands. "The Roman woman. She gave me this somehow."

"Tonight."

"Weeks ago. I never understood, never truly knew. Until this night." Her tortured gaze rose to meet his. "So many impossibilities I learned tonight. Things I did not want to believe."

A beam of moonlight silvered her face, the tracks of dried tears on her cheeks, and his heart wrenched. Seamless, this pain, stretching from her to him in an unbroken band.

"I've come to learn this world is far more treacherous than I ever understood." His mouth twisted. "And this world has ever been my enemy."

"Is that why you did it? Why you made that bargain? Because you see everyone as an enemy?" Her eyes were gleaming and fierce.

Leo clenched his jaw. "He offered me what I wanted most. Power."

"*He* being the Devil." A rasping laugh broke from her. "I cannot believe I am saying these things. And that they are true."

"What would you do?" Leo threw back. "When presented with everything you ever desired?" He stepped closer, hot anger and fear pulsing through him. "*None* of us are pure and virtuous. If someone appears before you and offers you your heart's deepest want, you take it. Just as the Hellraisers did. Just as I did."

She pushed herself up to standing, and it was all he could do to keep himself from helping her to her feet. "But the *cost*, Leo. A businessman knows you cannot get something for nothing. You taught me that."

Heat spread along his back. He felt a burn also climb up his calf. "We didn't consider the cost."

"Your soul."

"And more." He continued to close the distance between them. As he neared, he saw the dirty hem of her gown, and the tips of her tattered slippers. She had run far from him, fragile as a moth wing. Yet she still stood before him, her chin tilted up, shoulders back. The delicate girl he wed had transformed into this storm-tossed but defiant woman. If he could claim even a dram of her strength as his doing, he might congratulate himself. He was in no humor for congratulations. Not when seeing the betrayal in her eyes left him bleeding and raw.

"You." His gaze pinned her in place. "It cost me *you*."

She swallowed hard. "Everything between us is lies. From the beginning, nothing but deception."

"Both of us were strangers to each other. But yes," he acknowledged, "I played you false. Not with another woman, but with my secrets."

"And made me part of them," she fired back. "The coins."

Shame burned him, bitter and acidic. "Yes."

"You *knew* how much I wanted to please you, and you used that. Used me."

Only barely did he keep his head from dropping in remorse. "I did. Whatever advantage I could seize, I did so gladly."

"*I* was your advantage. Your aristo wife." Her words were knives, cutting him to pieces as he stood. It surprised him that his blood did not splash upon the gaudily painted columns, bright red against the blue.

"So you were. But not anymore."

She stared at him. The anger tightening her face warred

with the sorrow in her eyes, the profound agony of betrayal. "What am I now? An inconvenience. An obstacle on your determined path."

He drew still closer, until a distance of a few feet separated them. "You are my wife." Within his chest, his heart hammered, forging words he must speak. He drew a breath. "I love you."

Briefly, far too briefly, wonderment blazed in her gaze, but she banked it, and turned away. Her voice was a wintry rasp. "*Damn* you."

"I *am* damned," he said. "But not from the loss of my soul."

She gave him her profile. "There's no profit in plying me with honeyed words, Leo. You have magic. You have wealth and power. Everything you want is yours."

"I don't have you."

"An acquisition."

"My *wife*. The woman I love."

Her hands flew up to cover her ears. "Stop it! I knew you were ruthless, but I never suspected you to be cruel."

He stepped around her until they faced each other. Gently, he pulled her hands down, and he felt the wild rush of her pulse beneath his fingers, the fact of her body was both a poem and torture—this living woman, this mortal creature who made him love and made him fearful, who made him strong and made him vulnerable.

"Not cruelty," he said. "The truth."

"There is nothing you can say that I will believe." She tugged her hands away. "You made certain of that."

He winced inwardly. "Hear this. Whether you choose to believe it or not. The power given to me by the Devil, the wealth created by it, everything I've gained since I made that bargain . . ." He steadied himself. "I renounce the lot."

For a moment, she only stared at him. "Renounce."

"All of it." His words grew bolder as he spoke, as conviction strengthened. "It means nothing to me. Only one thing, one *person*, I want. You."

Her eyes widened. "You would give it all up . . . for me."

"Yes," he said immediately.

Yet she shook her head. "How badly I want to believe you."

"If it means spending the rest of my life destitute, performing penance, I'll do it." A corner of his mouth tilted up. "When there's something I want, I'm a tenacious bastard."

She did not return his smile. If anything, she looked more agonized, a woman on the rack. "I wish I did not love you."

Savage primal pleasure coursed through him, even as he burned. She loved him. In all his life, he never expected it, never thought it could be his. Yet to have *her* love him, her out of all women . . . such wealth he could not fathom. And he would seize it, for he was greedy for her.

"But you do," he said. "Just as I love you." He needed her mouth, her taste.

She saw his intent as he stepped closer. Want and fear mingled in her eyes. She tried to dart around him, making for the way out, but he moved quickly. His hand shot out to grip hers.

His fingers brushed against her ring. Images suddenly besieged him—creatures of foul shape, with leathery wings, jagged long teeth, curved claws, and yellow eyes. He could smell the rot of their flesh, hear their shrieks of hatred.

"Stay." He shook his head to clear away the images.

She pulled hard on her hand, trying to free herself. "Is this how it's to be? Using force to keep me?"

"Hate me if you have to. But don't go outside." He drew one of his pistols.

She froze in place. "Why? What's out there?"

Then the shrieks sounded, not merely in a vision, but here. And now.

Two creatures darted into the building. For a moment, Anne could only stare, for these were the beasts of a fever dream—grotesque fiends that had vaguely human shapes, with monstrous faces and horns. Serrated teeth crowded their mouths, and instead of hands and feet, they had claw-tipped talons. Ash-colored skin, sticky yellow eyes alive with rage.

Demons. She looked upon actual *demons*.

And they wanted her and Leo dead.

The demons rushed toward them, their claws scraping at the painted floor. Fear tightened her throat. She looked around wildly for something to use as a weapon.

"Behind me." Leo roughly shoved her back, putting himself between her and the advancing creatures. Fluidly, he drew his pistols, aimed. Fired. The powder exploded in a flash, filling the pavilion with two loud booms.

One of the beasts immediately crumpled to the ground, a hole in the center of its forehead. The other screamed and stumbled, then lurched to its knees. It clawed at the wound on its shoulder, black blood pouring down its arm.

Leo flipped the pistol in his left hand, holding it by its barrel. He rushed forward. His arm swung out as he clubbed the demon with the heavy butt of the gun. The creature toppled back, lashing out with its talons.

Anne winced as the demon's claws caught Leo across the thigh, but he made no sound of pain, did not hesitate in his movements. He swung the pistol again. It slammed into the beast's head, and the demon shrieked in outrage. Claws striking out, it tried to fend off Leo's attack, but Leo was relentless, wielding the pistol like a brutal club. He bared his teeth, savage, as he struck the demon. Again and again.

She had no love for the creature, but she turned away as its thick blood splattered on the ground and Leo's clothes and face. Its screams came fainter, wetter, subsiding into a gurgle. Then it fell quiet.

Turning back, she saw Leo standing over the body, his face dark with fury. Blood everywhere. He looked wild and fierce, terrifying and unquestionably male. Her heart seized, partly in fear, partly in amazement. She barely recognized the man she had married. And yet this seemed his truest self, standing over his fallen enemy.

His gaze rose and met hers. She saw it in the savagery of his storm gray eyes: he had just killed for her. This wasn't the first time, and it would not be the last.

He holstered his pistols, then held out a hand for her. Despite, or perhaps *because of,* what she had just seen, she hesitated.

"There will be more." His voice was chipped obsidian. "We must leave."

"Why have they come?"

His face became a hard mask. "Because I've turned my back on the Devil. I'm no longer his bondsman, but his enemy."

Anne gaped at him. She did not know what to think. Could he be telling the truth? He had woven so many lies, choking them both in the shroud of deceit. Burying them alive.

Instinct forced her to move. If physical safety could be found anywhere, at this moment, nowhere was as safe as being at Leo's side. She hurried forward and took his hand, knowing full well that she could trust him with the safety of her body but not her heart.

He looked down at their joined hands. His jaw tightened,

his expression enigmatic. And then they were hurrying outside.

Inhuman screams sounded in the night, the noise of giant, leathery wings beating the air. Anne pressed back as four winged demons swooped down. She clapped her hands over her mouth to silence her reflexive gasp. Only once had she seen beasts like this—in a medieval painting depicting the terrors of Hell. She had shuddered delicately at the painting, grateful that such monsters were not real.

But they were. And they now dove down to attack.

Leo released her hand. In a blur of movement, he took the musket that hung on his back, and aimed it at one of the demons. He fired. The demon screeched, then fell to earth. It lay still upon the ground as its blood coated the gravel path.

"Three left," Leo muttered. He glared at his firearms. "No time to reload. Damn me for not being a soldier. If Bram were here . . ."

Anne knew a well-trained soldier could prime and load a pistol or rifle in a single minute. She had seen demonstrations of the skill. But adept as Leo was, he did not possess this aptitude.

He slung the musket onto his back once more and looked about for another weapon. There was little time, though. The remaining demons saw their compatriot dead and new fury resounded in their shrieks. They dove down, heading straight for Leo.

She had to do *something*. Would that she had a weapon of her own . . .

Anger, fear—they coalesced within her, both cold and hot. She felt it gathering in the labyrinth of her body. Vivid blue energy. It had burst from her when she had no control, in moments of panic. She had thrown Leo across the room with it. Yet it belonged to her, was part of her. A weapon given to her by Livia. She was not so powerless.

Anne fought to summon this power as the demons flew toward her and Leo. She grasped at it, but it was strange and new, slipping from her hold.

One of the creatures dove down, raking Leo's chest with its claws. He grunted in pain and staggered back. The other two, scenting blood, swept low to join the fray.

Fury scoured Anne. And suddenly *there* it was, the power, potent as a storm.

She flung up her hands. Waves of energy poured from her in an arctic blast of air. She muscled for command, her body aching as she fought for control over the magic. It threatened to overwhelm her.

No. She had been powerless before, in so many ways. But no longer.

Gritting her teeth, Anne directed the energy toward the attacking demons. They roared as squalls pushed them back, their wings beating against the ferocious gale. Anne shoved them away from Leo, gaining him distance.

He glanced over at her, brow lifted in surprise. Clearly, he did not expect her to come to his aid.

She could not examine her motivations now. Her heart still bled. But this was a battle they must fight together.

Clenching her teeth, she sent another surge of energy through her body. One of the demons went careening backward into the branches of a nearby tree. Boughs splintered and snapped. A thrill of bloodlust shivered through her. She wanted to hurt these beasts, cause them pain.

Leo bent to load his musket, but he had only gotten as far as pouring powder into the barrel when a demon attacked. Anne moved to push it back with her power, yet Leo acted faster. He gripped the musket's barrel and swung out. The stock slammed into the demon's leg, and the crack of shattering bone echoed over the manicured grass. Whatever foul magic had created these beasts, they still possessed corporeal bodies—muscle and bone. They could still be hurt.

She readied herself to hurl more energy at the demons. Then she fell backward, thrown to the ground by Leo. His body covered hers. A loud crash rang out.

Peering up from beneath the heavy shelter of Leo's body, she saw a thick, jagged tree branch on the ground behind her. The demon she had pitched back into the tree shrieked in frustration as it hovered nearby. Anne glanced back and forth between the branch and the demon. It had hurled it like a spear, intending to hit her. And would have, had Leo not flung her down and shielded her.

It would not have been a scratch, the damage from the thrown bough. The jagged branch would have pierced her chest. Killed her.

Leo rose up onto his elbows, his body a lean weight atop hers. "Hurt?"

She shook her head.

The outraged demons howled. Anne already knew the sound. It meant they planned to strike again. Leo also seemed to recognize the creatures' noises. He rolled off Anne, then helped her to stand.

Shoulder to shoulder, they readied themselves for the next attack.

The three beasts dove down. Anne summoned her magic to push them back. Two could not withstand the force of her energy, flapping hard against the tempest but still finding themselves shoved away. The third was bigger, stronger. She could not hold him back. It swooped close, a terrifying winged force of claw and tooth.

Leo swung at it with his musket, but the demon flew out of reach. They were locked in this dance, back and forth, the demon lunging near, Leo pushing it away as he brandished his weapon.

Anne's glance fell on the gravel path beneath her feet. Her answer.

Swirling her magic, she used the energy's force to scoop up gravel. Then she flung it with all her strength toward the demon. It shielded itself from the onslaught, throwing up its arms to cover its face. But its wings were spread wide. Unprotected.

Gravel tore through its leathery wings. It gave a scream of pain and anger as membranes perforated. It could no longer keep itself aloft. It spun as it crashed to the ground.

Leo wasted no time. He ran to the creature and clubbed it with his musket stock. Over and over. This time, Anne *did* watch as Leo turned the demon's head into a mass of sticky pulp. The creature twitched, then was still.

Infuriated, the final two remaining demons charged. Anne hurled the force of her tempest at them, but the maddened creatures plunged forward. She crouched low as one dipped down, reaching with its taloned feet, and the stink of the thing as it swooped close nearly made her gag. She came out of her crouch to see Leo holding back the other demon, swinging with both his fists and his musket.

The first demon charged her again, and she bit back a hiss of pain as it cut her arm. Leo saw this. His face twisted in fury. He ran toward her, but the other demon held him back, its wings beating at the air, claws slashing.

Terror, exhaustion, and anger all seethed within her. This nightmare world—she wanted nothing more to do with it. Energy coalesced through her limbs, the force of a hundred storms. When the first demon rushed her once more, she let out a primal, furious scream, a battle cry, as she flung out her hands and unleashed the tempest inside.

"I have been lied to, manipulated, betrayed," she said through clenched teeth. "Made fearful. *No more.*"

The beast made a frantic, enraged sound as it fought against the gale. But Anne's wrath could not be contained.

She let everything run riot, letting slip any control she might have possessed. The demon struggled, and then, with a shriek, it was caught on the storm she had created. Like a leaf, it spun on the wind backward. Higher. It clawed uselessly at the air to stop its mad flight. She was unrelenting.

Anne continued to blast the creature with the force of her magic, and it tumbled back through the sky. Toward the nearby towering Pagoda that rose ten stories above the ground. The demon tried to stop its ascent by clinging to a gilded dragon on the corner of one of the Pagoda's roofs. The ornament snapped away, and the demon was flung high, higher. Until it reached the very top of the Pagoda.

It saw Anne's intent and let out one final scream of outrage. She refused to yield. Manipulating her magic, she brought the demon up, then dropped it—directly onto the Pagoda's spire. Skewering the demon. The spire stabbed through its chest, and the creature's dying howl rose up to the dark night sky before trailing away into silence.

The last remaining demon looked to where its compatriot lay dead. It turned panicked eyes to Anne, then to Leo. She reveled in seeing the creature's fear.

With a frightened yelp, it spun around and flew away. Its wings beating against the air, it disappeared into the darkness like the last vestiges of a bad dream.

The dream, however, was quite real. Demons' bodies lay strewn about, becoming only carrion, their inky blood spread on the ground and splattered on Leo's clothing, his face and hands.

In the aftermath of violence, the silence became its own war. Anne felt the magic within her recede, its blue energy a quieting storm, and as it ebbed, she was left shuddering and dizzy. The ground rushed to meet her.

Strong arms wrapped around her, holding her steady.

She caught the metallic scent of blood, the warmth of Leo's body, the fierce beat of his heart.

"I have you," he murmured. "I have you."

She struggled to push away from him.

"Stop fighting me. You haven't the strength to stand on your own."

"Give me time, and I will."

Yet he did not release her, and of their own volition, her arms came up to wrap around his hard, wide shoulders. She leaned against him, raging at herself for allowing this moment of peace. For letting him comfort her. He was the source of her torment, not her solace. Yet the past few hours and the horror of what she had just witnessed left her shaken and stunned.

My God, the things I have done.

"You fought well," he said, his lips against the crown of her head.

"I did not know . . . I could do any of that." She drew in a shuddering breath. "Surprised myself."

"And me."

Yet she did not like the warm humor in his voice. He had no right to it, to the intimacy of such tone and words. For it felt like a blade of ice through her heart. She pushed away again. This time, he let her go.

Even in the darkness, she saw his wounded, wary gaze. But he did not reach for her as she stepped back.

"There will be more." He glanced at the demons' bodies. "This was a test. To know what kind of enemy I am to the Devil."

"*Are* you his enemy?"

His hand brushed against the tears in his coat, revealing deep gouges in his flesh, and the wetness that gleamed darkly on his fingers was both the blood of the demons and his own blood. Her heart contracted painfully to see him hurt.

"This proves that I am." He clenched his hand. "I've forsaken the Devil. He has nothing for me, nothing I want."

"What *do* you want?"

His gaze was level as it met hers. "You."

A throb of longing pulsed through her. She saw how he wanted it to be. He wanted her to run to him. To throw her arms around him and declare that all was forgiven, and they could return to how it had been between them, two strangers finding an unexpected bond.

She wanted the same. But it could not happen. Not in the span of a few hours—if ever.

"It's not so simple."

"Tell me what I have to do. I'll do it." His words were forceful, not a plea but a statement of intent. She almost smiled at this. Leo never saw obstacles—only ways over or around them.

She answered him with the truth. "I do not know."

His jaw tightened, but he did not press her harder. "Where were you going?" When she hesitated, he added on a growl, "I've just killed five demons. That should give you *some* measure of trust."

"Four," she said. "You killed four. *I* killed the fifth." She could hardly believe that she, a woman of genteel birth, who'd never known bloodshed beyond an occasional reading of the *Newgate Calendar*, had not only fought against demons, but actually slew one—and happily.

Leo's mouth tugged into a small smile. "That you did."

"To the Black Lion Inn," she said at last. "In Richmond. Lord Whitney is there. He said . . . he could help, when I was ready."

She waited for Leo's outburst of anger. It did not come. Instead, he nodded tightly. "Whit severed his tie to the Devil. He'll have answers."

"I am glad someone does," she said, weary, "for I've none of my own."

Glancing around, Leo frowned. "Damn horse got spooked and ran off." He planted his hands on his hips. "I've been to the Black Lion. It's less than a mile from here. Have you the strength to walk the rest of the journey?"

She had never known such exhaustion, her limbs made of lead, her head thick and shoulders aching. Yet this was nothing compared to the weight in her chest, a heaviness so profound that she felt as though she observed the whole world from beneath miles of granite. She wanted only to run away and hide, to throw her arms over her head and surrender.

Instead, she took in a breath of cold night air. Straightened her shoulders.

"I am strong enough," she said.

Chapter 15

Cold morning mist lay chill upon the ground and draped the tree branches as Leo and Anne trudged along the road toward the inn. Difficult not to see this mist as a winding cloth, wrapped around the world as it was made ready for burial.

Leo was not a man given to flights of imaginative fancy. He dwelt in the real, the possible. Even when he used his visions of the future, he sought out truths that he might gain more profit, more power. He had never been a poet, nor aspired to be one. Pretty words and fanciful images meant nothing in Exchange Alley. And when he had spoken tender words to Anne, he had been plain, blunt. He could offer only that.

Yet now he saw the frigid morning fog as a shroud, and the thought could not be dislodged.

As he and Anne walked, they passed farmers with carts heading into the city, their wagons loaded with carrots, turnips, chickens, to be sold in Covent Garden or Fleet Market. The farmers looked askance at two obviously well-dressed but filthy strangers plodding wearily down the road. Clicking their tongues at sway-backed jades, the farmers moved past Leo and Anne quickly.

The sun continued to rise, but it offered no warmth. Anne shivered, wrapping her arms around herself.

He held out his arm. "Come. I'll keep you warm."

She shook her head. "I am well."

"Your lips are blue." When she still refused to come nearer, he cursed and, after removing his brace of pistols and musket, whipped off his coat. The movement pulled hot lines of pain through him, his wounds crisscrossing his body, but he ignored this. Instead, after replacing his weapons, he stalked over to Anne and settled his coat over her shoulders. It was dirty and torn, but better than nothing.

She did not thank him, yet at least she kept the coat on, clutching the lapels close. On her, the garment was huge, sleeves hanging down past her knees. She looked so damned fragile, shrunken. Appearances deceived, however. Anne's resilience and courage were an inevitable surprise. He should have known that his genteel bride was so much more than a dainty ornament, or a means of entry into the world of the elite.

He said none of this. Anything he offered her now would be rejected. Yet that did not mean he had given up. Resolve burned hotter and brighter than ever. Someway, somehow, he would make her his again. Even if it took the rest of his life.

Which might not be much longer. The Devil's methods remained cloudy to him, yet he knew with hard-edged certainty that the attack in Kew Gardens was merely the beginning.

He had to find a way to end this.

With that in mind, he resumed his walk toward the inn, though he kept his pace slower, to accommodate Anne's exhaustion and shorter stride.

At last, a two-story building appeared, a painted sign of a black lion swinging over its door. A boy slept in front of the door, waiting to receive travelers' horses. Leo stepped over him and Anne did the same as they went inside.

A man smoking a long-stemmed pipe sat by the fire in the taproom. At his feet curled a large orange cat, slumbering luxuriously. The man raised his brows at Leo and Anne's appearance.

"Lord Whitney," Leo said.

The man appeared as though he might protest divulging this information to such nefarious-looking characters.

Leo set a bag of coins on a nearby table. It jingled heavily.

The man took out his pipe and pointed its stem upward. "Third door on your left."

Leo took the lead as he climbed the creaking stairs, Anne close behind him. They reached the first floor and crept down the corridor, as silently as the aged, protesting floorboards allowed. From behind one door, someone snored. From behind another came the sound of a mattress creaking against the ropes, its rhythm unmistakable.

Anne deliberately did not meet Leo's gaze.

He moved past that door, until he found the one he wanted. Testing the doorknob, he found it locked. Impatient, he wanted to pound the door down, but he also did not want to awaken the entire house. He was just about to knock lightly when the door opened. Just wide enough for a saber blade to jut out, its point touching his throat.

"And a good morning to you, Whit."

The saber lowered. "Step inside. Quickly."

Leo and Anne slipped inside. The door shut and locked behind them. They found themselves in a snug bedchamber, gray in the morning light. Whit stood in the center of the room, bare-chested, wearing only a pair of breeches. No doubt about it, Whit *had* grown thinner these past months, his muscles standing out in stark relief. As if the apathy that had once imbued him had burned away, leaving behind a man lean with purpose.

Movement by the bed drew his attention. Leo had a fleeting impression of white cambric, dark, sleek limbs, and then Zora stood beside her lover. Her black hair lay in thick waves around her shoulders, and her eyes were darker still. And full of fire. She stared at him and Anne warily.

"Can we trust him?" the Gypsy woman asked. As she spoke, small tongues of fire engulfed her hands, throwing light and shadow.

Anne gasped, and even though Leo had seen a display of Zora's power once before, it still made him start, witnessing it again.

Gazing at the lacerations on Leo's body, the bloodstains on his skin and clothes, Whit answered, "Now we can."

The innkeeper fetched coffee and rolls, and his wife brought a basin, a water-filled ewer, and linen towels, all of which were placed upon a table in front of a looking glass. Then, with more coin lining their pockets, the couple scurried out to leave their guests in private.

Zora bandaged the cut on Anne's arm, a task Leo wanted for himself, but his wife's wary gaze held him back. He watched Anne splash water on her hands and face. A simple, domestic act, and one he had witnessed many times at home. But home was far away, and the life they had shared there lost.

For now.

The water was only slightly dirty when it was Leo's turn to bathe. Soon, it turned dark with blood—the red of his own, and the sticky blackness of the demons' blood. He needed to clean the wounds on his body, so he shucked his waistcoat and then his shirt, letting them drop to the floor as he stood at the table.

Anne gasped. He met her gaze in the mirror, saw the horror on her face as she beheld for the first time the markings of flame upon his back.

Shame crawled over him, hot and viscous. An unfamiliar emotion.

"That answers my first question," drawled Whit, leaning against the wall. He had thrown on a shirt, and crossed his arms over his chest. "Your soul still belongs to the Devil."

"How do you know this?" asked Anne. Her voice was thin, tight.

"He had marks much the same on his body." This, from the Gypsy woman. She strolled to Whit and ran a hand over his shoulder, then down his arm. Possessive, her touch, as if laying claim to Whit and his body, and speaking of deepest intimacy. Judging from the flare of heat in Whit's gaze, he welcomed his woman's proprietary touch. "Here, and here."

Leo's gut twisted with want. Not so long ago, he and Anne had touched each other the same way. After the fight in Kew Gardens, he desired nothing more than to hold her tightly, wanted that now, confirming that they had both emerged from the battle alive and sound. He couldn't—not without her fighting him.

"The marks have grown," Whit said. "And they'll do so until you are covered by them."

"What happens then?" Anne pressed.

Leo already knew the answer. "Then I'm his entirely. Irredeemable."

Anne pressed her fingertips to her mouth, her face growing paler still in the watery morning light. Her gaze moved over the markings, and Leo forced himself to hold steady and motionless beneath her perusal.

"There is but one way to prevent that," continued Whit. "To remove the markings completely. You must reclaim your soul."

Bracing his hands on the table, Leo felt tension knotting his muscles, all along his arms and across his back. "I've already renounced the Devil."

Whit studied Leo's wounds critically. "That I can see. But it isn't enough. A man may say a thousand words, make a thousand vows, yet none of it matters in the face of deeds."

"That much, I know." Rather than continue to feel Anne's hurt gaze, Leo busied himself with cleaning and dressing his wounds. He washed them ruthlessly, not sparing himself any discomfort as he scrubbed. Yet he made a poor martyr, for physical pain meant nothing in comparison to the bleeding ache within.

He could not fully reach the lacerations on his back, and struggled to clean them. When Anne approached and plucked the cloth from his hand, he held himself very still. She refused to meet his gaze. But she was gentler than he had been, dabbing at the cuts, and then finally taking strips of linen and wrapping them around his chest and back.

He remained motionless, soaking up her touch, her care. It did not matter that Whit and Zora were in the room, as well. He was aware of only Anne. Her hands, her breath across his skin, the small crease between her brows as she secured his bandages. She felt as close as another mortal being could be, yet impossibly far away. He knew her so well. He knew her not at all.

Turning his head slightly, he saw Whit and Zora watching this small scene. Both wore expressions of pity.

Pity was an emotion he always refused. It was for weakness and those who lacked resolve. Not once in his life had he turned away when the challenge seemed too great. This would be no different.

"Tell me how to reclaim my soul," he said.

"Each *geminus* maintains a vault of souls," began Whit. "Souls it has acquired through nefarious means."

Leo's gut clenched. Robbins had thought he'd seen Leo at Exchange Alley—working late, Robbins had believed. It hadn't been Leo, but his *geminus*. Little did those men of business know that they had, in fact, traded their souls to the Devil. Damning themselves without realizing it.

"*Geminus*," said Anne. Finished with her tasks, she moved away—though he wanted to grab hold of her, he kept his hands ruthlessly at his sides—and perched on the edge of the bed. "That . . . other Leo."

"The dark part of himself created when first the Hell-raisers made our pact with Mr. Holliday," answered Whit. He gave a wry smile. "That's what the Devil likes to be called. The *geminus* serves Mr. Holliday, and holds Leo's soul for its master."

"Then we kill the *geminus*," said Anne.

"Killing the *geminus* means killing Leo," said Whit. "So long as it remains in possession of Leo's soul, any injury or wound it sustains, *he* is hurt, as well."

The memory of pain throbbed through Leo, recalling how he had tried to throttle the creature and nearly choked himself to death. And the injuries the *geminus* incurred when Anne had thrown Leo into the bookcase. Bruises covered his torso, ugly purple beneath the white bandages.

His hurt body only emphasized how gravely, danger-ously wrong he had been, and yes, his pride suffered. *Damned fool*, each laceration and bruise accused. *Blind, arrogant imbecile.*

He held up his shirt, intending to put it back on, but it was tattered and stained. Whit rummaged through a valise until he found a fresh shirt, and tossed it to Leo. Fortunately, they were of a size, and the shirt fit well enough. It provided some cover, yet now that Anne had seen his markings, it felt as though nothing could ever hide the evidence of his hubris, the spectacular failure of his judgment.

"So we cannot kill the bloody thing," Leo bit out. "There must be another way to get my soul back."

"If your *geminus* operates as mine did," said Whit, "then there may be a means of doing so. Within its vault is *your* soul. Should you get into that vault, you can reclaim your soul and the curse is lifted."

"Sounds simple enough," Anne said.

Zora made a huff of sardonic amusement. "*Nothing* is simple, where *Wafodu guero* is concerned."

"For one thing," added Whit, "the vault is not fixed in its location. Zora and I discovered this the hard way in a tavern in Oxford. The vault lies behind any door the *geminus* so chooses. And only the *geminus* may access it. It may open a door, any door, to get inside the vault, but if you try to open the same door, all you will find is an ordinary room."

"But I could force the *geminus* to open the door," said Leo, "then enter right behind it, without the door closing."

"Even if you could force the *geminus* to do that, it has power to keep you from going inside. You will find it impossible to enter."

"Goddamn it." Leo paced, frustrated. "There *must* be a way to get into that vault." He whirled to face Whit. "How did *you* get inside?"

"*I* didn't. Zora did."

"And only then through the use of Valeria Livia Corva's magic," added the Gypsy woman.

Anne straightened. "The ghost?"

"A powerful sorceress, as well," said Whit.

"It was she who gave me this." Zora held up her hands, and flames suddenly danced along her fingertips. She smiled wickedly. "Very useful when fighting the Devil."

"She gave me something, as well." A fast, hard current of cold air gusted from Anne's raised hands. The flames surrounding Zora's fingers guttered and dimmed.

Leo and Whit exchanged glances. "Extraordinary women," Leo murmured.

"The finest that walk this earth." Whit smiled then, his old gambler's smile, full of rakish charm, only now he sought only the favor of his woman, not the cards.

Damned strange to see Anne—quiet, studious Anne who loved maps and known truths—the possessor of magic. Yet fitting, somehow, for it showed outwardly the strength he knew she possessed within. Seeing her fight the demons using her power . . . if he hadn't been battling for his life, and hers, he would have found the sight thrilling.

Even now, it made his pulse race faster, his breath catch. He was *awed* by her.

As she lowered her hands and the summoned wind died down, her gaze met his. She had to see the pride in his eyes, the fullness of his heart, for she gave him the smallest of smiles, and he smiled in return. As though they shared a secret pleasure, a gift only *they* could truly appreciate.

A filament of pleasure gleamed within him. All was not lost. She could be his again.

Then she seemed to remember precisely *why* she had been given this power, and her smile faltered.

It was enough. For the moment. He'd capture any hope. What he needed now was a means of reclaiming his soul. The rest he would seize later.

"Then we require the ghost," he said, turning back to Whit. "Livia. She needs to be here."

Yet Whit shook his head. "She has not appeared to us, not since yesterday. If she showed herself to you recently, it must have tapped her power."

"How long does it take for her to regain her strength?" asked Anne.

Zora shrugged. "A day, two days. When it involves magic, rules and time mean nothing."

Another impediment. Leo took up his pacing. Anne's smile offered him the slenderest of hopes, and he refused to let anything stand in his way. "If she's been fighting against the Devil all this time, she alone holds the most information, the most power. Proceeding without her would be a mistake."

"So, we must wait," said Anne.

Leo forced down a growl. He did not want to wait. Impatience burned him, hotter than any fire. "I want to summon the bloody *geminus* and get this over with."

"The moment you do," warned Whit, "a horde of demons will descend, and *that*"—he nodded toward the pale strips of bandages that showed beneath the shirt Leo wore—"will appear nothing more than kitten scratches in comparison."

Snarling in frustration, Leo slammed his fist into the wall. Fissures in the plaster spread out in jagged lines, and a satisfying pain radiated up his arm, but it did little to ease his anger. He pulled his arm back, ready to strike again.

A strong hand clasped his wrist, stopping him. Whit's hand, with its long gamester's fingers, and the gleaming signet ring that proclaimed him a peer of the realm. Leo wore no such ring, and never would. Yet it did not matter to him anymore. Distinctions such as nobleman and commoner . . . what did they mean in the face not only of eternal damnation, but the loss of the only love he had ever known?

He stared at Whit, this man who had once been a close friend, then an enemy and now . . . an ally.

"You aren't alone in your sentiment," Whit said, empathy in his gaze. "Not long ago, I felt the same way. But battering yourself to jelly solves remarkably little, I have discovered."

"Not that you didn't try," said Zora.

Whit added in a voice low enough to be heard only by Leo, "And such displays can be rather . . . unsettling to those who care about us." He glanced meaningfully toward Anne.

Leo followed Whit's gaze to Anne. She stood beside the bed, her hands clenched, her mouth drawn into a taut line. Concern darkened her eyes and paled her cheeks as she stared at him.

He had done enough to cause her fear. Slowly, he lowered his fist. Whit released his hold, and a sigh seemed to move through the room.

"A wise investor knows when to bide his time," Leo said, gathering calm. "Act too soon, and what could've been a promising venture becomes far too costly. Disastrous, even."

"No help for it, then," said Anne. "Until the ghost, Livia, returns, we've got to wait to make our plan."

Words such as *we* and *our* kindled fresh fires of hope within him. That was all he needed. The slimmest chance, the faintest possibility. He had built empires for himself upon grains of sand. With a few words from his wife's mouth, he had enough to sustain him for the long battle ahead.

Anne lay atop the covers in only her shift, staring at the low-beamed ceiling. Ashen morning light filtered through worn curtains, cracks in the ceiling and the unmistakable gouges from rats in the timbers. Despite her exhaustion, sleep refused to come, so she counted the fissures in the plaster, hoping to lull herself into, if not slumber, then perhaps a stupor.

Yet her mind would not quiet.

After the conclusion had been reached that they must await the reappearance of the ghost, it had been decided that what Anne and Leo next needed most was rest. She had been swaying on her feet, her eyes hot, her body aching. Zora, a woman she knew not at all, had immediately gone to find her a room of her own. And when the Gypsy returned to lead her away, Leo had stared at her hungrily. But he let her go.

Anne was glad of that. She had boiled away the last of her strength, leaving an empty urn, and though her mind demanded that she keep him at a distance, her heart and body craved him—even now.

Rolling onto her side, she watched a fly form obscure shapes in the air as it buzzed across the room. Zora sat on the floor by the window, her legs tucked beneath her. She frowned over what appeared to be a child's primer, and her lips silently, slowly formed the shapes of words.

Anne looked away. The day crept toward its zenith, and sounds of life penetrated the walls. Voices in the taproom. Horses outside. A carriage, a child's cry. They seemed near, and yet distant, echoes from dreams of other lives.

What would the men in the taproom say, were she to hurry downstairs and proclaim that the Devil was real, that magic was real, and she herself possessed it? They would call her mad. And if she demonstrated her new power, they would run away in terror, or perhaps revive the custom of burning witches.

Her mouth tugged in a sardonic smile. Let them try and burn her. She would blow out the flames with a wave of her hand.

Unless they bound her hands. Then she might be burned. Already, she thought she could smell her flesh being charred, flaking away from bone to be borne aloft on currents of heat.

Leo would come to her aid. Shoot them all down, or use his fists to knock them senseless, then cut the ropes binding her to the stake and take her far away to safety.

She shifted onto her back. *No indulging in fantasy, in fairy tales. The world is not so kind as to give us heroes and rescues—not without a price.*

"Unquiet thoughts make for a poor lullaby." Zora spoke softly, her voice smoky and subtly accented.

Anne turned her head to look at the Gypsy. Zora set the primer on the floor and crossed her wrists in her lap. Odd that the Gypsy would choose to sit on the floor rather than the nearby chair, yet she looked perfectly comfortable. Her dark gaze moved over Anne, clever and astute, rich with a worldly knowledge Anne could only envy.

"I hated him, too," Zora murmured.

Anne frowned. "Leo?"

"Whit." The Gypsy shook her head. "That *gorgio* fascinated me, yes, but I knew what he was, what he had done. He'd taken so much from me—my family, my freedom. I wanted nothing to do with him."

"But I thought . . . you seem so very . . . in love." It hurt Anne's throat even to say that word, *love*, yet she had seen the way Lord Whitney looked at Zora, the way he touched her, and there could be no other word to describe it. He would do anything for Zora, and she for him.

Zora's gaze warmed, and her mouth curved into a small, private smile. "Oh, most terribly. Yet he spilled more than a little blood to earn it."

This conversation was stranger than Zora sitting on the floor. Anne did not know this woman. In truth, she and the Gypsy could not be more different. The rings gleaming on Zora's fingers and the ropes of shining necklaces draped across her bosom seemed like emblems of distant, exotic lands.

Yet there was a point of convergence for her and the Gypsy: Hellraisers.

"I don't want Leo's blood spilled." Anne shuddered to recall the angry lacerations over his body.

Zora shrugged. "If, *Duvvel* willing, we survive our task, you won't have to see him again. If that's what you want."

"I don't know what I want." Anne turned to look back at the ceiling. She lay her forearm across her eyes.

"Hard men to love, these Hellraisers." Zora's words were wry, yet tinged with deeper emotion. "Harder still to *not* love them. But I think there is a reason why Livia chose to give magic to you and I."

"Because we might get close to the Hellraisers."

A definite smile sounded in Zora's voice. "Because we're strong."

The door opened. Someone entered the room. Anne did not remove her arm from where it lay. Only one person would come inside—and she knew the purposeful sound of his footfall. He never tiptoed anywhere. Certainly not with her.

"The door was locked," Zora said.

"I had the innkeeper give me another key."

Of course he did. Leo could make anything happen through force of will.

Untrue—he had not made Anne love him. That, she had done all on her own.

"I want to be alone with my wife," he said.

"I don't think she wants to be alone with *you*," answered Zora.

Before Leo could retort, Anne spoke. "It's all right. And I'm certain Lord Whitney would rather have you with him than sitting on the floor in here."

"I left him in the taproom," said Leo.

Anne thought she could hear reluctance in Zora's movements as she rose. But the Gypsy walked quietly from the room, shutting the door behind her.

Anne and Leo were alone.

"Here's some stew and bread." As he said this, she heard a bowl being set down atop a table, and the rich scent of cooked meat and the yeasty aroma of freshly baked bread drifted through the room.

"I've no appetite."

He expelled a breath. "Think what you will of me, Anne, but don't starve yourself out of spite."

Taking her arm away, Anne looked over to where he stood near a small table. Arms crossed, feet braced wide. He had borrowed some of Lord Whitney's clothing—a serviceable green coat and waistcoat, in addition to the shirt, but no stock, so the collar of his shirt fell open to reveal the strong sinews of his neck, the shadow at the base of his throat. Hair wet, undone, and slicked straight back. Yet he had not shaved. Golden stubble lined his cheeks. He was dangerous as a buccaneer, and blade-handsome.

Yearning and need throbbed through her. And sorrow.

"Spite? Is that what this is? Spite?" She sat up, and the room tilted. Truly, weariness took a toll. And, she admitted to herself, hunger. "How very petty of me. To be out of temper when I discover that my husband is in league with the Devil. And had been lying to me for the whole of our marriage. What a dreadful virago I am."

His expression hardened. "Don't," he growled. "Sarcasm doesn't suit you."

"As truth ill becomes *you*."

Snarling in frustration, he dragged his hands through his hair. Anne watched his every movement with a greedy pain. She wished she could despise him. How simple everything might be.

"It was a mistake," he ground out. "A goddamned mistake."

"Putting too much sugar in one's tea is a *mistake*. Giving one's soul to the Devil in exchange for dark magic deserves a grander sobriquet."

He crossed the room in two long strides, until he loomed over her. "You're a woman possessed of a good imagination. Imagine this: You are offered your heart's desire. What you want more than anything in the world. The cost of this gift is never mentioned, only its advantages. All you have to do is hand over the smallest trinket, and you finally possess that which you've always coveted." Anger and need darkened his eyes as he stared down at her. "Imagine it, Anne. Put yourself precisely in that situation and *then* judge me."

She stared up at him. This fierce storm of a man, devastating as a hurricane. She did as he asked; she envisaged herself in his position. Months ago, before she had met him, what might she have wanted so badly? A place of her own. A husband, family.

She *did* have those things, and lost them. Both because of Leo. But to keep them, to keep *him* . . .

The other Hellraisers were men of wealth and aristocratic privilege. Leo had wealth in abundance, but not the proper breeding. She knew so much about him now, how much he craved access into a world that barred him entrance, his pride. His need for acceptance.

All of those things he had been offered. Few could have resisted the temptation. Saints, perhaps, and Leo was far from beatification. God knew *she* was no saint.

"The lies, Leo," she said at last. "All those untruths I swallowed, like a credulous patient gulping poison instead of medicine."

"What was I to tell you? How could I even begin to

broach the topic? 'Lovely day at the Exchange, my dearest, and by the by, I made a bargain with the Devil.'"

She shoved up from the bed, shouldering past him. "Do *not* be flippant about this. You've no right to ridicule me."

He let out a breath. "True. I've only my self-abnegation. And your hatred of me. Both justly earned."

"I don't hate you." She turned to face him.

He brightened, and the hope in his gaze made her heart break all over again.

"I want to despise you." She knew she was being cruel, yet the cruelty was for herself as well as him. "It is not merely the lies you told, but the fact that you deliberately used me. Collecting coins for you. Having me believe I was gratifying some secret wish, a shared confidence for you and I alone. And I was so bloody eager to give you whatever I could. To help forge our wedding vows into a true marriage." She shoved her knuckles into her eyes, forcing back the tears that wanted to fall. When she felt in control of herself again, she let her hands hang down at her sides. "None of it was genuine. Just a manipulation."

He did not look away, did not flinch. Though it was clear that each word she spoke wounded him. Anger drained from his gaze, leaving behind regret and pain.

"True, again." His voice was a harsh rasp. "I used you, Anne. Most grievously. I've no excuse but my own greed. There's naught I can say but . . . I am sorry." He swallowed hard. "From the depths of my heart, I'm sorry."

She wanted to go to him. Comfort him. Never had she seen him in such pain, or with such aching want. Yet she kept herself rooted to the floor, the cool of the warped floorboards chilling her feet.

"I do not know what between us is real. What is illusion." She forced words from her burning throat. "Did you ever care for me, Leo? Or was I simply a puppet?"

He moved stiffly to the window, and braced his hands

on either side of the glass. His distant gaze seemed to barely see anything outside. Cold light carved him into sharp planes.

"At the onset," he began, "my motives were mercenary. Perhaps even more so than one of your typical aristo marriages. I saw you as a key, a way to open doors that had been closed to me. Ours was not a love match."

His words hit her like thrown rocks, yet she anticipated the blows. "That, I know. Each of us gained something from the marriage. It was a business deal. Commodities exchanged." She blinked as a sudden ray of sunlight pierced the gloom and knifed into the chamber. It could not hold out against the clouds, though, and shrank away until only its afterimage remained burned into her sight.

"Still," she continued, "I thought that, in time, we came to share something. Something beyond . . . the boundaries of commerce and trade."

He turned back to her, his expression fierce. "We did. We *do*."

"How can I know? What can I trust?"

"Trust *this*." He stalked across the room to her. She knew his intent, and stayed precisely where she stood.

She thought he would grab her roughly, crush her to him. Certainly his gaze burned and his visage tightened with hunger. But he was not cruel, nor brutal.

Stepping close so that their chests met, he threaded his fingers into her hair, cupping the back of her head with exquisite tenderness. He tipped her head back. Ravenous, reverent, his gaze moved over her face, as if seeking to commit every inch of her to memory. Slight tremors shook his hands, or perhaps it was she who trembled.

He lowered his mouth to hers, brushing his lips across hers, relearning her feel. Her eyes drifted closed as he took the kiss deeper, lips opening, urging hers to part. She wanted this so badly. When her own mouth opened, allowing him inside, a sound midway between a moan and a growl curled up from deep in his chest, a sound of profound need.

She tasted him, and his flavor was delicious, bittersweet. For he was familiar and strange, wonderful and terrible. Her hands came up to grip his tight biceps. This was as much touch she would allow herself, though she wanted to wrap her arms around him and hold him close.

My God, how tenderly he kissed her. His lips spoke to her; she was the center of everything, the origin and the destination. Sweet and profound.

"Trust this," he whispered against her mouth. "You seek truth. Here it is."

"A kiss can lie," she whispered back.

He shook his head. "Not mine. I've not the art of a seducer. Nor the words." He pulled back enough so that their gazes met, and locked. "In all that has happened, in all that I had, *you* were the truest thing. Only you."

She felt herself bleeding inside, torn and agonized. What he wanted from her, she did not know she could give. "Leo . . ."

Abruptly, he released her and stepped away. Her hands hung in the air as he tugged off his borrowed coat. Waistcoat and shirt followed, all of them tossed to the floor without thought. Until he stood before her, bare-chested but for the bandages.

He turned, and she saw—for only the second time—the markings on his back. The pattern of flames twisted across his shoulders, emphasizing firm muscles. They were almost beautiful, the markings, but for their sinister connotation. They showed he remained the Devil's possession.

"The marks have grown," he said, keeping his back to her. "From the first day to now, they have spread over me. I didn't know why, not until this morning.

"When they cover you, your soul is utterly lost." The markings coiled down from his shoulders, along his back in a V-shape. A single tongue of flame wound down the length of his spine. Yet the skin of his back was not fully covered by the images. His lower back remained mostly bare, as did the upper curve of his buttocks, just appearing at the waistband of his breeches.

"Even with my gift of prophecy," he said over his shoulder, "much of what I do on the Exchange involves hours of research, and careful consideration of available facts and knowledge. But instinct is vital, too. I trust my instincts. Always have. They seldom lead me astray."

He faced her, chin high. "And I trust my instincts now when they tell me that those markings would have covered me by now . . . were it not for you."

She blinked. "Me?"

"You saved my soul." He spoke plainly, with no embellishment, no uncertainty. "Had you not come into my life, had you not been who you are, my soul would now belong to the Devil. I know this as I know my own heartbeat."

Slowly, she walked toward him, and he held himself very still. She moved past him, until she faced his back.

Her hand brushed over the slope of his shoulder. He inhaled sharply at the contact. Beneath her touch, his muscles tightened, responsive and alive. He radiated heat. With careful deliberation, she traced the markings, each image of flame drawn upon his skin.

"I wish . . ." She followed the marks, trailing down between his shoulder blades, along his spine. The capability of this man, his will made flesh. "I wish you valued yourself more."

"When I'm with you," he rasped, "I do. I see what I can become, the better man I might be."

"Might be," she echoed. "But *will* you become that man?"

He shook his head. "The one future I cannot see is my own."

"Yet you envisioned mine. You touched something that belonged to me, and you saw." She placed her hands on his shoulders and turned him to face her. Releasing him, she picked up a scattering of pins she had removed from her hair, then placed them in his hand. "Tell me what you see now."

Reluctance tightened his mouth. "Anne . . ."

"Tell me."

He exhaled. Then his gaze grew distant—the same distance that had come into his eyes when they stood on the banks of the Thames, and he had taken a ribbon from her hair. Fresh anger surged. He had used his magic against *her*. It felt like a violation.

His gaze sharpened again. "It was . . . unclear."

"No prevarication," she bit out. "*Honesty*, Leo. Or there is no moving forward."

His eyes narrowed. "I *am* being honest. I saw more demons, and a struggle. I was there, too. But the where and when of it—that I couldn't tell."

Her uncertain future held only one certainty: another battle. What transpired between then and now, and what came after—assuming there *was* an after—that lay in her hands.

She stared down at them, her hands. Not so long ago, they were as dangerous as hothouse lilies, and just as delicate. Now, they contained power. Truly for the first time in her life, *she* had power.

And she would make use of it.

Chapter 16

"What do you want?"

Anne looked from her hands to stare up at Leo. How could she answer that demand, when she could not see through the tempest engulfing her heart? She wanted to pull him close. She wanted to fling him from her. She wanted solitude and she wanted intimacy. It seemed impossible that one person could contain such a multitude of contradictions—yet she did.

She needed to test him, test herself. If she read his innermost self, what would she find there? A text of devotion, or more deceit? She did not know if she could gather the tatters of her own heart and step out into the storm. Or perhaps the silken ties that bound her to him were gone forever. One way to know for certain.

She raised herself up on her toes and kissed him. Deeply.

For a moment, he held himself still, as if afraid to respond and drive her away. Even with tension thrumming through his body, she sensed his restraint, allowing her to find what she needed to discover.

Desire flared through her, and she grew bolder. He groaned as the kiss heated. Not tender, but hungry, their mouths opening, tongues slick. She gripped his shoulders. Their bodies pressed flush against each other. Beneath the fine material of her shift, she felt his whole body—every plane and hewn surface, each sinew underneath satiny flesh. As she burned hotter, his caution ebbed. His large hands cupped her behind, bringing her tight, hip to hip.

Hunger tore through her, stronger than sense or wisdom. Her heart still ached. Words of apology and remorse might suture his betrayal, but the wound remained, and its pain throbbed in time with desire.

She never knew that one could desire someone this way—shredded by loss and sorrow, consumed with wanting. An appetite that grew even as she devoured more and more. She must learn the secrets of his heart, and this urged her on, demanding more.

Gasping, she broke the kiss. Yet she had only just begun. When she tugged him toward the bed, he went willingly, face dark, expression stern.

"Take off your clothes." Her terse command surprised them both.

He obeyed, unhesitating. His gaze held hers as he tugged off his boots and undid the buttons on his breeches. These he peeled from his body, and then, save for the bandages, he was naked.

"I've never seen you this way," she murmured. "In the light." Nowhere to hide. Nothing to conceal or disguise.

He understood this moment's significance. He let her look her fill, and look she did.

She discovered that her husband was stunning. Lean and muscled, his arms hewn, shoulders wide, the surfaces of his chest, scattered with golden hair, the taut ridges of his torso that led to a hard, flat stomach. The line of hair that trailed from his navel. The long, firm muscles of his thighs, the indentations above his buttocks. He was no soft aristocrat, no pampered gentleman. Years of struggle had fashioned his body into something fierce and tough.

She wanted to curse the bandages for obscuring him with their lattice. *This* was the body of the man with whom she had shared so much pleasure, such profound intimacy. It frightened her, a little, to see what she had known and touched and kissed, as though she had fallen asleep with a hunting dog at her feet and woken up with a wolf.

For all that, he was human, too, as evidenced by the intriguing scars and small collections of freckles. A man of flesh. Her gaze touched upon the scar on his shoulder, given to him by Lord Whitney—a reminder of the tapestry of deceit that had been woven by Leo's hands.

Something on his calf drew her attention. More markings of flame climbed up the thick muscles.

"Why two sets of markings?"

He glanced away, and she saw the hard beat of his pulse in his throat. "Those came later. The *geminus* offered me more power."

Which he did not refuse, clearly. "When?"

"After I made the other investment for your father," Leo said. "It knew I was wavering. Sought to bind me to the Devil with further temptation."

That was not so long ago. After the riot at the theater, after both she and Leo had been endangered by the evil he and the other Hellraisers had unleashed. Yet he had given in to the Devil subsequent to all this.

She dragged her gaze back up to his face. He looked like a man ravaged, passion and yearning and regret in his eyes.

Her resolve held. Many questions remained unanswered: what he wanted from her, whether *she* might salvage the care she once felt for him. She would put them both to the test.

Urging him back, she pressed him down when the

backs of his knees met the edge of the bed. He sat, then leaned back on his elbows when she pushed against his shoulders.

He lay like that, braced on elbows and forearms, feet upon the floor, staring up at her with eyes the color of storm clouds. His cock strained up toward his navel. His fingers gripped the coverlet. Only his ruthless resolve seemed to keep him from leaping on her, claiming her.

She bent over him, bracing her hands on the bed, and kissed him hungrily. He reached for her. She grabbed his wrists and lowered them to the bed. His fingers curled into the bedclothes. Giving in to her demands.

For all the deception, on an intrinsic level, they knew each other. And this caused her hurt to renew itself all over again, reminding her of what had been sacrificed.

She wanted to push him as far as she could.

Pressing her body to his, she rubbed her breasts against his chest. The fine material of her chemise provided little barrier. He was solid and hot beneath her. Sensation sparked outward from the taut points of her nipples, and against her belly she felt the thick, hard shape of his cock.

"Is this what you came for?" she challenged, breathless as she teased them both. "Why you chased after me? The softness of my body when the rest of your world is hard and cold?"

With a look of tortured pleasure, he clenched his teeth. "More than this. I searched for you because I wanted *you*, in any way I could have you."

She took him in her hand. His response was a hiss, and an upward push of his hips. From crown to base, she stroked him, her grip tight. The silken feel of him in her hand made her shake with desire.

Abruptly, she released him and pushed back from the bed. He stared up at her, breath coming fast and hard.

"Is this your revenge?" he rasped. "To leave me wanting?"

"If it was, would you let me go?"

"It would destroy me."

"Yet if I needed to leave, if it was the only way to ensure my happiness, would you?"

He swallowed hard. "Yes."

Damn him. If he were a brute, unrepentant and selfish, this would be simpler, painless. Yet he wasn't. He was Leo, and she loved him. After all this, she loved him still, and nothing hurt her more.

The choice to stay or go was hers. Yet she could not leave.

"If my happiness demands selfish gratification?" she pressed.

"*I* will give it to you."

She climbed onto the bed, grazing her hands along his thighs. He was her supplicant now. She pushed him down, so that he lay back, his head upon the mattress. "And you'll ask for nothing in return."

"All I want is the chance to give you pleasure."

With his gaze hot upon her, she braced her knees on either side of his head. Her quim was inches from his mouth.

She had never been so blatant in her demands. Her eyes challenged him as her body pulsated with need.

Prove yourself, she said to him wordlessly. *Prove to me that all is not lost*. His gaze holding hers, he gripped her thighs. Slowly, reverently, he brought her lower, until his lips pressed against her.

Anne swallowed a gasp, yet she could not keep silent when his tongue traced a glossy line from her opening to her pearl. He did this once more, and she cried out from the pleasure.

Though she wanted to let her eyes drift closed and float in sensation, she kept them open, watching Leo as he tasted her. With deep, lush kisses and licks, he feasted upon her, creating marvels of pleasure with his mouth. He drank from her as though she were the rarest and most precious delicacy, one he was determined to savor. And all the while, his gaze stayed on hers, burning bright.

Tremors shook Anne's thighs as the climax built, then crashed over her. He persisted, sucking upon her. In this way, he was both worshipful and commanding, for he coaxed her to bliss over and over, and she could not stop him, did not want him to stop, needing only pleasure and more pleasure and not the labyrinth of questions and uncertainty that lay beyond pleasure's ruby haze.

Shuddering with another release, Anne pulled away, feeling the echo of his fingers as he unclasped his iron hold on her thighs. He'd never looked fiercer with want, his eyes hot, his mouth slick with her.

"I would give you that," he rasped. "Every day, every hour."

"And what for you?"

"Whatever you will give me."

She edged backward and removed her chemise. In that cool gray morning, she was as exposed as he, naked in every way. Yet she felt stronger than ever.

Her knees pressing into the bed, she straddled him. Though he thrummed with want, he stayed as he was, lying back, feet on the floor and hands clutching the coverlet until his knuckles were white.

"This isn't a promise," she whispered.

"I know."

She steadied herself over him, her hands braced on his chest, the head of his cock at her opening. At the touch of her wetness, he gave an animal growl.

His eyes were heavy-lidded yet fiery as she held herself above him, savoring even this small contact. And then she could wait no longer, and sank down onto him. She moaned at the sensation, thick inches of him sliding into her, filling her.

She paused for a moment, drinking in the feeling of him inside her. Looking down at him, she expected his eyes to be closed as he retreated into physical pleasure. But his eyes were open and fixed on her face. As if memorizing her.

Hot tears gathered in her own eyes. She wanted to be selfish and think only of herself, but the slick, sleek marvel of their joining, and the look of sorrowful rapture on his face, spoke otherwise. She had sought to test him, test herself, and now had her answer: their sex could never be merely two bodies pursuing mercenary pleasure. They needed balance, giving and taking.

"*Anne*," he said, hoarse. He finally released his grip on the coverlet, his hand coming up to brush away her tears.

Using the back of her hand, she wiped her eyes, forcing the tears back. She did not know how much time she and Leo had left. She knew nothing at all. Only him. Only now.

She took his hand still cupping her cheek and moved it to her hip. Uncurled the fingers of his other hand and placed it on her other hip.

"Hold tight," she whispered.

His eyes blazed.

She rose up, and lowered herself down. Hot sensation spread through her. She moved again. And again. Each rise and fall filled her with gleaming pleasure. Watching Leo beneath her, seeing the beat of his heart under the hard curves of his muscles, and the brightness of his gaze—she had never felt such a combination of ecstasy and suffering, and the darkness brought the pleasure into stark relief.

His hands gripped her tightly, his hips rising to meet hers with thick, potent thrusts. The tempo increased, flesh to flesh. She ground herself into him, shameless in her demands. Her tight, throbbing pearl rubbed against him, and he angled himself to reach her exactly as she needed.

Sounds came from her. Wild, unrestrained sounds. They mingled with his deep growls as their pace sped. And not once did their gazes part.

"Leo," she moaned. "God."

"Just like that," he answered, panting.

She dug her fingers into his chest, leaving bright red marks. Release came like a hurricane, a storm of pleasure that wracked her every part, harrowing her with sensation. She did close her eyes then, tipping her head back as she lost herself to the climax.

The pulsations had barely dimmed when she felt herself gathered up and carried easily across the room. There was a crash and clatter as Leo shoved everything, including the food he had brought, off the table. He sat her on the table's edge. At his wordless urging, she wrapped her legs around his hips, her hands clutching his shoulders, body already primed for more.

"I feared I would never feel this with you again," he rasped. "That I had lost you forever."

He gripped the table, gaining leverage, and thrust. Hard. She arched into him. He plunged into her again, and once more. The table shuddered from the force of his movements, just as she shuddered, yet she was caught in a maelstrom of pleasure from the fierce heat and power of him as he sank into her over and over. He was relentless, and she reveled in it. In him.

Another orgasm tore through her, harder than the first. She cried out. A moment later, he groaned, body stilling. Head bowed, he gasped against her neck, and his breath fanned over her skin.

They stayed like that, him still deep within her, their bodies fused.

"I love you, Anne." His voice was deep, vibrating

through her. "Even if the Devil drags me off to Hell, I will never stop loving you."

She said nothing, only wrapped her arms around him and wished for answers that would not appear.

Leo woke with a start, and found Anne curled against him, his arms wrapped around her. She was soft and warm, deeply asleep. Darkness filled the room. He closed his eyes and allowed himself to soak up the feel of her, her supple pliancy and the silk of her flesh. It had been far too long since they had lain like this, completely at ease, unguarded—yet he knew it was an illusion shaped by fatigue. Though he had loved her body with a soul-draining intensity, she would not permit him this closeness were she not exhausted.

Pain, it seemed, had a limitless supply, for he felt it anew, cutting through him. He had always taken whatever he wanted, yet there seemed nothing he could do to make Anne his once more.

A soft tap sounded at the door. This had been what had awakened him moments earlier.

Naked, he eased out of bed, grabbing his primed pistol as he did so, and padded noiselessly to the door. Likely demons would not knock, nor common thieves, but he'd take no chances.

Whit's voice came from the other side of the door. "Livia has returned."

Leo opened the door a bare crack. "Is she in your room?"

"She appeared for only a moment. Doesn't like populated places like inns. We're to meet her by the river as soon as we can."

Leo nodded, and closed the door. He turned to find Anne sitting up in bed, already pulling on her chemise.

Though he was used to dressing in the dark, she was not, so he lit a candle. It guttered, until Anne gave it a pointed stare, and the flame steadied. More evidence of her strange new power.

In the pale yellow light of a single candle, they noiselessly dressed. The air in the little room felt filled with broken glass, each inhalation a study in pain. They were two strangers who had shared the deepest intimacy. He helped lace her into her gown, now stained and limp, and she thanked him with a small nod.

Dressed in his borrowed clothes, Leo put on his brace of pistols and slung his hunting musket onto his back. He had reloaded all of his weapons, ready for whatever might come. As Anne moved past him, he gently took hold of her arm.

She gazed up at him, stronger than he had ever seen her before, her hazel eyes clear.

"However long it takes," he said quietly. "From this life to the next. I will find a way to regain your trust."

"You have it," she murmured. But she held him off with an upraised hand when he stepped closer. "I don't know if it is enough. What we had . . . is broken."

"I'll fix it. Make it as it was."

She shook her head. "It can never go back to what it was. That is irrevocably lost." She glanced down at his hand on her arm. "We have to leave."

He did not want to, but he let her go, and they both left the room. At the doorway, she turned, then waved her hand. The candle winked out, throwing the chamber into darkness once more.

Down in the taproom, he purchased some bread, cheese, and apples, and had them packed into a hamper. "You need to eat," he explained at Anne's questioning look.

"What about you?"

"Take care of yourself first." He had been hungry before. It had not killed him.

The inn stood some hundred yards from the riverbank. They walked together, passing a lone cottage, and Anne ate as they moved toward the water. The night was cold and still, a thick blanket of clouds pressing down, smothering sound.

Beneath the branches of an oak, close to the water's edge, stood Whit and Zora. They kept close to each other, hands linked and voices low in shared confidence. The distance between Leo and Anne felt wide and echoing— but he had spoken truly. No matter what it took, no matter the time, he would find a way back to her, fashioning a bridge from his bones and blood if necessary.

"Where is our ghost?" Leo asked. "Do we summon her?"

"I am not *summoned*," came the specter's voice from the darkness. Light gathered around the roots of the tree, an unearthly glow, and it gained strength as it grew.

Though Anne, Whit, and Zora seemed more familiar with the sight, Leo stared as the shape of the Roman woman emerged. There was still much of this hidden world he did not know, and it struck him again how reckless he and the other Hellraisers had been, dabbling with such potent magic, skirting the edges of unfathomable power.

"I choose to come when I so desire," the ghost said, her voice sharper as she came into focus. Leo had seen her a handful of times in his dreams, a plaguing presence urging him to turn away from the Dark One, as she called it. He would have dismissed visitations as nothing but a restless mind had not his fellow Hellraisers confessed to having the same dreams.

Now he was awake, and here she stood. Or floated, rather. For her sandals hovered above the ground as she drifted toward him and the others. Unease prickled along his neck.

She stared at Leo, mistrust and haughtiness in her dark eyes. "The emblem of the Dark One obscures him. He is no ally."

"He *is*," Anne said, surprising him. "He has renounced the Devil."

"Words." The ghost scoffed. "Any child may recite them, without thought to the meaning."

"I'm no child," Leo rumbled. "My words are backed by my deeds."

"He fought against demons, Livia," added Whit. "He has proven himself."

Leo and Anne's gazes met, for he *had* proven himself to her. Yet she insisted there could be no regaining what they had once shared. God, how he hoped that was not true.

"That determination shall be made by me," pronounced the ghost.

"Tell me what I need to do," Leo said through clenched teeth, "and it will be done." This was far more than wresting a place for himself in the upper ranks of Society. The opinions of a few weak-chinned aristos did not matter. Let them think him a baseborn guttersnipe. They might print the foulest slurs in all the newspapers, create belittling caricatures to be flung across the most distant shores. None of that carried significance.

Only now, when he stood on the brink of not only losing his soul, but the only woman he ever loved, did he understand this. His pursuit of status had been a fool's trade. He did not even *like* most of the gentry, and yet he sought entry into their ranks. A hollow ambition that would leave him broken and alone.

All that would change. Had already changed.

Everyone—Anne, Whit, Zora, and Livia—stared at him now. Fissures appeared in Livia's wariness, but all Leo cared about was Anne, and fighting to recover what had been squandered.

"This fight we soon face," said Livia, "the stakes are far greater than the fate of a single soul."

"I know."

"Such confidence. Will you be so assured when your life is imperiled?"

One thing had not changed: Leo did not like to be questioned. He bristled. "Whatever is necessary. If that means my death, I accept the consequences."

The ghost continued to stare at him, judging, assessing. Finally, she nodded. "All things have a genesis and a culmination. The journey ends where it truly began."

"We must go to the ruined temple?" asked Whit.

"No," said Leo. "To London. To my home."

They rode east, passing through Chiswick, the buildings growing more numerous and closer together. And as they ventured farther into the city, signs of turmoil abounded. Broken glass and shattered wood littered the streets, and more than once they passed gangs of roving men who threw rocks and challenges, their eyes bright with wildness.

One such gang surrounded Leo and the others. "Pretty group of toffs," the leader snarled. Torchlight gleamed on his shaven head. Sometime during the night's rowdiness, he had lost his wig.

The leader reached for the reins of Zora's horse, but before anyone could act, Whit had his saber out and pointed at the man's throat. Leo aimed his pistols toward the rest of the gang.

"I can only shoot two of you," Leo said to the mob. "Three, if you count my musket. But you might be one of the three."

"By nature, I'm a gambler," added Whit. "Are any of you?"

Muttering amongst themselves, the mob edged away and its leader stepped back. They retreated into the night, yet tension still hung over the street.

"Your efforts are appreciated," said Zora. "But it would've been a small matter for me to reduce him to ashes."

"A woman wielding flame like a weapon might attract undo attention," noted Whit, "even amidst this chaos. Besides," he added, bringing his horse up beside hers so he could lean close, "it gratifies my male pride to play savior every now and then."

Leo glanced away as Whit kissed Zora. Seeing their ready trust and affection felt like rusty nails pounded into Leo's heart. His gaze met Anne's, who had also looked away from the open display of tenderness.

Spurring his horse on, Leo said with a growl, "When you're done making love in the middle of the street, we've got my soul to reclaim and the Devil to thrash."

He heard their horses behind him as they followed. Anne pushed her mount so that she rode beside him.

Passing Hyde Park and the genteel neighborhoods, the roving gangs thinned, but those who were on the streets moved quickly, heads down, as if anticipating attack. No sedan chairs were out, a rarity. A tense air of retreat clung to the wide streets and the imposing surfaces of Mayfair mansions, and few windows were lit. These were the prime hours for London's elite to make their rounds of evening diversions, yet no music filtered down into the avenues, no laughter or voices engaged in lively conversation.

Only a night had elapsed since Leo had ridden these streets in mad pursuit of Anne. Yet it felt as though decades had passed.

Saint George's struck the half hour as Leo and the others headed into Bloomsbury. His house was dark, save for a few candles burning in the front chambers, constituting the servants' attempt to make life appear somewhat normal.

·

Leo quickly dismounted and strode over to help Anne down from the saddle. She did not flinch from his touch, but she did not lean into it, either. Still, he took pleasure in his hands around her waist, and her slight weight as he swung her down. He did not know how much longer he would have to hold her like this, so he would take from it what he could.

Two grooms warily emerged from the mews behind his house to take their horses. As the sweat-flecked animals were led away, Leo said to the servants, "Once they are tended to, remove yourself from this place at once." He tossed them each a sovereign. The men's eyes widened, but they nodded in agreement.

Standing at the foot of the stairs leading to his front door, Leo stared up at his house. Three years ago he had purchased it; for three years it had been his nominal home. Yet the colonnades and handsome brick exterior moved him not at all. It was a building, nothing more. Only when Anne had come to live under his roof did he feel any sense of excitement when seeing its façade, and only then because he knew he was close to seeing her at the end of a long day.

He had bought this place to serve as a dare to the elite. His challenge: *You cannot make me disappear or slink off to the gutter. I am here. See me. Respect and fear me.*

And the magic given to him by the Devil served to shore up his challenge. It made sense that this house—the emblem of his desire for approval from those he did not truly esteem—now was to be the battleground for the fight for his soul.

Anne stood beside him and also looked up at the house. Trepidation tightened her mouth. Yet she glanced over at him and seemed to sense the swirl of emotion within him. Cautiously, she reached out and took hold of his hand.

He stared at their linked hands, feeling a tightness in his chest that came not from fear but from wonder. Whatever happened in the coming minutes and hours, he had this, this shared moment that *she* had crafted. Even when her hand slipped from his, he continued to feel her strength resonating within.

When Whit and Zora joined them, Leo drew a breath. He mounted the stairs. A gaping Munslow opened the front door, all sense of professional demeanor gone in light of the strange vision standing at the top of the steps: the master of the house, laden with weapons and wearing another man's clothing, the mistress in her torn and dirty gown, the errant Lord Whitney, and a Gypsy. Not precisely the sort of gathering one found in Bloomsbury minutes away from midnight.

The footman recovered enough to say, "Welcome home, sir." He held the door open, and the group moved inside.

"You and all the other servants," Leo said. "Gather your belongings and leave immediately."

Munslow stared. "Sir? Have we displeased you?"

"Not at all. But this place is not safe, and in a few minutes, it will be even less so." He handed the footman a key. "This is to my strongbox in my study. Take all the money you find there and dole it out amongst the servants. I'm trusting you to be fair in its distribution."

"Yes, sir," Munslow said, his face still frozen in shock.

"And if I'm still alive in the morning," Leo added, "I'll be happy to give anyone a character so they may find further employment. Go now," he said when the footman could only gawp at him.

Wearing a look of utter bafflement, Munslow headed belowstairs. Presumably to tell the other servants that the master had gone mad.

"Word will get out," murmured Anne once the footman had gone.

Leo understood. Servants told tales amongst themselves, and gossip spread from household to household. What one servant might learn would soon reach the ears of their masters. By the time lords and ladies made their morning calls the following day, everyone would know that Leo Bailey had lost his mind. Which could imperil future trade transactions. No one wanted to do business with a madman.

"I can't find it in myself to give a damn," he answered.

The chandelier overhead was unlit, and a single candle illuminated the entryway. Shadows engulfed the house, swallowing up the expensive trinkets and costly furnishings. A clock on a mantel measured time in relentless ticks. He thought of all the chambers in this house, chambers in which he had hardly ever ventured, rooms full of objects but empty of life. His house was a sugar sculpture that decorated the dining tables of the elite—ornate, extravagant, utterly useless. Existing only to be admired, but never truly used.

He never saw, not until this moment. "How did you stand this place?" he asked Anne now. "Hour upon hour, day upon day."

Her eyes were dark but clear. "If I wanted the man, I endured the house."

The things he made her suffer, the strength she had to weather it all—it was a wonder he could stand to be within his own skin.

Though his heart beat hard at the thought of the struggle to come, resolve was iron in his spine. Soon, the servants would be gone. When they were, Leo would take back what he had foolishly squandered. He might not survive, but he had never backed down from a fight. And none was so important as the battle that lay ahead.

Chapter 17

Anne's throat was tight, as though an unseen hand gripped her, slowly constricting. There seemed not enough air, no matter how she tried to breathe it in. Yet it was only fear, and she forced herself to calm. She could not face the approaching challenges if she collapsed in a faint.

Once the servants had cleared the house, she followed Leo toward the study. Lord Whitney and Zora remained in the front hallway. As Anne trailed after Leo down the corridor, she heard the hiss of steel as Lord Whitney drew his sword. A blaze of light that meant Zora had summoned her magic. The Gypsy did that so easily—conjuring up her power and wielding it with such confidence—it was clear she had used it many times in battle.

Both Zora and Whit made ready for the fight. They would form the defense against intruders when the inevitable assault happened.

Pressing her hand against her mercilessly pounding heart, Anne could scarce believe that this elegant Bloomsbury house would soon be the site of a pitched battle. It made as much sense as calling the house a home—for it was just as ill-fitting a title. She had never been at home here. Only Leo had made it bearable.

She kept her gaze on his wide shoulders as he walked toward the study. He appeared so strong, so potent. Surely he would survive this. He had to. They could not return to how it had once been between them. Yet he meant far too much to her to lose him.

He reached the open door of the study. They did not go in, but saw that a lamp had been lit. True to Leo's command, his strongbox sat atop his desk, the lid open. The strongbox had contained hundreds of pounds, well beyond what any servant might earn in several years. The men and women who had served him might not have employment, but they had been well compensated. Perhaps it might buy their silence.

Leo turned to her. His mouth flattened into a grim line, the angle of his jaw hard with determination. She'd never seen him more resolute. A warrior on the brink of combat.

Words formed on her lips, yet she could not say them. They gazed at each other in silence. The candle in Leo's hand flickered and cast shimmering shadows upon the walls. He looked both golden and dark, a terrifying figure from the depths of dreams, and it amazed her that this tough, fierce-eyed man had given her such pleasure only hours before. Not merely pleasure, but the truth of his heart.

Would it be the last time they ever made love? The dawn would have her answer, but dawn was far away.

"Ready?" Leo closed the study door, and he and Anne stood in the corridor outside. They had agreed that this place offered the right location for their needs, with few avenues for getting in or out. A battle would take place here, in this hallway covered with French silk damask.

She exhaled shakily, wiped her hands on her skirts, then nodded.

He started to speak, then stopped. He moved quickly. His arms came around her, pulling her close. And then his mouth was on hers.

Anne sank into the kiss, as hungry and demanding as he. They consumed each other, straining tight, savoring taste and sensation as those about to undertake a fast luxuriated in the flavor of the final morsel of food and last drop of wine. She tasted him and inhaled his scent and felt the hard, lean length of his body, knowing she might never experience these sensations again.

"Anne," he rasped against her mouth. "My unexpected gift. A gift I never earned. But I'll have you however I can, for as long as I can."

She did not think she had pieces of her heart left that were big enough to break, yet they shattered anyway.

He ended the kiss, releasing her as if by force of will. She let him go, but the distance between them tore through her as they stepped back.

"Please," she whispered, "do this now." She could not stand prolonging this.

He steadied himself, standing even taller, then spoke the words that sealed their fate. "*Veni, geminus.*"

The candle went out, and everything became darkness.

Leo held himself still as the scent of burnt paper filled the hallway, acrid and brittle. And then there was another shadow in the corridor, standing just behind Anne. It held his shape, his size.

Immediately, Leo placed himself between Anne and the *geminus*. For that's what it was. He did not need light to identify the creature. He recognized it now with the same certainty as he knew his own handprint.

"'Tis past the time of negotiation," the *geminus* spat. "My master does not look kindly upon the slaughter of his minions."

"Then he shouldn't have sent them to be slaughtered,"

answered Leo. His eyes grew adjusted to the dark, and saw the hazy echo of his own face twisted in a sneer.

"A poor strategy on your part, summoning me," said the creature. "We know where you are now. At this moment, hordes of demons approach. There shan't be enough of your carcasses remaining for the night soil collector to gather."

"We have reinforcements," Anne said.

Leo's heart swelled to hear the strength in her voice, no trace of the fear she surely felt.

The *geminus* chuckled. "A mortal man stripped of his power and a Gypsy girl with a mountebank's skill hardly amount to reinforcements."

An unearthly shriek echoed through the house. The windows rattled. The ground shook. It sounded as though dozens of knives were being sharpened, then Leo realized it was the scrape of talons upon stone.

Demons. Approaching.

The *geminus* laughed again. "For a man given the gift of prophecy, you've shown remarkably inferior planning."

"There is one ally you have not considered," said Leo.

"The other Hellraisers are not your friends."

"Not the Hellraisers."

"Who, then?"

"Me," said Valeria Livia Corva.

Light exploded, filling the corridor with radiance. The Roman woman emerged from a brilliant nimbus, hands upraised and ready, hair wild, and she fixed the *geminus* with a hard, unrelenting stare.

Radiance from Livia threw everything into high relief. The creature recoiled, and it unsettled Leo deeply to see a look of naked hatred upon his double's face—as though Leo himself shrank back in fearful loathing.

"We've more than enough power to face you," said Leo, "and whatever else comes crawling up from Hell."

Snarling, the *geminus* lifted up its hands, preparing to

work its own magic. Yet whatever it attempted to do, the effort failed. It glared at Livia.

"No retreat for you," she said. "This mortal home is your trap, until I decide otherwise."

The *geminus* sneered. "You cannot harm me. Unless you seek to hurt *him*." It flicked its gaze toward Leo. As it did so, it drew a poniard from inside its coat. Before Leo could stop it, the creature jabbed the point of the blade into its own left hand.

Anne cried out as Leo hissed in pain, gripping his now-bleeding hand. He moved quickly, knocking the poniard hard from the *geminus*'s grip so that it stuck in the wall. Even this small blow resonated in his body, the force of his own strike against the creature echoing in his hand.

Despite the loss of its weapon, the *geminus* chuckled. "Threaten as much as you please. The mortal and I are joined. He is my hostage."

Much as Leo wanted to plow his fist into the creature's smirking face, he restrained himself. Anne looked equally murderous. Yet the next move had to be Livia's.

"You are not so protected as you believe." The ghost moved closer to the *geminus*, which glowered defiantly at her approach. "To the Dark One, you are nothing but a puppet. We shall make appropriate use of you."

Latin words streamed from her mouth, and with her hands she made complicated patterns in the air. The *geminus* seemed to understand her intent, for it tried to dart past Leo, but he grabbed the creature before it could flee down the hallway. He ignored the sharp pain in his own arm as he held fast to the struggling *geminus*. Livia had to finish her spell before the creature could be set free.

He felt the change, an echo of her magic threading through his body, but the *geminus* felt it even more strongly. Its movements grew stiff, mechanical. In slow increments, its struggles against Leo's hold quieted. It stared down at its body as if it were a strange, phantom limb.

"What iniquity is this?" it cried.

"A taste of your own poison," answered Livia. "During my living years, I learned my own share of dark magic. You and your master seek to command others against their will. Now you share the same experience." She nodded at Leo. "Release it."

Leo uncurled his fingers from around the *geminus*'s arm, careful to stay close lest the thing make another attempt to flee. But it did not run. Instead, limbs moving with sharp jerks, it turned to the study door. Its hand curled around the doorknob.

"Reconsider," it said over its shoulder, words growing thin with panic. "All is not yet lost. There is still time—"

"We know already how trustworthy your master is," Leo spat, hating to hear the *geminus* using his own voice to bleat like a coward. "Do as you're commanded."

The *geminus* made another sound of protest, but it opened the door to the study. Yet the room that lay just across the threshold was not Leo's study. It was a stone-walled chamber with a high, vaulted ceiling. The books were gone; his desk was gone. In their place were rows and rows of heavy wooden shelves, and trestle tables running the length of the long chamber. On the shelves and the tabletops were objects the size of oranges. They each cast light, some more brilliantly than others.

Leo knew without being told that what he saw were *souls*. Human souls. All of them held captive in this chamber. The cold stone walls formed a grim prison, pitilessly enclosing the radiance of the souls' humanity. Yet as Leo looked upon them, greed stirred. Shimmering and precious, the souls were rare prizes that inspired covetousness—even within him.

Leo had been one of the reckless. Somewhere in that impossible room, his own soul waited.

* * *

Anne stared, hardly believing what she saw. Here was the vault of souls that Lord Whitney had described. The souls themselves were beautiful and shimmering, far lovelier than any gem torn from deep within the ground. Even standing some distance from them, she could feel their power and potential radiating outward, sending flickers of energy through her body.

The sight of so many souls trapped within the gloomy, oppressive chamber made her heart wilt. Already, a few of the souls faded, their light dimming. She did not know what would happen when their brilliance disappeared entirely, but it must certainly mean disaster.

"How did you come by so many?" she could not help asking the *geminus*.

It forgot its momentary horror, and looked smug. "Mortals are such fallible, gullible things. I learned this well during my profitable visits to the Exchange. They throw their souls away for mere trifles. Money, power. Love."

She stared at the shelves and shelves of souls, fighting despair. If this was the handiwork of a single *geminus* in only a few short months, imagine what many more of the things it could do in the span of a year. Hardly a person would walk the earth who still possessed their soul. And if the Devil could harness the power of all of these souls, power that Anne herself could feel . . . no wonder he must be stopped.

Leo strode toward the door to the vault, but could not move into it. He seemed to face an invisible barrier; his hand pressed empty air as though pushing against glass. Curling his hand into a fist, he threw a punch. The blow simply glanced away.

The *geminus* laughed. "Another excellent scheme. The vault is there, but what of it? You cannot go inside."

"We knew that much," muttered Leo. Yet it was in his nature to try anyway.

"Then you know no mortal may enter."

"Conversely," Livia said, "*I* am not mortal."

Anne held her breath as the ghost darted toward the vault. For this had been their intent, what they had planned beside the river in Richmond. When Lord Whitney had retrieved his soul, it had taken Livia's magic to gain Zora entry into the vault. That spell had cost Livia much of her power, but now they had a simpler option. She herself would gain entrance into the vault, and secure Leo's soul.

Yet when the ghost tried to pass across the threshold, she actually stumbled back. A look of bafflement crossed her face. She attempted to enter once more. Again, she met an invisible barrier. She stared down at her hands and body in confusion.

The *geminus* gave another ugly laugh. "Perhaps I ought to have made myself more clear. No *human* may enter the vault, be they living or dead. Ever since the Gypsy's essence was smuggled into another vault, alterations have been made."

Anne's heart sank, and Leo bared his teeth in frustration.

The Roman was not deterred. "No solid surface has yet barred me," she said, eyes hard and determined. "Not since my imprisonment between the realms. This night shall be no different." She rushed toward the wall beside the open door, and passed right through.

Anne anxiously looked into the vault for Livia's reappearance on the other side of the wall. The ghost did not materialize.

"Where is she?"

Livia appeared a moment later, emerging from the wall. Her face was set in a dark scowl. "All I find beyond that wall is a library. No vault. No souls. Merely useless books. If there is a way in, I cannot find it."

As the *geminus* continued to laugh, Leo cursed, long and floridly, and even Livia looked crestfallen. Desolation was a crushing weight in Anne's chest. For all their plans and hopes, for everything they had been willing to sacrifice, everything that had been lost—Leo's soul still belonged to the Devil, and there was nothing any of them could do to get it back. He was lost. They had failed.

They *could not* fail.

"Almost admirable," the *geminus* chuckled, wiping its eyes. "A fiasco, of course, but extremely inventive. 'Tis a shame that none of you shall serve my master. He would make excellent use of you."

Another unearthly scream rattled the windows. From down the corridor came the sounds of the front door being shaken, heavy bodies throwing themselves against the wood. Glass shattered. Zora shouted out a warning, and the clang of Lord Whitney's sword rang out. Demons howled, rage and bloodlust in their uncanny voices.

"Of course," said the *geminus*, mockingly solicitous, "you are welcome to join your friends in their useless battle. But know that you fight for nothing. And once my master's soldiers destroy your mortal body, your soul spends eternity in bitterest suffering."

"Hers won't," said Leo, nodding toward Anne. "That is all that matters." He drew a pistol and pointed it at the *geminus*'s heart. "I'll take you to Hell with me."

"Leo, no," cried Anne.

The *geminus* tried to grab the weapon, but Leo knocked it back. It pressed against the wall, steeling itself for the death shot. The shot that would kill it, and Leo.

She must act. Resolve straightened her shoulders as she reached deep within herself, searching for the power she desperately needed. Fury and fear roused it, and she drew it forth, the bright blue energy within herself.

Shutting her eyes, forcing herself to concentrate, she seized the power and sent it forth in a blast. Anne stretched her hands out, guiding her magic. Harsh, cold wind poured out in a gale, the force so strong that Leo was knocked back against the far wall. Paintings toppled down with a crash.

Leo fought and kept himself upright. The walls groaned with the force of the tempest Anne unleashed. She had no doubt she could tear the house down to its very foundations.

"Anne," Leo shouted. "Stop and get out of here! Before it's too late."

Demon screams could be heard above the roar of her storm, and the whole house shook—from her, from the massing beasts. But she would not relent, nor run. She had a purpose.

Anne stretched her hands toward the vault, guiding the tempest. Powerful wind swept to the open door . . . and went right through. The storm met no barrier as it rushed through the doorway and across the threshold.

"No!" shrieked the *geminus*, yet it already was happening.

Her teeth bared, Anne fought to direct the wind. It poured into the vault, scouring it, rattling the shelves within, even tipping the heavy tables lining the middle of the chamber. Souls were caught up in the storm, picked up by the powerful winds so that they danced upon the air, glimmering and shining like fireflies. The sight almost distracted her with its beauty. Yet she could not waver from her purpose.

She shouted with effort as she forced the tempest to return to her. It felt like struggling with an entire herd of wild horses, her arms shaking, sweat filming her body.

Anne pulled hard on the energy, calling upon every reserve of strength. The wind swirled through the vault and then, finally, rushed toward her.

Torrents of biting air churned out of the doorway, back into the corridor. As they battered her, souls also came flying out, borne aloft on the wind. The hallway filled with dozens and dozens of shining souls. Their radiance filled the corridor, spreading light.

The *geminus* gave a furious scream. It clawed at the air, attempting to grab the souls as they crossed the threshold. Yet they evaded the *geminus*'s grasp, flying away in all directions. Searching out their owners.

The final soul came spiraling out of the vault, gleaming brighter than the others. Instead of winging off to find its possessor, it stopped in front of Leo. Anne dropped her hands, and the tempest abruptly halted. Enervated, fascinated, she swayed on her feet as she watched Leo look wonderingly upon the soul. It bathed him in warm radiance. He gazed at the soul, awestruck, reverent, and reached out a shaking hand. Slowly, like a wary animal, the soul approached.

It was *his* soul.

All of the souls had been lovely, but Leo's was so beautiful, so full of brilliance and possibility, tears gathered in her eyes.

Movement in the corner of her sight caught her attention. She turned to see the *geminus* leaping to intercept the soul.

Livia flung out her hand, and the *geminus* stumbled back, forced away by unseen magic. Though Leo winced from this impact, he remained standing, and held himself still as his soul drew nearer. Yet it hovered inches from his chest, as if uncertain.

"My vow to you," Leo whispered, speaking to his own soul. "Never again will I give you away. I promise."

Anne held her breath, waiting. She had done what she could. This moment belonged only to Leo and the soul he had relinquished. She had the distinct impression that the soul was assessing Leo, judging him. Seeing into the deepest part of him, where there could be no manipulation, no falsity. Only Leo, and the truth of his heart.

Leo, too, waited, his expression torn between hope and fear. He had never looked more vulnerable, and her own heart ached for him. As if sensing her emotion, his gaze found hers. *This is because of you*, his eyes said. *Whatever comes afterward, it is* you *that made this possible.*

With a sudden, darting movement, the soul shot forward. Right into Leo's chest. He sucked in a breath, his whole body going rigid. Radiance filled him, an inner light that shone brilliantly. A smile of profound amazement and peace curved Leo's mouth. Even as the light dimmed, the smile remained, and Anne felt the paths of tears tracing her cheeks.

"We've done it," she murmured, awed.

He turned silver bright eyes to her. "*You* did it, Anne." He drew himself up fully. "And I will thank you properly. Later." Turning to the snarling *geminus*, he gave a predatory grin. "The gloves are finally off."

The *geminus* ran.

A look of utter panic on its face, it shoved past Leo, past Anne, and plunged through Livia as it sped toward the front of the house. For a moment, Leo could only stare in astonishment. He had not anticipated the creature would run.

But he would not allow it to escape. He sprinted after it. Anne's footsteps sounded behind him.

The spectacle in the entryway nearly stopped him in his tracks.

"Oh, my God," whispered Anne.

Whit and Zora faced a pack of demons—scaled beasts with long, beaked faces and serrated tails that gouged the floor and walls wherever they struck. Numerous creatures swarmed through the collapsed door. Whit struck at the demons, his saber engulfed in flame, and Zora brandished a whip of fire. Both Whit and Zora made impressive sights as they combated the monsters, their movements sharp and deliberate, felling the seething horde as it tried to advance.

Of all the sights Leo had anticipated seeing in this marble-floored, elegant foyer, he never thought to observe a battle between flame-wielding humans and vicious beasts from Hell.

Immediately, Livia joined the fight. More demons swarmed into the house through the windows, and the ghost used her magic to hurl them aside like so much kindling. Some of the creatures sprawled on the ground and lay still, but others instantly clambered to their feet and charged.

A demon rushed at Whit, approaching him from behind. The entryway echoed as Leo shot the creature, its dying scream merging with the bang of the pistol.

Whit spun and saw Leo standing at one end of the foyer. Whatever he saw in Leo's face made him smile. "So it's done."

Leo nodded. This was not the moment, nor had he the time, to examine how he felt now that his soul had been restored. Yet he sensed its presence within him, a wholeness that had been missing for so very long. Right now, what he felt was the need for vengeance.

He looked for the *geminus*. Blocked from escaping by the thick mass of brawling demons, it vaulted over the banister and ran up the staircase. Leo glanced back and forth between the ascending *geminus* and the battle going on in the entryway to his house.

Another surge of demons attacked. Whit swung at one

beast with his fiery blade, and the creature's head went rolling. The snap of Zora's whip severed the arm of another, and Livia hurled demons to the walls and ceiling. Plaster dust rained down in clouds as Leo's costly house was being decimated—and the sight filled him with vicious satisfaction.

"We have this front," Whit yelled above the chaos. "The *geminus* is yours."

Leo glanced up at the *geminus*. It had reached the top of the stairs and was starting down the hallway. Frustration welled—even if Leo ran full-out, he wouldn't be able to catch the damned thing.

"I need your trust," said Anne.

"You have it," he said without hesitation.

Her eyes widened briefly at his immediate acceptance. Then she drew in a breath as if steadying herself and lifted her hands. Suddenly, Leo found himself surrounded by powerful currents of air. It was everywhere, all around him, and then it was beneath him. He started as he lifted *up off the floor*, his boots hovering above the marble floor.

Holy hell, he *flew*.

For a moment, he struggled against it. Then he saw Anne, and how her eyes widened with wonder at her own power. This was her doing. He was borne aloft by the wind Anne conjured.

Her awe did not last, for the *geminus* was getting away. Leo forced his body to relax. And then the stairs scrolled under him as he was lifted higher. The sensation was amazing—air all around him, flying up the staircase like a hawk. But all too soon, it was over, and his feet touched down at the top of the stairs, the wind dispersing.

He glanced down to Anne, still at the foot of the staircase.

"Go," she called.

He did. Leo kept his gaze trained on the *geminus*'s

retreating back as it ran down the corridor. It sought escape, yet every door it approached banged shut on a gust of wind. More of Anne's doing. But her power did not reach the last door in time, and it ran inside. Into the master bedchamber.

The sounds of combat retreated as Leo sprinted along the hallway. His lone focus was the *geminus*. Reaching the doorway of the bedchamber, he growled when he saw the creature pushing the mattress aside to uncover the loaded pistol Leo always kept beneath the bed. Of course, the damned thing knew his secrets. It was *him*. Or had been.

Leo stepped inside. The *geminus* waved its hand and the door slammed behind him. He tugged on the doorknob. It would not move. He was barricaded inside with the *geminus*.

It had transformed from his double to his distortion, its features twisted, snarling mouth full of jagged teeth, its eyes solid black and awash with bitter hatred. Looking at it sickened Leo, knowing that what he saw now was his own darkness, his own hate.

He and the *geminus* faced each other, both with weapons drawn and aimed.

"The opportunity was yours," spat the creature. "To rise above your station. To possess unlimited power. But, vulgar peasant that you are, you pissed it all away."

"I never needed magic to forge my way in the world."

"You could have had *more*."

Once, that was all he wanted. More of everything. More wealth, more influence. More respect. But none of those things held value. Not when he couldn't find peace within himself. Only Anne had given him that.

"I have everything of value."

He fired. The *geminus* shot at the same time. Yet at that precise moment, the house shook with a massive impact.

Both bullets missed, Leo's hitting one of the bedposts, the *geminus*'s lodging in the door frame.

Before Leo could grab his musket, the *geminus* launched itself at him. Talons now tipped its fingers, and as he found himself grappling with the creature, its claws raked across his face. He barely felt the blaze of pain. All he knew was this fight, a fight he must win.

He and the *geminus* rolled across the floor of the bedchamber, slamming into furniture, trading brutal punches. This was a fight unlike any other he had known. The brawl during the theater riot was a nursery game by comparison. Now, he and the creature were vicious, relentless, determined to prevail by any means. Leo took punishing blows to the face, the chest, to any part of his body the *geminus* could reach. And he attacked the creature with the same ruthless cruelty.

A shriek sounded close by. Leo spared a glance to see that a demon had flown through a window, and now leapt forward to join the fight. The damned monster stood over him, slashing at his undefended back. Pain flared. He hissed as the demon screeched triumphantly. Though he struggled to hold both the demon and the *geminus* at bay, he was only one man.

Suddenly, the demon was hurled across the chamber, the solid bedchamber door flying off its hinges and plowing straight into the creature. As they flew through the air, the demon's wing scraped across the *geminus*'s shoulder, sending it rolling across the floor. Both the door and the demon smashed through a closed window, the glass shredding the monster as it flew. It screamed once as it fell, then came a thud as its body hit the ground outside.

Leo glanced over toward the doorway. Anne stood there, hands outstretched. Her hair spilled over her shoulders, and her eyes blazed with righteous fury. *She* had torn the door from its hinges, throwing it and the demon across the room and through the window. She had protected him from secondary attack. And she looked ready to face any and all enemies.

"Behind you," he panted.

Anne whirled around as four demons advanced, claws out, eager for blood. Dodging their talons, she held them back with sharp, targeted blasts of wind. It amazed Leo that she was the same woman who had shaken with terror on their wedding night, yet it made perfect sense. That fierce spirit had always been within her, merely waiting for the proper time to make itself known.

"Admirable, yes," hissed the *geminus*, getting to its feet, "yet futile. Like your friends downstairs, she will be slaughtered, and you shall spend eternity reliving her last agonizing moments. Over and over again."

Rage, brilliant as an inferno, tore through Leo. He slammed his fist into the *geminus*'s sneering face. The creature spat blood, then struck back.

As Leo and the *geminus* were locked in combat, he heard Anne holding back the onslaught of demons, throwing the monsters into the walls, thrashing them with her power. Exhausted and battered as he was, his whole body aching, he drew strength from hearing her fight. Though they were each engaged in their own battles, he felt their unity of purpose, of heart, and felt a surge of power course through him.

Staggering to his feet, he hauled the *geminus* to standing and rained punches upon it. The creature tried to fight back, but Leo backed it into a corner. Desperate, furious, the *geminus* struck out with its claws. Yet it weakened.

The *geminus* suddenly launched itself at Leo. He acted instinctively, grabbing hold of its lapels. He swung its head toward the marble mantel. A wet crunch sounded as its head collided with the stone. Blood coated the marble, a dark smear dotted with clumps of hair, and the *geminus* fell to the carpet.

Leo strode over to where the creature lay on its back. It stared up lifelessly, its gaze already glazed and vacant. Taking up his musket, Leo placed the muzzle directly between its eyes and pulled the trigger. The smell of blood, brains, and gunpowder filled the room.

He did not waste time standing over the body. In two strides, he was beside Anne, still holding back the demons.

She glanced from him to the *geminus*. Though she blanched at the grisly sight, a small, victorious smile curved her mouth.

"An ungentlemanly fight," she said.

"I'm no gentleman." He swung his musket around, holding it like a club.

"Oh, I know that *very* well."

The remaining demons, seeing the *geminus*'s inert body, turned and fled. Yet sounds of combat continued to rise up the stairs. The battle was far from over.

He walked to Anne, and held out his hand. When she took it, sliding her palm against his, he felt a hot, purifying *rightness*.

Together, they headed downstairs to join the fight.

Chapter 18

Chaos reigned at the foot of the stairs. Aside from the riot at the Drury Lane Theatre, Anne had never seen such destruction. The few pieces of furniture lay in splinters. The chandelier hung crookedly, swaying like a glittering pendulum above the melee. Demon bodies were everywhere, sprawled across the marble floor or slumped against the walls.

In the midst of this stood Lord Whitney and Zora, standing back-to-back. Hard to believe that Lord Whitney had ever been one of the idle elite, wasting time and money at the gaming tables, for now he fought like a born warrior, his fire-wreathed sword hacking down three demons.

Zora, too, made an awe-inspiring sight as she snapped her flaming whip, felling two creatures and pushing back two more who sought to advance. Distant crashes in the front chambers of the house revealed Livia locked in combat with more demons.

"This cannot be Bloomsbury," Anne murmured as she and Leo stood at the top of the stairs.

He quickly readied his pistols and musket, tamping

down the powder and loading the bullets. "It's the first circle of Hell."

And so it looked. Two humans fought at the center of a dozen writhing, snarling demons, with a specter providing reinforcement.

Leo brought his musket up to his shoulder, took aim, then fired. A demon attacking Zora fell as the bullet shattered its chest. The Gypsy woman looked up and offered a nod of thanks.

"The _geminus_," she called up, "is it dead?"

Lord Whitney glanced toward Leo, then answered before Leo could. "Aye. I suffered the same wounds sending my _geminus_ back to Hell."

Anne and Leo hurried down the stairs. Leo used his pistols to take down two more demons, then wielded his musket like a club, knocking the monsters down with brutal efficiency.

"Most of the demons have fled," Lord Whitney shouted above the din. "These are the holdouts."

"They'll regret their obstinacy," growled Leo.

Anne guided her magic, throwing demons into the walls. The creatures twitched, then fell, landing in broken heaps. She directed gusts of wind to take up tongues of flame from Zora's whip and set several of the demons alight. Their screams echoed in the vaulted room as their bodies burned, filling the air with noise and the stench of charred flesh.

And then, suddenly, the humans outnumbered the demons. Only two monsters still lived. With terrified screams, the demons clambered toward the door, anxious for escape. Anne and the others found themselves standing in the middle of the entryway, panting and bloodied, but alive. Leo's coat was torn, revealing angry gouges across his body, he had a cut across his cheek, and crimson dripped down his hand to mingle with the black pools of demon gore. Yet he stood tall amidst the destruction.

"The final retreat," Zora said, staring at the open, empty doorway.

"A wise decision." Leo glanced at the walls.

Anne gasped. Fire crawled up the walls in a blazing webwork, catching on draperies. The banister became a line of flame leading up to the first floor.

Zora's whip of fire immediately disappeared. "Apologies."

Yet Leo merely shook his head. "Couldn't be helped. But we need to get out. Now."

Smoke filled the entryway, and Anne coughed as it saturated her lungs. She took Leo's offered hand, and together they ran from the house. Lord Whitney and Zora followed, with Livia meeting them on the sidewalk outside. The street glowed in the lurid illumination. Soon, the fire inside the house would find its way outside.

Anne turned to Livia. "We cannot let the house burn, or it will spread to the other homes."

"Air will merely encourage the fire to burn," the specter answered.

"I've another idea." One she was not certain would work, but she hoped the natural science lecture she had attended long ago had been accurate.

Closing her eyes, Anne focused all her energy on the power within her. She held out her hands, calling to the air. She sought not to *create* air, but to draw it *into* herself. This was a new challenge, one beyond anything she had attempted before. It took every ounce of her will, fighting to drag the air out of Leo's house. Her teeth clenched with the effort and sweat dampened her clothing as she struggled.

She cracked open one eye. Her heart leapt to see the flames within diminish. Yet it took far more strength to smother the fire than she knew she possessed. Abruptly, the burden lessened. Anne glanced over to see Livia also working to draw out the air. The ghost's head was thrown back, and her image flickered, taxed almost beyond endurance.

With a final, hard pull, Anne and Livia stifled the fire. The last tongue of flame guttered, then went out.

Anne sank to her knees. She felt herself carefully pulled to her feet, and she leaned back into Leo's firm, strong body, weary beyond imagining.

He murmured her name, lips pressed against the crown of her head. She felt utterly spent, and he formed a solid wall behind her, around her. She fought against a wave of exhaustion, released in the aftermath of battle. It was over. Finally.

Leo tensed. She felt his every muscle contract into readiness. "Hell," he growled, looking off into the darkness.

She turned her head to see what set him on edge. Her own body stiffened when she beheld the new threat.

Three silhouettes. One long and lanky. Another shorter, but ready for combat. And the third, tall and broad-shouldered, with the distinct posture of a battle-hardened warrior.

Like omens of disaster, the Hellraisers emerged from the shadows.

Here, then, was the biggest threat of all.

As Leo watched the men he once considered friends stride toward him, he understood how dangerous the Hellraisers truly were. He'd been one of their numbers, capable of anything.

All three men carried swords, and as they appeared out of the darkness, their faces wore similar expressions: hard, determined, pitiless. Even Edmund, the most affable of the Hellraisers, looked ready for violence. John appeared as though he wanted done with this pesky annoyance so he might return to more important matters. And Bram, with his cold eyes, his long dark coat flaring behind him, resembled the tough, merciless soldier he had been after returning from the brutality of war.

Leo gathered Anne close, sheltering her with his body. None of the Hellraisers would touch her. He would wet the cobblestones with their blood before he allowed any of them to hurt his wife.

Damn it, he hadn't the time to reload his firearms, and he wasn't trained to use a sword. Bare hands, then. He knew plenty of strategies for fighting against an armed enemy. Even enemies he once thought of as his brothers.

They faced one another in the middle of the street: Leo, Anne, Whit, Zora, and a flickering Livia standing against Bram, Edmund, and John. Yet despite the uneven numbers, it would be a fatal mistake to think the Hellraisers at a disadvantage. Leo had fought beside them enough to know the threat they presented now.

"Never believed you so weak," Bram said on a growl.

"Not weakness, but strength," countered Leo. "The same strength that's in each of you."

John snorted. "This isn't the Exchange, Leo. You can't wheedle your way into our favor."

"Leo does not *wheedle*," Anne said, rousing. Strength gained in her, and though she kept close, she stood upright on her own. "He is trying to save your cursed souls."

Edmund started, as if suddenly becoming aware of her presence. "You . . . know about everything? And yet you remain at your husband's side?"

"Where else should she be?" rumbled Leo. Yet he knew that Anne's continued presence next to him counted as one of the greatest marvels of his life—if not *the* greatest marvel. "It was *she* who finally managed to reclaim my soul."

He turned slightly and pulled at one of the tears running along the back of his coat. The tear went all the way down, through his shirt, to his flesh beneath. Tugging on the slashed fabric, he revealed his shoulder.

Anne gave a small inhalation, Whit chuckled lowly, and Bram muttered a curse. For the skin on Leo's back was unmarked. The images of flames were gone. He knew he would find the same on his calf.

"A soul is a very little thing." John sounded unimpressed. "Compared to what we might have, the power we can wield, who requires a soul?"

"Even the greatest emperor has one," Whit said. "Without it, he becomes nothing more than a tyrant."

"I'm certain I've no soul to save," countered Bram. "What I *do* have is pleasure in abundance, and that is my only necessity."

"Bodily pleasure," said Leo, "but what of your heart?"

John made another dismissive sound. "Marriage has transformed you into the veriest weakling."

Gazing at Anne, he saw the ferocity in her face despite the exhaustion beneath her eyes, her torn and dirty gown. And her arm, around his waist. "It has made me far stronger than I could have ever dreamed."

Her grip tightened, sending another pulse of energy through him.

Bram rolled his eyes. "Enough of this maudlin twaddle." He raised his sword. "You have chosen your allegiance just in time to die." Assured as an officer, he commanded, "Hellraisers, advance."

Leo braced his feet wide, making himself ready. Whit brandished his saber, and the fiery whip reappeared in Zora's hand. Anne, weary as he knew her to be, still prepared herself for battle, her chin tilted and hands upraised as she stood beside him.

Edmund's gaze continued to move back and forth between Leo and Anne, and Whit and Zora. Leo saw what Edmund saw: men willing to fight and die for their women, and women just as ready to do the same for their men. A pained look crossed Edmund's face.

Both John and Bram edged forward. But Edmund remained where he stood. "I . . . I cannot."

"Edmund," snapped Bram over his shoulder. "This is no time for tender sentiment. Move. Now."

Leo watched, warily amazed, as Edmund slowly lowered his sword. He wore an almost baffled expression. "No. This must stop."

Clever as always, John said, "Do you want to lose Rosalind? For surely you will if these traitors have their way."

Yet Edmund shook his head. "I never truly had Rosalind. Since I received my gift, she has not been the woman I wanted, the woman I loved. Merely an empty shell that looked like Rosalind." He stared at Whit and Zora, and then Leo and Anne, his gaze hollow with longing. "I merely own a *thing*. But I do not have love. And I know . . ." His voice thickened. "I know that the Rosalind I love would hate the life I've given her."

"Edmund," said Leo, but he did not know what he could tell his friend. If Leo were in Edmund's place, if he had Anne but not Anne, missing the crucial essence of who she undeniably was . . . Leo could not endure it.

"You mean to turn traitor, just like these two?" John snarled. "Take up arms against us?"

Carefully, as though releasing an adder, Edmund set his sword upon the ground. "I've no wish to fight you. All I seek is to relinquish my gift that I might set Rosalind free."

Bram and John hissed in frustration and anger, but Leo felt the blossoming of true hope. With Edmund as an ally, surely they could defeat the Devil. He might wish to retire from the battle, but Leo knew that Edmund was too gallant to turn away from such an important fight. It might take a little while, yet he would come to their aid. In this war, they needed every ally, every advantage.

And Edmund was far too good a man to be damned. Of

all the Hellraisers, he had been the one who preferred laughter to rowdiness, friendship over debauchery.

Edmund moved toward Leo. "I will need your guidance."

"You have it." Leo held out a hand.

"No," growled Bram.

"He is our *enemy*," John snarled. Swift as a viper, he lunged forward, sword upraised and aimed at Leo.

Leo moved to dodge the blow, but it never came. Instead, the tip of John's blade protruded from Edmund's chest. Edmund had leapt in front of John, blocking him from running Leo through. And had taken the sword strike intended for Leo.

Anne gasped in horror, and flung out her hands. A blast of wind tossed John backward. Both Leo and Whit ran forward. But they were too late. Edmund stumbled for a step and sank to his knees. John got to his feet, still holding his sword. Blood streaked the metal, and he gazed at it dispassionately.

Gently, Leo lowered Edmund to the ground, careful to support his head. Edmund's wig slid off, revealing his closely shorn hair. Leo tore off his coat and wadded it up to press against the wound, but blood spilled from Edmund's chest and back, coming up in pulses as his heart beat out his life. Already, Edmund turned ashen, his eyes glassy.

"Help him," Leo shouted to Livia. Out of all of them, the ghost possessed the most power.

Yet Livia only shook her head as she hovered near. "Were my strength not so diminished, even then I could do nothing. I've no authority over life and death."

"He's not dying," Whit insisted.

"And you . . . call yourself a . . . gambler," gasped Edmund. "Terrible at . . . bluffing."

"I'll fetch a surgeon." Leo started to rise, but Edmund gripped his hand with surprising strength.

"Give me this . . . one favor."

"Anything."

Edmund fumbled weakly to pull his shirt up from his

breeches. Helping him, Leo tugged on the fabric when his friend's strength failed.

"On my . . . right hip," Edmund whispered.

Leo examined his hip. "You are not wounded."

"And the . . . marks?"

He saw only pale flesh. "If they were there, they have gone now." Edmund's sacrifice had done that, restored his soul.

A small smile appeared on Edmund's mouth. "She is . . . free. Make certain . . . she is . . . cared for."

"I swear it."

"And I," added Whit.

"Tell her I . . ." Edmund's words trailed off, and his chest went motionless. His hand fell away from Leo's, lying on the blood-slick cobblestones, the wedding band on his finger gleaming dully.

Only when he had closed his friend's sightless eyes did Leo surge to his feet. John stared back at him, his expression tight. Bram was a dark, motionless figure, his face wreathed in shadows.

"You damned coward," snarled Leo. He hardly believed what had just happened. Only a few weeks ago, they had all sat around his table, taking a meal together. And now Edmund lay dead in the street, murdered by his friend.

"I take all threats seriously," said John.

"He was no damned threat to you." Leo's hands were wet with Edmund's blood.

"*Everyone* is a threat. Especially you."

Leo dove for Edmund's sword. He hadn't training in the weapon, but the need for retaliation would make him a quick study. All that mattered was avenging Edmund.

Seeing the fury in Leo's face, John edged backward. For the first time that night, John seemed uncertain, his gaze flicking between Leo and the others. All of them, even Anne, stood ready to fight.

Everyone jumped back when a thick column of smoke suddenly appeared in the middle of the road. Not smoke,

Leo realized, but a concentration of darkness, drawing in all light as if consuming it. The shadows swirled, then collected into the form of a man.

The darkness dissipated. A figure stood between the Hellraisers and Leo. Though Leo had seen this man only once before, he recognized him immediately. Immaculately groomed, he wore a gentleman's suit of ash gray satin, his dark red waistcoat covered in rich embroidery and gems. He wore a fashionable bag wig, tied with black silk. A ring, topped with a large, black stone, adorned one of his slim white hands. In every way, even in his upright posture, he looked an elegant, wealthy gentleman.

But he was no gentleman. He was not a man at all.

"My dear Hellraisers," he drawled, his diamond white gaze glancing down at Edmund's body, "this was not how I envisioned our reunion."

The Devil had returned.

Anne had not yet recovered from the shock of seeing Sir Edmund Fawley-Smith murdered by the Honorable John Godfrey. The poor man had surrendered his life trying to protect his friends. He had been run through like meat upon a skewer. His blood was everywhere. And there had been nothing she could do to help.

Now his lifeless body sprawled upon the ground, and someone, some*thing* had appeared. Her every nerve tensed, and chill spread through her body. For she knew instinctively who stood before her, wearing the guise of a nobleman. She had seen too much to be astounded, and yet there was no way to prevent the shock that froze her in place. To have heard so many times about the Devil, and now, to *see* him made real . . . If Anne lived to see the dawn, she doubted she would ever forget this sight, burned as it was into her mind.

She sidled closer to Leo, threading her fingers with his.

"Two of my Hellraisers gone in a single night." The Devil

shook his head, a disappointed tutor. "Edmund offered me little, but you, Leo, you could have been such a wonder."

"I'll live with the disappointment," he answered flatly.

The Devil offered a chill smile. "Not for much longer."

Anne stiffened. She did not care for those ominous words.

"I believe it was one of your natural philosophers who said, *Actioni contrariam semper et æqualem esse reactionem.* For every action, there is an equal and opposite reaction. The loss of two Hellraisers, and their power, means that the two remaining Hellraisers shall have *more* power." The Devil curled his fingers as he turned to face Bram and John. Black energy gathered in his hands, seemingly drawn from the night itself.

Both men drew upright, as though preparing themselves. John looked eager. Bram's expression was opaque. He had not spoken since Edmund's death, and continued to maintain his silence. Yet he did not turn away from the Devil's offer.

Good God, Anne already felt Bram's menace. She could not begin to fathom what he might become if further corrupted. And John had already proved himself a villain. With more power at his disposal, he would transform into a monster.

Sensing this, both Leo and Lord Whitney sprang forward, swords upraised as if they meant to strike down the Devil. Yet before either could land a blow, energy poured from the Devil's hands, directed toward Bram and John. At that same moment, a flash of light streaked in front of Bram.

It was Livia, crying out, "Stop!"

Her cry cut off abruptly as the dark energy pierced her. The energy pulled her into a small, single point of light, shrinking to almost nothing. Momentum carried this tiny gleam back, and into Bram. It sank into his chest, then vanished. Bram staggered back, his hand pressed between his ribs, looking down with a bewildered glower.

Livia was gone.

But Anne could not wonder at the ghost's disappearance. Though somehow Livia had managed to deflect the Devil's magic from going into Bram, John had not the same protection. He would not want it, for he wore a rapturous expression as dark energy coursed into him. The Devil was imbuing him with greater power—and he gloried in it.

Leo cursed and started forward again, sword upraised. The Devil snapped his fingers, and the sword spun out of Leo's hand.

Seeing this, Lord Whitney also moved to strike, but the Devil flung him back with a flick of his wrist. Zora cried out and ran to him, sprawled on the sidewalk nearly fifty yards away. Anne breathed out in relief when she saw him stagger to his feet, though he favored one leg as Zora helped him stand.

Shouts sounded down the street. As if coming out of a trance, the city finally roused. Men's voices called out, and feet and hoofbeats pounded against the cobblestones.

The Devil lowered his hands, and gave an irritated growl. "Do what you must," he barked at John. "See my work come to fruition. And you." He turned to Bram. "I will see you again very soon. As I will all of you."

With that, shadows engulfed him, and then he was gone.

The sounds of approaching men, and the rumbling of the wheels of fire wagons, drew closer.

"We must go," Bram said on a growl to John.

Yet John seemed reluctant to leave. A sinister smile crossed his lean face. "I can take them. The things I can do now . . ."

"*Immediately*, John." The order in Bram's voice could not be disobeyed, not even by John. Both men turned and hastened down the street, away from the oncoming commotion. Before he disappeared into the darkness, Bram turned and stared back at where Anne and Leo stood. His hand lingered on his chest, over his heart—the place into which

Livia had seemingly disappeared. And then he sped off, melting into the shadows.

"Don't want to be here, either," Leo muttered, "when there are questions that demand answers. Come." His hand clasping Anne's, they hurried toward Lord Whitney and Zora. "Can you run?" he demanded of the other man.

"Aye."

"Then we move."

"What about Edmund?" Anne asked.

Leo looked grim. "He will be found, and . . . tended to."

The four of them ducked into the mews just as throngs of men crowded the street. Anne and the others ran down the dark streets, and time blurred as she forced her body to move through the night-shrouded city. Finally, they reached a weedy, overgrown burial ground. Some of the headstones tilted precariously, and a freshly dug grave awaited its occupant.

Gasping for breath, she braced her hands on her knees. She felt Leo's warm hand on her back, steadying her. Brittle earth and dead grasses crunched beneath their feet as their group drew together in a close circle.

The wind shook the bare branches of the trees, the sound mournful, ominous. Surely the Devil would come for them again, send more and more demons, run them all to ground. No wonder Lord Whitney had such caution and alertness in his gaze. He and Zora were hunted, as she and Leo would be. And the four of them together presented a substantial target.

"We have to part," Leo said, as if hearing her thoughts. "Safer that way."

"There is a band of Rom near the Scottish border," said Zora. "They will take Whit and I in for a time."

"And what of you?" asked Lord Whitney.

"I'm a saddler's son," Leo answered with a small, wry smile. "That makes me well versed in being inconspicuous."

Anne almost laughed at that. Leo could never be

inconspicuous. He radiated presence, whether he was dressed in silk or tattered muslin. She had known that from the moment they had exchanged marriage vows—he was a man of uncommon strength.

"I shall believe that when the proof stands before me," said Lord Whitney. Clearly, he also knew Leo well.

"We cannot run and stay hidden forever," said Anne.

"And we won't," Leo answered. "A bigger battle is coming, and we must be there to fight it."

"What became of Livia?" asked Zora.

"No idea," said Leo. "But of a certain, we will need her for that battle."

"It's to happen, then." Anne rubbed her hands on her arms against the chill. Leo moved to offer her his coat, then stopped when he realized he had none to give her. His borrowed coat was now soaked with Edmund's blood, pressed uselessly to the fatal wound. "The fight between us and the final two Hellraisers."

"That it will," said Lord Whitney, somber. "I do not know what happened with Bram, but John's power has grown terribly. Of that, I am certain."

"With his influence in Parliament," muttered Leo, "God knows what kind of chaos he will lead us into."

"We've faced demons," Zora countered, "and won."

"John and Bram are by far more dangerous." Lord Whitney spoke with certitude. "They are the demons we know."

"Then that should make them easier to vanquish," said Anne.

"I know my own evil," Leo answered. "Defeating that was the hardest thing I've ever done. It will be the same for John and Bram. The darkness, it countermands everything. Devours everything."

She shivered at the hard-won experience in his voice. "It cannot be hopeless," she said, trying to convince herself as much as the others.

"There will always be hope," Leo replied.

Silence fell as each of them considered what lay ahead. It was to be a struggle, one they were not confident of winning, yet they had to try.

At last, Lord Whitney extended his hand to Leo. "It does my heart good to have you my ally again."

Leo took the offered hand and shook it solemnly. "The loss of our friendship haunted me, Whit. I'm glad to have it back again."

After releasing Leo's hand, Lord Whitney offered Anne an exquisite bow, and kissed her knuckles. "Madam, you surpassed my every expectation."

"I surpassed my own, as well," she answered, then added feelingly, "My greatest thanks, Lord Whitney."

"Whit, if you please. Those who slay demons at my side I consider my greatest friends." He added lowly, for her ears alone, "And for what you have done for Leo, I consider you an angel."

"Hardly an angel." She was all too human, too fallible.

"Whatever you call yourself, you've earned my gratitude. And *his* soul."

The moment Whit released her hand, Anne found herself pulled tight to Zora in a fierce embrace. "Sister," Zora said, "I take back everything bad I ever said about *gorgies*."

Anne was not certain she wanted to know the bad things Zora might have said about *gorgies*, whatever they were. But she returned the Gypsy's embrace, knowing that she could rely on her far more than any of her own kin.

As Whit and Zora headed off into the night, a pang of sadness threaded through Anne.

"I hardly know them," she murmured, "yet I will miss them."

"We'll all meet again." He took her hand in his. "We're an army now. The four of us fought together, and won."

"We won *this* battle. But what about those yet to come?"

He brushed his thumb over her ring, and waited. After a moment, he exhaled. "It's gone—my power to see the future."

"You miss it," she said flatly, fearing his regret.

Yet he shook his head, and his eyes were bright in the darkness. "Its loss holds no value. There is only one thing, one *person*, I cannot lose."

Emotion burned her throat, and she struggled to speak.

He thought her silence meant doubt, and he continued, his words low and fierce. "Tonight, I saw my friend murdered. Edmund sacrificed himself for something he wanted desperately. Something he saw in *us*."

"Love," Anne whispered.

Rare uncertainty knotted through his voice. "You said that we can never get back what we once shared. Do you still believe that?"

After a moment, she spoke. "I do."

He seemed to turn to marble, his face and body rigid.

"You and I," she continued, "we aren't the same people we were. Both of us have changed."

"I love you. *That* hasn't changed."

"And I love you," she answered. "But *my* love has changed. It's stronger now—because I know who you truly are. Just as I know who I am."

"You are remarkable."

She *felt* remarkable. "And you are a very complicated man."

"A complicated man and a remarkable woman shouldn't be apart." He gazed at her as though he did not ever need to look upon anyone or anything else.

This man had fought demons and his own dark self this night, yet here, with her, he showed his vulnerability. To her, this made him all the more powerful.

"We cannot go *back*," she said, "but we can go *forward*. We can build something even stronger than before." She stared at the rips in his shirt and the bloodstains. "I don't know what the future holds. We'll face it together, though."

Even the shadows could not hide the blaze of pleasure in his face. He drew her close, and kissed her. Despite the chill night, his lips were warm and firm. "My love," he murmured, "the future is *ours* to write."

Sussex, England, 1762

The Gypsy girl cheated.

James Sherbourne, Earl of Whitney, could not prove it, but he knew with certainty that she cheated him at piquet. She had taken the last three hands, and his coin, brazenly. Whit did not mind the loss of the money. He had money in abundance, more, he admitted candidly, than he knew what to do with it. No, that wasn't true—he always knew what to do with money. Gamble it.

"How?" he asked her.

"How what, my lord?" He liked her voice, rich and smoky like a brazier, with an undercurrent of heat. She did not look up at him from studying her cards, arranging them in groups and assessing which needed to be discarded. Whit liked her hands, too, slim with tapered, clever fingers. Gamblers' hands. His own hands were rather large, more fitting for a laborer than an earl, but, despite their size, he had crafted them through years of diligence into a gamester's hands. He could roll dice or deal cards with the skill and precision of a clockmaker. Some might consider this a dubious honor, but not Whit. His abilities at the gaming table remained his sole source of pleasure.

And he was enjoying himself now, despite—or *because of*—the cheating Gypsy girl. They sat upon the grass, slightly removed from the others in the encampment. Whit hadn't sat upon the ground in years, but he did so now, reclining with one leg stretched out, the other bent so he propped his forearm on his knee. Back when he'd been a lad, he used to sit this very way when lounging on the banks of the creek that ran through his family's main country estate in Derbyshire. Years, and lifetimes, ago.

"How are you cheating me?"

She did look up at him then. She sat with her legs tucked demurely beneath her, a contrast from her worldly gaze. Light from the nearby campfire turned her large dark eyes to glittering jet, sparkling with intelligence. Extravagantly long black lashes framed those eyes, and he had the strangest sensation that they saw past his expensive hunting coat with its silver buttons, past the soft material of his doeskin waistcoat, the fine linen of his shirt, all the way to the man beneath. And what her eyes saw amused her.

Whit wasn't certain he liked that. After all, she was a Gypsy and slept in a tent in the open fields, whilst he was the fifth in his line to bear the title, lands, and estates of the earldom that dated back to the time of Queen Elizabeth. That merited some respect. Didn't it?

"I don't know what you are talking about, my lord," she answered. A faint smile curved her full mouth, vaguely mocking. The sudden desire to kiss that smile away seized Whit, baffling him. He enjoyed women—not to the same extent as his friend Bram, who put satyrs to shame and even now made the other Gypsy girls at the camp giggle and squeal—but when gambling was involved, Whit usually cared for nothing else and could not be distracted. Not even by lush, sardonic lips.

It seemed he had found the one mouth that distracted him.

"I know you aren't dealing from the bottom of the deck," he said. "I have had the elder hand twice, the hand with the advantage. We know what twelve cards we both have. Your sleeves are too short to hide cards for you to palm. Yet you consistently wind up with one hundred points before I do. You must be cheating. I want to know how." There was no anger in his words, only a genuine curiosity to know her secrets. Any advantage at the card table was one he gladly seized.

"Perhaps I'm using Gypsy magic."

At this, Whit raised one brow. "No such thing as magic. This is the modern eighteenth century."

"There are more things in heaven and earth," the girl answered, "than are dreamt of in your philosophy."

Whit started at hearing Shakespeare from the mouth of a Gypsy. "You've read *Hamlet*?"

Her laugh held more smoky mystery. "I saw it performed once at a horse-trading fair."

"But you *do* believe in magic?" he pressed. "Gypsy curses, and all that."

Her slim shoulders rose and fell in a graceful shrug. "The world is a labyrinth I am still navigating. It is impossible for me to say I *don't* believe in it."

"You are hedging."

"And you're *gorgio,* and I always hedge my bets around *gorgios.*" She gazed at him across the little patch of grass that served as their card table, then shook her head and made a *tsk* of caution. "They can be so unpredictable."

He found himself chuckling with her. Odd, that. Whit thought himself far too jaded, too attuned only to the thrill of the gamble, to enjoy something as simple and yet thrilling as sharing a low, private laugh with a beautiful woman.

She *was* beautiful. Perhaps under the direct, less flattering light of the sun, rather than firelight, she might not be as pleasing to the eye, though he rather doubted it. Her cheekbones were high, the line of her jaw clean, a proud, but proportioned nose. Black eyebrows formed neat arches above her equally black eyes. Her mouth, he already knew, was luscious, ripe. Raven dark and silken, her hair tumbled down her back in a thick, beribboned braid. She wore a bright blouse the color of summertime poppies, and a long, full golden skirt. No panniers, no stiff bodice or corset. A fringed shawl in a vivid green draped over her shoulders. One might assume such brilliant colors to jar the eye, but on the Gypsy girl, they seemed precisely right and harmonized with her honey-colored skin.

Rings glimmered on almost all her slim fingers, golden hoops hung from her ears, and many coin-laden necklaces draped her slim neck. Whit followed the necklaces with his eyes as they swooped down from her neck to lie in sparkling heaps atop her lush bosom. He envied those necklaces, settled smugly between her breasts.

Whit had a purse full of good English money. He wondered if this girl, this cheating, sardonic siren, might consider a generous handful of coins in exchange for a few hours of him learning the texture and taste of her skin. Judging by the way she eyed him, the flare of interest he saw shining in her gaze, she wouldn't be averse to the idea.

"For God's sake, Whit." Abraham Stirling, Lord Rothwell's voice boomed across the Gypsy encampment, tugging Whit from his carnal musings. Bram added, "Leave off those dull card games for once and join us."

"Yes, join us," seconded Leopold Bailey.

"We've wine and music in abundance," said Sir Edmund Fawley-Smith, his words slurring a bit.

"And dancing," added the Honorable John Godfrey. Someone struck a tambourine.

The men's voices blended into a cacophony of gruff entreaty and temptation. Whit grinned at his friends carousing on the other side of the camp. True to form, Bram had his arms around not one but three girls. Leo and Edmund busily drained their cups, whilst John received instruction from a Gypsy man on how to properly throw a knife.

Hellraisers, the lot of them. Whit included. So the five friends called themselves and so they were known amongst the upper echelons of society, and with good cause. Their names littered the scandal sheets and provided fodder for the coffee house, tea salons, and gentlemen's clubs, their exploits verging on legendary.

Bored with London's familiar pleasures, the Hellraisers had all been staying at Bram's nearby estate, spending their days hunting, their nights carousing. Yet they had soon tired of the local taverns, and the nearest good-sized town with a gaming hell was too far for a comfortable ride. It seemed more and more lately that the Hellraisers grew restive all too quickly, Whit amongst them, seeking novelty and greater heights of dissolution when their interest paled. He was only thirty-one, yet he could gain excitement only when gambling. Lounging in the gaming room of Bram's sprawling estate, Whit and the others had considered returning to the brothels, theaters, and gaming hells of London, but then Bram had learned from his steward that a group of Gypsies had taken up temporary residence in the neighborhood, and so an expedition had been undertaken.

The Gypsies had been glad to see the group of gentlemen ride into their camp, even more so when liberal amounts of money were offered in exchange for a night's amusement. Trick horse riding. Music. Dancing. Fortune-telling. Plenty of wine. And cards.

"How much wine have you drunk?" Whit called to Leo.

It took a moment for Leo to calculate, swaying on his feet. "'Bout four or five mugs."

"Ten guineas says you don't make it to six before falling arse over teakettle."

"Done," Leo said immediately. The nearby Gypsies exclaimed over the absurdly high amount of the wager, but to Leo, and especially to Whit, the amount was trivial.

Whit smiled to himself. Leo was the only son of a family who made their fortune on the 'Change, and he was the only one of the Hellraisers who wasn't a gentleman by birth. He felt this distinction keenly and, as such, met any challenge with a particular aggression. Which meant that Leo took any bet Whit threw his way.

"Your friends seem eager for your company," the Gypsy girl said wryly.

Whit brought his gaze back around to her. "We do everything together."

"Everything?" She raised a brow.

"Nearly everything," he amended. Bram might have no shame, but Whit preferred his amorous exploits to be conducted in private. He wondered how much privacy he could secure for himself and the girl.

A striking older Gypsy woman walked up to where he and the girl sat and began scolding her. Whit could not understand the language, but it was clear that the older woman wasn't very pleased by the girl's behavior. The girl replied sharply and seemed disinclined to obey. The older woman grew exasperated. Interesting. It seemed as though Whit's saucy temptress proved as much as a termagant to her own people as to him. Though Whit wasn't exasperated by the girl. Far from it. He felt the stirrings of interest he had believed far too exhausted to rouse.

"My granddaughter, Zora," huffed the older woman. Her accent was far stronger than her granddaughter's. "Impossible. 'Ere the fine gentlemen come for *dukkering*, and she does not *dukker*."

"What's *dukkering*?" asked Whit.

"Fortune-telling," the girl, Zora, answered. A fitting name for her, perfumed with secrets and distant lands. "Is that what you want, *gorgio*?" She set down her cards, then held out her hand. "Cross my palm with silver, and I shall read the lines upon your hand. Or I can use the tarot to tell your future." She nodded toward a different deck of cards sitting nearby, upon a scarf draped over the grass.

"I don't want to know the future," he said.

"Afraid?" That mocking, tempting little smile played about her lips.

"If I know the future," he replied, "it takes away all of the risk."

This made her pause. "You like risk." She sounded a bit breathless, more than the heat of the nearby fire reddening her cheeks.

He gave her a smile of his own, not mocking, but full of carnal promise. "Very much."

Zora turned to her grandmother and spoke more in their native tongue. With a loud sigh and grumble, the older woman trundled away.

Whit seized his opportunity. "I can give you five times what you'd win from me if you tell me how you keep winning at cards."

"I thought you enjoyed risk," came her quick reply.

"There's a risk in cheating, as well. Someone might catch you. And if they do catch you, who knows what they might do. Anything at all."

She gazed intently at him, then shook her head, firelight lost in the darkness of her hair. "No. It would be too dangerous to give those skills to a man such as you."

"A man such as me?" he repeated, amused. He set his cards down upon the ground. "Pray, madam, what sort of man am I?"

Her fathomless eyes seemed to reach deep inside him. He felt her gaze upon—*within*—him, a foreign presence in the contained kingdom of his self. After a moment, she said, "Handsome of face and form. Wealthy. Privileged. Bored. Throwing years of your life upon a rubbish heap because you seek something, anything to engage your restless, weary heart and prove you are still alive."

Whit laughed, but the sound was hollow in his chest. He didn't know this girl. Didn't know her at all, having met her for the first time earlier that very evening. She certainly did not know him. He was an *earl*, for God's sake, with a crest emblazoned upon his carriages. No fewer than three substantial estates belonged to him, all of them staffed with small armies of liveried servants.

She lived out of a tent. Whit wasn't sure she even wore shoes.

Yet a few words from her cut him deeply, far sharper than any surgeon's blade, and much more accurate. Why, he wasn't even aware he bled, but he was certain he'd find droplets of blood staining his shirt and stock later as he undressed for bed.

His solitary bed.

"If you won't divulge your secrets with the cards," he said with an insouciance he did not quite feel, "perhaps I can tempt you to reveal other, more personal secrets." There could be no mistaking his intent, the suggestive heat of his words.

She drew in a sharp breath, but whether she was offended or interested, Whit couldn't tell. Despite her insight into him, he possessed none of the same insight into *her*, making her as opaque as a silk-covered mirror. When his physical needs required satiation, Whit knew women of pleasure in London, Bath, Tunbridge-Wells. Actresses, courtesans. He knew their wants, their demands, the systems—both crude and elegant—through which they negotiated their price. A mutually beneficial relationship, and one he could navigate easily.

When it came to offering a night of pleasure to a fiery Gypsy girl, here, Whit found himself happily at a loss. Happily, because he had no idea how she might respond, and the inherent risk made his pulse beat a little faster.

"Would you see me financially compensated for revealing those personal secrets?" she asked, her own voice sultry.

"Absolutely," he said at once. "If that is what you wish." He moved his hand toward the purse he kept tucked into his belt, but then he stopped in surprise when she reached over and clasped his wrist. Her grip was surprisingly strong, surprisingly arousing. He felt her touch spread like a lit

fuse through his body, beginning the reaction eventually
leading toward explosion. Whit stared down at her hand,
her dusky skin tantalizing against his own lighter-colored
flesh, then up at her face as she leaned close.

"*Romani chi*s are not your *gorgie* whores, my lord. Especially me." Her voice was steady, yet her eyes were hot.
"I may lie *to* you, but not *with* you. Not for coin." She released her grip and sat back, and Whit felt the echo of her
touch. "If I were to take any man to my bedroll, it would
not be for money."

Which seemed to imply that she *might* share her bed
with a man, only without any sort of monetary inducement. That sounded promising.

Before Whit could speculate on this further, Bram staggered over with his arm hooked around the neck of a
Gypsy man. The Gypsy looked a little alarmed to be so
close to the tall, somewhat inebriated stranger, but could
not easily break free.

"Taiso here just told me something very interesting,"
Bram said. "He said that a few miles from here is a Roman
ruin. Isn't that right, Taiso?"

· The Gypsy man nodded, though from eagerness to rid
himself of Bram or ready agreement, Whit couldn't tell.
"Aye," Taiso answered. "To the west. On a hill. Many old
columns, and such."

"Bram, if your estate is nearby, wouldn't you already
know about a Roman ruin?" Whit asked.

Apparently, this had not occurred to Bram. He frowned.
"Must be a new ruin."

The Gypsy girl, Zora, snorted. Whit found himself
smiling.

"We should go investigate," Leo said, ambling forward
with John and Edmund trailing.

"No!" yelped Taiso. "Ye oughtn't go there. 'Tis a place
of darkest magic. The haunt of *Wafodu guero*—the Devil!"

"So much the better," said Leo. "We're Hellraisers, after all."

Edmund and John chortled their agreement. "This place is getting deuced dull," Edmund added.

Whit didn't think so. Though he was uncertain whether the tantalizing Zora might share a bed with him, he wanted to stay with her longer, even if it meant simply talking. He couldn't remember being so engaged in a conversation for a long, long time.

"It's settled, then," declared Bram. "We go to the ruin."

Cheers of approval rose up from Leo, John, and Edmund. Bram fixed Whit with a stare that held far more strength than one might expect from his inebriated state.

"You're coming, aren't you?" Bram asked. The question verged on a command. In some ways, Bram styled himself the de facto leader of the Hellraisers, even though, as a baron, he ranked beneath Whit. Yet Whit had no desire to lead this band of reprobate men—he wanted only the thrill of the gamble—and so left the decisions to his oldest friend.

Yet it was all a ruse. Bram mightn't say so, but he *needed* to have Whit with him during their many escapades, and if Whit refused to go, Bram would stay.

Whit looked at Zora, who watched the whole exchange with an incisive, speculative gaze. "What say you, Madame Zora?" he asked. "I could go to the ruin, where the Devil is rumored to reside, or remain here, with you. Shall we wager it on the flip of a coin or turn of a card?"

Her expression turned opaque. "The disease of your boredom has nearly claimed you if you can't make decisions for yourself."

He didn't care for the edge of censure in her tone. Whit spent much of his time avoiding anyone who might reproach him, which was why he hadn't seen his sister in nearly a year. It was not this Gypsy girl's business if he liked to gamble. It was no one's business but his own.

Resolved, Whit smoothly got to his feet. He hadn't been imbibing at the same rate as his friends, so the world remained steady as he stood. "Let's see where the Devil lives."

Bram exhaled, as if holding a breath in anticipation of Whit's answer. Seeing Whit make his decision, Bram grinned his demon's grin, the same he made whenever he was on the verge of doing something truly fiendish—like that time he entertained an entire troupe of ballet dancers in his London town house.

Zora arose to standing in a sinuous, graceful line.

"A kiss for luck," Whit said to her. He stared at her lips, the color of a rose just before sundown. He needed to know her taste, her warmth, when his own world felt so flavorless and cold. God, he wanted that, wanted her mouth against his, and the sudden strength of that want hit him like a cannon.

At that word *kiss*, her gaze went directly to his mouth. And heat and heaviness shot directly to his groin. Desire gleamed in her eyes.

Which she quickly shut away. Her expression cooled as her gaze moved up to his eyes.

"It would be a shameful thing to kiss you in front of my family. But I will wish you *kosko bokht*." There was something almost sorrowful in her words, in her eyes, as she stared up at him.

He felt it then. An icy sense of premonition sliding down his back, like a cold hand tracing the line of his spine. Though he was not a superstitious man, just then some strange other sense of foreboding tightened his muscles and bones. He had the oddest desire to stay in the encampment and avoid the ruin.

"Time to ride, lads," Bram commanded. He and the other men strode off to where a Gypsy boy had brought their snorting, impatient horses.

Whit laughed at himself, shaking off the sense of dread

as he might hand a rain-soaked greatcoat to a servant. Nonsense, all of it. As he'd said earlier, this was the modern age, and the Devil and magic did not truly exist.

He reached out, requesting Zora's hand, and after she slowly gave it to him, he bowed over it and pressed a kiss to her knuckles. Her eyes widened. Beneath his lips, her skin was silk and warmth; he barely resisted the impulse to lick her to learn whether she tasted as spicy as her spirit.

Their eyes met over their clasped hands. "Farewell, Madame Zora."

"Be careful, my lord."

"There's no amusement in careful."

"There is more to life than amusement."

"If there is," he answered, "I have yet to encounter it."

She slid her hand from his, and her gaze also slid away.

"Whit!" came a chorus of voices from across the encampment.

He gave her one last, searching look, as if trying to etch her image on the metal of his mind. A silent entreaty for her to meet his gaze one final time. Yet she would not, staring fixedly at the ground, and the flickering firelight turned her into a distant gold-and-ebony goddess. He wondered if he might ever see her again. The thought that he might not filled him with an inexplicable anger.

He made one final bow, as sharply elegant as a rapier, then turned and strode off. Whit swung himself up into the saddle. Bram and the others kicked their horses into a gallop. Whit's horse wheeled and danced in a circle as he took one last glimpse of the Gypsy encampment, of *her*, before he set his heels into the beast's flanks. They darted off into the night.

The *gorgios* were gone, having left some hours ago. Yet Zora could not be easy, could not still the beating of her heart or whirling of her mind. She paced as everyone else in the camp amused themselves with music and stories. It had been a good night. The wealthy *gorgios* had thrown coin around like handfuls of dust, and the mood amongst the families was high and celebratory. Even the best day of horse trading and *dukkering* at a fair could not bring in as much money.

Zora alone could not enjoy the remains of the evening. She walked up and down the camp—careful to keep her path behind the men who sat around the fire, as custom and belief demanded. Amongst the Rom, it was considered dangerous for a woman to pass in front of a seated man, though no one explained the reasons why in a way to ever satisfy Zora. That had been her way, since her earliest years—Zora demanding why, and the answer: *because*.

"Sit, girl," commanded Faden Boswell. "Ye make my head spin with yer to-ing and fro-ing."

Zora ignored him. Faden claimed he was the king of their group, but he talked more bluster than he did enforce order. Everyone knew that Faden's wife, Femi, held the reins of control and made the major decisions.

"She's thinkin' of her handsome *gorgio*," teased Grandmother Shuri. "With the pretty blue eyes and deep pockets."

"He is not *my gorgio*," Zora said immediately, yet she knew the truth. She *was* thinking of him. Whit, his scoundrel friends called him. A suitable name for a man possessing much intellect, yet also ironic, for he squandered his wits on ephemeral pursuits. What drove a man to live from one game of chance to the next? He had wealth, privilege, friends—though those friends were as wicked as demons. Yet he staked his happiness on the brief excitement of the wager.

It troubled her. *He* troubled her, far more than she would like.

There was passion in him—and no true channel for that passion. Nothing that engaged him fully.

No, that was not true. He seemed very much engaged and passionate when he looked at her.

Zora suppressed the shiver of awareness that danced through her as she remembered him. Grandmother Shuri was right. The *gorgio* Whit was indeed a most handsome man, and extremely well formed. He might be a scoundrel of the worst order, but it left no toll upon his face and body. Tall, his broad shoulders admirably filling out his costly coat, his long legs encased in close-fitting doeskin hunting breeches and high boots polished to brilliance.

And his face. She recalled it vividly as the firelight painted him a dark angel. Unlike other wealthy *gorgios*, he wore no wig but pulled his deep brown hair back into a queue. She imagined what his hair might look like loose about his shoulders, and knew he would appear a very incubus, sensually tempting a woman to wickedness. He had a square, strong jaw. A bold, aristocratic nose. Full lips. Dark, slashing brows above eyes the color of the sky at midday. Sharp, those eyes, and hungry.

Hungry for her. He made himself very plain. He wanted her for a night's pleasure. And, God preserve her, she wanted him, too. That lean body. Those clever hands. But she'd spoken true. She was no whore, and would not take his coin in exchange for her body. Even if he had not offered to pay her for the privilege, Zora knew that such affairs with *gorgios* were dangerous for young *Romani chis*.

She might not have taken him to bed, but she had not wanted him to go, either. She enjoyed talking with him, the way in which he truly seemed to listen. He was not afraid or dismissive of her opinions, not like other men—especially Jem, her former husband. Whit's mind was sharp, and he played the bored rogue, but she saw in him a yearning for meaning, for connection to something real, beyond the gloss and polish of his wealthy, wastrel life. She had that own yearning for herself, for a life away from telling fortunes and speaking in deliberate riddles. There had to be more than that.

There had been a palpable connection between her and Whit, which was indeed strange. Two people could not be more different. He lived trapped within walls, and she had the freedom of the road and the sky. He was a wealthy *gorgio* man of privilege, whilst she was a *Romani chi* who wore her wealth around her neck and upon her fingers. The sun and the moon. Yet the connection had been there, just the same.

She could not quite dismiss the disquiet she felt when he and his attractive, scapegrace friends decided to visit the Roman ruin. She might not adhere to the old folk beliefs of her family and the other Rom—it all seemed rather superstitious and silly to her, frankly—but something seemed deeply unsettling and wrong about the fact that the one *gorgio* who lived nearby had never heard of the ruin before tonight. Almost as if . . . it had been hiding, waiting for him and the other men.

"Ach," she growled to herself. "Enough of this." She had grown weary of pacing like a cat and would divert her restless thoughts.

Zora threw herself down onto the grass and shuffled her tarot deck. She did not believe the *dukkering* cards could actually tell the future, just as she did not believe the lines on a person's hand foretold anything. When she *dukkered* for the *gorgios*, she let them focus on the cards or their hands, while she actually read their faces, their postures and silent, subtle, unaware ways that revealed who they were and what they desired. Easy for them to think she had the gift of magic. But all Zora truly had was a knack for seeing people and telling them what they wanted to hear.

Still, dealing the tarot for herself usually soothed her. The proscribed patterns in which the cards were laid. The pictures printed upon their faces, older than history. Calming.

After shuffling the cards several times, Zora began to

lay them out in the ten-card cross with which she was most familiar. She did not pay much attention, simply allowing her mind to drift as her hands moved, setting down the cards. When she did finally bring her attention down to the cards, what she saw made her gasp aloud.

Evil. A great evil is coming, unleashed by the five.

Zora shivered. The warning was plain, spelled out in the cards.

She shook herself. Yes, the tarot had its meaning, and she knew what each card was supposed to represent, but they were merely suggestions, not actual truth. Not genuine prophecy of what was to come.

She quickly gathered up the cards she had laid, shuffled them again, then laid them out once more in the cross formation.

Her breath lodged in her throat.

The cards came out the same. Exactly the same. The five of swords. The inverted knight of wands. Culminating in the fifteenth card of the Major Arcana: the Devil. Zora stared at his horned, goatish face contorted in a sinister grin, batlike wings outstretched, as he presided over two figures chained at his feet. A pentacle marked the ground where the chained figures knelt.

Coincidence. That was all it could be. She would prove it.

She scooped up the cards and shuffled them a third time. And for the third time, she set them out. By the time she turned over and placed the final card, her hands shook.

The same. Each and every card. Their meaning clear: *A great evil is coming, unleashed by the five.*

Her heart pounded, her palms went damp, and her mouth dried. She never believed it possible, and yet . . . it was. The tarot predicted the future, a terrible future. Which meant—

Zora jumped to her feet. She ran to her family and the other families who made up their band. At her approach, the men stopped playing their fiddles and took their pipes from their mouths, and the women left off their gossiping. They all stared at her, and she knew that her face must be ashen, her eyes wide. She likely looked like a phantom.

"We have to stop them," she announced without preamble.

"Who?" asked Litti, her mother.

"The *gorgios* who went to the ruin." Her hands curled into fists by her sides as she fought to keep her voice level. "I have seen it. The cards have shown me. If we do not stop them, those five men are going to let loose a terrible evil."

No one laughed. Everyone knew that Zora put no faith in *dukkering* or magic. Yet it was for that very reason that they all took her seriously now. In fact, looks of pure terror filled their faces and the firelight shining in their rounded eyes turned them glassy and blank. Zora stared at them, at the men, and they stared back.

Not a single man moved.

Impatience gnawed at her. She took a step closer. "Why are you all sitting there like frightened goats? Get up! You must ride after the *gorgios* and stop them!"

The men exchanged glances until, *finally,* Zora's cousin Oseri stood up. Zora exhaled in relief, but her relief was short-lived. From the terrified expression on his face, it was clear Oseri had plans only to hide in his tent.

"The *Wafodu* is too great," he stammered. "The evil will hurt us."

"So you are going to do nothing?" Zora demanded.

The men all shrugged, palms open. "What can we do against such powerful, bad magic?" someone bleated.

"Anything!" she shot back. But every last one of the men refused to move, while the women crossed themselves and muttered prayers.

There was no hope for it. With a growled curse, Zora turned on her heel and walked into the horse enclosure, but not before grabbing a crust of bread from the cooking area

and slipping it into her pocket. It was said that bread held
the Devil at bay, and she needed every bit of assistance she
could scrounge. She also had her knife, tucked into the
sash at her waist.

"Where are you going?" Zora's mother cried.

Zora did not stop until she slipped a bridle onto one of
the horses and then swung up onto its bare back. Once
mounted, she trotted forward until she stared down at the
trembling men and women of her Romani band.

"I'm doing what needs to be done," Zora said. "I'm
going to stop those lunatic men before they do something
we shall *all* regret."

Despite her fear, she kicked her horse into a gallop. She
had never faced anything like this in her life, and had no
knowledge of what awaited her. How might she prevent the
evil from being set free? All she knew was that she must.

Atop a rounded hill, the ruin formed a dark, jagged
silhouette against the night sky, like a creature rising from
the earth. As the riders neared the hill, Whit felt himself
drawn forward, pulled by a force outside himself. He did
not know *why* he had to reach the ruin, only that he must,
and soon. His companions must have shared the feeling,
for they also urged their horses faster, their hooves pounding beneath them as thunder presaged a storm.

At the base of the hill, all of the men fought to control
their shying, rearing horses, trying to urge them up toward
the ruin. None of the beasts would take the hill, though it
was surely traversable by horse. The men alternately
cursed and cajoled. Yet the horses refused to go farther.

"On foot, then," grumbled Bram.

After dismounting, as directed by Bram, the men gathered up fallen tree branches. Bram used skills honed during
his time fighting the French and their native allies in the

Colonies and quickly made torches from the branches. He set them ablaze with a flint from his pocket.

"Don't we look a fine collection of fiends," drawled Whit. For that is what they resembled as light from the torches bathed the men's faces in gaudy, demonic radiance.

At this notion, they all grinned.

"Shall we investigate, Hellraisers?" asked Edmund.

"Aye," the men said in unison, and Whit felt almost certain he heard a sixth voice hiss, *Yes*.

They climbed the hill, using torchlight to guide them. The shapes of toppled columns and crumbling walls emerged from the darkness, gleaming white and dull as bones. Everyone reached the top and surveyed the scene. Whatever the building had once been, its glory had long ago faded, becoming only a shade of its former self. A strange, thick miasma cloaked the ruin, its dank smell clogging Whit's nose, and it swirled as the five men prowled through the ancient remains. Examining a partially standing wall, he touched the surface of the stone. A cold that seemed nearly alive climbed up through his hand, up his arm, and would have gone farther had he not pulled back.

Their murmured voices were muffled by the heavy vapor, but Leo said, loud enough for all of them to hear, "What the hell is this place?"

"Appears to have been a temple," answered John, their resident scholar. He crouched and brushed away some dirt until he revealed what appeared to be a section of stone floor. "See here." He pointed to the ground as everyone gathered around. Holding his torch closer to the stonework, he indicated the faded, chipped remains of mosaic lettering. "*Huic sanctus locus.* 'This sacred place of worship.'"

"Worship of what?" asked Leo.

"Bacchus, I hope," said Bram. He gazed critically around the ruin, the torchlight turning the sharp planes of his face even sharper, his black hair blending with the night. The light gleamed on the scar that ran along his jaw and down his neck, a souvenir from his military service. "It's dull as church up here."

"What were you expecting?" said Whit. "It's a *ruin*, not a bordello." He thought of Zora, her refusal to take his money in exchange for a night in his bed, and wondered if he would ever see her again. He decided he would, and planned to return to the Gypsy encampment on the morrow, though he did not know how pleased she might be to see him.

Bram made a noise of displeasure and paced away, kicking aside a few loose rocks in his impatience. Whit, John, Edmund, and Leo all exchanged rueful smiles. Of all of them, Bram pushed the hardest for yet greater depths of debauchery, as if continually trying to outpace something that chased him.

The friends broke apart to drift separately through the ruin. Whit ambled toward a collection of five columns that had all toppled against each other, barely standing but for the tenuous support they gave each other. Fitting, he thought. He found himself possessed by the oddest humor, a moody melancholy that sought some means of release. Too late he realized he should have placed a wager with Leo as to what the ruin might have once been. The opportunity was gone now. Perhaps there was something else here upon which he might gamble. Leo had not gotten to a sixth cup of wine back at the Gypsy camp, so that bet could not be won or lost.

A gleam at the base of the leaning columns caught his attention. He slowly neared and peered closer. Yes, something dully metallic appeared on the ground. As he edged closer, he saw that the metal was, in fact, a large, thick rusted ring, the size of a dinner plate. Whit thought at first the ring simply lay in the weeds. A second ring, exactly the same, lay some three feet away. Closer inspection showed the rings were attached to something in the ground. Whit crouched to get a better view.

"Come and have a look," he called to his friends.

The men assembled around him, and the light from their collective torches revealed that the iron ring was affixed at one end to a large, square stone block. Whit handed his torch to Edmund and cleared away the rocks, weeds, and debris that nearly obscured the block, with Bram and Leo assisting. Soon, the block was completely uncovered. It was roughly three feet across and three feet long, with a metal ring set at each end.

"Looks like a door," said John.

"If it's a door," Bram answered, "then we should open it." His voice sounded slightly different from normal, a deeper, harsher rasp.

At once it seemed to Whit to be not only the most sensible thing to do, but the most essential. A burning need to see what was behind the door seized him, as strong as any need to gamble. He gripped one iron ring, and Leo gripped the other after giving his torch to Bram.

"On my count," said Whit. "One, two, *now*!"

Both he and Leo pulled with all their strength. Whit's muscles strained and pulled against the fabric of his shirt and coat, against the doeskin of his breeches as he dug his heels into the ground and fought to wrench open the heavy stone door. He grunted with exertion through his gritted teeth. *Pull, pull!* He had to get the door open.

Bram, Edmund, and John shouted their encouragement, their eyes aglow with the same fevered need to breach the door.

A deep, heavy wrenching sound rumbled up from the ground, as if the very foundations of the world were being rent asunder. Whit and Leo pulled harder, encouraged by the sound. Inches of stone emerged up as the stone slab rose in clouds of dust. Suddenly, with a final growl, the stone broke free from its earthen prison.

Whit and Leo heaved the block to one side, and it thudded on the ground, barely missing John's toes. But John didn't complain. He, like the other Hellraisers, was all too captivated by the sight of the opened door.

A black square, the doorway, and through it the scent of long-buried secrets came wafting up. It wasn't a damp smell, rather hot and dry, the scent of singed fabric and burnt paper. Whit grabbed his torch from Bram and thrust it through the doorway in the ground. The firelight illuminated precipitous stone stairs that disappeared into the gloom.

"A hollow hill," murmured Whit.

"I've read about them." John gazed avidly down. "From ancient legends about fairy kingdoms."

They paused for a moment, each taking in the wonderment of an actual hollow hill. In silent agreement, they descended the stairs. Their boots scraped over the stone, and the sound echoed as they delved farther. They found themselves in an underground chamber. Whit could not imagine what kind of ancient tools had the strength to carve a large chamber out of solid rock, yet somehow, some ancient laborer had done just that. The room itself was almost entirely bare, just a floor and sloping walls that arched overhead. Whit was surprised at the height of the ceiling. He was a tall man, yet he did not have to stoop or bend in the chamber. Instead, he stood at his full height as he and his friends slowly turned in circles as they gazed at the incredible room hewn from a stone hill.

Yet the chamber was not empty.

"We have a companion, lads," said Whit.

At one end of the chamber, on a crude seat carved from solid rock, sat a man—or at least his skeletal remains, remarkably preserved given that they had been buried in this chamber for what had to be over a thousand years if the age of the ruins above was any indication. Whit and the others pressed closer to stare at this new discovery.

"He's wearing the uniform of a Roman centurion," John whispered. "His helmet has the horsehair crest, he has medals upon his chest, and—this is astounding—his wooden *Bacillum Viteum* stick has not decayed." Sure enough, a knotty stick rested in the crook of the centurion's arm.

"I'm more interested in *that*," said Whit. He pointed to what the long-dead soldier held in his bony hands. A bronze box, the size of a writing chest, with images of twining snakes worked all over its surface. The centurion gripped the box tightly, holding it snug against his breastplate. Whatever was inside the box must have been extremely valuable, valuable enough to consign a Roman officer to death.

Bram stared at the box, then at the faces of his friends clustered around. He grinned fiendishly as he placed his hand upon the box. "Let's have ourselves a look."

Whit stared as Bram forcibly pried the box from the skeleton's grip. The bones cracked as the box was wrenched free, yet Whit did not wince at the sound. All he wanted was the box, to learn what it contained, and he gazed avidly as Bram began to open it.

Be careful, Zora had warned him. Yet he shoved her warning aside. The answers to everything were inside the box.

As the lid opened, the flames from the torches were suddenly sucked inside the box. The chamber plunged into darkness.

GREAT BOOKS,
GREAT SAVINGS!

When You Visit Our Website:
www.kensingtonbooks.com